I0679613

STAR LEGIONS

THE TERRAN WARS

WARRIOR KING

BY MICHAEL G. THOMAS

© 2018 Michael G. Thomas

The right of Michael G. Thomas to be identified as the Author of the Work has been asserted by him in accordance with the Copyright, Designs and Patents Act 1988.

First published in the United Kingdom in 2017 by Swordworks Books.

All rights reserved. No part of this publication may be produced, stored in a retrieval system, or transmitted in any form or by any means, without the prior permission in writing of the publisher, nor be otherwise circulated in any form of binding or cover other than in which it is published and without a similar condition including this condition being imposed on the subsequent purchaser.

All characters in this publication are fictitious and any resemblance to real persons, living or dead, is purely coincidental.

ISBN 978-1-912799-00-8

Typeset by Swordworks Books
Printed and bound in the UK & US
A catalogue record of this book is available from the British Library

Cover design by Swordworks Books
www.swordworksbooks.com

STAR LEGIONS

THE TERRAN WARS

WARRIOR KING

BY MICHAEL G. THOMAS

PROLOGUE

The Hall of Heroes, Laconia

The Arachne fighting machines were as big as bulls, and yet walked upright on eight legs. Spindly limbs extended out from the flanks of their grotesque looking bodies. The robotic machines fused the elegance of a well-trained warrior with the terror of the greatest monsters of ancient myth. Each Arachne was constructed from gleaming metal and festooned with ribbed plates around their bodies to protect the vulnerable electronics held safely inside. Their heads pushed up from the front of the torso with glowing red eyes, giving the impression of some soulless beast.

Once close enough, they reared up from the ground, with four legs supporting their weight. The other four reached out in front with long talons, each as big as a sword and twice as sharp. The arms moved and began a complex series of patterns almost impossible to discern to the naked eye. They were ready to fight.

"Monstrous beasts," Agesilaus muttered. He rose from the

ground and twisted about at the waist to face the approaching metal warriors. Agesilaus looked every part the Laconian warrior of old. He was a big man, at almost two metres in height and encased in bronzed effect armour, "I will crush each of you in turn."

The nearest of the three machines hissed something intelligible, and then they began advancing towards Agesilaus with a clattering of metal feet, and the clicking of movable armoured plates. The scarred warrior pointed towards the approaching machines and laughed at them as if they were little more than a group of children.

"It's time to join your friends in the Underworld."

They moved into position, with the machines advancing towards him from three directions. Agesilaus was not afraid, and certainly had no doubts as to his ability to fight. More important to him was the location. This was the Hall of Heroes, a vast open-air arena, built to accommodate hundreds of warriors, and dated back to time in the city's distant past. It was not a place for public entertainment and amusement as on other worlds, but for the warriors of Laconia to train and fight. To be here was an honour, even for a prince such as him. Spacecraft might travel between the stars, while legions of soldiers battled a multitude of alien species with energy weapons, yet the Hall of Heroes remained unchanged from the days now long lost. Unlike other similar buildings, it was cut directly into the rock of the mountain, giving it a primeval look and feel. Some said it was the remains of a dormant volcano, or perhaps even the birthplace of one of the Terrans' ancient gods that had resided upon the independent sanctuary world of Olympus. Tall stone statues of nameless warriors surrounded the open space, each in a different pose, yet armed and equipped in the same fashion and facing off against a hundred races.

"Fight me!" he shouted, taking a step towards the machines, "I'm waiting!"

One by one they pointed their weapons towards him. They lacked firearms, but that didn't stop the Laconian warrior from activating his shield as they closed the ground. A Laconian might be the strongest and bravest of the Terran soldiers, but each understood individual prowess meant little if it resulted in one's death. And he knew these machines were not just programmed as sparring bots, they would fight to kill. Anything else was simply wasting his time.

It begins!

The three machines lurched ahead, swinging their weapons in sequence. It was fast, precise, and terrifying. Agesilaus covered the last few metres, then dropped down, and slid underneath their limbs. One machine was now blocked by the other two, and as they slashed at him managed to strike each other first. Agesilaus came to a stop and turned to face them.

"As uncoordinated as a Medes legion. Is this all you have?"

Agesilaus dropped into a low stance, his feet wide apart and legs bent. The time for playing was over, and he readied for the mortal combat. As always, he bore the traditional weaponry of his people's, the heavy infantry of the Laconian state. In his right hand the infamous Asgeirr-Carbine, the Laconian close quarter weapon fitted into the fist and lower right arm of a warrior. It combined a razor-sharp blade and a cut down pulse carbine. The entire unit was compact and very light, and though short ranged was also very powerful. It was capable of blasting an enemy apart with gunfire, while the blade could penetrate even the toughest armour. The mobile shield generator added substantial weight to his back, and only a man in peak physical condition could ever consider using one. The shield projector unit in his left arm was heavier than a rifle and emitted the phased shielding that could protect a man from gunfire, and even blades.

Here it comes.

One machine surged forward with all four talons slashing away.

And here you will fall.

The other two came in close behind, but not so close that they'd make the same mistake as before. Agesilaus swayed with the machine's movement, matching its timing into almost a dance. His armour looked heavy, but it was a technological marvel, combining layers of metal and polymers to keep it flexible and padded, and capable of becoming as hard as ship armour once struck by a weapon or missile. The Arachne struck with two blades, but the Laconian warrior was nowhere to be seen. The thing twisted about, but Agesilaus was even faster than the machine.

Be where your enemy is not.

Agesilaus sidestepped the attack, pulling his right arm back to attack in a punching action. The Asgeirr-Carbine blade pushed out from its housing, and he stabbed it into the torso of the machine with the strength that could have shattered a man's skull. Two of the blades snapped back towards him in a reflex action, and one caught his upper arm. Though a glancing strike, the blade was razor sharp and cut into the flesh. Blood ran freely from the wound, but that seemed to push the Laconian on to greater feats of strength and power. He pushed once more, and the monofilament punch blade forced its way deep into the machine's side, close to the vulnerable systems inside.

"Be gone…you foul thing!"

A pulse of energy from the shield generator fitted to his back surged through cables running from the bottom on the unit and down to each arm. The energy enveloped the Asgeirr-Carbine, running through the blade and into the innards of the machine, quickly turning the internal components to a molten mess. Agesilaus withdrew the blade as the internal components of the machine exploded in a pulse of blue light. The blast was so great it knocked him flat on his back. He lay there for a second, shook his head, and laughed. He turned his back on the remains of the eight-legged machine as it collapsed to the ground, lifeless and spent.

"Is this the best you have to offer?"

To his surprise both machines stopped, as though frozen and reduced to stone by the gaze of the mighty Gorgon. Even Agesilaus felt a moment of panic, half expecting his own body to succumb to the monster's powers. Something deep down told him the stories were simply that. And yet he'd seen things that made him doubt they were merely the imagination of storytellers. He might still be a young man, but as a Laconian soldier he'd fought all manner of enemies, from the Terran soldiers of Attica, to the monstrous Taochi that served as part of the Imperial Army. Built like an upright bull, but with a strongly muscled upper torso, and arms almost three metres tall. They famously eschewed firearms in combat and could take on a dozen Terrans in combat. Yes, there were monsters in this world, and he had no desire to see his life ended as a heap of stone. He spotted a new figure moving out onto the floor of the famed arena, and his attention was instantly drawn to the different shape.

What is this new treachery?

The sun was low in the distance, and he had to squint to pick out the shape. Deep down he already knew what it was, and that instantly changed his approach to the melee. It was a man, and he carried a weapon, a rifle in two hands across his body.

"Agesilaus. If you still pray to the old gods, now is your last chance."

Agesilaus licked his lips and focussed his attention on the newcomer. He remained a wary distance from the fighting machines, though, as just one well-aimed cut could end his life there and then. They could be in range in less than two seconds, and he needed to be ready.

"Who sent you?" he asked bitterly, though he knew who it was. The figure slowed and then stopped. He looked relaxed, yet kept his hands on the weapon and ready to fight.

"You already know the answer, Agesilaus. Now it is time for you to make a decision."

"Let me guess." Agesilaus completely ignored what the man was saying, "Leotychides, the bastard son of Agis sent you."

Agesilaus shook his head and started his breathing regimen. It was something all full Laconian warriors practiced when going into battle. They were trained from seven years of age in the ancient and mystical arts of war and physical prowess. The process was known as the Agoge, and completion of it was a requirement to becoming a full citizen. He'd studied and practiced stealth, loyalty to the state, military and individual training, hunting, dancing, singing and much more.

"Does it matter? You will be little more than a memory."

The man walked closer and onto the sandy surface of the fighting space. Agesilaus pointed his right arm at him and roared so loudly, every soul within the structure would have been unable to speak over the sound.

"How dare you step on this sacred ground! Only a full-blooded Laconian that has worked their way through the Agoge may ever present themselves to this field of battle. And you are no Laconian."

The shadowy shape stopped, and then appeared to split apart from one man into ten. All were armed, each carrying something different. There were rifles, carbines among a few. But the majority carried primitive weapons such as swords and spears. They must have been there to make up the numbers, but Agesilaus knew too well that numbers had a strength of their own.

"And what does that make you? The lame princeling, and son of a failure. I bring a message from my patron. This is your last chance, so choose your fate wisely."

The sun moved a little higher, but Agesilaus was becoming accustomed to the burning light. He could now see they were men, and each wore the minimal armour of the stratiotes. These were the common mercenaries used by Terrans for hundreds of years, for everything from scouting or guarding fortifications. They wore no obvious uniform, their disparate clothing and equipment the only thing they had in common with each other. The leader was different, and now had he managed to pick up the accent. It was well disguised, but he'd recognise the sound of a Plataean anywhere, one of the puppets of the Boeotian League, the rising rivals of Laconia.

"Lay down your shield, and we can end this quickly."

The voice came from behind the line of mercenaries. He was protecting himself at all costs.

"Coward," Agesilaus muttered, moving his feet in the sand-covered floor. The man laughed and called back at him.

"Leave Laconia today, Agesilaus, or be buried in this field. Either suits us just fine."

Agesilaus shook his head and placed himself into a fighting stance. His left foot was forward, legs slightly bent, and his weight central and balanced. It was a strong fighting position, allowing him to advance or retire in an instant.

"I would be honoured to be buried in this place, the hall of my ancestors."

He tried to sound confident, but with ten enemies moving in on him, he knew that even his skills might not be enough. Skill amounted to little when numbers were involved. His shield and blade could only be in one place at a time. Three of the enemy moved off to his right, training their rifles on his flank.

They are moving to my unshielded side. I am betrayed!

He tried to adjust his stance, but there was no way he could completely protect himself, and remain capable of fighting those advancing towards him with raised weapons. At the same time, the remaining seven advanced to within twenty metres. They raised their weapons, ready to charge. One more figure emerged and formed up between the two robotic warriors. He was dressed in the common garb of a Laconian citizen, and yet carried a carbine across his chest. Atop his head he wore a helmet of the fashionable Phrygian style. This type of helmet derived its name from its shape, the high and forward inclined apex, resembling the caps often worn by warriors of the Phrygian and Thracian peoples.

"Remember Pylos, my old friend. Hundreds of your kin laid low by commoners with rifles. A pulse round cannot tell a coward from a hero. All it takes is a single point to pierce your heart, and your future will be forfeit."

"Then forfeit it will be. You consider yourself Laconian, and yet you speak a never-ending stream of words. Fight, or leave. Do not kill me with boredom. A Laconian speaks with his actions, not this rhetoric."

The man snorted in derision, and then moved his arm in a gesture Agesilaus had never seen. At once the two remaining robotic fighting machines activated, rose up tall and surged ahead, passing the mercenaries on each flank. The armed soldiers filed behind them, weapons raised and ready for combat. Agesilaus braced for the attack, but then spotted the soldiers to his right taking aim. Tiny flashes marked the moment they opened fire, and then the hellish battle began.

"So, it begins."

Agesilaus twisted and lifted his arm up just as the mercenaries with rifles opened fire. The pulse rounds slammed into his shielded side with heavy thuds. The shimmering circular energy shield deflected the pulse rounds with flashes of light. A weaker man would have dropped his arm, but years of training and practice gave him the physical and mental strength to keep the shield up. He twisted to the right, ducked down behind the shield, and pushed out his Asgeirr-Carbine out to his flank. It spat once, and the projectiles slammed into the face of the central figure. The man stumbled backwards and vanished from view, but was quickly replaced by yet more of his comrades.

"Fight me, you cowards!"

More shots struck around him and pinned him in place. If he moved even a metre he would be struck, yet he could see the fighting machines coming right for him. They would be with him in seconds, and then it would be over.

"Watch out!" yelled one of the mercenaries, "Behind you."

Agesilaus lifted his right arm, and took quick aim at his tormentors. Years of training had honed his body into something close to a machine. He took aim, firing a burst from his carbine as the shape dashed among the group of mercenaries. It moved fast and soon moved off to his side. In less than a second, two of them fell to the ground. One gun went off, and then the shooting was over.

"Kill him!" shouted the leader of the mercenaries, even though now he was nowhere to be seen, "Now!"

He could see the figure moving about as though practicing

some complex dance, but Agesilaus knew who it was. A smile drew across his face as he watched two mercenaries fall to the ground, and a third spun about screaming. The Arachne fighting machines moved in close, and as before, their arms starting to whir about in a pre-set sequence. Agesilaus drew up his body into a fighting stance, readying for the fight to come. With his flank secured, he could now fight as he wanted to. Up close and personal.

"Let's dance!"

The machines reached him, and as before their powerful limbs crashing down in crude cutting actions. There was no subtlety or strategy, merely rapid attacks against any targets they could find. Agesilaus took most of the blows on his shield arm moving in between them. They continued to hack away, but he ducked and pulled to avoid their blows, forcing them to cause light damage to each other. One slashed at his ankle, but ribbed plates of metal protected his legs, his chest and back were hidden behind the muscled cuirass of plastic and metal. They left deep dents in the plating, but he remained upright and unhurt.

"Watch your back!"

Agesilaus dropped to his knees. The group of men were coming right at him. They were a motley group and little more than a mob. They must have thought he was weak and trapped. He stabbed up into the body of the first machine, sending a pulse of energy into its torso, just as his ally leapt through the air with the grace of a goddess. She landed atop the last remaining machine and sank a short blade deep into its body. She then summersaulted backwards and landing besides Agesilaus just as her weapon glowed white and exploded. The broken machine crumpled to the ground.

"Fools!" Agesilaus lifted his right arm, "Now pay for your

hubris."

The last remaining mercenaries rushed the pair. Two opened fire with crude pistols, but were unable to breach Agesilaus' shield, even at this range. His Asgeirr-Carbine mowed them down with ease, the weapon firing on full automatic. Just three remained, and as they came closer, the female warrior leapt among them with a long dagger in each hand. It took a few short movements, and they were dead. She turned back to face him and smiled.

"Kyniska. Your skills continue to improve."

She playfully bowed before him, and then reached out to his arm. Blood ran from a deep gash in the flesh, and yet when she touched him he did not flinch.

"As do yours, Brother."

"We must always work to keep our bodies and minds at their peak."

He said it in such a serious and stoic tone that Kyniska burst out laughing. She was the epitome of Terran beauty, tall, athletic, and with a mischievous look in her eyes. Her limbs were strong from the same physical training as the others in the Agoge. Like Agesilaus, her feet were bare, as were her head and arms, leaving them unrestricted when in combat. She wore a short crimson robe that ran from her shoulders down to her thighs, leaving her long legs exposed and vulnerable. Like Agesilaus, she wore a beautifully constructed cuirass that followed the shape of her chest and stomach perfectly. A brown belt with multiple sheaths ran around her narrow waist. Unusually, her hair was not black, but a dark red, with hints of blackness at the roots. Kyniska was a young woman in her mid-twenties, and a perfect example of the strength and skill so regarded in Laconia. She remained single and unattached, a reminder of her fierce will and independence.

"What was that?"

Agesilaus looked to the right and nodded towards the bodies. Kyniska slipped away and moved along them, prodding each one with her blades. One by one they remained still until she reached a poor wretch who made the mistake of moving. Without hesitating, she slashed the blade across his throat, and the man tipped over as the blood drained from his body. Finally, she looked back at him.

"Dead men tell no tales."

"Indeed not."

Then the body rolled to the side, and the man with the Phrygian helmet rose as though climbing from his grave. He moved quickly and managed to slash horizontally with a short blade, catching Agesilaus in the chest. It would have cut him in half, had it not been for the exquisite cuirass that he wore. Sparks flew from the impact, and Agesilaus stumbled backwards. The man was now upright, and the rising sun showed off his form in every detail. Kyniska raced to his side, and before he could move, she slashed at the backs of his legs. The cuts were quick and accurate, sending him to the ground on his knees, screaming in pain.

Agesilaus moved back to the man, glanced down at his chest, and shook his head.

"If you were a true Laconian, you would know your puny weapons are no match for our armour."

The man spat on the floor, and that stopped Agesilaus in his tracks.

"You dare defile the Hall of…"

Before he could say more, the man reached for a weapon on his flank. Agesilaus wasted no time, and slashed at the man's throat with a powerful reflex action. The blade of his Asgeirr-Carbine cut the mercenary's head clean from his body and sent it crashing to the ground.

"A sneaky man." Kyniska bent down to pick up the man's head. She showed no signs of weakness, as expected for any Laconian citizen. Blood ran down onto her hand and forearm as she removed his helmet and cast it aside.

"I've never seen this man before."

Agesilaus looked at the head for a moment and then shrugged.

"He meant nothing to me before today, and I will never remember his face again."

"True." She dropped the head to the floor as though it were little more than garbage. Their eyes met as Agesilaus ran his fingers through his finely groomed beard. He sported a full beard, as was common amongst the full citizens of the state. It pushed out into a beautifully groomed point, in contrast to his busy crop of black hair that was now a mess of sweat and blood from the short and violent battle.

"Who would dare send assassins against me?"

He deactivated his shield and lowered his weary arm. At the same time, the blade in his right hand pulled back into the Asgeirr-Carbine. A grim smile spread along his face as he double-checked their foes were truly incapacitated.

"There is only one that would be so brazen, and so cowardly as to send others to do what he would never dare try."

"Leotychides?"

Agesilaus nodded slowly.

"There is nobody else."

"Then we find him...and we kill him. Tonight," Kyniska said through clenched teeth, "For too long has he sought to deny you your birthright." She made to move, but Agesilaus grabbed her with his arm and held her firmly.

"Not now...not today. We do not enter a battle until we

know it is already won. Remember the words of our friend Lysander."

Kyniska hesitated, knowing deep down that her brother was correct.

"Lysander is no fool, Brother. You are correct. His attention to detail is legendary. The moment of battle is just the last act in a long play."

She rubbed her cheek, leaving a long bloodstain along her fair skin.

"Leotychides is a master of deception and scheming. He would only have launched this attack against you if he could guarantee success. He undoubtedly had a plan, and it would result in our deaths, disgrace, exile, or a combination of the three."

"Agreed. Now…what do we do about this mess?"

Agesilaus stretched his aching muscles and laughed.

"Let us leave politics and talking to the diplomats, Kyniska. I never finished my exercises, and it is our duty to ensure our minds and bodies are ready for any challenge. Want to join me?"

Kyniska placed her blades back in the sheaths on her side, and moved in front of her brother. He lifted his hands up in front of him and readied himself for the fight to come.

"I'd like nothing more…Brother!"

Without warning, she leapt from her coiled-up stance and directly at him. She seemed to rise up into the sky like some demonic beast, and as she covered the ground, a great smile spread across Agesilaus' face.

"That's my girl." He leapt to the side to avoid her blow. She hit the ground lightly, rolled forward, and brought her blades down and onto his weapon. Sparks flashed as the burred edges ran along each other.

This is how Laconians fight. On the field of battle with weapons drawn, and face-to-face.

CHAPTER ONE

Median Battleship 'Vairya', The Ionian Territories

Waiting deep inside the armoured behemoth was the warlord and tyrant, a Medes noble hated and feared in equal measure. He commanded legions of warriors, and entire fleets of ships from a hundred different worlds. His reputation was known to every soul within a thousand parsecs, and now he was ready for war. He was a noble of the highest order, tasked with defending the border colonies of the great Median Empire. The greatest empire in recorded history, and one that had attempted two invasions in less than a century against the worlds of the Terrans. His domain encompassed a bewildering array of systems, as well as billions of citizens of many different races. From the bullish warriors or the Taochi, to the machines of the Robotic Domains, all called him Master, or suffered a cruel and terrifying fate. He was no mere mortal, but a noble Satrap of the Empire, his name Tissaphernes.

The great Satrap was dressed head-to-toe in the finest clothing money could buy in the Empire; fine silks from the

Eastern trading colonies, and the best Terran body armour that could be found in the Ionian Territories. He'd even appropriated a pair of Laconian shoulder plates, and had them modified to fit his narrow frame. Some might think he was Terran from the amount of military equipment he wore, and yet his robes and tunic were clearly of Medes style and cut. One might make the mistake of thinking him a provincial noble out to make a name for himself. But that would be a mistake of the highest order. As Satrap, he was a literal god to these people, a position of authority guaranteed to him by birth, and by his ruthless rise to the top. None were above him, save the God King himself, and some considered him a possible heir to even that lofty position.

We have arrived.

Tissaphernes opened his eyes slowly as the dark command chamber slid aside. He was a Medes, one of the great warrior tribe that dominated the Median Empire, the arch enemy and rival of the Terrans. After centuries of rule, the Medes had supplanted or married into the noble families of their territories, cementing their position of power. Tall, thin, and almost elfin in stature, he could never have passed for a Terran soldier, although compared to most Medes; he was a towering figure and the right hand of the God King himself. Yet for his lack of physique, he remained a figure of awe and authority onboard the battleship. For the last three hours he'd kept apart from the rest of the crew. He enjoyed the peace and quiet, but also the ability to see and communicate with the other commanders in the fleet, without needing to involve another soul. He had no friends on this ship, or even in this fleet. And that didn't bother him at all. He was the master of all, and every one of them knew it.

Excellent. For months I have waited for this day. The Terrans will suffer like they have never suffered before. Their bodies will decorate my ships, and they will know that the rebel colonies will yield...or they will fall!

Just thinking of the pain he would inflict on his foes forced a smile to spread along his face. He had no love for the Terrans, and he desperately needed to prove his worth to the God King. His power might be unrivalled, but the God King liked to keep his Satraps busy by making them vie for his attention and patronage. Only through proving his worth could he seek advancement, and he had his eyes set on the greatest prize of all.

My ships will turn their world to ash.

Tissaphernes looked to the lines of automatons on the command deck, and then exhaled a long, satisfied breath. The ancient battleship had the look of some great predatory sea monster, with its crustacean like hull, and a pair of long bow sections that had much in common with pincers. Multiple curved layers of armour surrounded the aft section, as well as the six gigantic engine mounts pushing out from each side. It was a thing of great beauty, as well as a design created to instil terror in all that saw her. Though few in number, these colossal warships served as the home for the Empire's most powerful leaders, and where one was found, death and destruction could be expected to follow.

"We have arrived within ten parsecs of the Terran world of Ephesus, my Lord," said a faint voice from outside the command chamber, "The fleet is assembled and awaiting your leadership. Our allies and mercenaries are here as ordered."

He took another careful breath before adding, "They await your commands."

"Finally," said Tissaphernes with a snort, "The Terrans and their Ephesian lackeys have lived the life of luxury for too long. Today is the day everything changes. All Terrans will rue the day they dared challenge me and the Median Empire."

He licked his lips with anticipation, and then spotted the nervous Sarvan waiting in front of him. He felt like drawing his blade to strike him down, but deep down knew he needed to contain his anger, at least for the next few hours.

"You know why we are here, Sarvan?"

The commander of the ship shook his head, but said nothing.

"The Ionian Territories were once the trading worlds and ports of the Empire. Our people grew rich as our trade fleets travelled the stars. Medes, Carians, and Terrans working together for the good of the Empire. It is through the power of the God King that any of this was possible."

He then snorted.

"And yet the Terrans turned on us, killed our people, and declared every world to be independent from the Empire. Now the years have passed, and they are strong and united as two super powers. The Ionian and the Aeolian Leagues."

Mentioning the names of the two regional powers seemed to make his blood boil. They were more than a problem for the Empire. They were also a check on his own power. He was Satrap of two massive satrapies that encompassed almost the entire border between the Empire and the worlds of the Terrans; to the right of his domain the great regions of Cilicia and Cappadocia, and then through the Su'bartu Maelstrom and onto the Core Worlds, and the home of the God King. He clenched his fists, visualising the worlds that blocked his access to open space from his own territory. With the rich territories of the Empire on one side, and the border colonies on the other, they acted like a wall to his ambitions.

Twenty-four colonies that should be mine, no…they will be mine. They are a stain on the honour of the Empire and must be brought to heel. And if they will not submit...they will burn.

He turned his attention to the ship's commander. The unfortunate wretch had no idea what to say or do, only to await his orders. Like a small animal he waited silently, as a loyal dog would do with his owner.

"My ship, Sarvan. Is my battleship ready for the battle to come?"

The command chamber finally opened up completely, revealing the deck of his ship in all its glory. Like everything else Tissaphernes touched, it was grandiose and excessive. Even his command chamber was raised like a throne above all others, constantly reminding them of his greatness. Lines of officers were on each side, gazing into their computer displays as they managed the hordes of crew on the vessel. This was not the compact deck of a Terran vessel, where a dozen men and women of high rank would command their vessel. This was a ship filled with automatons, the massed ranks of the Empire. They would function without question, no matter the task or how difficult. An n officer approached, and then bowed down low before him.

"The ship is ready for battle, my..."

"The ship?" asked the Satrap in a stone-cold tone.

He then shook his head slightly and waited as the Sarvan lifted his gaze and looked to Tissaphernes, doing his best not to look into the man's eyes.

"You mean my ship?"

The Sarvan appeared almost relieved to be asked the question. Obeying was easy for an automaton, but showing initiative was something removed from their programming when born. They were there to unquestioningly follow orders, and nothing more.

"Yes, my Lord, your ship. The new automatons have

completed repairs to the bow batteries. The damage to the lower decks was extensive, and the...restricted timetable made it difficult. Losses were heavy, but all systems are back to full function. I am..."

"Losses? What losses?"

"Seventy-seven of your automatons lost their lives during the repairs. One of the primary weapon batteries experienced a malfunction and was..."

He swallowed uncomfortably, recalling the faces of the dead and dying. Tissaphernes looked back at him with cold, uncaring eyes. He didn't appear to be affected by the news, or register that there had been even a single loss during the major repair work. The Sarvan inhaled deeply and pushed himself to continue his report before he was censured.

"The radiation leaks were substantial, and in the last two days we've suffered from unexploded munitions."

"Good. That is the news I wanted to hear," he said to the stunned Sarvan. The senior automation did his best to hide his horror. He might be in charge, but he was still one of them, and he felt their loss, even if Tissaphernes did not.

"This ship must be fully functional. The Terrans will not give up without fighting. They might be treacherous, self-centred scum, but they know how to fight. That is the price of spending their lives at each other's throats."

He rubbed his chin as he smiled.

"At least I hope they don't. An unwilling opponent is a dull opponent."

"My Lord, your ship is fully operational. Armour, shields, and weapons are all ready for battle and operating at a high level of efficiency. The mercenary ground troops are waiting on the launch decks for your orders. Your ship, and the entire fleet awaits your command to make the final jump to the target."

A smile formed up along Tissaphernes' face as he looked at the squirming individual. He then turned his attention to the legion of officers on the deck. Though the ship was packed with people and technology, not one of the officers had access to anything more than their own system or section on the ship. Only he, and the ship's captain had access to all external data and communications. It gave the impression that the battleship was more like a floating relic than a warship.

"That is good. Today is a glorious day…is it not, Sarvan?"

Not one of the automatons moved from their posts. The Sarvan opened his mouth, and then hesitated. He might be the captain of the biggest ship in the fleet, but he was also the thirteenth captain in the last ten years. Sarvan was merely a rank and a title awarded to one individual on the ship, and it could be taken with the slash of a blade. He was so insignificant that he had no idea how many of his predecessors had already lost their lives. A small number of his kin managed to reach the position of Sarvan, but the number that had lived an entire lifetime as commander of a warship was miniscule.

"Well?" Tissaphernes asked.

He licked his lips nervously before he answered.

"My Lord. It is indeed a glorious day. You will have your vengeance, as promised."

Tissaphernes watched the Sarvan carefully. After all these years, he was sure he'd developed an excellent sense of understanding for these weakling automatons. In theory, they were utterly loyal, but he had seen them fail before. He now operated with a zero tolerance for failure and wondered how reliable this new officer would be. Then a shape at the far end of the deck caught his eye. It was barely visible, yet he knew a senior guard was heading for the massive doors and checking on a new arrival.

Finally. She is here.

"Good. My fleet is ready for battle, but there is one piece missing from this puzzle. Now, where is my new right hand? I need my Darbabad if this battle is to be the success I know it will be."

The Sarvan stepped aside and pointed back along the deck. At the far end the doors were wide open, and in the centre a single figure. Something about this individual marked her out as much more powerful and more important than any of the Sarvans. She walked smartly along the deck, four officers marching behind in perfect rhythm. Seeing her approach was greatly relaxing. He trusted few people with the most important tasks, but when it came to the command of massive battles, he knew his own limitations. He was a grand strategist, not a naval commander.

"Very nice," said Tissaphernes, "Yes…Very nice."

The woman moved closer, and then stopped before him. The Sarvan bowed and stepped aside, leaving the two to look at each other. She was a mature Median noblewoman with well over eighty years of age to her name, perhaps even more. She was as tall as Tissaphernes, elegant and dressed as always in her smart Imperial Navy uniform, tall black boots and black gloves. Her long white hair ran down past her shoulders, yet she looked half of her age. Her uniform served as a reminder that she did not operate as a provincial officer, but as one of the God King's chosen cadre of elite commanders.

"The renowned Darbabad Forouzandeh. Exactly the person I need. You honour me by your presence."

She bowed her head, but it was a modest gesture, and nothing like that of the Sarvan.

"Satrap Tissaphernes. It is some time since we last met."

"Indeed. I am sorry to hear of the fate of your ship. The

Boubak will be long missed. Another victim of the Terran criminals."

She looked at him suspiciously. He'd never been much of a friend to her, and even now she found it almost impossible to trust him. Yet he was one of the twenty-six satraps established by Cyrus, the greatest of the God Kings. The satraps had never been kings, but viceroys ruling in the God King's name. They carried power and influence greater than any Terran could dream of.

I must listen to him, if not trust him.

"Quite. And you are no stranger to their wiles and violence, are you not?"

His nose twitched, and though he tried to hide it, he could tell she'd noticed.

"Very true. The Terrans are pirates and bandits, and for too long have preyed upon our generosity. That is why I have called you here, just one jump from the richest world of the Ionian League."

The Darbabad remained silent, waiting for him to continue. Tissaphernes had expected her to speak, but she would not be intimidated. As a Medes noble that could expect to be treated as a minor god, he was both annoyed and intrigued by this attitude.

"Today we will avenge our lost comrades. Walk with me."

The two moved along the deck, and through the next set of doors. It didn't take long until they reached a circular room devoid of any decoration. There were no other officers or crew in the place, and for a second the Darbabad lowered her hand to her side, as though preparing to reach for a weapon.

"I had this reconstructed from the remains of the salvaged Terran Titan taken in battle after the brutal fighting at Cunaxa. What do you think?"

Darbabad Forouzandeh looked at the markings and design.

"It's a non-functional observation system. I don't quite see how this is…"

The light dimmed in the room, and then the walls around them vanished. In their place was the area of space around the great fleet.

"Incredible," she said quietly, "You managed to get the system live and working in this battleship. Your engineers are to be commended. I would like to see this kind of technology aboard my own vessel."

Tissaphernes feigned humility as he nodded to her.

"Witness my grand fleet, Darbabad Forouzandeh."

The assembled Carian fleet was a sight to behold. Squadrons of ships from multiple worlds provided everything that could ever be needed to wage a war between worlds. Ships as small as destroyers were dwarfed by the lines of sleek Carian cruisers and battleships. Small groups of heavily armoured landing ships waited inside formations of destroyers, ready to smash through a planet's atmosphere and deposit hundreds of warriors to the surface. There were even contingents of slave ships from the Leleges regions, with their infamous Quadrireme slave galleys. These powerful, yet primitive ships made up for their lack of technology and firepower with hundreds of crew manning their manual weapons.

"Impressive. One thing you can rely upon with a Medes fleet is numbers."

It was a passive aggressive comment, and one that Tissaphernes didn't like to hear. Against his people the ships were powerful symbols. But they always suffered when up against equal numbers of Terrans. Memories of battles with his hated foe drifted into his mind, and he visibly shook his head to send them away.

"A well led Median fleet can defeat even the strongest foe."

Darbabad Forouzandeh was sensible not to push this further. All this talk of ships and fleets paled to insignificance compared to the mighty Vairya they now walked aboard. The powerful ship sat behind an entire squadron of Elamite battleships, each the equal of anything the average Terran colony could muster for battle.

"You are not wrong, Satrap Tissaphernes. And I have seen the reports of the Ionian colonies. There are rumours they intend on combining the Leagues into a regional Empire allied to other Terran colonies. Combined they will be able to challenge your own territories. I cannot imagine the God King would be pleased with that."

She smiled, and he knew she was toying with him.

"I have returned from my mission to Pharnabazus."

Mentioning the name of his rival made his blood chill. The two warlords loathed each other, and their bitter feud extended beyond any ambitions they might have over the Terrans.

"And?"

"He will consider joining you in a campaign against the Terrans. But he has conditions. One of which is that the God King must provide Imperial forces to assist."

"Of course he has conditions. Is his fleet ready?"

Darbabad Forouzandeh smiled.

"He has the numbers to match you, and he is building news ships every month. My agents confirm that he plans on using it very soon."

"I see. So he grows stronger over time. And with each passing month, our glorious God King demands action. Who is his target? Me or the Terrans?"

Darbabad Forouzandeh shrugged.

"Only Warlord Pharnabazus knows that answer."

"Quite."

Darbabad Forouzandeh said nothing, and merely watched him speak.

"A common threat is all that can pull our people together."

His voice trailed off, and then he stopped, leaving Forouzandeh wondering if it was now time for her to speak.

"Now…what do you ask of me?"

Their eyes met, each trying to work out the plan and schemes of the other. Tissaphernes knew the woman had lost the favour of many in positions of power in recent months, but she remained in demand for any that needed a war leader. There were none with more experience, or bore a greater list of victories than the renowned Darbabad. Any regional leader, be they Medes or Terran, would pay handsomely for her skills.

"I will bring all twelve colonies in the Ionian Territories under my control, as well as the twelve colonies in of the Aeolian League. Twenty-four rebel colonies brought to heel."

"A bold endeavour, Tissaphernes. This is something your forebears have tried and failed to achieve in the past. That will require a vast outlay of cash and warriors. You will need both Pharnabazus and reinforcements from the Core Worlds to do this."

That was a biting remark, and he almost lashed out at her impertinence.

"The God King will provide resources where he feels they will be of benefit. That is why I need to make a show of things, to make him understand that with minor assistance, I can transform the Empire and move ahead of the other satraps."

"And this is why you requested my presence? To aid in your strategy?"

Tissaphernes shook his head.

"Not entirely. I have my own plans for the future, and I do

not need help with them. But I am no Darbabad, and fighting a war is not a good use of my skills. I require a woman of unique abilities to lead my primary fleets in battle, and to provide me with a military strategy that will defeat my foes."

He smiled at her, and this time she could tell he was actually being honest. Tissaphernes was a plotter and a schemer. But she had also spent enough time around him to understand when he was being deceitful.

"This fleet is ready, but I will not strike our enemies until every piece is positioned on the board." He nodded towards her, "And you are the final piece."

Even Darbabad Forouzandeh looked surprised at his words. It was rare for the mighty Tissaphernes to admit he needed help.

"I want you to lead the fleet into battle from this ship, the most powerful vessel in my arsenal. Vairya will be your flagship, and you will destroy the Terrans utterly. As your ships crush the Terrans, my ground troops will assault their colonies, worlds, and space stations until they bring control of the Ionian Territories back to me."

Darbabad Forouzandeh remained completely calm and unemotional, though she found the challenge to be rather titillating.

"Will you do this one thing for me? Will you be my Darbabad?"

She licked her upper lip provocatively. It was a substantial offer, and one that would leave her answering to none other than the satraps of the Empire. She could do as she pleased, and attain her wildest dreams of avarice at the expense of others. She was no conventional Medes officer. She was from the Carian satrapy, one of Tissaphernes' two territories. Caria had been the domain of the traitor Cyrus, and that had left an indelible mark on the honour of the region. Many saw the Carians as loyal and trustworthy defenders of the Empire. But just as many that saw their dealing with the Terrans as a reminder of their moral flexibility.

"And if I do this for you?"

Tissaphernes shrugged.

"What is it that you desire?"

The Darbabad walked away from him and ran her hands along the inner walls of the ship. She moved several metres before stopping and looking back at him. He could see she was interested, but also that she had no need to aid him. She now had her own ships, as well as a charter to travel the Empire at will.

"I will lead your fleets, Tissaphernes. And I will destroy your enemies, one by one. Whoever they are."

Their eyes met, and the great Satrap nearly stepped back upon seeing the fire burning in her eyes. He'd hoped beyond hope that she would aid him, but she seemed far more interested than he'd ever anticipated.

"And your price?"

"My old ship, the great Boubak fell in battle against the Terrans at the Eternal Fortress. The price is that you will give me this ship and its entire crew."

He gasped at hearing that.

"Vairya? My flagship? This ship is no mere trinket, Darbabad. It was granted to me upon becoming Satrap of Lydia. It is a mark of my status and position in the Empire. To give her to you would allow you to usurp my authority."

To his surprise, the Darbabad turned away from him and looked as though she might leave.

"No, Tissaphernes. It will be my flagship."

He hesitated as movement out in space caught his attention.

His assembled fleet was a mighty host, though obvious to any commander that it was made up primarily of warships. There were few transports among their number, and any of the warships could only deploy so many warriors into battle. A long line of Elamite battleships moved into position ahead of the fleet. They were all different colours, with ships from dozens of different worlds. A handful even bore the markings of the Imperial Fleet, though they also the markings of Tissaphernes.

There they are.

Lights flashed as dark beetle like shapes arrived in the middle of his fleet. They were ugly ships, and nothing like the vessels already arrayed. He counted them as they came in until satisfied that every ship he'd paid for had come to serve him.

My Mulac mercenaries, excellent.

He looked back at the innards of his flagship, slowly shaking his head. It wasn't something he wanted to do, but unlike Darbabad Forouzandeh, his interests were much greater than that of ships. He wanted star systems, armies, fleets, and one day perhaps, the title of God King.

I play the long game of strategy. I can find more ships. When I am the God King, I can have a hundred Vairyas built for me.

Tissaphernes did the unthinkable and lowered his head for a moment. He needed to sound sincere, and she needed to believe she had won this victory. Even so, he checked to make sure there were no automatons anywhere near him. The last thing he wanted was for a single one of them to see even the smallest sign of weakness. To them he was a god, and that had to remain.

"Very well, Darbabad Forouzandeh. You strike a hard deal, and I will expect you to fight even harder for me. Fight these battles, and lead my fleets to many victories."

She raised her eyebrows, but still said nothing.

"Do this for me, and Vairya is yours...in perpetuity."

Now she smiled at him and nodded towards the assembled vessels. She was clearly happy, though Tissaphernes was disappointed to note that she seemed far from surprised. He didn't like to see anybody think they'd beaten him in some way, and already he was coming up with new plans to come out on top.

"Good, very good. Now. I am correct in saying that you have several captured Terran vessels?"

Tissaphernes nodded, though taken aback that she was already thinking of the coming fight. But then he remembered her reputation, and why he had brought her here to meet the fleet.

"Yes, we have some. I captured a number at Lydia, and others have been taken from the battlefields of a dozen stars. Why, do you have some ideas?"

Darbabad Forouzandeh lifted a single eyebrow in mock amusement.

"Tissaphernes. I started planning for your campaign a month ago."

His mouth opened a little, and try as he might he could not stop himself from laughing. It was a low booming voice that spread through the innards of the massive open space. This went on for many seconds until he finally quietened down.

"Good. I expected nothing less. Now tell me, why do you need it?"

"I need to sacrifice one before battle begins. And that will grant me the window I require to succeed."

Tissaphernes turned and began to move away, and then signalled for her to follow him. He might have handed her his ship, but he was still in charge, and intended on making sure she knew that every single day.

"In that case, Darbabad Forouzandeh. The fleet is yours. Now tell me of your plan? I want to know how you intend on snuffing out my foes."

"I will beat them for you. But before we can do that, we must bring them to us. To wear them out and drain their strength before you strike. We will trade soldiers, colonies, and ships as the price to bleed them. But we will avoid engaging their forces in major battles."

Tissaphernes hesitated, and then smiled.

"You have learnt your lesson well from the Black Legion."

She almost smiled at hearing that.

"The Black Legion was defeated in the end, was it not?"

Tissaphernes had not expected this approach, and he'd never truly considered the Black Legion had been beaten. After all, they'd been able to leave the Empire and to return to whatever lives remained for them. Even so, he decided to see where the Darbabad Forouzandeh was planning on taking him. He gave a gentle flourish of his hand for her to continue.

"The God King evicted them from his lands, without needing to destroy them in battle. It was a smart, and well considered strategy, and beyond the capabilities of the Terrans. I will do the same, but on a vastly larger scale."

Tissaphernes looked to her, checking for any sign of betrayal.

"You will provide the Terrans with victories and allow them to live?"

Darbabad Forouzandeh nodded slowly.

"Yes. And in doing so we will starve the Terrans of people, weapons, and funds. We will let time and the vastness of the Empire engulf and envelope them. But first they must be drawn in."

"And how do you intend on doing that?"

Darbabad Forouzandeh looked at him carefully, trying to size up his thoughts on her plan. He seemed receptive, but his reputation for anger and violence was well deserved. She was no coward, but she also had no intention of being killed on a whim.

"I will strike these Ionian colonies hard and fast. They will be forced to plead for aid. Once they are fully committed can we proceed to phase two."

That seemed to intrigue him.

"I see. Now tell me more about this phase two."

CHAPTER TWO

Light Cruiser 'Shrike', Ephesus Prime

The devastation wrought throughout the peaceful Ephesus System began with the arrival of just one ship. A proximity alert activated on the command deck of the light cruiser Shrike as its passive sensors detected the object. Kybernetes Vasilis Christos stepped towards the ship's tactical officer and pointed to the distant shape.

"What is that thing doing here?"

The tactical officer shook her head as she looked more carefully.

"I don't know, Sir. It's a small frigate and bears the marks of the Laconian fleet."

"Laconian? What are they doing so far from home? Very strange."

"Yes, Sir. It is showing no signs of life, and is heavily damaged. It must have drifted here. The hull is as cold as ice."

"Possibly. Tag and pass it on to Command. They can send a unit to investigate. At least it's not drifting in any of the shipping lanes."

"Yes, Kybernetes."

"Sir," called out the auletes, the ship's communications officer, "Command confirms the next grain shipment will arrive in four minutes, and they request we scan them upon arrival."

Christos sat back in the command chair.

"Understood. Helm, lay in intercept course, and ready our scanners."

He turned his attention to the mystery ship. The imagery from the onboard cameras was quite grainy, be he could still make out the scorch marks running along its hull, and numerous holes marked damage from recent fighting. His attention was soon pulled away as seven flashes alerted him to the arrival of civilian transports.

"New contacts. It's the Mudrāyan grain ships."

"Ahead of schedule. That is just typical. Scan them."

"Yes, Sir."

As their FTL engines shutdown, they coalesced into great bulk transport ships. They were bigger than almost all military ships and looked centuries old. Their markings were from the Mudrāya Satrapy, a breakaway region of the Empire that still supplied the lowest costs food materials to most of the nearby colonies. As their attention shifted to the grain ships, all interest in the derelict Laconian ship faded. The vessel drifted into position almost half a million parasangs from Selene Theta, the eighth moon that orbited Ephesus Prime. The small vessel was little more than a ghost ship, its hull cold to the night. The ship rotated slightly as it was pulled closer and closer to the small moon. Had anybody been paying attention, they might have spotted the small antenna pushing out from its hull, and the slowly rotating scanners showing that some systems were active.

"Another glorious day on patrol," he said with a sigh. He then leaned back in the seat just as Kentarchos Alexis returned to the command deck of his warship. That made him sit up straight.

"Kentarchos, the ship is yours."

Alexis nodded politely and moved to take his place. In a past life he'd been a mercenary, fighting for both sides in the brutal wars between the League and Attica. Now he lived his retirement out as a ship commander in one of the safest sectors in the galaxy. At least that was what he thought. He'd been busy assisting one of the engineering teams for the last hour, and upon his return found the deck as he'd left it. It appeared to be a day like any other, with little of interest outside of the hundreds of ships plying their way along the numerous shipping lanes.

"Anything to report, Kybernetes?"

Vasilis Christos shook his head.

"Nothing. Unless you count the arrival of seven grain transports over Ephesus Prime. Oh, and there's an outbreak of food poisoning on one of the Median tourist liners from the Cilician Gates. They've been put into quarantine until a medical frigate can send in a team."

He was a by the book officer. As executive officer, he was the right-hand man of the Kentarchos, and responsible for ensuring the commander's orders were carried out as quickly as possible. This freed up the Kentarchos' time to concentrate on the bigger picture. Vasilis was an ex-Arcadian soldier and veteran of many military campaigns decades earlier. There was little this man hadn't seen, from pirate raids on the distant outer worlds, to fleet engagements between the Terrans. Kentarchos Alexis shook his head as he sunk down into his command seat and rubbed his weary eyes.

"A food poisoning outbreak, Christos? At least they're all stuck aboard the one ship. I'd not want to be there on the planet in those circumstances."

He almost chuckled as he slowly turned in his chair. The displays inside the ship were relatively modern, though the vessel did at least have a partially integrated virtual observation system. Less sophisticated than the systems used in capital ships, it was still very effective. Christos tapped one of the displays and brought up imagery of the other newly arrived ship.

"We also identified this Laconian derelict. It showed signs of damage and was entering a decaying orbit. We've flagged it as a shipping hazard, and tugs are due to assist in the next ten hours."

Alexis stretched his legs and sighed.

"It really does get exciting out here, doesn't it?"

Ephesus patrol was perhaps the most boring postings possible in the Ionian Territories. The twelve systems were some of the richest in existence, and the safest. This was a consequence of their unique and unusual position in the galaxy. They owed their success to being Terran enclaves on the border of the outer territories of the Median Empire. He'd be lucky if he ran into a smuggler, or even the rarer sight of a pirate or corsair. Nothing happened in this area, not with both Imperial and Terran ships patrolling the shipping lanes.

Christos shrugged.

"This is Ephesus. Nothing happens out here that would warrant our attention."

What would I give for some action? Anything would be better than another day of this drudgery, Alexis thought.

He ran his eyes over the shipping reports once more, and

then stopped.

"Wait, bring up the details for the derelict."

In seconds the schematic spun about before his face. He watched for a moment, and then tapped the next unit. At that moment, he shot upright as though he'd seen a ghost.

"These antenna, they are never deployed during FTL transport. And look, two of the short-range scanners are in different positions with each image."

Christos looked at the imagery, and then gasped.

"They're running short-range tactical scans. But why?"

"I don't know, but I don't like it."

He ran his hand through his light beard one last time, and then pointed towards the other vessel.

"I don't like this, not one bit. Helm, lay in an intercept course and get us there fast."

"Yes, Kentarchos."

Christos spun the model of the ship about on the screen.

"You think this could be hostile?"

"Maybe. I don't like taking chances. I want data locks placed on her. And get in touch with Command. They need to know of a possible threat to local space."

"Ah, well. It's time to move onto the entry point. Here's to another day of peace in Ionia!"

"We're on the way, Kentarchos."

The elegant Raptor Class light cruiser activated its thrusters and began the slow and gentle process of moving into higher orbit. Her outer hull was painted in a beautiful pattern of yellow and orange, with accents along the dorsal sections in bright gold, almost silver-coloured trim. Her sleek design combined the armour and firepower of the Terran ships, with the manoeuvrability and elegance of Medes vessels. Shrike was a small ship, little bigger than some of the more modern destroyers used by the Terrans, and yet her size betrayed her capabilities. She was a hybrid in every sense of the word, her styling much in common with cartilaginous fish. The ship's forward hull was quite bulky, but with a long, sleek tail which large thrusters were fitted to in the style of fins. A small number of turrets marked the position of the vessel's powerful plasma weapons, though as usual they were all stowed behind thick gun port plates.

Shrike was one of six Raptor class cruisers on patrol over the jewel of the Ionian Territories, the great harbour of the Ephesus System. There were other similar patrols around the moons and other planets, making this one of the safest shipping havens in the known galaxy. Here the three colonised planets serviced more ships and trading convoys than the rest of the worlds in the Ionian Territories combined. As well as being a great trading hub, they were also a place where Terrans met Medes, as well as a hundred other races in relative peace.

More important to many visitors, Ephesus claimed to be one of the great wonders of the known universe, and because of that it enjoyed pre-eminence among its peers. Seven of these great, artificial constructions were known to exist, the majority in territories under the control of the God King and his satraps. The great Star Temple of Artemis formed an entire city on the capital world of Ephesus Prime, one of the most famous religious and tourist locations in the galaxy. It was a region free from the war and violence that seemed to pervade most regions of space.

"Kentarchos!" Christos yelled, "You are not going to believe this."

"Try me."

Christos pointed nervously at the array of screens in front of them. Pulses of multi-coloured lights marked the arrival of ships from FTL travel. One came in, but then more and more followed until there were nine. And still they came.

"Carian ships. Cruisers, destroyers…and troop ships. It's a small fleet. They are advancing with their gun ports open, and it's heading directly for…"

"Ephesus Prime," Alexis interrupted, "This cannot be. We've maintained the peace for more than a century. What fool would dare break it with full-scale war, and with such a pitiful little fleet? We could annihilate these vessels in…"

Another flash marked the arrival of yet another ship, a massive Super Elamite battleship carrying the markings of the Carian Royalty. The ship was a monster, dwarfing every other vessel in the sector. It made even the biggest freighters seem minute in comparison. Alexis almost lost his voice as he read the name of the ship as it appeared on the various screens.

"Vairya!"

He looked back to his Kybernetes who appeared equally stunned.

"Yes. It's Tissaphernes' ship all right. He's broken the treaty coming here! Like any of us should be surprised. The man is a traitor, right down to his rotten heart."

When he looked back, he noticed six much smaller Elamite battleships flanked the battleship. The difference was so great the standard ships looked little more than cruisers alongside that behemoth; enough they were as big as the largest Terran battleships. More than a dozen squat, ugly looking vessels flanked it. They looked more like beetles than spaceships, their hulls protected by a shell-like structure, and spindly legs fitted with weaponry pushed out to their flanks.

"Mulac assault ships. But they are not designed for space combat."

Then he gulped, realising the magnitude of what was

happening.

"They can only be here for one thing."

A dark mood filled the ship as the handful of officers realised what was happening in their beloved star system, each all too familiar with the reputation of the Satrap Tissaphernes.

"Auletes! Contact Ephesus Command, and send them all of our data. They need to know the Satrap is here, and he's brought an entire fleet with him. Helm, plot a course for Ephesus, and activate the FTL drive."

A bright burst of light struck from one of the newly arrived ships. For a second it seemed as though it would hit Shrike. Instead it slammed into Vulture, one of the other identical Raptor Class light cruisers. The stern tore apart before any shields could be powered up. More shots slammed into the wreckage, each projectile ensuring not a single soul would survive.

"She's gone, Kentarchos," said Christos. Alexis looked at him and then gasped at the destruction brought by the surprise attack, and the utter brutality of the assault, "I'm detecting no lifeboats in the area. Should we move in to…"

"No, there will be time for rescuing survivors when this is over. Activate our engines now, and get into a defensive formation ahead of them! Use the FTL drive if you must."

We will tell their story. And come back for the bodies…if any of us lives to tell the tale.

He shook his head, simultaneously tapping the communications node fitted inside his ear. It was a simple piece of short-ranged technology, but reliable and almost impossible to jam unless within a few metres. His voice spread to every member of the crew, no matter where they were on the ship.

"This is your Kentarchos. Ephesus us under attack. This is not a drill. I repeat; this is not a drill. We are moving on an intercept course, and will rejoin the Ephesus defence perimeter."

The ship shuddered as the FTL drive powered up. In a fraction of a second, they were moving at incredible speeds, along with the other four surviving light cruisers. They would need seconds to reach their destination, rather than the hours it would take under normal drive. He licked his lips before giving the order he'd never expected to give. The swirling lights stabilised, and the engines cut, dropping them out of FTL travel. The other four cruisers were right next to them and already turning to face off against the newly arrived ships.

"Battle stations! Get the shields up! Jam their systems, and activate all countermeasures."

He glanced across to Christos who was already calling out orders to the other officers. When finished, he turned his attention back to the Kentarchos. He nodded quickly, confirming they were ready.

"It's time to show these Carian scum who's in charge in this sector. Nobody opens fire in the vicinity of Ephesus and gets away with it!"

The lights shifted in shade as the interior of the ship transformed to war mode. It was far from subtle, with everything from the interior lighting to the display screens changing palette and tone. Gone were the cool yellow and beige lights that gave the vessel a warm and comfortable glow. Instead everything looked red and serious, as the situation demanded. No opportunity for surrender had been given by the new ships, and no demands given.

"Open up all gun ports, and roll out the guns!"

There was a moment of confusion and horror that paralysed every single person on the ship. But then he shouted orders without needing to give it a moment's thought. Most of the crew were Ionian Terrans and had seen little or no combat. That was not true for her senior officers, however. Each was experienced in war, and though they had come here to escape the violence and destruction of battle, they remained intimately familiar with it. There were few officers on the command deck, but those that were quickly leapt into action. More shots tore into the formation of ships, but the quick reaction of her crew saved them from certain death.

"Shields powered up," said the Kybernetes as he checked with the other officers, "I've brought the reserve cells online and powering up. Looks like we're going to need them. We've got light gunfire coming down on our squadron."

He pointed to central screen that showed imagery of the planet and surrounding area.

"Orbital platforms are preparing for battle."

"Preparing? They should always be ready for battle. That's their only job."

He shook his head as he watched the screens. The platform were big, designed to operate both as supply posts and transfer stations, as well as powerful batteries that could bombard any vessels entering the system.

"And where the hell are our damned fighters?"

A cursory look towards the orbital platforms confirmed their shielding was powering up, but there was still no sign of the embarked fighter units launching into space.

"Activate the VOB."

The inner walls of the command deck seemed to vanish as the molecules on the metal plates changed to provide video information from outside. It wasn't a complete three hundred and sixty-degree system as used on bigger ships, but it provided half of the information to the front and sides, as well as above and below the position of the senior officers. Now he could see the newly arrived ships in all their glory, and it sent a shudder down his spine as he realised the mortal danger they were in.

"Transfer additional cover to the port side, and bring us about. Open gun ports, and prepare for battle. Contact all patrol vessels, and ensure they're ready for battle. I want everything we have in high-orbit to move to standard defence pattern alpha."

The Kybernetes hesitated.

"Do it. Do it now! Time is not our friend. Not today."

The man could barely speak as he passed on orders to the gundecks. It took a few seconds longer than it should have before he looked back.

"All gun crews are ready."

"Good. Now, target the…"

He ran his eyes along the growing number of approaching ships. Many were firing and selecting mainly civilian ships. Anything that came too close to the other ships was soon cut apart. He tapped his communication node.

"The flagship. Turn everything we have on her, and fire a broadside. Now!"

It took another three seconds as the ship made the subtle course changes. The other four vessels did the same, matching their heading and speed. The entire flank of Shrike and the other ships vanished behind a flurry of plasma shots. The bright pulses of energy surged towards the massive vessel and struck all around its bow. Some missed, but at least a third hit their mark.

"No damage. Their shields are down to sixty percent. We'll never be able to damage that thing without help."

The Kentarchos watched on stoically, looking at the approaching ships.

"Very true. But our job is not to destroy this fleet, is it?

Remember the Hot Gates. The Laconians could never win that battle, yet they fought it knowing they would die."

They looked to each other, and Alexis knew immediately when his Kybernetes understood what he was saying.

"The job of the perimeter force is to delay the arrival of their reserves, and to motivate our friends and allies to join us in battle."

"Exactly. We will attack their flagship, and force them to deal with us. We will buy time with our lives."

"Of course. We have five squadrons arriving in thirty seconds. Komes Katarios is in command and leading the Ephesus cruiser wing."

A stream of gunfire glanced off the flank of the ship, some of the shots managing to create small gaps in the shielding. The helmsman quickly adjusted their course, and then positioned the intact dorsal shielding against the incoming fire.

"Shields are down to thirteen percent. Another hit and we're gone," said the tactical officer, "I think we..."

At that moment the first three squadrons arrived in a series of bright flashes of light. One moment they were little more than a blur, the next in position and ready for combat. They deployed ahead of the battered light cruisers, presenting their main gun batteries towards the enemy. They were a mixture of light and heavy cruisers, with torpedo boats as escorts. The formation was tightly organised, based on the drills they'd performed many times before. One by one the torpedo boats activated their forward launch tubes and prepared to open fire.

"Finally," said Alexis, "Now we'll give them a fight. By Hades, they'll wish they'd never bothered a soul in this system."

A smile formed along his face as he watched the huge warships manoeuvre for the battle. Their engines glowed bright as they moved into weapons range. They were still outnumbered by the new arrivals, but these were no slave ships from the Median Empire. The free men and women of the Terran worlds could not be compared to the whimpering automatons manning the Imperial vessels. He had no doubt in his mind that the Terrans would prove their worth.

"Smash them," he said, raising a clenched fist.

The torpedo boats started first, sending a wide pattern of powerful warheads towards the Carian vessels. But as they unleashed their arsenal of weapons, it became clear that Ephesus would not give in without a fight. The first of the shots struck the enemy flagship, as well as two of its escort vessels.

"Beautiful," said Kentarchos Alexis, "These Carians have made a big mistake. Terran ships do not yield to these Medes' lackeys."

Even as he spoke, the enemy fleet began to lose cohesion. Long energy beams from heavy cutters tore apart small ships, volleys of plasma exploding against armour and shields. Bursts of laser fire from Terran ships punches scores of holes in the armour of Median vessels, with so many shots striking them that some vanished under the bright red bombardment.

"Komes Katarios has broken through their line. She's taking the heavies in with her."

"That's my girl," said Kentarchos Alexis, "Katarios does exactly as she promises."

The Kybernetes double-checked one of the displays before calling back over his right shoulder; he'd seen something unexpected and looked surprised.

"The Carian fleet is splitting up."

"Good. That means the Komes has done her job. Now we can chase down the stragglers, as a pack of wolves hunt down the weak of the herd."

"Uh…Kentarchos. They're splitting up."

"Excellent news."

"No…it's not panic. I think this is a tactical withdrawal to pull in our heavy ships. If you look, the main division is moving to higher orbit around the flagship."

"And the others?"

Christos leaned in closer for a better look before answering.

"The others are heading for the moons, and down to lower orbit over Prime. We have a chance to hit them."

Kentarchos Alexis considered his options, but before he could give the order, the holographic image of the Komes appeared. The woman wore her breastplate over her clothing, and it looked as though she'd been rushed to get to the battle; for all that, the look on her face was fierce and without compromise.

"This is Katarios, commander of the Ephesus Defence Forces. You will stand down from this incursion immediately. I will not allow…"

Her image crackled and faded. It was then replaced by an entirely different signal. Christos checked with the other officers before shaking his head.

"Not good. The enemy flagship is overpowering the Komes. They're sending in a stronger signal, and it's being bounced between every one of their ships."

"Switch to direct laser comms, then," said Alexis, "We have to retain command and control in this battle."

"Sir. It's from her commander. You're not going to believe this."

"Put him on."

The holographic communications emitter flickered as it changed from the corrupted image of Katarios to somebody entirely different. Kentarchos Alexis rose from his seat as he looked upon the face of his foe. He was tall and much thinner than any Terran.

"The Satrap Tissaphernes," he said quietly, and then looked to his second-in-command, "I should have known the Medes wouldn't be able to stay away for long. This satrap is the scourge of Ionia."

He wore no obvious armour, instead a soft crimson robe with yellow trim that hung from his shoulders down to just below his knees. The top of his head was hidden beneath a tall, almost conical hat. A soft white belt made of plaited fabric ran around his waist, and at his side a curved scabbard hid a bejewelled blade. As Alexis examined the Medes man, he could just make out the shape of scale armour at his sternum, confirming that under the robe he was probably attired for battle.

"This is a trick. He's dressed for battle, and yet he's hiding under this farcical clothing. He wants us to think he is soft and weak."

"He is a Medes," said Christos, "They are soft and weak."

Kentarchos Alexis shook his head

"Don't be fooled by these people, Christos. What they lack in physical strength, they make up for with numbers and guile. There is a reason their Empire is greater than anything our own people have ever achieved."

They both looked back to their tormentor.

"Greeting, Terrans of Ephesus. Lay down your arms, and surrender this system, or see every one of your colonies cleansed with fire."

Alexis gasped.

"He truly wants war this time. Why?"

Though the image remained of the Satrap, the voice of the Terran commander returned, along with her crackling and partially corrupted image.

"The Ionian Colonies are neutral. You have no business being here, Tissaphernes. Your actions risk war between our peoples. Remember Salamis, Plataea, and the Hot Gates. You do not want a repeat of those debacles. Your God King does not suffer fools. Your domain is..."

Tissaphernes' expression shifted at the mention of the God King, and for a fraction of a second it even looked as though he was a little nervous.

"Wherever I travel, I become the God King. My words are his words, and my actions are his actions. You supported your Terran friends in attempt of the God King's life with the usurper Cyrus. Now you will pay for your crimes. Choose now. Surrender, or death."

The image vanished, and Komes Katarios took his place. She looked equally stunned and angry at what she'd just heard. Alexis and the other officers waited with bated breath at what her orders would be.

"You all heard this madman. Tissaphernes is a treacherous leech, and his word can never be trusted. Defend the colonies. Fight to the last ship! We will never..."

Her image vanished as quickly as it had arrived. It then shuddered, returning with significant damage and decay.

"Capital ships will join me in an attack on the enemy battleship division. We will hold them back so that the light squadrons can engage the landing ships. Do not let them reach the surface!"

Alexis breathed a sigh of relief at hearing this. He was no coward, but being given orders to attack the primary fleet would mean the end of his own ship in no short time. He wiped his sweaty brow and pointed to the imagery in front of him. At the same time, the doors to the command deck opened, and in rushed four more officers. They said nothing and moved to their stations. One bore a bloodied bandage on her forehead as she dropped behind her computer display. Alexis pointed towards the VOB system, and the formation of Carian and Mulac vessels now descending at speed from their position directly above them.

"This is it. We're going to smash into their formation before they can reach low orbit. Give me all the speed you've got. Auletes, put me on with the rest of the squadron."

He looked ahead as multiple formations of light cruisers and destroyers moved together into a great shoal of warships.

"Ready yourselves," he said over the communication node, "The Battle for Ephesus has begun!"

CHAPTER THREE

Ephesus System, Ionian Territories
The great trading colonies of the Ephesus System were no easy prize for an invader. For centuries many a pirate and warlord have passed the great colonies and tested their mettle against the defences. The systems and its planets were well guarded by scores of ships bearing the colours of the Ionian League, while the elite Ephesian fighter squadrons protected the skies over the colonies. Even if a foe could reach the surface they would be hard pressed to deal with the substantial fortifications on the ground.

Ephesus Prime was the jewel at the heart of this shining paragon of wealth and success. As the most heavily inhabited colony world, it was something truly special, a rich world in one of the richest areas of the galaxy. Technologically advanced, and home to the wealthiest traders and shipping companies from dozens of different races. The planet was a bizarre dichotomy of large oceans and great swathes of arid landmasses. The desert climate was common throughout most of the world, complete with canyons, rocks, and sand. The coast featured trees, plants, and animal life, giving the cities a tropical paradise look. What the rest of the planet lacked in foliage and greenery it made up for with a consistently dry stable environment, and free from natural storms. This combined to create the perfect location for the manufacture and maintenance of ships, as well as the logistics of moving freight. Massive mega cities filled with tall buildings and rich apartments were built into the cliffs and looked out to the grand oceans.

As expected, the space battle over Ephesus was a bloodbath. After fifteen minutes of fighting, a number of capital ships were already on their way down to the planet below. Kentarchos Alexis watched with sadness as a grand looking cruiser, emblazoned with the markings and colours of the Ionian Territories dropped out of sight. Flames poured from its flanks, and entire sections tore away as it breached the planet's atmosphere. The Terran ship was not alone, though, as ships from both sides fought to a standstill, smaller ships and transports trying desperately to break into lower orbit.

"Helm, thirty-degree roll and start a retro burn!" Christos ordered.

The engines roared as the ship performed an impressive roll in the middle of the battle. She was so fast that a stream of fire from a Median cruiser completely missed her. Shrike spun to her portside and then vanished behind two Terran armoured destroyers. The change in course and speed threw off the enemy scanners, so that when she reappeared they'd lost their locks.

"Perfect," said Alexis as they moved out and directly behind a small Carian frigate. The ship was damaged and trying to escape the fighting. He watched multiple Terran fighters strafe the ship and then turned away. A smile formed ever so slowly across his face.

"Starboard gunners…wait for my command."

The ship continued to roll, and for a moment her underside faced the enemy ship. Shrike's gunners held their fire as ordered, and slowly the light cruiser rolled her flank into position. The dozens of men and women waited patiently, their sights filled with the shape of the damaged destroyer. Though advanced, the individual gun batteries were still managed and operated by skilled professional crewmembers.

"Fire!"

The flank of Shrike lit up with white and blue flashes as gun after gun blasted away. Shots slammed into the frigate at a range of two hundred metres. With the shielding gone, the damage was catastrophic. But then they were gone and raced into the maelstrom of yet another battle. More fighters and ships streamed past as the organised battle quickly turned to chaos. Kybernetes Christos moved along the deck, checking the combat stations. Dekarchos Alexis remained in his seat, watching as ships and fighters engaged in the bloody battle.

"Good, very good. Wait…I can see a squadron of landing ships breaking out."

He pointed to his left, below the point where a dozen ships were engaged in a close-ranged gunnery duel. It took a moment, but then the shapes of a group of the large black vessels appeared. Their engines were burning brightly as they used every ounce of power to push themselves down to the planet's surface.

"Helm, follow them down."

Alexis then tracked the numerous vessels nearby. He could see a small number of light ships, but he wanted the fighters and gunships.

"There!"

He activated his communication node and spoke to the commanders of the fighter units.

"This is Dekarchos Alexis of the Light Cruiser Shrike. You have a formation of landing ships breaking through at sector Sigma Six. Follow my waypoints and provide fighter cover for my assault."

A wave of acknowledgements arrived, though from less fighters than he would have liked. At that moment Shrike's engines pulsed with power, and they accelerated towards the damaged vessel. This was one of the heavily armoured landing ships, with its black, beetle-like hull and curved slabs of thick armour. The shielding pulsed and flickered as a squadron of Terran fighters screamed overhead, firing shield smasher missiles. Every hit reduced the strength of a small section of the shields, creating an opening that could be attacked.

"There, that's the spot! Target the breached shields and fire!"

Shrike was already in position, along with her four sister ships. They were flying almost vertically and directly towards the planet. The enemy vessels were now completely black, silhouetted against the brightness of the planet far below. The bow-mounted heavy cutters activated in a short burst of energy. They drew a narrow beam to the target, and then sat there, cutting through the metal and bulkheads in the same way industrial mining lasers were used. Two more light cruisers joined in, followed by a torpedo boat. These unusual ships were based on frigates, but with their forward and lower hull weapons replaced with torpedo tubes. These massive weapons could hurl high-powered plasma shots, or conventional munitions such as anti-ship missiles and torpedoes.

"Wow!" Christos said, "Look at that!"

A blast of energy that looked like a tiny star erupted from the front of the torpedo boat and slammed into the damaged section of the enemy cruiser. It penetrated deep inside its hull, exploding in a flash of incandescent light. The ship broke apart as the three Terran light cruisers circled around it, continuing to fire. There was no mercy as they ensured its shattered hull could never recover. They raced past, each putting another volley of plasma into its burning hulk. No sooner were they past it when they ran immediately into a screen of Carian destroyers trying to provide a perimeter for ships coming in behind them. They were surrounded by groups of small Median light fighters.

"These people never give up, do they?" Kentarchos Alexis said through clenched teeth. He was about to continue when a pair of the agile fighters spun past pursuing a pair of Terran fighters. One came in too close and was hit by gunfire from Shrike's port side.

"Nice shooting," said Alexis, "Very nice shooting."

"New contact!" Christos said in a shrill shout, "Five ships just came out of FTL. They're right beneath us."

"Show me."

Both looked down as the floor shifted and changed until it looked completely transparent. Right below them were five battleships, each a different colour, and firing streams of light in all directions. Terran vessels scattered, smashing through the defenders like predatory fish breaking up a shoal.

"They've locked onto us!"

"Evasive action. Shift all power to lower shields," said the Kybernetes, "Helm, bring us around and right down their throats."

Alexis gritted his teeth as the helmsman put the light cruiser into a deep dive and increased power to the thrusters. The change in course and acceleration was substantial, and not even the internal dampeners could negate all of it. Ahead a squadron of cruisers moved in fast to hit the battleships from the side.

"Nice flying. Bring us around to join the others attacking from their flanks. We'll hit their engines and then move on to the next one. Divert the shields back to the bow."

"Yes, Kentarchos."

The light cruiser was a nimble vessel, and they avoided the raging battle above as they moved into position. Fighters screeched past, flaming trails following them as missiles chased in all directions. The VOB system gave a perfect view of the target ahead as they moved in to attack

"Are the gunners ready?"

"Yes, Kentarchos. Flank plasma batteries are ready to fire."

"Good. This is it. Be ready."

The light cruiser formed up along her comrades and moved in quickly towards the target. Gunfire glanced off her shielding like hail on a winter's day. Occasionally, one would knock out a shield panel, but another would shift its overlapping layer to cover the gap. Plasma shells exploded in bright cascades of colour, showering the cruiser in patterns of light.

"Ready to fire," said the Kybernetes.

Alexis opened his mouth to give the order as another shape coalesced right in front of him. His eyes opened wide, as he realised exactly what it was, and the threat it represented.

"That's a Median Battleship. Take evasive…"

It was too late. The ship fired before they could turn away. Pulse cannons cut into the hull of Shrike, but the heavy cutters did the truly terrible work. They slashed like swords through the ship, tearing up compartments, destroying weapons, and triggering a hundred fires. Incredibly, the brave crew managed to roll away from the ship, but the damage was done.

"Kentarchos!" Christos yelled, "Systems are failing everywhere. Weapons and shields are gone. Engines are heavily damaged. We need…"

A trio of Median Azarakhsh Imperial heavy gunships dropped down from almost a kilometre away and opened up with their arsenal of weapons. Pulse cannons bit deep into the damaged ship, while the pair of pulse rotary cannons sent hundreds of rounds against the broken armour. They pulled away at the last moment, but not before releasing a cloud of anti-ship missiles from the missile cells.

"Brace for impact!" Kybernetes Christos shouted, but it was all in vain.

They crashed through the shattered armour plates and exploded in three locations. Entire sections of Shrike were torn away, leaving a burning hulk to drop down from orbit. Alexis couldn't believe it. One minute they were hunters, racing around the battlefield to find their quarry. And now his ship was a wreck, and he was fleeing like the rest of his people. He knew what he had to do, and he had to do it quickly.

"This is the Kentarchos. Shrike has been crippled. All crew abandon ship. I repeat. All crew abandon ship."

The ship was falling apart, through incredibly the command deck and a handful of other compartments remained intact for now. Alexis deactivated his harness and rose from his chair. Kybernetes Christos kept shaking his head as he looked to his commander.

"I don't know what we could have done differently. How could…"

Alexis grabbed his arm and pushed him away from the centre of the deck.

"Enough. Get to the boats, now!"

They staggered away as the last few systems began to fail. Luckily for the bridge crew, they were able to reach one of two emergency exit hatches fitted into the walls of the command deck. Bright lights flashed around them, marking their position even in the lowest of light. A second door on the other side of the airlock, a metre away led to the inside of the lifeboat. A pair was attached to each flank of the deck, a design feature that continued at fixed points along the length of the ship.

"May the Gods save our comrades," Alexis said as he stepped inside, "None of them deserved this."

As the door slid shut, the gravity system finally faded. The last thing Alexis saw was the side of the command deck vanish and replaced by the frigid vacuum of space, and then the lifeboat burst away from the stricken vessel. He could see the ship falling apart, and it almost brought a tear to his eye. That was until he looked back at his crew. Some bore cuts and marks from the battle, yet each looked angry and determined.

"We're going down, and fast." Christos wiped blood from a cut across his forehead.

"Make for the Omega Nine complex and get us down fast. This battle is not going to end in the skies of Ephesus."

They looked out of the small windows and down to the planet below.

"The lifeboat carries armour and weapons. Get yourselves ready. Ephesus has not fallen. Not yet!"

CHAPTER FOUR

Olympian Shipyards, Ephesus Prime
Security Chief Elli Selene never expected to see her world turned to fire and ruination in a single day, and certainly not by those they considered friends. She leaned back in the soft chair, watching the line of ships from her position in the raised observation platform above the Hestia Shipyard. The platform, a small, semi-circular section jutting out from the main foyer, granted her the perfect view of the six massive dry docks, with their long metal walkways, cranes, and all manner of equipment. Each bay contained a waiting ship, well lit from powerful lamps fitted to the walls and ceiling. Some ships were there for reconstruction work, but the majority for the cut-price servicing and upgrades offered by the Ephesians. This was one of twelve similar facilities built into the Northern cliff face of the Dodona Peninsula, each named after one of the old gods. They were known collectively as the Olympian Shipyards, after their namesakes, and their reputation was known for thousands of parsecs in all directions.

Elli her earned her living in this region working for the rich corporations and guilds. Those that understood such things might notice the markings on her vintage Corinthian helm lying on the seat next to her. They were subtle, but confirmed her reputation with a dozen corporations, as well as multiple colonies. She worked for a small mercenary unit that operated out of Ephesus Prime, working aboard the civilian freighters that plied the worlds of the Ephesus System. She was one of thousands of similar people on Ephesus earning their living from the trade convoys along the numerous shipping lanes. In a past life she'd served as a stratiotes to half a dozen different warlords, even doing a tour with a unit of border corsairs.

What's that sound?

Elli knew something was going on well before it happened. She looked to the left and then to the entry point back into the station. She was sure she could hear footsteps. She'd been an attractive woman before half of her face was burnt in a major raid a decade earlier. Surgery and reconstruction efforts had hidden the worst, but she'd never look the same again. Now in her late thirties she looked every part the gung-ho stratiotes. She was taller than most, with dark brown curly hair, pale green eyes, and her dark skin a reminder that she spent as much time as a mercenary on the surface of Prime, as she did onboard freighters.

A siren activated, and she turned her attention to one of the large display boards on the wall next to the doorway back inside the facility. She couldn't make out the words, but she recognised the alert warning icons. It was a warning to ground personnel that an unidentified vessel had entered Ephesus space. One technician looked at it and shook his head. That immediately piqued her interest. The station was quite small, and led to a passage that ran directly to the elevators down to the shipyards.

"What's happening?"

The man turned and looked back at her, surprised there had been somebody nearby. He stared for a few seconds before he could make out her shape in the corner, partially hidden in the shadows. Then his eyebrows rose in recognition.

"Selene?"

She nodded in reply, and he took a few steps closer to check. Though seated, there was something suspicious about her. The way her hands rested near her side and next to her rough looking brown leather coat. She wore a light tan bandolier across her body, a sure sign that she was a gun for hire.

"It's a proximity alert. Something is happening up there."

He looked up to the ceiling, but Elli kept her eyes on him. She knew the place well enough to know there was nothing above them save the high ceiling, and long metal ribs that stretched throughout this part of the facility.

"Something?"

"Who knows? I need to get back. All work crews are being recalled."

Without saying another word he rushed away, leaving her alone. She'd been resting in the lower deck shipyard of the Omega Nine complex for most of the morning, waiting for repair work to be finished on her ship. Her job was to ensure nobody stepped inside the vessel without authorisation, and from her vantage point she could see every soul that came within a hundred metres of the battered old spaceship. The repair work was a long, laborious task, but she was in no hurry, for now.

Well…that was odd.

Elli reached to her side and pulled out her pistol. It was a military issue pulse weapon, based around the guts of a standard issue Doru rifle. The stock was gone, replaced with a folding section little more than an L shaped piece of metal. The barrel and muzzle were three centimetres long and helped to reduce the size and weight. After a few moments, she raised her gaze and looked back down to her ship. The three-hundred-metre-long ship was certainly an ugly vessel, yet the hammerhead design with its wide bow and flared engines looked friendly, in a bizarre sort of way.

"Selene! They're here!" A voice shouted from far below. It was someone working on the landing gear. Elli moved to the metal railing for a better look.

"Who is here?"

She turned her head, but remained seated. A grubby looking mechanic emerged from behind a stripped-down cargo shuttle. This was one of the less salubrious locations aboard the complex. Then the alarms sounded, and at first she assumed it was a drill, unlikely to be something more serious. But when she spotted five fully armed Phriconis soldiers hurrying past her, she knew something was wrong. They moved to the wide elevator system and stepped inside.

"Penatarchos. What's happening? I thought this was a proximity alert?"

The soldiers readied themselves for combat, waiting inside, but the officer in charge must have recognised her because he waved over to her.

"Elli. Landing ships are coming this way. Get to the shelters, now!"

"Where are you going?"

"The docking gates are still open. We're moving down to help with the defences."

Elli rose from her position and walked towards them. She knew how long it took for the elevator to activate, and stepped inside as the unit shuddered, beginning its rapid descent to the lower level.

"Sir," said one of the soldiers, "This site is off-limits to civilians."

Elli shook her head with amusement as she pushed inside.

"If there's trouble, you're gonna need my help."

One of the heavily armoured soldiers grumbled, and then tried to push her back, but to his astonishment she grabbed his arm. Her grip was firm, and as he tried to pull his arm back, he found it locked in her vice like grip.

"Hey! Civilians are not allowed this way. Military only!"

The man was clearly stunned by the movement from a civilian, much to the amusement of his commander.

"Get out of here!" The man again tried to push her. Elli sighed and instantly reacted to his aggression. She took no mercy on her aggressor and pulled the man's arm towards her, throwing him off balance. Before he could recover she slammed his head into the wall. He'd have been knocked unconscious had it not been for the helmet, although the impact was still enough to send him crashing to the ground in an ignoble mess. One of his comrades laughed at him as he helped pulled the fallen warrior back to his feet.

"Don't mess with Elli. She's no civilian," said the Dekarchos.

"Listen to him next time." Elli laughed, "Now tell me... what's going..."

A mighty roar drowned out her voice, blotting out all noises. Then the elevator shuddered violently just before it struck the lower level.

"Everybody out!" said the officer.

They needed no encouragement and leapt out onto the metal flooring of the shipyard facility. Small numbers of technicians and mechanics were running in the same direction.

"Orders from Command. We need to get to the outer docking gates. Reports of intruders coming in."

The unit started to jog away from the service area towards the inner dock. Their arms rattled and clunked as they moved, as opposed to the gear worn by Elli made no sound of any kind. They rounded the last bulkhead in the massive berths and to the vast open space before the array of inner docking gates. The doors were still open, and led into another large chamber almost as big, before reaching the final set of gates that led out to the warm air of Ephesus. A man stumbled and fell as he rushed away from the gates, and a friend helped lift him to his feet. Elli hesitated, spotting the bloodstains on his chest and moved towards them.

"What's going on? Do you need help?"

The wounded man looked up at her, and she saw the pain in his eyes.

"The Medes are here. Get as deep as you can!"

His friend pulled him away, and left Elli wondering what was happening. But then she felt the massive vibration in the ground, followed shortly after by a great booming sound. She lacked the communication node in her ear that connected to the command network. It was a minor loss, but right now she would like to be patched into the military network to understand what was going on.

"Elli!"

She twisted around. The leader of the spatharii was waving his arm towards her. Another squad ran past with their rifles in their arms and still pulling on their body armour.

"Get over here now. We could use your help."

Elli nodded and raced to join the others. They moved towards a bulkhead door system that was wide enough for three of them at a push. They stepped inside and into the dark, slightly damp smelling passages. Elli knew of the outer bunker complex system, but she'd never been there before. Based on the debris and refuse scattered about, it looked as though few others had in recent years. They inched through the sections and reached a more open area. There were dozens more soldiers, and this was the moment Elli realised things were much more serious than she'd expected. To her right was a bunker built from a composite of stone and metal. A horizontal slit ran from left to right, providing a panoramic view of the basin below the outer defences. She could see where the rocks ran down to a wide shingle beach, and the warm, gentle waters of the ocean.

"What's the situation, Komes?" asked the Pentarchos.

The heavily armoured commander with the markings of a Komes leaned against the stone wall and wiped his brow. He looked nervous, but deadly serious as he spoke.

"Come with me…all of you."

They followed the officer through the armoured doors and out onto the balcony installed just in front and below the horizontal slit. They stared up into the sky.

"That is not good," said one.

Elli shook her head.

"Wow. So…it's true. This is an attack."

A hundred dark objects filled the sky, long black trails following many of them. Every few seconds flashes and pulses of light marked the denotation of powerful warheads, or perhaps the destructions of ships.

"Look," said the Komes, "to the North East."

Elli followed the direction he was pointing in, and then almost staggered backwards. The massive shape of a warship was falling from the sky. It was impossible to identify as it was wreathed in fire and flames, and it dropped down at high speed.

The very air and clouds around it seemed to push out of the way to allow it to enter the area. Before it was completely visible it came under attack from a hundred directions. Laser fire and missiles struck it repeatedly, though few seemed to do much in the way of damage.

"Command reports eleven ships are falling, with most breaking up on the way down. That's not our concern, though. What we…"

"Komes!"

A soldier leaned over the edge and pointed off to the horizon, and far out to sea. A streak of light extended out from the massive ship and struck one of the air defence towers built into the cliffs. It exploded in a terrifying blast of energy and metal. More shots hit the ground as though the entire continent was under attack by a focussed lightning storm.

"Something is coming in…and fast!"

The aerial bombardment was already a sight to behold, but the soldiers had spotted new threats, and Elli sensed the panic. The soldiers defending the colony were well trained and equipped, but not experienced warriors. And she knew from her past adventures, experience counted above all else in such situations.

"Gods!" yelled one, "It's an invasion!"

Without giving any commands, the soldiers instantly responded. Rifles and carbines pushed out in front of them, with some resting on the edge of the ledge to support the weapons. Elli activated the augmented lens fitted to her helm.

"Wait. There's a lifeboat, and it's got Terran markings on it."

The Komes nodded as she spoke.

"Command confirms it. We've got survivors from one of our cruisers. They're coming in hot."

"Uh…what about those?" asked the Pentarchos.

A series of flashes above them marked the arrival of multiple ships. They were big vessels, and based on the amount of fire they were taking, far from friendly.

"They're coming out of FTL in the upper atmosphere. That is a risky move. A very risky move."

Elli's eyes narrowed as she squinted. The biggest looked suspiciously like the Elamite battleships she'd encountered previously, huge vessels bristling with weapons and landing decks for fighters and landing craft. The ships carried dozens of gun batteries, as well as six gigantic cutters in the central hull section. Other craft dropped away from it, and soon at least a dozen, perhaps more, were coming down to the surface. Gunfire lifted up to meet them, and soon both sides were exchanging a flurry of shots.

"Dropships, dromon gunships, and landing craft," she said almost as a whisper. A spatharios grabbed her arm. His armour shifted about as he moved, a telltale sign that he'd rushed to get there.

"Dromons, you said?"

"Yeah. This is an invasion force, all right. And look…right behind them."

A trio of large black ships, each with the look of a black armoured hornet swept in low and fast. Long white contrails streamed behind them. Dozens of similar craft headed off in other directions, but these three were heading right for them.

"Mulacs!" hissed one of the soldiers.

As Elli looked at the ship, hundreds of small dots flickered along its hull. It took a fraction of a second for her to realise what it was.

"Get down!"

Half of them dropped to the ground, but just as many watched with in surprise and horror as the projectiles hurtled down to the ground. Charges of plasma smashed into the rocks and defences, exploding in a shower of incandescent light. Elli kept low as more shells crashed all about them. Plasma weaponry might lack the elegance of pulse weapons and laser fire, but it was by far the most destructive.

"Everybody back into the defences!" said a voice, "Hurry!"

Elli looked up as another blast hurtled a pair of the soldiers against the wall. The impact was so great the two were knocked out in an instant, perhaps even killed. She started to crawl her way back inside when a plasma round struck the wall behind her, blowing open a great chunk. She lifted her arms to protect her face, but the firing continued. An arm grabbed her and yanked her inside. Alarms sounded, and the few remaining looked broken and terrified.

"I'm getting out of here!" A spatharios threw down his helmet and prepared to leave."

"Stand your ground, soldier!" Elli snapped.

The man looked at her, shook his head, and turned away. With a single fluid movement she whipped her pulse pistol from its holster and fired. The shot hit him in the back of the leg, and he collapsed in a heap. He turned looked at her with an expression of terror and rage.

"Now…anybody else feel like running?"

They looked to her in horror, not one daring to move away.

"Where is the Komes?"

A young female soldier popped her head out of the breached wall and then jumped back in as a fusillade of bullets struck all around her.

"Two of the ships have landed! The third is trying to land up top."

She gasped, as though the mere effort of exhaling was now too much for her.

"Mulacs! Hundreds of them! They're coming down the boarding ramps."

Hearing that name sent a shudder of fear through Elli's body. As if to emphasise the danger, a volley of shots struck the fortification. Not the powerful blasts from spaceships, but the telltale effect of small arms fire.

"I've faced them before. We need to be ready. They are tough, but they won't keep fighting if we stand up to them."

She'd come across them. There was no actual race of Mulacs as such. It was actually a generic name used for many different species of mutants, pirates, and mercenaries. These creatures had little useful skills outside of combat, violence, and piracy. And these were exactly the roles the Medes paid them for. Mulacs frequently acted as scouts and raiders for their forces. In more recent years they'd carved out their own territories in the border regions and proved a constant scourge to shipping companies.

"Get into position, now!"

CHAPTER FIVE

Olympian Shipyards, Ephesus Prime

The space battle above the planet continued to rage, both sides fighting desperately to gain control. With each passing moment multiple landing ships broke through to the planet far below, pursued by fighters and gunships. It was a brutal affair, with the losers plummeting from the stratosphere and down to the surface. Smoke trails arched in all directions as both sides continued to sustain heavy losses.

One landing ship lost power a kilometre from the surface. It dropped down to the coast like a flaming comet. Elli covered her face and turned away as the craft smashed into the coastline, exploding with the intensity of a small star. The light quickly faded, to be replaced by the shouts of the defenders rushing to their allocated positions. As they fanned out through the massive docking gates and barricades, they came under fire. Gunfire struck the armour of the still open gates, sending sparks and flames in all directions.

"Dropships coming in!" shouted an unseen soldier. Another

called out far on the right, "I see more heading in from the North."

The shipyards possessed heavy defences, but all were reliant upon being manned in an emergency. Some of them moved to the slits in the walls and pushed out their guns ready to fire. Others headed for the steps leading to the high levels, just as many waiting around looking panicked and confused.

Elli ignored them for now, turning her attention to those outside. Behind the thick walls she was relatively safe, and used the time to scan and tag any suitable targets before submitting them to Ephesus Command. A lot of craft were in the area, and she could see dozens of attacks along other parts of the cliffs and the cities. More heavy Mulac vessels were depositing their ground troops all over the colony. There was nothing she could do for them, though, and right now she needed to protect those around her.

"Okay. We hold the docking gates, and we'll stop any of those cold-blooded monsters from getting in here. The air-defence turrets will take care of anything coming in from above, but it's down to us to stop them breaching the gates."

Something heavy slammed into the ground, and all of them flinched other than Elli. More powerful blasts continued to strike, though did little more than fill the sky with dust.

"We dig in and hold this place. Mulacs take no prisoners. They are foul beasts that will mutilate and kill any they find. So we will show them no mercy. Understood?"

A few of the soldiers answered, but most seemed stunned by what was happening.

"Do you understand?"

This time she shouted at them, and more of them answered. Her eyes ran along the odd group of individuals as she counted their number, as well as their equipment and weaponry. Some were partially equipped, but the armour and weapons were enough to divide them up. The Terrans made use of two main types of soldier, the stratiotes and the spatharii. The first type was the most common, with light armour and ranged weaponry. They were the heavy infantry, with tough armour, shorter ranged weaponry, and various types of body shielding.

"Good. Now…I see them, two groups moving out of the large transport. Stratiotes, you will deploy to the two forward bunkers where you'll have the best field of view. Keep your heads down, and fire when they're in range. The rest of you stay with me."

The stratiotes hesitated, so she pointed off to the two bunkers.

"Go! We have to hold them back, unless you want to be food for Mulacs!"

The stratiotes scurried away and began positioning their long Doru rifles along the slits and loopholes in the fortification. Seven heavily armoured warriors remained, waiting for her orders. Elli made to leave, and then spotted the people clambering out of the broken lifeboat. One nodded and began to move away.

"I'll take care of them. You handle the defences, Security Chief."

Elli smiled grimly.

"Then get back here. I need every soldier that can carry a weapon. And you look like you can handle that thing."

She laughed, indicating towards the Xiphos Assault Carbine. It was smaller than the Doru rifles, though looked much heavier. A thick strap system hung from his armour to help take the weight of the weapon, and its integral shield generator. It was also a pulse weapon, but shorter and squatter. The front was covered in a cowling, hiding all but the three muzzles that pushed out to the front. The weapon's magazine extended up from the top and curved slightly forwards. She'd seen them before, and other mercenaries knew them as Boeotian Blasters, due to the fact that the Boeotians used them for all their regular heavy infantry. It was a hybrid design, and one she'd not yet seen in action.

"Will do." The man swung the weapon to his side. It slid down over his thigh to his right, leaving his hands free. Now she could see the iconography on his breastplate, and it showed the face of some great hideous beast. Unlike the Laconians, the majority of Terrans chose their own armour and shield designs.

"Nice Gorgon."

He smiled as he moved away. Elli then bent down to a fallen warrior. The burnt body was a young woman, perhaps in her early twenties. The markings on the armour were no longer visible due to the scorch marks. To the other waiting soldiers' horror she pulled the strap locks and removed her chest armour.

"You can't take her…"

Elli ignored them and tugged at the shaped cuirass. It was almost identical to the men's armour, though with slightly more pronounced chest plates. She pushed it over the top of her own gear and then nodded to one of the men.

"Help me."

He moved the straps on the armour until it finally locked into place. With her bizarre mixture of clothing and armour, as well as her mismatched helmet, she looked unlike any of the others there.

"All of you, with me!"

They filed after her, through the narrow gaps and onto the escarpment. The horizontal slits gave them ample space to place their carbines and pistols, and they quickly readied themselves for battle. From there it was easy to see the rocky slope that ran down to the water, as well as the circling spacecraft busy firing at the defences.

"Stay low and wait until they're close enough that you can see their faces. Understood?"

"Yes, Sir!"

Each moved into position, readying for the assault. The more lightly armed soldiers were already firing their rifles down at the approaching shapes. Elli kept her head down low, looking down at the first of the landed ships. Multiple Median fighters circled overhead and fired down at the dock. She was so busy she didn't see the craft above her as it hovered over the walls. Elli looked up as it unleashed dozens of thermal charges. They crashed into the towers and walls with a ripple of thunderous flame. Explosive charges tore breaches in the outer walls, creating a dozen entry points for an attacker.

"Hold the breaches!"

Guns blasted away at the spacecraft, but it remained aloft long enough to deposit its fighting machines into battle. Elli took aim with her combat pistol as the things dropped down towards them. They moved relatively slowly, lacking the skill or initiative of the Terrans, yet they were tough and heavily armed.

"Combat drones!" screamed one of the soldiers.

The robotic shapes dropped down from the sky as the metal beasts descended onto the battered walls and into the breaches. One struck the man and squashed him as though he was little more than a mound of mouldy branches. The robotic warrior rose up tall and powerful, and then activated its weapons. A man rushed up towards it with a blade in one hand that crackled with energy. It was specifically designed to deal with machines, but he'd left it too late. The thing spun about and unleashed all of its weaponry on the man. He disintegrated in a cloud of flesh and armour. Elli dropped the magazine from her weapon and loaded in another without looking.

"Keep firing!"

Sparks glanced off the artificial warrior as it tried to move closer. The machine was of a similar size to a Terran, but much broader in the upper body. It lacked complicated hands, instead equipped with low velocity pulse weapons and blades. Clearly designed to be resilient but limited in their abilities. After all, who wanted machines that could turn on their own side?

"There's more of them!" yelled one soldier. Elli spotted him, but before he could fight back, a machine grabbed him and threw him out through one of the breaches. Terran warriors circled around the nearest machine, blasting away. Shot after shot hit the thing, but most resulted in little more than sending off streams of flame and sparks. Elli ducked behind a fallen soldier and took aim at the centre torso of the machine. Her gun fired over and over, punching small holes in the plates.

"Kill it!"

More shots struck the machine, but two of the Terrans scattered and ran as the robotic fighting machine continued to blast away.

"Here it comes!" A stratiotes leapt away from the open gates. The incoming lifeboat approached the outer dock gates. A long trail of black smoke followed it in, yet somehow the thing was still flying.

"Get out of the way!" Eli shouted.

The Terrans ran as fast as they could to the sides of the inner dock. At that moment the enemy surged inside. Four others joined the robot, and together they moved away from the breached structure and further inside.

Is this how it all ends?

* * *

Alexis braced for impact and looked out of the tiny windows. He could see broken white and yellow lines as gunfire bit into the sky. The defence was impressive, but he doubted it would be enough to hold back a full-scale assault. Smoke trails marked the position of aircraft, spaceships, and missiles, though he found it impossible to tell them apart. He could see the massive landing ships circling the powerful fortifications that seemed to rise up in all directions, as many were already on the rocky beach areas, or atop the shattered walls of habitation wings and docking areas.

I'm seeing the fall of Ephesus.

And then they were inside the gates. A group of machines turned to face them. They opened fire and shredded the front of the lifeboat, but it was too little, too late. The lifeboat screamed through the gates and crashed through the machines, slamming hard into the ground. It skidded off into the distance and jammed underneath a crane gantry. Dockworkers raced to assist it, the automated turrets blasting away at distant enemies. The lifeboat hit the side of the outer docking gates with a speed. If it hadn't been for the retro thrusters, Alexis and the others would have been turned to jelly. The skids tore off as they burst through the closing doors, and the next bulkhead tore off most of the right-hand side of the craft. Alexis closed his eyes as the craft finally came to a stop. He slowly opened his eyes.

We survived the crash. I don't know how, but we did!

Incredibly, the transport passenger compartment remained completely intact, though a number of small fires quickly spread through the craft. Alexis tried to move, but the harnesses tugged at his body, pinning him into position. He held his breath and then looked to the others.

They're alive...but not for long.

Smoke quickly filled the inside of the lifeboat and it was soon impossible to see more than a metre in any direction. Alexis shook his head, immediately regretting his automatic reaction. A dull pain filled his head, and he stopped moving. He'd sustained minor injuries back on Shrike, and the last thing he needed was to collapse while trapped inside a burning lifeboat.

"The port thrusters are still burning," said a young female survivor, "The cockpit is going up in flames. We have to get out!"

Dekarchos Alexis reached for the emergency door release and pulled hard. "Stay in here and you die."

The door panel pushed out several centimetres, and then locked into position.

"What?" Alexis tried again, pulling the lever twice, but smoke began flooding the interior, and those without masks or helmets were coughing and choking.

"Get back!"

Alexis had no idea who was outside, but he stepped back into the smoke, pushing the others with him. The door shuddered and then split apart. More shots struck the metalwork before a heavily armed spatharios pushed his head inside.

"You're clear."

"Let's go!" Alexis said. One by one they stumbled from the shattered lifeboat and landed face first on the ground. Once there he lay still, breathing in what he assumed would be clean air. Instead he found he was lying down in the maelstrom of a terrible battle. He rose back to his feet and found his trusty Kybernetes right there beside him.

"Okay, this isn't what I expected."

Both looked on as a motley collection of Terrans fought a valiant and one-sided battle against beasts and machines. He reached for his sidearm, but it wasn't there.

"Dekarchos!"

As he turned to his right, his Kybernetes was there holding out a pistol. It was one of the weapons fitted inside the lockers in the lifeboat. Though nothing compared to the weapons of the infantry, it was better than nothing.

"You might need this."

A shot streaked past overhead and clattered against the wreckage of the lifeboat. Alexis ducked down. He clutched the Terran pulse pistol as he removed the safety and prepared to fight. A junior officer ducked alongside him and lifted a pistol.

"What's the plan, Dekarchos?"

Alexis activated the faceplate of his helmet and then pointed towards the now sealed dock doors, and the dozens of warriors engaged in battle.

"We need to get these people out of here. The outer dock is lost. You saw the numbers landing outside. We need to fall back to the central Shipyard Citadel."

Before he could say another word, a trio of large robotic machines pulled apart the broken outer wall and stepped inside. They were bigger and slower than the other combat drones and seemed to shrug off the gunfire as though it was little more than rain. Shots struck against their armour, but they merely moved their extra limbs around to the front to act as additional armour. Their low velocity guns hammered away, cutting down men and women with every burst.

"To me!"

Alexis ducked down and gasped as a woman ran into position ten metres from the machines. A dozen spatharii were with her, five carrying shield packs on their backs. They formed up in a loose line as their generators activated. Oval shields of pure energy appeared in front of the warriors, and they pushed ahead, forming a loose line. Others joined at the flanks, and soon a wall of pulsing shields faced off against the machine.

"Join them!" Alexis shouted.

His officers rushed to the back of the line and pushed their weapons through the gaps in the shields. The machines tried to move forward, but blasts from the heavier weapons forced them back.

"Don't give them an inch!" said the woman, "Fight!"

Something flashed up on a gantry near the broken wall. Heavy gunfire cut down from the position behind the machines and blasted off a leg, yet still the machines fought on. One rose up to try and surge forward, but a rocket slammed into its back and spun it around. The other machine turned around to fire at their unseen enemies, exposing their backs. Their gunfire cut the hidden soldiers apart, and Alexis gasped as they fell from their ambush positions.

"Now! This is our chance," Alexis ordered, "Hit them hard!"

He bent down, dropped his pistol, and picked up a heavy carbine. The weapon was slick with blood, but he ignored that, and pointed it towards the back of the machines. The things swivelled about, blasting away, quickly killing three more of the stratiotes. The Terrans broke ranks and surged forward with weapons blazing. In seconds, the machines were wrecks, with broken metal and parts lying strewn along the dock floor. Alexis and Elli met in the middle, and for a second there was an awkward silence.

"Dekarchos," said Elli, "Nicely timed."

"All citizens withdraw to emergency shelters. Warriors and militia to your stations."

More shapes appeared along breaches in the outer walls, but accurate rifle fire pinned them down. Alexis checked his weapon and moved closer to Elli.

"Thank you." He answered with a smile, "The outer dock is lost. We need to fall back."

Elli nodded quickly.

"I know. Withdrawal commands are being sent throughout the colony. This looks like a full-scale invasion."

Alexis considered their situation for a moment. He knew the layout of the colony, and specifically the structures on this landmass quite well. The spaceports and docks were positioned all along the coast, watched over by a single massive structure that rose tall and mighty among them.

"The Citadel?"

Elli nodded.

"It can hold a million souls, and its layered walls are strong. We can hold out indefinitely."

There was no time to relax, though, as the last remnants of the outer doors and walls broke apart. Explosions crackled in a hundred places as demolition charges created breach after breach. The Terrans stepped backwards, and behind the line of shimmering shields. Then the black shapes emerged. They wore dirty looking clothing, with loose folds covering up armour. Light occasionally glinted off their armour, quickly confirming that they were armoured and prepared for battle.

"Mulacs!"

The largest of the group clambered over the rubble and then stopped as scores of his comrades raced past. He looked across to the Terran and threw back his hood, revealing a rough, almost reptilian face. He was of similar build to a Human, but with a broader chest and substantially greater muscle mass. He wore some kind of respirator device built into a crude metal facemask. Elli reached down and plucked the Boeotian's Xiphos from his dead hands. She took aim and pulled the trigger. The recoil was so much that she almost fell over backwards. Five or six Mulacs were instantly cut down, while the others scattered before its terrible fire.

"The dock has fallen," she shouted, "Get back to the tunnels. We need to reach the Citadel!"

Shots crashed around them, and two stratiotes were cut apart. The remaining Terrans put down a fearsome volley back at them, but still they came. Other soldiers, including many turncoat Terrans in dull, black armour, soon joined the Mulacs. They moved slowly and carefully, blasting apart anybody standing in their path.

"Run!" Elli screamed, "Run for your lives!"

CHAPTER SIX

The Great Marketplace, Laconia

Agesilaus and Kyniska moved along the street past one of the largest outdoor markets on the planet. Hundreds of citizens walked along the stores, Helot indentured workers trailing behind them, carrying their purchases. A few citizens looked towards them as they passed, but so far there had been no trouble. Since the violence in the Hall of Heroes they were keeping their heads down, in case anybody else was looking to cause them harm.

"Just like any other day," said Kyniska, "You wouldn't think somebody had just tried to assassinate the brother and sister of the Basileus."

"He's not Basileus anymore, Kyniska. Our brother is dead, and with him gone, so is any influence he had left. We must be careful. We have rivals and enemies everywhere. Laconia is not what it once was."

Kyniska stopped and looked at her brother's gleaming eyes. There was no easy way to tell their eyes apart, even when a deep-seated rage continued to burn through Kyniska.

"I know that. We're still the siblings of the old Basileus. We deserve more than this. He deserves more."

"I am not disagreeing, but we cannot act. Not yet. We have no more status than any other Laconian. Survey the ground, and watch our enemy's move. I promise you, he will act upon his hubris soon enough, and at that moment we will be ready to strike."

Kyniska shook her head, pulling her head covering up closer to hide her face. She nodded towards the distant public buildings. Both gazed upon the bright lights that danced about the beacon aloft the tall stone tower. It was usually barren and ignored by all, but not today. The top pulsed and flashed with light, announcing the warning to every Terran city, planet, and colony.

"This is a rare occurrence," said Agesilaus, "I have never seen its kind before. There are no expected meetings of the Apella, are there? But the beacon has been lit and here we are. This is a sign from the Gods."

The light rose up from the tower and into the sky. It was a beautiful, majestic moment, and as he watched the show of sheer power, so did thousands of others. The air seemed to crackle with the raw energy, and many gasped at the enormity of the thing. With each pulse of colour, the tower repeated the message, a warning to all Terran colonies. The energy flashed and crackled with enough power to cripple or destroy any vessel that strayed into its path. The tower was the tallest and most significant part of the ancient Skias, the building used to make critical decisions on behalf of Laconian citizens.

"The last time the beacon tower activated the Empire was on the move."

"I know," said Kyniska, "And the God King torched world

after world on his rampage. Even the Attican homeworld was shattered in the fighting. Perhaps the new God King wishes to return and finish what his ancestors started."

Agesilaus snorted in reply.

"In that case, his timing could not be more perfect. Our people have been fighting each other for years. We're weak and divided, colonies are still recovering, and the people are sick of fighting and the poverty that goes with it. We're easy targets."

"Come on, then. We need to get to the Skias. Something is happening, something serious."

Agesilaus nodded.

"Yes, and if the Empire is on the move, we need to be there to fight. Our safety is nothing compared to that of our people."

He followed her as they merged back into the crowds. Both wore their chiton, as did the rest of the citizens heading towards the Skias. It was a common form of clothing, dating back to the days of the Ancients, and worn by both sexes, but especially men. It was a sewn garment, unlike the female peplos, a draped garment held on the shoulders by a fibula. The two wore Laconian cloaks at their shoulders, as well as pilos hats. These were a common conical travelling hat in Illyria and many of the other Terran colonies. The pilos was the brimless version of the petasos and made from felt. Attached to the pilos was a sun veil that hung around the sides of the face and neck, making it almost impossible to identify them as little different to the thousands of foreign workers known as perioikoi. They were the members of an autonomous group of free but non-citizen inhabitants of Laconia. Concentrated in the markets, ports, and other trading areas of Laconia and Messenia colonies.

"Wait," said a Laconian heavy infantryman.

Kyniska almost pushed him aside, but Agesilaus grabbed

her as a dromon assault carrier swept overhead. Two more followed close behind, circling lazily over the city.

"Wait," he whispered, "The city guards are being brought in. That means a potential security threat. I suspect war is close at hand."

The two hesitated, but then the dromon came in closer, as though heading directly for them. The big flying machine looked like a mutated flying monster, with short wings, and powerful engines burning hot. It settled along the street and citizens quickly stepped away, but there was no panic or fear shown by any of them.

"See," said Agesilaus, "Nothing but business as usual."

Laconia was a military state, and soldiers and their war machines were frequently spotted moving about their business. A large group of children rushed up to watch as the underside ramp dropped down to reveal its cavernous interior. Clouds of dust or steam shrouded the ramp as a tracked infantry carrier moved slowly down. Some of the children shouted excitedly until a pair of Laconian soldiers told them to move aside. On any other world they might have argued, but not here. They stepped aside, but only enough to let it through. The vehicle trundled past, while Laconian infantry fanned out and then moved off into the city. The tall vehicle kicked up a cloud of dust behind them as it turned the corner, stopping alongside a similar parked vehicle.

"You're right, Brother. Something major is happening."

She then shrugged coyly to him.

"Meetings and politics are no friends of mine. Give me a pistol and a blade any day over that folly."

The tower let out a howl as the energy transmission intensified. From the ground it gave the impression of directly communicating with the heavens, which in part it was. The clouds pushed away as the energy pushed off into space and far beyond.

"The Apella meets infrequently," said Agesilaus, "And only when something significant warrants attention. But the beacon means much more. We should be there...and soon."

They approached the ancient square structure, though Kyniska was far more interested in the myriad of people and alien species waiting in large groups outside. Only full citizens were allowed inside, as well as citizen representatives of the allies. They passed an army transport, a large wheeled machine with an open-top bed on the rear. Atop were eight fully armoured spatharii. It skidded to a stop, and as one they leapt from the sides and fanned out into the streets. The duo moved to the main street that led up to the civil buildings, soon finding their progress slowed by the throng of people. Directly ahead was the Great Skias, perhaps the oldest of the remaining buildings in the city, apart from the Hall of Heroes. It had been there for hundreds, perhaps thousands of years. It was one of the many civic buildings, but when it came to matters of state, nowhere was more important.

"I've been inside the Great Skias on hundreds of separate occasions, but today is something different. I haven't seen these numbers since the war with the Attican Alliance. It must be the Empire...it must."

Kyniska's eyebrows rose. Like most Laconians, politics was an anathema to her. And yet she understood its role in their world. The rights of citizens, the creation of alliances, and the declaration of war must all be deliberated and decided upon in this one place. If it were to be done any other way, it would be the domain of tyrants.

"Whatever it is, it's important that we're here. Brother. The beacons are only lit when outsiders threaten Terrans. This is no local disturbance. Something is coming."

The exterior looked little different to the many temple buildings in the city, its stone outer structure primarily consisting of tall Doric columns. These large pillars rose up tall to the red tiled roof. A massive triangular pediment ran the full width of the building, and upon its surface a detailed sculpture of gods, men, and monsters engaged in battle.

Agesilaus looked to the path leading down from the raised part of the city. Like all of the civic buildings, they were positioned on the highest point and with a good view in all directions. The capital was unsparingly flat, but with a small range of hills that were dominated by the great Hall of Heroes positioned at their centre.

"Look," said Kyniska.

Both raised their gaze to the sky, and the shape of three large vessels that had just arrived over the planet. They must have been in low orbit to be visible this far away, yet were instantly recognisable to them. They were far from elegant, with long bulky hulls and layer upon layer of armour in every direction. Some had even described them as looking like lobsters that had been stretched to twice their length, and then had their tails removed. Banks of gunnery batteries ran along the side, and on multiple levels.

"Kataphrakt Heavy Battleships," said Agesilaus, "The heart of our fleet and only present when war is imminent. What are they doing above the capital? We are at war with nobody of consequence. Is the Empire already here at our doorstep?"

The massive ships moved slowly from view, and in their place appeared multiple squadrons of fighters that proceeded to patrol the stratosphere. Long white trails marked their progress as they followed their present course high up in the sky. There was nothing immediately suspicious about what was happening, but it still left Agesilaus feeling uneasy.

"If I'm not mistaken, those are ships from Lysander's fleet."

Kyniska's eyes lit up at the mention of the man. Agesilaus knew the way she felt about him, and even he felt a tinge of discomfort in knowing he'd arrived.

"Lysander? You think he is coming here?"

"We shall see. If he is, then all will be drawn to him. As always."

Agesilaus hesitated for a moment. He'd been inside dozens of times before, but he'd never seen such a throng of people. As he paused, he could make out the tens of thousands who remained outside, adding their voices to the growing din. The citizens of the capital had been summoned, and they were all keen to get inside. He took a step closer and then heard the howl of horns. He twisted at the waist and looked down at the group advancing along the wide path to the building.

"Virtual Citizens," he said under his breath, "So, it is true. The entire League will be voting."

Kyniska seemed particularly intrigued by the machines as they moved on past.

"Voting? In that case the Elders have already made their decision. Didn't you always say they present two cases, one of which will never be chosen?"

"Indeed." Agesilaus tried not to laugh, "It is important the citizens feel their voice will be heard. But unlike the Atticans, we leave leadership to those with age and experience. Better to be ruled by the Five and their Council of Thirty, than to the baying mob."

Both watched the synthetic machines move through the crowd. They were the same size and shape as a man, though more lightly built. They were not designed for war, or even for the rigours of labour. There were twelve, and all of them moved in perfect timing with each other. Each carried a ceremonial shield bearing the Corinthian Pegasus on the front. They looked little stronger than a malnourished labourer, with thin, barely visibly synthetic muscles, and almost transparent skin.

"Why are you here?"

One of the chrome machines stopped and looked towards her. The face was completely flat and featureless, save for a pair of artificially generated eyes. They pulsed once, and then were replaced by that of an old man wearing traditional Terran garb. He sported a beard little different to most of the Laconians present, and behind him was a civil building that she'd never seen before.

"Lady Kyniska." The machine then lowered its form into a gentle bow, "I bring the collected wisdom of the Corinthian Collective to the deliberations of the Congress of Allies. We have petitions to present."

Kyniska pulled the veil over her face, but it was too late. Already others were talking, and she knew word would travel fast. The siblings had more than enough enemies in the city, and without their armour and heavy weapons, they'd be easy picking if trapped in the open. The machine lowered its head politely and then moved to join its comrades. Kyniska pointed further off into the distance where other groups of artificial beings were advancing. Some of the Laconian citizens gave way for the machines, but many simply blocked their progress so that they could get inside first.

"You're right. Something big is happening today. There must be representatives from every world, colony, and city in the entire League. Did you hear what he said about the…"

"Petition? Yes, I heard. If all the League is here, then it will be something significant. But first we have Laconian business to attend to. Family business."

He turned his attention to the ancient structure, pausing as a trio of much older men moved past. None would dare impede their progress, from one of the many indentured workers in the capital, through to full-blooded citizens. Age and experience was revered in the city, as much as military prowess and strength. Finally, they were able to follow the others into the colossal structure. Guards in full military attire waited at every entrance. Their armour gleamed and crimson cloaks flowed in the gentle breeze. Their shimmering shields pulsed and flickered, and yet they remained motionless, and might easily have been statues, had they not been scrutinising every individual that entered.

"This is the day, Brother. Are you ready?"

Agesilaus laughed.

"Of course I am. Has there ever been a time when we were not?"

The siblings entered building, but as they reached the steps leading down into the large open space, Agesilaus slowed down. It was only a fraction, but he was clearly slower than everybody else. Kyniska could see his lameness was much more pronounced when moving down the steps into the main chamber of the Apella, the assembly building of the Laconian state, than when he moved on open ground. The motors in the limb whistled and whined, soon drawing the attention of some of the older men. Many knew who he was from the sound from his leg.

"Now," said Agesilaus.

Both threw off their cloaks to reveal their faces beneath. Gasps spread through the old building, instantly confirming that many had known what had happened.

"I knew it. They knew, and they did nothing."

"Politicians," agreed Kyniska, "Offers of power and positions of responsibility will buy their silence. Even Laconians."

"Disgusting that they would fall so low. It is time for change, for true leadership."

Kyniska nodded towards a group along the opposite side, all watching with eyes like daggers.

"Leotychides," Kyniska muttered, "The filth is always here, and parading like a cockerel in front of the assembly. He has no honour showing his face here after what he did to us."

Whispers spread as the two moved further inside the crowd. Kyniska leaned close to her brother and spoke quietly in his ear.

"Are you sure it was wise not pushing a blade into his throat? It is time to bring him down. Will you bring his crimes before the Gerousia?"

Agesilaus placed a hand on her arm.

"In time, Sister. Let him dig his own grave first. Leotychides is a man of words, plotting, and scheming. That will be his undoing. For now, let him dig."

Kyniska's nostrils twitched, knowing he was right. Her gut instinct was to attack, but to do that in this sacred place, and without presenting evidence or witnesses, would bring harm to her brother, and to her family. The two walked on down the steps to the covered seating area close to the front. The inner ring was reserved for the great nobility of the planet, and to the Laconian State. Once there, they looked around at the others moving inside. The Gerousia was able hold thousands of individuals, and yet it was only to be used by Laconian citizens. Yet today there were the machines from other worlds in the League.

"This is all very irregular, Brother."

A Laconian official called out to the assembled citizens.

"The Gerousia!"

A hush fell over the hall as the twenty-eight elders of the Gerousia entered the place. They were the Laconian council of elders, with every one of them over the age of sixty. Only they could debate measures to put before the people for popular vote, and each was chosen from one of the major Laconian colonies. They were the most powerful officials in Laconia, with only The Five higher in seniority. Each wore the traditional garb of the Laconian noble, something that hadn't changed in hundreds, perhaps thousands of years. They entered the place and sat in their allocated positions at the front of the hall. Two seats remained empty, both in the middle of where they were positioned. Behind them came the twenty-ninth figure, a young man who looked utterly lost compared to the elder statesman. Standing alongside him was another man, older but in different dress to the others.

"Kneel!" Agesilaus whispered as every soul in the building bowed down low. Kyniska hesitated, and then joined in. The Laconians bowed to no one, but their Basileus, more commonly known as kings to other societies.

"Agesi," Kyniska said quietly from her low position, "And he still has that puppet Aristodemus at his back."

The young man moved into one of the two remaining seats, and then signalled for all to sit. One by one they sat down, and then waited until one of the oldest of the old men rose to his feet. At that moment the crowd rose back to their previous position. Kyniska watched the assembled men, especially those near the Basileus.

"Oreetes. I knew it would be him. The old fool has been trying to put Leotychides on the throne for years. Watch your back, Brother."

Agesilaus nodded slowly, without looking towards her to avoid drawing attention. Oreetes turned slowly from right to left, checking on the numbers assembled. One of the others also rose to his feet.

"Silence, Oreetes. Wait for The Five. No meeting of the Apella may take place without their guidance and oversight."

Oreetes merely increased the volume of his voice and drowned him out.

"We cannot wait for the Ephors, or for anybody else. Events conspire against Laconia and our allies. Our colonies are impoverished since the war, and far across the expanse lies the Great Enemy. Every day his strength grows, while the worlds of Terrans diminish. We need leadership more than ever to rebuild Laconia in this region. This is an opportunity, and one we can use to make Laconia the superpower of this galaxy. I say we can wait no longer. We must elect our new Basileus to aid the loyal Agesi in leading our people."

Many in the crowd shouted back at him, trying to silence him, and for a moment he was drowned out by the shouting. Even Agesilaus laughed as he watched the old man's discomfort.

"The popular assembly have already..."

"Enough!" said a voice far above the line of old men. All attention shifted to the booming voice as he entered the building and stopped at the highest point. In walked a group of ancient elders, each so old that just walking along the steps proved almost impossible. They continued to move slowly, and then past the noble men of the Gerousia. They then waited in front of them, standing like sentinels in front of the council of elders.

"I don't like this. All of The Five are here. That is... unsettling."

At the same time, he shifted his eyes to his hated enemy. Leotychides. The two exchanged looks, but everything he needed to know he could see from the man's face. The guilt was as plain as if he'd shouted it across the great building. Leotychides might be partially related by blood, but both of them knew what had transpired. There was no love lost between them, but as Agesilaus gazed into his eyes, he knew their time was coming to an end.

You tried to kill me once, Leotychides. You won't get a second chance.

* * *

Outer Dock, Ephesus Prime

A Mulac heavy transport circled overhead, before sustained fire from a trio of fighters set it on fire. The blazing wreckage spun from the sky as the pilots struggled to keep it airborne. Elli cheered as the craft clipped an outer wall of the dock. The spacecraft was tough, but the impact tore off the starboard wings and sent the machine spinning out of control. It vanished from view for a moment, followed by a bright flash and a booming explosion.

"Yes!"

More explosions followed shortly after as both sides continued to pummel the other with gunfire and missiles. Elli wanted to turn back and fight, but they were fighting on borrowed time, each minute giving their enemies opportunities to bring in yet more troops. The retreat from the outer dock quickly turned to a rout as the ceiling and part of the walls collapsed. Elli and the others had already passed the inner dock and the burnt remnants of a transport ship. They were moving along one of the principal skywalks that connected the dock areas with the other parts of the colony. Bodies littered the halls, a consequence of the violent orbital assault. More joined the retreat until they found their way blocked by a shattered starship. The walls and roof were gone, leaving this part of the facility completely open to the elements. Mulac snipers crawled over the broken exterior sections and fired down at those inside.

Not much further.

Elli scrambled over the broken masonry, leant back to avoid gunfire, and then spotted her pursuers. She lifted her weapon and blasted away as two Mulacs rose from cover. More shots hit the enemy soldiers, but time was quickly running out for the defenders.

"Keep moving!" She leapt over a fallen technician, "We can use the service shafts to get away from the dock. Follow me. I know the way."

More people joined them as they retreated from the fallen structure. Air and dust blew inside as more the facility fell apart from the constant bombardment. Shells slammed into the ground as Elli ran, clambering over the rubble. She pointed towards a small opening ahead that led down into the shadows. It was small and would easily have been missed by anybody else.

"There!"

They moved quickly, with Elli and the two naval officers at the front. As they clambered over the last pieces of rubble, they discovered it was guarded by three stratiotes hiding behind the outer pillars, and firing erratically with their rifles at any distant targets. As Elli moved closer, a shot whistled past her face, narrowly missing her head. She quickly lifted her hands and remained still, as enemy soldiers poured in from behind.

"We're Terrans. Let us through!"

She leaned out again, and for a second deactivated her plate on the front of her helmet. They could see her, but one continued to point a rifle at her.

"Come on, then. Hurry!"

Elli wasted no time and broke from cover. No sooner had she stepped out than more shots from the advancing enemy hit around her. The trio fired back, quickly forcing the enemy back into cover.

"Run!" she yelled.

One by one they rushed through the small doors into the service complex. The others followed close behind as shots landed nearby. Alexis was close behind her, as well as a handful of fully armoured and some of Alexis' crew. It was a small group, and half the size they'd left the dock with. They all bore marks of the battle from dirt and blood on their armour and clothing, to cuts and lacerations. Some carried rifles and others firearms, but as many remained unarmed. No sooner were they all inside when the few remaining defenders swung the doors shut and activated the locking bars.

"Nothing is getting through there," said the cocky young soldier.

Elli placed a hand on the bars and shook her head.

"No chance. We need to blow it. Who has a spare rifle?"

The young soldier held out a bloodstained Doru rifle.

"Will this work?"

Elli deactivated the faceplate on her helm and smiled at him. Her face was covered in damp perspiration, and a fresh cut on her cheek left a smudge of blood on her skin.

"It will."

With a few presses on the device, followed by an adjustment to the cooling pack, and she was done. The gun was already beginning to emit a hum, much to the surprise of the others.

"Uh...what are you doing? That will cause a burnout. The gun won't work once you've burnt out the core."

Elli laughed.

"It will do more than that. Now...let's go!"

A few hesitated, but as Elli jogged past them, they soon moved. The passages through the rock of the mighty cliffs were dark and cool, but there was something reassuring about being so far inside the hard material. It took longer than expected before the gun overloaded. By the time they reached the next passage, the ground shook, and the more experienced soldiers planted themselves again sturdy stone walls.

"Brace yourself," said Alexis, "This is gonna get dusty."

The rumble continued, and for a few seconds it felt as though the ceiling might come down on their heads. A few panicked and ran off into the distance. Elli and the other more experienced among them simply waited. Clouds of dust filled the passage as the weapon detonated, bringing down the door, tunnel, and everything else within ten metres. Alexis wiped the dust from his helmet and turned to Elli.

"Interesting little trick. Where did you pick that one up?"

She grinned before reactivating the protective plates on her helmet.

"You'd be surprised what you learn after a few months in the trenches."

"I bet."

The motley collection of soldiers and civilians continued forward through the rabbit warren of tunnels that led throughout the mountainside. Elli remained focussed on their destination, and it wasn't away from the fighting. Even so, she felt much safer now that they were underneath the perimeter wall of the Citadel zone. They clambered into the next section, pausing as dust and small rocks dropped down from above.

"They've breached the tunnel complex," said Alexis, looking up, "They're hitting the colony with some dammed heavy weapons."

He then moved alongside his executive officer who

continued shaking his head.

"If you ask me, this is no invasion. It's a reprisal. They want to see the place burn."

More rock continued to drop down, but as the dust cleared, a path ahead became visible. It looked more like a bridge cut into the rocks, and parts were now missing where they'd broken away. It was still more than enough to follow safely. As they were about to move, a gust of wind created a clearing in the dust.

"Wow," said Alexis, "That is pretty impressive."

They looked up to the vast defences that could be seen far ahead. They were still half a kilometre from the main fortification and its thick inner walls, but this area consisted of scores of towers and blockhouses built into the rock, as well as a mighty fifty-metre-tall wall that ran in a semi-circle around the Citadel. Each end buttressed into the side of the mountain, giving the effect of being one stone structure. Hidden gunnery positions kept back any stray enemies that moved too close and bought them time to prepare.

"Yes, it is," said Elli, "And we'll never see it if we do not hurry."

The mixture of military and civilian personnel hurried along the broken path and walkways, moving deeper into the colony and away from the Mulac assault. The stone rock passages were weakened in all directions and torn open in a dozen places. At almost every point the remaining alarms and security systems announced the arrival of yet more enemy forces at multiple points along its length. Finally, the tunnel moved upwards, and voices from other Terrans increased in volume. Shapes began to move, and then they reached breached doors that led into a mass of people and confusion. Signs for the public transportation system flickered continuously, the thump of bombs and bombardment cannons filling the air.

"What do we do now?" Alexis asked, "We can't fight from down here."

Elli pointed into the distance. Most of the lights no longer worked, but it was possible to make out the shapes of people trying to force open the automatic doors that led out onto the maglev track system.

"We'll take the express highway to the inner ring half a kilometre away. It rises up over a hundred metres, and cannot be breached. We should join the main line. The walls are the thickest, and it's the rally point for the battle. We've been drilled for this for decades now."

Alexis looked confused.

"And what about this place? Surely we can't let it fall without a fight. The outer wall is still strong, isn't it?"

Elli shrugged.

"The outer wall is a curtain wall. Parts of it haven't been maintained in years. It's more for show than anything else. We'd be more useful at the main defences."

"Perhaps. But then what will happen to all these people? They will be massacred as they try and get to the inner walls."

A single unit of lightly armed stratiotes filed past. They looked young and inexperienced. Yet they moved quickly away from the crowds and towards the shafts that rose up to the defensive positions inside the outer wall. Elli instantly felt a pang of guilt as she watched them go. But then her mind turned to the Citadel, and its primary defensive walls. It was a mighty structure, and rumour had it the inner walls had never once fallen to an enemy attack. That had seemed significant in the first few minutes of the battle. Now it seemed a pointless anecdote that would soon be forgotten.

"Come with me," said Elli, "Let's see what's going on first

before we make plans we might regret."

They moved closer to the crowds, and Elli shouted as loudly as she could, but there was simply no way to move more quickly through the underground passages. The space and air battle had been so swift that every route underground was so full it was almost impossible to make any progress. Large groups of soldiers and civilians pushed and shoved, desperately trying to get from the commercial and trading parts of the colony to the strongest defensible position within fifty kilometres. The mighty Olympian Citadel. They finally reached the huge vertical sliding doors that led to the maglev system. It was a grand looking place, with large staircases leading to the many platforms. It was always busy, but now it was streaming with people. Elli pushed to the front and then stopped.

"What's going on?"

A scruffy man in overalls, and with a sling across his upper body, shook his head. He then looked off to his left where the entire wall was gone, and they could see outside. Spacecraft continued to battle it out, but the long streams of black smoke served as the cruellest reminder of the danger they were in.

"The expressway has collapsed. The cars are piled up right there. We have to use the freight lines to get inside the fortress."

He lifted a hand to his weary face and almost broke down in tears.

"The Mulacs are coming in too fast. I can't get them all out."

Elli grunted with frustration, and then turned back to the other soldiers in her group. Shells struck outside, shaking the ground, and sending dust down from unseen gaps and cracks.

"They need time to get into the central citadel. If we leave, the Mulacs will overrun the outer walls and then get into the tunnels. All these people will die."

The soldiers stared blankly at her, wondering what she was

asking of them. She turned her attention to the man in the overalls.

"How long until you can get all of these people out of here?"

The man scratched his head as lights from one of the automated rail cars appeared off in the distance.

"Three more runs. Ten minutes round trip. I need thirty minutes to get them all out safe."

Elli placed a hand on his arm, doing her best to look reassuring.

"I'll buy you an hour. Get to work."

He looked stunned, but the look on her face told him she was serious. As he moved away, Elli turned her attention to her band of stray soldiers. Others carrying weapons moved nearer to hear what she had to say. She might not be the biggest or best equipped of them, but she exuded a confidence that drew people in.

"Okay, listen up. The tunnels are truly screwed. These Medes are coming hard, but they're really spread out. That won't last for long."

She pointed to the crowds of people waiting to use the service rail cars.

"The only way these people are getting out of here is to wait for the next cargo trains. They need at least thirty minutes to get out. We have to hold back the Mulacs coming up from the docking gates until then."

A stratiotes shook his head repeatedly. He was young, perhaps early twenties or less. He wore an Ephesian tunic, and a light breastplate that was marked and dirty. He lacked a helmet, and it looked as though his rifle had never been used.

"No way, man," he said nervously, "No way am I staying back here. We'll leave with the others. If we go out there, we'll be killed in seconds. Just no."

Alexis opened his mouth to speak, but Elli stepped in front of him. The crackle of gunfire was getting louder.

"Go, if that's your choice, soldier. But there are no more trains. Will you sacrifice civilians to escape with your life? Can you live with that shame?"

He lowered his head, but remained where he was. Christos, and a few of the exhausted looking crew of the crashed lifeboat checked their weapons and then moved to the breached wall. Alexis made to follow them, and then nodded to Elli.

"My crew were nearly all killed in battle over our home. But each of us will be damned if we leave our comrades to die in this colony. We're soldiers, and it's our duty to help them. And doing this we'll help ourselves."

Christos pulled back the loading bolt and pushed in another clip into the side of his pulse rifle. He might have been a Navy man, but he had no issue with fighting in the rubble with the others.

"Ares himself will aid us in this fight. I am sure of it. We didn't fight in space only to give up down here."

He pointed to the less motivated of the group.

"I'll be damned if I'll turn my back on them. And you know what will happen to you if the Medes win, don't you?"

The other stratiotes looked to each other nervously. Christos laughed before explaining.

"Slavery. You'll spend the rest of your life serving drinks on pleasure barges to fat Medes nobles. Or maybe you'll be lucky, and they'll get you to join the robots in the silver mines."

"Not me," agreed Alexis, "We'll fight to buy time for these people. They are our kin, and they need our help."

"Then let's go," said Elli.

They streamed away, following the broken path up and out

of the ruined transit station. As the small number of survivors from the docking gate battle moved up towards the surface, they once again heard and saw the terrible signs of battle. On one side was the colossal fortification that circled around into the massive curved wall. So tall it looked like an artificial mountain from where they were.

"Incredible," said Christos, "It never looked that big from the sky."

Elli looked up at the outer walls of the mighty Citadel, and her chest filled with pride. There were fewer more impressive fortifications than this ancient bastion. Carved into the rock, the Citadel was half man-made and half natural wonder. Then she spotted the shapes moving through the sky. A trio of Zafar Imperial light fighters screamed overhead, strafing the ground. Their pair of pulse cannons made short work of any poor soul caught out in the open. As they pulled away, the defence turrets built into the outer walls opened fire. The multiple batteries of pulse cannons filled the sky with bright light. In seconds, they managed to catch one craft and sent it tumbling from the sky.

"Yes!" Vasilis Christos yelled, "Bring them all down!"

He was so busy looking back he didn't see the Azarakhsh Imperial heavy gunship moving in low. It was coloured green, with light grey accents on its hull and wings. It was much bigger than the fighters, and built around a vertical lifting fan at the centre of its hull. Pulse cannons extended out from chin mounts, while a pair of pulse rotary cannons hung beneath its short, angular wings.

"Scatter!" Elli said, but Christos was absorbed in the gunfire still chasing away the enemy fighters. He panted for breath, looking towards her instead of the new target. Elli's eyes opened wide as she spotted the shape well before it was audible. She knew what it was, even from the silhouette, and it struck terror in her heart.

"Run!"

Some of the others saw what she was pointing at.

"Is that one of ours?" asked a young stratiotes, "What if it…"

Elli instantly threw herself at the young man, also managing to throw Christos off balance. The trio crashed to the ground, rolling down the broken stone steps as the gunship opened fire. Its guns tore holes in everything they touched, while missiles slammed into the walls. The gunship then screamed away, leaving Elli atop the stunned looking Christos.

"Uh…thank you."

Elli rolled off him and reached for her fallen weapon. Then she looked back at him.

"This isn't space, Kybernetes. There's no spaceship to keep you safe. One stray bullet is all it takes to end your life. Remember that."

A ripple of gunfire caught her attention. Perhaps five kilometres away sat a large Median warship. Though embroiled in battle, it was still able to continue its bombardment of the defences to soften them up for the assault.

"We need to get to the outer walls. There, the outer bastion!"

They looked down the rocky hill towards what remained of the outer wall.

"That's it?" Alexis asked, "You said it was a wall."

"It's more a barrier than a wall. Most of the structure is part of the old North Ridge with some crenulations, abandoned bunkers, and that…"

She pointed to a squat looking structure pushed up like a small artificial knoll. It was well inside the outer defences and showed signs of heavy damage from the fighting.

"It has firing positions on all four sides, and it will take atomics to bring it down. That, my friends, is where we make our stand."

She didn't look to see if they were coming and raced up the ramp to the rear. It passed over a deep ravine that ran all around the bastion. Alexis was next, and he hesitated as he looked down at the wide trench encircling the position.

"A moat. In all my life I'd never have expected to…"

"Get inside!" Elli shouted, "There'll be time for sightseeing later, as long as you're not dead!"

CHAPTER SEVEN

The Great Skias, Laconia

The arguments had gone on for almost an hour now as Oreetes berated the assembled citizens over his plans. He'd spent an age describing the weakened defences of Thebes, the broken Corinthian fleet, and the annihilated ports of Attica. Everything he talked about concerned assembling vast new armies of Laconian regulars and marching to war. And for all this time and effort, nothing had been resolved. The representatives from the Terran allies had even handed over their petitions for more ships to defend their shipping lanes, increased garrisons, food aid, and more. Each time it appeared that they might be making progress, the arguments would intensify. Agesilaus couldn't believe the nonsense he was hearing as he whispered to his sister.

"This is madness. What are we doing here?" he said bitterly, "Were we not called because of some great and terrible calamity?"

Kyniska shrugged, and then shouted at the top of her voice.

Her tall figure and booming voice echoed as though she was using a powerful form of amplification.

"Enough of this bickering. Tell us now…why has the beacon been lit?"

The shouting slowed and then stopped, as one by one the people looked to her. At the same time, one of the Ephors rose up tall and proud, and this time even Oreetes sat back down. He was frail, and yet the marks on his face and arms served as reminders that this was once a healthy and strong young man. He would have tangled with Laconia's enemies using his hands, fists, and weapons the same as the others. Each cut and wound a badge of honour to him and the state. Between them they wielded a power greater than every other institution of the state. Each bore the authority and respect of a leader and a general.

"News has arrived from the defeated and cowed Attica."

He said the words slowly and deliberately so that every single soul could understand. Horns sounded, and all attention shifted to a new arrival towards the back of the building, and at the highest point. All looked back apart from the Ephors who refused to pay much attention. Sunlight glinted from the man's armour as he emerged from the arched entrance and into view. He was a monster of a man, dressed in clothing that most Laconians would find excessive. His armour gleamed, and at his flanks moved a small entourage in full armour.

"Lysander," whispered one citizen, "He has returned."

Many cheered as the soldier moved down the steps, his excessively long crimson cloak trailing behind him. It was all theatre, and even Agesilaus shifted uncomfortably at seeing the legendary general. Every single man and woman rose to their feet as he walked closer to the young Basileus and the waiting Ephors. Then he bowed down to the youngest man in the sacred place.

"My Basileus."

He then looked to the Ephors who gave him the nod to continue.

"The violent resistance movement of Attica has ended, and as promised, we have allowed a limited restoration of their cities and democracy. They are cowed by our power, but they have not been destroyed."

Oreetes and two of the other elders rose up in protest.

"You were sent to crush them, not to aid them."

Lysander sighed with frustration.

"Then you do not understand the subtleties of strategy, old man. A destroyed state is a vacuum, and something will replace it. Better to weaken them, and have them as allies, than to leave it to the Gods to decide."

Oreetes shook his head as he listened.

"Hubris. Never declare your abilities to match or surpass the divinity of the Gods."

Those few words seemed to resonate with the older individuals, but then he squandered any favour he'd earned with his next words.

"You did bring the remains of their treasury here? Laconia has great need of funds to rebuild after the wars."

"Money!" shouted one citizen, "That's all you think about, Oreetes!"

Lysander smiled and nodded towards the silent Ephors.

"Of course I did. The funds were part of the war reparations. All of it is now in the hands of the Ephors, as the law dictates."

He turned away from the man, and looked up to the other dignitaries, focussing on Kyniska.

"The beacon has been activated due to automated distress calls being sent between all Terran worlds. The distress call brings new and troubling news for all of us."

Every soul in the building watched him in silence. Lysander might not be of noble birth, but he was a celebrated general, and a man with a long and successful career. News of his victories were responsible for dozens of new plays, stories, and theatrical projects created by perioikoi artisans all over Laconia. He was as celebrated as many of the ancient Gods, yet looked down upon by many for the exact same reasons. Laconians liked their victories, but excessive veneration of an individual was usually avoided. Lysander paced slowly as he spoke, his oratorical skills clear for all to see.

"As I returned from Attica, I heard news from the Ionian Territories. The transmission is broken, but already being sent to dozens of colonies. My technicians quickly repaired the damaged signal and sent it here, for the ears of the Ephors."

He nodded towards the elders, and in doing so cemented his role as general on their behalf. It was a minor, but important distinction to make. For no man in Laconia could consider himself higher than The Five, not even the dual Basileus.

"The Ionian Territories might be part of the Empire, but these colonies were founded by many of our own families. Laconians have built up great cities, and along with other Terrans have shown the Empire how we can achieve greatness far beyond their own abilities. These transmissions brought me grim and terrible news, however, news that left me and my commander stunned. May I present this to the people?"

The Ephors looked to each other. There was silence as they made their decision. There was no greater power in Laconia than that wielded by the Ephors. Each nodded, and Lysander waited until all five had played their part. It was an odd arrangement, but one every Laconian understood well.

"The Trinity," said Kyniska with great reverence as she

spoke the ancient chant, "the people, the Gerousia of thirty elders led by the two Basileus. And at the top, as the Gods themselves amongst mortal…the Ephors."

She looked up at the sky and noticed clouds were forming over the massive open-topped building. Her eyes widened as she watched them move closer, spreading darkness over parts of the city. Agesilaus nodded at her.

"They are the arbiters of law and order, those who guide through knowledge and wisdom. Three legs of the trinity, strength, experience, and stability, the Laconian Trinity."

His expression softened as he looked back towards Lysander.

"The Trinity has served our people for many generations."

Lysander moved out into the open space and stopped. He removed something from the side of his tunic and dropped it to the ground. Just before it struck the stone, it expanded and then grew until it showed a projection of a planet.

"Ephesus Prime, the jewel of the Ionian Territories. As you know, this is one of many regions colonised by Terrans, and its position along the border of the Median Empire has proven lucrative for all of us."

A mumble of agreement spread through the chamber. Though the city, colony, and its empire were founded on strength of arms, trade still brought in the bulk of its wealth. There were now more perioikoi, or foreigners on Laconia than there were citizens.

"Look," said Kyniska, "What has happened?"

Agesilaus' eyes narrowed as he concentrated on the shifting images. They transformed to show the surface of the planet, and dozens of broken and burning buildings. Long columns of black smoke rose up high, creating colossal skies of choking fog. Agesilaus rose from where he sat and called out to Lysander. Their eyes met for a moment, and an unspoken conversation took place, unseen to the others around them. They'd been friends from childhood and trusted each other implicitly.

"When did this happen?"

"A matter of three days ago, Agesilaus. The heralds from the colony told me that a massive fleet operating under the flag of the Median Empire did this. The Great Enemy has returned, and its satraps have declared war against all Terran colonies within their Empire. The peace treaty between Laconia and the Empire has been torn asunder, and they act as we, the great Laconia, no longer exists."

That sent a great gasp through those in the building. One of the Gerousia pointed to the imagery and shook his head.

"For too long we have warned of the growing power of the Empire. Twice they have invaded our lands and destroyed cities, stations, and even entire colonies. Our dead number in the millions, and still this enemy persists in wanting our destruction. They have marched on the greatest Terran cities, and burned them to the ground."

"And twice the Terran armies and navies had massed together and beaten them back," said Agesilaus, "Though we can claim no glory in the first war."

"It is true," agreed Lysander, "We cannot claim glory for the victory of Marathon. That is what happens when history passes us by."

That drew much ire from the assembled Gerousia. Few liked to be reminded that Laconia had refused to send warriors to aid Attica in its time of need. And yet against the odds they'd attacked, even though weaker and outnumbered. Few agreed on the facts of that day, other than that the enemy was vanquished, and the worlds of the Terrans spared for many more years. The young Basileus who had until now remained silent, pointed to projection.

"What happened to the colony? Has it been destroyed?"

A silence filled the open space before Lysander nodded slowly, and then replied.

"The colony remains, though how much is not entirely clear. The last reports show Mulacs and other mercenaries launching assaults against more than a hundred locations. It seems about a third of the colony was taken in the fighting, but the Ephesians are no Thespians. They fought hard and retook most of the cities, spaceports, and docks. The colony is partially under Terran control, but there is now a massive blockade."

That sent a ripple of anger and horror through the crowd. Arguments quickly started, even when the Ephors attempted to regain control. The young Basileus tried to silence the crowd, but he was too small and quiet to get much attention. It came to the legendary Strategos Lysander to quell the rage and anger.

"I know. Trust me...I feel your anger. But there is more, much more."

The imagery of the city, and then the planet faded. It was replaced by a three-dimensional map of the Terran colonies scattered all along the border of the Median Empire, like fleas on a dog.

"The Medes are readying for war, and two of their greatest satraps have declared their intention to retake every Terran city. Ephesus will fall, and so will dozens more worlds. And once those are gone...they will come for us."

He licked his lips, watching those shaking their heads.

"Pharnabazus, Satrap of Phrygia has broken his truce with us, and it appears he is joining forces with Tissaphernes of Lydia, the great betrayer. A union between these two could prove catastrophic. Between them they have the troops and ships to bring all Terran worlds to their knees."

The map shifted to show the border region. Many of the old colonies were shrouded in flames, signifying they were under attack.

"These two satraps have sent small fleets to raid Terran worlds and colonies, and the latest reports show massive casualties. Some of the colonies are already evacuating and preparing for the long crossing back to our own territories."

The crowd was silent, and now the Basileus could be heard. The Ephors listened to him carefully, though few could miss the shape of Aristodemus leaning over and whispering into the Basileus' ear.

"The Medes are powerful, but they have been divided for decades. They fight each other for power, and for the favour of the Great King. But recent mercenary campaigns against them have unified their commanders, and they have numbers that we can only dream of. We can ill afford a mistake that could leave the worlds of our people destroyed. Only together can we hold them back."

He hesitated, and when he next spoke, his voice almost squeaked as he tried to sound strong and forceful.

"I advise we sent envoys to every Terran world, from Attica to Pella. We must rally all Terrans to the cause of our common defence before these two satraps can mobilise an unstoppable host."

Many in the crowd roared their approval, and taking advantage of the moment, Leotychides stepped forward. Some of the Gerousia nodded in approval, and that started an involuntary growl deep inside Agesilaus' throat. Leotychides lifted his hands and shouted to get attention. Kyniska grabbed Agesilaus' arm, but he still shook his head.

"Not yet. Listen to what he offers first. It will be the coward's way out. Of that I can promise."

"I agree with the Basileus." Leotychides smiled towards the young ruler. There seemed to be a sneer forming along his face, and yet many seemed to only notice the fake, warm tones coming from his voice.

"As son and heir to the late Basileus Agis II, I announce my intention to serve as co-Basileus. Together, the two of us can guarantee peace and stability for this world…and beyond."

He almost laughed but caught himself at the last moment.

"As co- Basileus of Laconia I would be honoured to command our forces if the Great Enemy dares to show his face on our territory. I would make sure we are ready for war, with new ships and equipment procured for our army and navy."

Many of the perioikoi outside the building could hear what was happening, and cheered along with his offer of defensive preparations. Construction of new hardware would mean plentiful work for the weapons factories and shipyards, though at a cost to the regime and its small number of citizens. Inside the great building, the Laconians seemed less than impressed by what he offered. Even Leotychides appeared taken aback by the sound coming from them. He lifted his hands up high, but was immediately interrupted by Agesilaus who pushed forward, almost stumbling as he struggled to keep his lame leg in check. The motors grunted, and yet he moved quickly enough to block Leotychides as he laughed at his lame opponent. It was a mistake, for all knew of Agesilaus and his noble deeds for the state. That one action seemed to backfire as many citizens stepped aside for the man, bringing him at least a few minutes' grace.

"You are not the son of the Basileus, Leotychides. It is common knowledge you were sired by the treacherous Attican, Alcibiades. You are nothing more than a bastard, and have no right to inherit the title. Laconia deserves more…deserves better."

Leotychides gasped in mock horror, and then pointed to Agesilaus' leg.

"If you'd been anybody but the brother of the Basileus, you would have been left to die. Now, if you…"

He tried to say more, but Agesilaus was now on the sandy floor and turned to face the crowd. He intentionally ignored the Ephors and the Gerousia, focussing his efforts on the citizens.

"It is true. I am lame. I was born with one deficient leg, and yet the artificers of Laconia gave me another chance. With their skills and technology, I was able to march, and I was able to fight."

To the horror of many of the elders, he lifted his tunic to show the motorised leg. It was bare metal, and each could see the motors, pistons, and artificial muscles and tendons that allowed it to move.

"This shows the skill of our people, not me. Unlike Leotychides, it is also true that I am the brother of the late Basileus. By our laws, this means I cannot inherit the title, and yet this bastard son of Alcibiades offers you what? Words and preparation for war?"

He shook his head as he worked the crowd.

"Since when did Laconia sit back and wait for her enemies to act? Are you not the same Laconians that bested the Attican Alliance in a long and bloody war? We are the most feared Terrans in the galaxy. Our warriors are the strongest, the bravest, and the most loyal. And yet we have something no other Terrans will ever have…"

The crowd visibly leaned in closer to hear his words.

"Loyalty. Each of us will stand firm in the phalanx, never yielding our place or dropping our shields. We are brothers to a man. And our kin in the Ionian Territories have called out for our help. And you would listen to the honourless Leotychides and his plans to do nothing?"

He struck his chest with his right fist.

"I, too, am Laconian, pure born and have proven myself in the Agoge. Even with my lame leg I fought in the phalanx, as did every man and woman in my unit. I have wounds from battle, and I would be honoured to withstand many more for my people. Make me your Basileus, and I will raise an army and take it to the enemy. I will crush the generals of this so-called God King, and I will bring Laconian law to the Ionian Territories. If…if you will let me."

That sent a chill through every soul in the building. Lysander moved to his side and reached out with his right hand. The two gasped forearms in a grip that told every single citizen in the building they were united in a common cause. Lysander then spoke, and every person listened intently.

"Agesilaus is a true Laconian. For too long the Empire has turned Terran against Terran. Let us not forget the treachery of Tissaphernes, and the murder of our generals. We are Laconians. Do we wait for the enemy to come to us, or do we take the war to them? We should mobilise the Laconian levies and prepare for war!"

Agesilaus smiled back to his old friend.

"I ask each of you to consider this, and allow me to serve as Basileus. Let me be your right arm against the Medes."

Several called out in support, but Lysander then called out to them, to mobilise their hearts and minds to the struggle.

"I support his claim to the throne, and his dream of victory against the Medes."

Scores of individuals rose to speak, but one in particular caught the eye of the Ephors. It was one of the robotic virtual citizens and represented millions of citizens in its own right.

The machine waited until one of the Elders signalled for it to speak.

"What do our comrades in the Corinthian Collective say?"

The machine remained still, yet spoke as though a woman was actually present. Its voice was loud and perfectly clear.

"My citizens wish to know where the money for this campaign will come from? A full Laconian war fleet will cripple our economy, and mustering our forces for an assault so far from home will leave our colonies defenceless."

Leotychides paced nervously, pointing to the machine.

"Yes...yes," he said in agreement with each and every point made.

"The fighting against the Attican Alliance has left our accounts empty, our ships worn, and many of our people remain wounded from the fighting. Laconia might be thriving, but the worlds of the League are weak, and many impoverished. Money and investment is needed if millions are not to starve."

That drew the ire of many of the Laconians. Some started to shout, but then Leotychides rose again to his feet. He must have smelt the opportunity and shouted before he could be removed.

"The lame Agesilaus would have us destitute while he plays soldier off in foreign lands. We should fight here, on land of our choosing. It is safer, smarter...and cheaper!"

He pointed to Lysander.

"Even our greatest hero could not do this without crippling our finances. I know you do not wish to hear this...but finances are what drive our war machine. We are ill prepared for another war. And if the Great Enemy comes here, we must be armed and ready for the fight. What leader would dare leave Laconia undefended?"

The Corinthian Collective representative nodded in

agreement.

"The Collective concurs. We would rather…"

Agesilaus lifted up his hands to interrupt the machine.

"I have one more thing to say."

He cleared his throat, and at that moment, Leotychides made the mistake of joining him on the sandy floor. Perhaps buoyed up by the support from the outsiders in the audience, Leotychides moved in front of his rival and tried to shout him down. Now they were alongside each other, it became apparent quite how much bigger Leotychides was. This was not helped by Agesilaus' shortened leg that had left him lame from birth.

He pushed Agesilaus backwards and then turned away to make a speech. It was a surprisingly violent act, and out of place in the sacred building. Agesilaus wasted no time in steadying himself, stepped back, and slammed his fist into Leotychides' face. It sent him crashing to the ground. As the man struggled to control the blood gushing from his nose, Agesilaus addressed those around him.

"Yes, I will go to war, but I will not take the wealth of Laconia with me."

He turned and looked towards his hated foe.

"And in wealth I refer to our citizens. Laconia has no need for coin, only in the strength and courage of its people. I make this pledge to you. I will go to war for you, but I will also go to war for all Terrans. I will begin a new era of Laconian hegemony. We will lead, and all Terrans will join in the fight."

Many of the Laconians gasped. The idea of victory without costs might have intrigued some, but the idea that other Terrans might fight for their Basileus rather than them might even have motivated some to want to join the campaign.

"…and I will take the minimum of resources. Give me thirty Laconian officers and any soldiers or ship's captains that wish to volunteer. They will earn no pay from the state, nor draw pension for their family should they be wounded or killed."

Leotychides burst out laughing, but Agesilaus continued.

"I will make arrangements for the rest."

The assembled men and women couldn't believe what he was saying. One Corinthian machine pointed at him, others rose to their feet shouting questions to the man promising them so much and for so little.

"You offer us the impossible, Prince Agesilaus. And yet you still have not explained to any of us how will you pay for this war?"

Agesilaus nodded, but unlike the others did not smile or show even the slightest grimace. He was the exemplar of Laconian ideals, calm and collected under pressure, and the difference between him and Leotychides was clear to all.

"Fighting in Terran space will leave stations ruined, and entire colonies at the mercy of our enemy. Remember the campaigns of Xerxes. He destroyed world after world, and even burned the capital world of the Attican Alliance. Even we, the blood enemies of Attica would not attempt to erase their culture from the history books. No...I will make the Medes pay for every coin. And I will bring back more wealth than any of you can imagine. Food and pay will come from their coffers, and I will continue to fight this war with resources gather by volunteers, or taken from the hands of our enemies."

Even Lysander seemed taken aback by Agesilaus' proposal.

"And what about soldiers? When I went to war with Attica, I took the strength of our fleet and ground forces. You cannot win this war with so few. Let me take command of this operation. I will..."

Agesilaus knew his childhood friend meant well, but he was also a colossus when it came to politics and war. The man would already be Basileus if he had an ounce of nobility in his blood. Instead, he'd become Laconia's greatest general, and never, ever heard the word no. Agesilaus knew deep down that if he wanted to be King, he would need to stand apart. And that meant showing the Elders, the Ephors, and the citizens that he was his own man, even at the price of becoming estranged from his friend.

It's now or never. Do it…or fade back into the shadows.

He could see the thousands of faces, many from worlds he'd never visited. The Ephors remained silent, liked demigods as they surveyed the events before them.

"No."

It was a single word, and yet at this very moment it had the power of an entire unit of soldiers roaring at their enemies. A silence spread through the building, and Lysander looked taken aback. He whispered to his old friend so that no others might hear.

"No? You can't do this alone."

Those were the worst possible words to use in front of Agesilaus. Like all Laconians, he was proud and often stubborn. But there was more to him. He'd been forced to work harder every day of his life. His lame leg had left him at a disadvantage, and yet he'd succeeded in the Agoge. He was strong, fast, and brave, and he could command the loyalty of those around him when needed.

"I am the only man here with the right to lead you in this campaign. Choose me as Basileus, and I will do what no Terran has done before. I will take the war to the enemy, and I will strip his resources to pay for our Terran legions. Laconians will feast on the carcass of the Median Empire, as the crows feast on the dead."

Scores of citizens rose to their feet, shouting in agreement.

Agesilaus turned to face the council of Thirty Elders, the Gerousia. As the people with the authority to place items on the agenda, he desperately needed their approval. Leotychides continued shaking his head, blood running down his chin.

"And I still offer the chance for victory with a defensive campaign, fought on the ground of our choosing. I am no bastard. I am the trueborn heir of the Basileus. The title is mine...by right!"

Agesilaus laughed, though there remained doubt in his heart. He knew this was his moment, and with the Gerousia and the Ephors present, he could force a decision once and for all.

"Leotychides is a gutter rat, nothing more. He speaks for himself and not for our people."

Leotychides walked around him, but Agesilaus ignored his predatory behaviour and focussed on the crowds. They watched intently.

"I am the brother of the late Basileus, and the only heir with both blood and fire in his heart. Basileus Agis will ready our forces at home, should I fail. I will take thirty officers, plus levied Helots to assist me. I will recruit forces as needed with the loot taken from the enemy. Do you support my claim?"

The old men spoke with each other, and though three argued loudly against Agesilaus, the majority were overwhelming in favour. Finally, one of them moved down to the five silent Ephors, and then stepped back to their place. A hush filled the structure as every individual watched with bated breath. And then they spoke as one. It was an eerie experience, their voices synchronised like machines.

"Agesilaus and Leotychides have been put forward as candidates to replace the illustrious and honourable basileus, Archidamus II. Saviour of all Laconia during the great planetary quakes, and the Helot revolt, a time when our planet, and the entire Laconian system were under threat. Who will replace him and continue his fine legacy?"

Every single soul rose to their feet, each chanting the name of their favourite. Agesilaus wasn't sure which was loudest, and with each passing second the noise grew louder. After what seemed like an age, the Ephors lifted their hands to silence them.

"Who chooses Leotychides?"

The shouts and cheers were loud, and when Agesilaus looked to his old friend Lysander, he could see the disappointment on his face. Agesilaus' heart sank as the Ephors turned towards him.

"Who chooses Agesilaus?"

The roar of support howled through the ancient building with such power it felt as though the walls themselves were trembling. Agesilaus was stunned at the support. When he looked to Lysander, his friend lowered his head, and then smiled.

He pushed me to do this…it was his plan all along. I am sure of it.

"So be it," said the Ephors, "As is our custom, Laconia will be ruled by two Basileus, or Kings in the new tongue. They are the first citizens of the state, and will provide military leadership in times of war."

He stepped forward as another moved to his side, with a simple crown in his hands. It was nothing fancy, and might easily have been made from iron. He held the device out in front of Agesilaus and placed it upon his head.

"Arise noble Basileus Agesilaus II. As dual monarch of Laconia, you shall provide leadership and inspiration for our people wherever you travel. May you lead our soldiers and allies to great victories and bring honour to Laconia."

He turned to the vast crowd, lifting his hands up high to

proclaim their new leader.

"Long live the Basileus!"

The shouting continued, and yet Agesilaus was not ecstatic. All he could think was about the projected campaign, and of the great victory he had promised them all. This campaign would require hundreds of thousands of soldiers, and hundreds of ships, but he'd promised to do it without access to the main assets of the Laconian state. He would be hamstrung from the very first day, and then what would happen to him, and to Laconia. His eyes met Leotychides, and he could see the hate swelling in them. It shouldn't have affected him, but Agesilaus took great comfort in his rival's fall from grace.

How did my forebears raise mighty armies to go to war?

He didn't need to give it a second's thought. Already he could see the great legions of the past, and their famous victories.

I will raise the greatest force of mercenaries ever seen. And with every victory my numbers will grow! In a thousand years people will still remember our achievements.

CHAPTER EIGHT

Gythium Naval Academy, Laconia
The sound of aulos filled the vast open space as twenty thousand warriors waited for their new commander. The warriors were lined up in an impressive formation, and a number of auletes called out with their ancient flutes. It was a scene reminiscent of something from another age, and yet this was how Laconia always went to war. A light wind caught the Laconian banners that surrounded the naval base. They fluttered gently, their movement the only sign that this wasn't a painting. Behind them was the great circular facility, with the scores of pens used to house small warships. Scores of heavily armed landing ships and dropships stood in front of that. The Gythium Naval Station was the largest naval facility on the planet, and home to the training units and simulators used by naval cadets and crews. It was also home to multiple fighter squadrons, and transport units used to ferry Laconia's warriors away from the planet, and to war.

"So, this is the grand army of Basileus Agesilaus," said

Kyniska, gazing out to the myriad of souls, "And this took just a few days. Your skills continue to surprise, Brother."

Agesilaus smiled, but said nothing. Kyniska marched alongside him, their long crimson cloaks blowing in the wind as they moved in front of the array of soldiers. They wore the full attire of Laconians at war, with their dark tunics, bronzed combat armour, and back-mounted shield packs. If they were attacked at that very moment, they would be able to fight, and fight well.

"Are they not an impressive force? I doubt any Terran state could dare stand against them on the battlefield."

Kyniska laughed at his joke and found him looking back at her with a look of pained indifference. The Laconians were the only Terran state to feature a full-time professional army, a feature that had given them hegemony of so many of their neighbours. These volunteers were not professionals, and yet Agesilaus implied they were a match for their Terran kin. It bordered on hubris, but as she looked at them, she began to wonder.

"What is so funny, Kyniska?"

She sighed and shook her head.

"They certainly look the part. But when it comes to the battlefield, will they fight? From what I've seen, they're as likely to turn on us as to fight for us. What loyalty do they owe Laconia? Contrary to what our enemies might think; this is no Laconian army."

Agesilaus chose not to answer and walked past the first of many tourma. The formations consisted of two thousand men and women. These volunteer soldiers carried their own grand war totems in the front ranks based around the cult of twins. Known commonly as the Dioskouri, the bronzed statues curled like snakes up the three-metre pole and into a pair of warriors clad in bronze. It was the closest thing to a battle flag and portrayed the Polydeuces as founding figures of Laconia.

Agesilaus simply nodded to the nearest officer as they passed the first tourma. The soldiers could easily have been mistaken for regulars. They wore the same armour as regulars, and even carried the same weaponry. They lacked the shield generators used by citizens, instead small bucklers that were much lighter and carried their own internal shield generators. Unlike the officers, they also lacked the crimson cloaks of the citizens.

"They might be Helots, but I have promised them so much more. It is my firm belief that every soul has the same potential. Given the correct motivation, I think I can make them the equal of any soldier."

Kyniska looked stunned, perhaps even a little insulted by what he had just said.

"Careful, Brother. The Helots are born to be ruled. Do not give them reason to expect more."

The next group looked almost identical, save for the large numbers of younger men and women present. The Terrans military units usually consisted of an even mix of ages and sexes, but not this one.

"The Mothakes. Bastard children of Laconian and Helots. I did not ask for their help, but almost two thousand were waiting here to volunteer. All of military age, and all lacking experience."

"Curious, very curious. You say they are of age, but only just, my Brother. Some look as though they have never seen a woman before."

"Or a man," Agesilaus chuckled, "And yet they stand here ready to fight."

Kyniska remained confused.

"They have their own liberty, do they not? Why would they volunteer?"

"Why not ask them yourself?"

Kyniska nodded and moved away from her brother towards the group. She looked at several in the front rank, and then settled on one young woman. She could have been no older than nineteen, yet stood upright, proud, and confident.

"Child. You are Mothake born, are you not?"

She lowered her head slightly, but was not cowed by the insinuation of her breeding.

"Yes. My father was a Laconian warrior, and my mother a Helot factory worker."

Kyniska smiled, but that didn't appear to make much of a difference to the youngster. She could see the bitterness in her eyes, something she'd seen many times before among the Helots.

"Then why volunteer to fight for the Basileus? He offers you war and possibly death. You are not a Laconian. You owe the state nothing but your labour."

Now the woman appeared confused.

"We are not here for Laconia. Are you not?"

Kyniska nearly stepped back in confusion. It was not the question she'd expected to hear, not with such gusto. This youngster was a believer, and that was very unexpected.

"Please explain."

"The Basileus. He has no army of his own, only a few ships and his guards. The army he is building will come from all across Terra, Arcadians, Atticans, Messenians, Megarans, Phocians, and more. They are not here to fight for Laconian. They are here for the Basileus."

Kyniska raised her eyebrows and waited for the explanation.

"He marches for the freedom of all Terrans, and to seek

revenge upon those who have ruined our civilisations. Is there a nobler cause than to seek war again the Medes?"

"Indeed, but are you prepared to fight, and to die for this cause?"

She looked at those around her, and then back to Kyniska.

"My father died in battle against Medes. He served as a mercenary with Clearchus. My family has promised eternal hatred of the Medes. If I cannot fight and die alongside my Basileus and my fellow Terrans, I will find another way."

Kyniska moved back to her brother's side, and continued walking in front of the massed regiments of soldiers.

"I concede. You were right…to a point."

He might have smiled back at her, but it was hard to tell even at this range. Marching right behind them was a single large bloc of warriors. As one of the dual Basileus of Laconia, Agesilaus was now entitled to a personal guard of three hundred Epilektoi. These were an elite bodyguard unit of the Laconians used to defend senior commanders at home and on campaign. Every one of them was a full-blooded Laconian with at least a decade's combat service. Kyniska enjoyed hearing their boots strike the ground, and as they reached the next tourma, she glanced back at them.

"They look good, my Brother. They will follow you wherever you send them. I believe these Mothake may even do the same. I remained unconvinced on the others, though. They have done little more than skirmish for our armies before. Will they be able to stand against an experienced Median host?"

Agesilaus gave her a look only she could understand, a mixture of surprise and uncertainty. She shook her head and turned her attention to the spacecraft. To their right was a line of Chelandion Dropships. Each of the hundred and ten-metre-long spacecraft sat menacingly in their designated bays, their loading ramps lying open and on the ground. They were all light grey in colour and bore the inverted V symbols along their hulls. They were squat shapes, with tiny cockpit areas, and bulging gun turrets pushing out under both sides of the nose. A single powerful engine ran from front to back on the upper hull, and two pairs of wings extended out from the front and back. These wings were tipped with additional thrusters that could swivel about to provide vertical take off and landing, as well as allowing them to hover over the battlefield.

"I can't believe Lysander was able to arrange all of this. His influence is considerable. He can't be happy the Ephors chose you to lead instead of him."

Agesilaus shook his head as he continued to step past the waiting line of spacecraft.

"Lysander is a loyal man, but he is not of noble blood. He could never expect to command when our Basileus was leading the campaign. The other Terrans would not fight for him and for Laconia. But they will fight for me if I can make this something new, and something different."

Kyniska looked at the faces of the Helots as they slowly passed them. There was an anger to them, and a resilience she'd never really noticed before. She had never thought that they might one day fight for any reason other than their orders. They'd operated with Laconian armies, but always in support. No basileus had ever risked using them for anything important.

"Lysander has managed to get the ships and transports for me. I don't know how, but it's a good start. If we're careful, I believe we can pull off a feat unmatched since the days of the ancients."

He stopped and placed a hand on his sister's arm.

"We won the war against Attica, but at what price? Every Terran colony is now weakened. Even we cannot risk a full-scale Laconian military campaign against the Medes. I have to use Helot volunteers, mercenaries, and any allies I can find. Our worlds are impoverished. Meanwhile, the Medes lie fat and comfortable, laughing at our misery."

"So you plan on doing what exactly? A call to arms for all mercenaries."

Agesilaus shook his head.

"No. I will call upon Terrans, as the warlords of old did when the Princess Helen was kidnapped. This will be a Pan-Terran campaign, not Laconian. All will benefit from our bounty, and at the expense of our common enemy. We will match the deeds of our ancestors, and put petty rivalries aside."

"A bold suggestion. But what about them?"

She nodded to their left, where the next groups of thousands upon thousands of Terrans waited in silence. To anybody else they might look like citizen soldiers, but she could tell immediately they were anything but. Officers barked their orders at the new recruits. Some of the soldiers did their best to look smart and precise, and just as many shifted about, some looking outwardly hostile towards their new commander.

"The Neodamodes?"

Kyniska smiled.

"Of course, I mean the Neodamodes. Somehow you convinced the council to let you take twenty thousand of our Helots for this campaign. This is madness, my Brother. Twenty thousand souls that would butcher us in their sleep given half a chance."

"There's a reason, my Sister. These are the most troublesome Helots on the planet. Many of them have taken part in revolts, and some were sentenced to life-time service in the death camps."

"And you think they will fight for us?"

Agesilaus stopped and turned to face the long lines of soldiers. They looked impressive, though they'd had just days to be given the most rudimentary drill. A few looked back at him with grim expressions on their faces. Kyniska lowered her right hand to her side, ready to draw a blade if required. Agesilaus did nothing of the sort.

"Yes. They will fight, and they will fight well."

"But why? They are little more than slaves. Every one of them is tied to the land and a single Laconian citizen. There's a reason they continually revolt against us."

Agesilaus ran his fingers through his beard and stepped towards the next group. The three nearest took a step back from him, as if expecting him to launch some sort of attack against them.

"See. Even now they recoil from us. We would be better leaving these Helots here, where they belong."

Agesilaus looked along the front rank of the soldiers. Many looked angry, but all were tough from their hard labour at the hands of their masters.

"Helots. You understand the terms I have offered you for this campaign?"

Scores of them nodded or shouted back in agreement.

"I will offer you nothing but blood, sweat, and toil. This campaign might take weeks, or even years. But I will promise you one thing. I will not ask anything of you that I will not do myself. We will go to war as brothers."

That sent a shockwave through the crowd of soldiers. Even Kyniska was shocked. Agesilaus could see his words had the same effect on all of those gathered in front of the ships. Some turned to speak with their comrades, and in seconds word spread in all directions.

"We will share the same food, the same beds, and the same

hardships. Laconian, Neodamodes, Helots. And anybody else that will fight with me. And those that return will come home with great stories, scars on their bodies, and the knowledge they are now part of a great kindred. Finally, every soul that fights with me will earn their freedom."

One by one the Helots lifted their weapons up high and started to shout. At first the words were hard to understand, but then a single name became clearer and clearer. Kyniska looked to her brother as he walked along in front of them. Each chant seemed to fill him with fire, and she was sure he looked taller than he had been just minutes before.

"Agesilaus... Agesilaus... Agesilaus!"

He turned towards her and winked.

"You see? There are things more important than wealth, or even honour to these people. Freedom is the most powerful gift I can ever offer them. Is there anything greater?"

The two moved along and continued the inspection, all the while the soldiers chanted Agesilaus' name. Finally, they came to the last unit of Helots and a waiting Chelandion Dropship. Though identical to all the others, this was not grey, but dull black, and with red markings showing the iconography of Laconia. Along its flanks it carried the personal markings of the Basileus. A small unit of soldiers waited at the base of its loading ramps.

"So where do we go now, Brother?"

Agesilaus stepped onto the bottom of the ramp and stopped. He looked back as his officers proceeded to issue boarding orders to the thousands of waiting soldiers. Many were already stepping inside their craft, and soon they would lift up to the sky to join the waiting transports.

"I need more soldiers for this war. Not rookie soldiers, but veteran mercenaries with experience fighting our enemies."

"Mercenaries?"

"Yes. And I have already sent out envoys to every ally we have in the League. Any that want to share in this campaign are welcome."

Kyniska lifted an eyebrow in mock surprise.

"You said you would do this without needing the use of regulars."

"No. I said I could do it without mobilising regulars. There's no reason why they cannot volunteer."

"Brother. You're close to being a Sophist."

There were few things more insulting to Agesilaus, and had it not been for the fact it was his sister, there might have been other repercussions.

"Perhaps you're right. Nobody said I couldn't ask for volunteers from our allies, did they? And I need a lot more soldiers if we're going to be victorious."

He looked at her for several seconds before saying what she'd expected from the start.

"I need more warriors. The kind that can whip these new recruits into shape before their first battle."

"Agesilaus…there's only one place you'll find mercenaries like that."

His eyes seemed to glisten as he nodded.

"I know. I've sold the last of our possessions at home. The house and our heirlooms are all gone as we agreed. It is not much, but it should be sufficient to obtain enough experienced souls to help us. Everything went…Save for this…"

Agesilaus reached inside his cloak and brought out a small golden statue. It showed a woman atop a chariot pulled by a pair of great horses. Kyniska gasped at seeing the old trophy.

"My prize from the great games at Olympia."

She placed a hand on the golden shape that represented her

acclaimed victory, the first ever for a woman. But to Agesilaus' surprise, she did not take it.

"Melt it down, and buy another warrior."

A tear began to form at the corner of Agesilaus' eye. He knew how much the victory had meant to her, and also what she was giving up to help him in this campaign. They left behind everything for this. If they were anything but victorious, they would return in ignominy. She grasped her brother's hand in the traditional hold at the forearm.

"Let's see what the last of our funds can buy us. Whatever happens, we will assemble our forces in five days and leave for the Territories. This will be an event unseen since the days of Agamemnon."

"Assemble them where? Some volunteers may be wary of assembling directly over Laconia."

A smile formed along Agesilaus' face as he listened to his sister.

"I know the perfect place."

* * *

Tartarus Trading Post, Neutral Space
One day later
Agesilaus marched confidently through the bustling streets that filled the floating city. His artificial limb whined as he moved, though with the noise from so many people there was no chance of being noticed. The metal appendage did slow him down, though, altering his gait enough to draw additional attention from those around him. The motorised leg had always been an encumbrance to Agesilaus. It allowed him to walk, to move, and to fight. But he would never have the luxury of grace or speed. A Laconian child would normally be modified at birth

or sent away to avoid staining the honour of their family. And yet Agesilaus had persevered, and now he seemed to use his leg as a badge of honour. A reminder that his deformity was not a weakness, but merely part of who he was.

As always, his sister was at his side. Tall, beautiful, her eyes watching every direction at the same time, she looked poised and ready to fight at the click of a finger. Traders and workers alike moved like a retreating tide as they passed on by. Behind the two nobles followed a small entourage of Laconian officers and their subordinates. All were fully armoured and bearing arms. Anywhere else it might have looked as though they were searching for trouble, but not here on Tartarus. Agesilaus had heard stories of the barbarity and decadence of the facility before, but the reality was something of a culture shock.

"Are you sure this is the place?"

Erasmos Epiphanios, one of the thirty Laconian officers he'd brought, nodded slowly. He was older than the two siblings and bore the marks of battle on his arms and face. His crimson cloak fluttered behind him, though never low enough to touch the ground.

"Yes, my Basileus. Our contacts confirm the most dangerous mercenaries are located here. They are not cheap and will not work for all that seek them."

That drew a grim look from Agesilaus.

"This place insults me," he said gruffly, "No Laconian should be forced to grovel in the dirt for warriors. What can we expect to find down here?"

Kyniska laughed at his complaints.

"Brother. It was you that said you could fight this war without the need for our military. The funds you've been gifted will buy us very little."

"Yes," he agreed, "Perhaps that was not the wisest move I

have ever made. Better to go to war with thirty loyal Laconians, than thirty thousand imbeciles."

Erasmos shook his head.

"I'd like a few more, my Basileus. Some say the Gods are on the side of the biggest tourma."

"I'm sure there are," laughed Agesilaus, "They are the people that write about war. They do not fight it."

The next street looked more like something in a filthy Theban city, rather than the heart of a high-tech station drifting through space. There was barely enough space for his group to push through. Traders, workshops, and stores filled with people and goods operated day and night. On top of the crowd, there were also the sounds and smells to contend with. As they moved into the next trading zone, a large group blocked their path. They were a mixed bunch of men and women, with a few reptilian Mulac mercenaries with them.

"Well, ain't you fancy!" The largest of the men stepped forward, "Level Nine is for select clientele."

The Laconians were barely visible in the low light, and two of Agesilaus' guards stepped ahead to protect their leader from potential danger. Guns pushed out from inside stores, but the Laconians moved not an inch.

"Stand aside," said Agesilaus, "My business is of no concern to you."

"Oh...really."

The man whistled, and dozens more individuals appeared from the buildings and storerooms. At the same time, many in the crowds melted away, doing their utmost to steer away from the coming trouble.

"My name is Megabates, and you've found your way into my district. Nobody hires from this station without going through the Mercs Guild first. And I'm the official representative for

Level Nine."

A smile spread across his round face.

"For a price, I service quality customers. The more you pay, the more access you get to the best of what we have to offer. Don't like it? Go back to the slums and pick up a few thousand automatons. If you want experienced Terrans, you come and see me."

He licked his lips with anticipation.

"But if you're here, then you already know that, don't you?"

A dark-skinned henchman moved to his flank. He wore half the armour of a spatharios. From the marks on his body he had seen a lot of combat or been a slave fighter in the pits. He looked at the Laconians in the shadows and muttered a barely intelligible question at them.

"Where do you think the Black Legion got most of their contracts?"

The man stared into the darkness towards the shapes of the soldiers. He could see the outline of Agesilaus, but little more. The Laconian Basileus, on the other hand, could see him perfectly in the reflected light. Megabates carried a short metal cudgel in his hands. The thing was unsophisticated, but he moved it in a manner implying he had plenty of experience. He was easily as big as Agesilaus, though years of good living had put substantial fat on his body.

"I know who you are," said Agesilaus, "I am here for the best you can sell me."

The man shook his head.

"A Laconian warrior forced to speak to me. I am honoured by your presence."

Megabates bowed before him, but it was a mocking gesture, winning no favour with Agesilaus. Kyniska took one step ahead, and the man instantly burst out laughing.

"You let a woman speak for you? I thought Laconians were the peak of warriors? That's what they keep telling me when they come for work."

One of Megabates henchmen stepped towards the Laconians. He was slightly off balance and stank of alcohol. Agesilaus recoiled at the smell, but remained exactly where he was.

"How much for this one?"

The man moved closer to Kyniska. He then made the fatal mistake of reaching forwards to grab her. Before he knew what was happening, she'd drawn a kopis blade from a sheath at her thigh, and then slashed upwards. The movement was beautifully enacted, and Agesilaus doubted he could have performed any better in the circumstances. The gleaming blade caught the light as it moved, glinting silver and gold, and it move higher and higher.

"Never touch me!" Kyniska hissed, as her blade cut deeply into the man's flesh, sending blood spray across the two nearest men. Screams filled the place as the man staggered backwards, yet Megabates remained where he was.

"Do you let women fight all your battles for you... Laconian?"

Agesilaus could feel a fire burning inside him, something that made him want to avenge an insult. In a lesser man it would have driven him to action, but he was far from that. It was easy to put it aside in his mind. The Agoge had drilled him well, and discipline was something he'd mastered at a young age.

"I do not let them...and yet they do."

Megabates hesitated, and in that instant Agesilaus could see the fool's weakness. It was written not just in his face, but also in the way his people looked to him. Not a soul among them had the intellect or gumption to provide any kind of leadership.

Arrogant and violent, but he is uncertain. His men look to him for leadership, and they will break once his will fails him. They are like a pack of wild dogs, brave together, and cowardly when frightened.

"We're looking for the best mercenaries on Tartarus."

"Yeah, who's asking?"

Agesilaus moved out from the shadows, and the light caught his armour at just the right moment. For a second it seemed to dazzle all of those around him. His robotic leg whined, but did little more than emphasise his role as a warrior basileus. He moved so close that the henchmen of Megabates could easily attack him if they so chose. The close proximity made them nervous, and several stepped away to put distance between them and the Laconian. Kyniska remained right at his side, her bloodied blade still hanging down from the one side, and called out to them on Agesilaus' behalf.

"King Agesilaus of Laconia is asking. And I offer you the chance for glory and wealth beyond your imagination."

"How many warriors can you provide?"

Megabates' eyes opened wide with greed.

"As many as the richest man can pay for. I have contracts with thirty separate units, and thousands of mercs on the books. What do you want? A few hundred automatons, or maybe a unit of spatharii to bulk up your numbers?"

He then turned away, showing his back to the Laconians.

"I don't deal with paupers from Laconia. Come back when you've got real coin in your hands. Pathetic."

"Megabates." Kyniska started to say more, but Agesilaus shook his head. Megabates then looked at them both and smirked.

"You can't be expecting much if you've sent your own basileus to negotiate."

Agesilaus took a single step forward and lifted his right

hand. The blade from his Asgeirr-carbine whisked out in a single movement and removed the man's head with minimal effort. He turned to face the other mercenaries before the bloodied stump even hit the ground.

"Take our message to your mercenary cohorts. I want only the best to demonstrate their skills to us within the hour. We will take the best three hundred you have to offer."

The group started to disperse, but Agesilaus called after them.

"Be under no illusions. This contract is no mere trifle. It will be the hardest fought for in their lives, and the rewards will match the risk. One hour."

And with that the Laconians were left alone, with the headless corpse of Megabates leaking blood out into the floor. Kyniska looked to her brother and shrugged.

"You think we'll find enough warriors here?"

Agesilaus started to move away from the body, and then looked to his arm. A communication device on his wrist pulsed. He tapped it, and a series of images floated above it.

"Contact from Basileus Agis. He has spoken with our allies on my behalf to look for volunteers."

"Has he succeeded?"

Agesilaus gazed at the imagery for a few more seconds."

"Unclear. I'm surprised he was able to act alone."

He ran his hand through his beard, considering their predicament.

"Perhaps your leadership has encouraged him to become the man he was born to be."

Agesilaus looked unconvinced.

"We will see soon enough. No matter what, we will meet at the rendezvous in four more days. After that, we travel to the Great Expanse, and to war."

CHAPTER NINE

Battleship 'Agamemnon', Aulian Nebula

Agesilaus could feel the enormity of the events he had put into play. Weeks earlier he'd been another princeling, and one never expected to do more than fight as an officer in the ranks of the army. He'd spent his days attending to the duties of his role as a Laconian citizen, which meant primarily physical and military training. There was also the additional practice of oratory and even some mathematics from travelling tutors. In short, everything that could be expected as a member of the Eurypontid extended royal family, one of the two ruling families of Laconia. He removed his helmet and ran his hand through his dark hair as he considered his position.

Soon we will be at war, a war that has not been seen for generations.

He shook his head, imagining what was to come. Any other man might be excited, but not him. He was conditioned to be calm and reasoned, and would not sacrifice his forces on a whim. He closed his eyes and concentrated on the pantheon of Gods. First in his mind was Ares, the god of war, but then came Athena, pillar of wisdom and justice. He felt as though he was among the pair, and if he concentrated harder, he might even be able to reach out and touch them.

I will not stop until we are victorious, or my life is taken from me. Of that I promise.

He had stunned his kin by having himself proclaimed as both Eurypontid Basileus, and a Strategos, roles that demanded every moment of concentration from him. He'd thought nothing of them at first, but each passing hour had revealed the significance, and the difficulty of what he had promised his people; a war against the Great Enemy, and yet with the minimum of expense from his own state.

I have put this invasion force together, and I will see the campaign through no matter what help I receive.

He tried to convince himself of his strong position, but deep down knew he'd put himself and his sister into a dangerous place. Enemies at home would be happy to see him fail, and now he was away from Laconia, they would be free to plot and scheme. But there was also the advantage that while away from home, he had a free hand in conducting this war. The Ionian Territories and beyond were desperate for help, and he could even move into the Empire itself, should troops and ships be willing.

We have a chance to reverse the course of history. Can we succeed where others have failed?

He turned his attention to the display screens situated throughout the command deck of his new ship. He would have preferred to leave home with an entire armada, but for now had to manage with what he had. He hoped beyond hope that his call to arms would be answered. As always, he wore the full panoply of war, with his cuirass, greaves, and additional plates covering his body. The long crimson cloak hung down limply behind him, and his tall Corinthian helm rested under his arm. It was an archaic design. Something about its shape reminded him of the old stories, and as basileus he thought it important to the new volunteers that he looked as they expected. A Laconian basileus of old, like the Lion Leonidas, renowned hero and basileus that fell at the Battle of the Hot Gates.

Kataphrakts alone will not be enough to subdue our enemies. Three battleships could achieve greatness, but greatness enough will not free our kin.

His gaze shifted to one of the larger displays showing the view to the left of his flagship. Sat alongside the sides of his vessel was a pair of the massive Kataphrakt Class mega battleships. One was the same design as his ship; another lacked the forward guns, instead equipped with two long gun decks on each flank, bristling with sixteen batteries per side.

They were advanced variants of the simpler and smaller craft used by most Terran states. They hurtled through space at impossible speeds, heading towards the fleet rendezvous point. The other two ships were identical vessels, each sporting the dark mottled colours of the Laconian fleet. Massive inverted Vs were emblazoned on each side, serving as a stark reminder of their origin. These were ships of war, and from the single most powerful Terran state that existed. More than that, after defeating the Attican Alliance a decade earlier, Laconia had shifted to become the dominant power in the galaxy, perhaps even close to matching the power of the Empire itself.

Dukas Aphrodisia Myrrine, the ship's commander, and Admiral of the fleet, checked the course details before moving her attention towards him. She was the epitome of an experienced naval commander, something Laconia had never truly given much thought or attention to. She moved closer to him, and then nodded towards the nearby vessel.

"These mega battleships are built for one purpose. Nothing else comes close, other than perhaps one of our Titans. Only Terrans could produce such ships."

Agesilaus smiled as he listened.

"Yes, they are true machines of war. But one cannot deny the beauty of their designs as well."

Dukas Myrrine reached out and pointed towards the flank of the nearest ship.

"The upgraded plasma batteries are less than a month old. According to the tests, they are almost fifty percent more powerful than the conventional batteries, and capable of shredding an Imperial cruiser in a matter of minutes. The upgrades more than make up for the reduced numbers of guns on our flanks."

Agesilaus found it hard not to smile. There were moments where he wished he could slip back into the ranks of the Army, and simply be treated as just another soldier. To stand shoulder to shoulder in the phalanx, and engage Laconia's enemies with physical strength, skill, arms, and teamwork. But that was not to be his fate, and he would embrace it, as he knew he must. Dukas Myrrine nodded towards the front of the ship.

"As for the guns, we have heavy cutters to the bow that more than make up for them. The old and the new combined together into one package."

"Yes," said Agesilaus, "These new battleships are a shining example of the military advancements and experience of all Terran designers and engineers. Only our people have the skills to produce such incredible feats of engineering. I appreciate the great gifts we have been granted."

Light flashed to the left, and both watched starlight bathe the flank of Harbinger, the ship that could easily be the twin of Agesilaus' flagship. As the light moved slowly from bow to stern, it glanced off the twelve colossal barrels that pushed out aggressively.

"Any Medes captain would baulk at the sight of her, don't you think?"

Dukas Myrrine nodded politely.

"Hopefully."

Though the heavy plasma cannons were small compared to the bulk of the ship, each was actually as big as a starfighter, and could launch a projectile capable of annihilating a corvette. Curved slabs of armour protected the upper sides of the hull, layered one on top of the other. Further to the rear the superstructure raised into a wide T shape that looked out over the rest of the ship. A long line of extra-heavy plasma cannons glistened in the light, while three massive cutter arrays pushed out from the bow. Seven launch bays on each flank provided points for fighters and landing craft to launch into battle. To top off the mighty arsenal of weapons was a single huge ordnance battery on each flank, each containing twenty-eight individual torpedo tubes.

"And there is Myrmidon...what a monster of a ship. What she lacks in flexibility, she makes up for with plasma cannons. I almost feel sorry for whoever feels her wrath first."

He then chuckled, something of a rarity.

"Almost."

Both gazed upon the double deck of gun batteries that filled the flanks of the ship with thirty-two heavy plasma cannons on each side. The design lacked subtlety, and its purpose obvious to anybody that gave it much thought. Finally, Agesilaus looked to the officers on his deck, and the displays showing tactical information for the system.

"How much longer until we arrive, Dukas?"

Dukas Myrrine activated the virtual observation system,

and the walls faded away to reveal outer space. The standard displays continued showing more specific data, but there was something entrancing about flying through space in what appeared to be a completely transparent warship. The nearest stars moved by slowly, but many remained exactly as they were.

"Less than a minute, Strategos. Reconnaissance drones report no signs of Boeotian ships. The sector is clear, as expected. I have to admit, I am surprised we have been left to travel unmolested."

The mere mention of the Boeotians made the veins on Agesilaus' forehead pulsates. They were perhaps the least trusted of all the Terran peoples. In the past, they'd yielded to the fleets of the Medes, and even fought alongside them when forced to. It had lost them many friends among Terrans, and he had no time for any of them.

"Good. I hoped we would be here for a short time. By the time they even realise we're here, we should be gone."

That appeared to surprise Dukas Myrrine, and Agesilaus could tell she was confused.

"You disagree?"

"I am merely surprised we did not send envoys before arriving, Strategos. They fought alongside the Empire when our very worlds were at stake. If it were not for the sacrifice of all Terrans at Platea, we might have seen Boeotian soldiers on Laconian soil."

Agesilaus' nostrils twitched uncomfortably. No soul had ever stepped foot on Laconian soil without being invited, and the very idea of enemy soldiers marching on its sacred soil filled him with barely concealed rage.

"Yes. You are not wrong, Dukas. But still, to be basileus requires me to take a step back and to see the entirety of the campaign I wish to conduct. Peace with the Boeotians will make my task easier, and if they do not know I am here, it will be much easier.

"Of course, Strategos."

"I hoped that four days should have been more than enough time to locate those looking for fortune and glory. We cannot afford to wait any longer before we leave. The lives of our kin far away inside the borders of the Empire depend on us. A day late and every world could be a burnt husk devoid of life."

He looked away and spoke more quietly. Clearly, he would have preferred Laconian forces, but today he had to accept whatever was given to him.

"And to warn them that I intend on bringing my fleet here, to witness the celestial events, and to ask for aid in our voyage. For millennia the Aulian Nebula has been offered sacrifices prior to great journeys. It would send a clear signal to all that join us of our divine mission. A united Terran effort to free our comrades far away."

Dukas Myrrine raised an eyebrow in surprise.

"The Boeotians are no friends of Laconia. I suspect they will stop any ships attempting to come to your aid, Strategos. Perhaps worse."

Agesilaus could see she had doubts, and perhaps there was something else she wanted to say before their arrival, and though little interested in long conversations, he felt obliged to ask.

"You want to ask me something, Dukas?"

The ship's Captain looked nervous for a second, but then she could see the eyes of her Strategos. He might be the supreme commander of the campaign, and also one of the two basileus of Laconia, but he was also a man. There was nothing tyrannical about him, either in his tone, or in the way he behaved.

"Only the reason for our destination. We could have assembled over Laconia before leaving. It seems a risky move assembling the fleet on the periphery of our only true enemy among our kin."

"Yes. We could, but they are not just our enemy. Every Terran state knows of the Boeotian treachery. I suspect many would welcome assembling here merely to tread on Boeotian toes."

He then nodded directly ahead.

"But there is something so much more than politics or war. Look at that, and force yourself not to weep…"

He reached out with his armoured hand and pointed towards the growing nebula. Even Dukas Myrrine gasped as she gazed upon the shapes and colours of the mysterious event.

"In the past, it was described as the birthplace of monsters, and to others a fortress for the Gods. It has been many things to many people…But you want to know why we're here?"

"Yes, Strategos. There is no great spaceport here, and no place to moor our ships before leaving. I still do not understand why we are here."

Agesilaus smiled back at her.

"You do not remember your history, Dukas. Do you not recall the great expedition that was assembled here so long ago? The mighty fleet that rose to the occasion upon being called together by the warlord Agamemnon?"

It took a second, and then the woman's face flushed with embarrassment. It was one of the founding stories for all of the Terrans. Perhaps the greatest story ever told by the Terrans, and one as relevant today as it had been so long ago. Though they might war with each other, they shared common religions, languages, and histories going back thousands of years. And this story, more than any other, now became so obvious to her that it was embarrassing.

"Of course, Strategos. How could I have forgotten? I feel such a fool."

He said nothing and waited for her to continue.

"In Ancient times this was known as Aulia, the port of the Gods. It was from here that the ancient ones travelled the stars. For centuries the heroes of old would come here before travelling on their great adventures."

"Exactly. And this is the place where Agamemnon himself arrayed his legions prior to war with Priam and his minions. To save the honour of his brother, and to seek revenge upon those who would take his wife as hostage. This is the place where the thousand ships sailed from, and into legend at the ten-year Siege of Ilium."

His eyes almost appeared to glaze over as he described those ancient events. They might have happened hundreds of years earlier, but to most Terrans they were considered more as myths than historical events; the time when the legendary Achilleus and Hektor battled beneath the city's mighty walls.

"We will follow in the footsteps of our forebears as we cross the Great Expanse."

He touched his beard, and for a moment looked lost in thought. When he looked back at her there was real fire in his eyes, the kind he would expect to see as he fought his enemies in close quarter combat.

"How is my ship, Dukas? Is Agamemnon ready for war?"

Dukas Myrrine seemed much more relaxed with this particular question, and moved along the deck pointing to various stations and command officers. There were far less personnel onboard a Laconian ship, and a much higher degree of technology and automation present; a certain reminder of the technological and martial prowess of the Laconian state.

"Yes, Strategos. I made sure the name was announced within an hour of the new crew moving aboard. She's fully manned by experienced officers, and has been checked from bow to stern. I have personally inspected every deck and station for operational efficiency. Any component operating below maximum has been replacement. In the last day five weapon arrays have been replaced due to faults from the factories, and new fighters are being prepped for the campaign. Volunteers pilots have been promised by our allies, but they are not with us yet."

She instantly spotted the uncomfortable look on the young Basileus' face. He had a great campaign to plan, and so far she'd seen few resources actually made available to him.

"Strategos Lysander has done us a great service in procuring such venerable vessels, but Agamemnon is a mighty prize, brand new, and a month from the shipyard. Unnamed, it is as though the Gods themselves knew you would need a flagship for the coming war."

Agesilaus wasn't so sure about that, but he was certainly happy to have her.

"She is indeed just what I need. And there is no better name for my ship than Agamemnon. What about the other battleships? According to my information they have seen long service."

"Correct, Strategos. The ships have had a hard life, but all systems are functional and combat ready. Their crews have done an excellent job in keeping them well maintained and operational. They are ships built for war, and they will not let us down."

Agesilaus squinted as he replied.

"Exactly as I want my warriors. No soldier worth their salt can offer me a thing unless they've bled and sweat on the battlefield. Experience, discipline, and training are what I need."

Dukas Myrrine nodded politely, and then pointed directly ahead.

"The Aulian Nebula reaches dozens of light years in all directions. It is causing havoc with our FTL system and has altered our jump vector. We will arrive three minutes ahead of schedule. The navigation computer estimates our arrival time will be in four minutes."

She could see the Basileus' lip move slightly, but he said nothing, instead turning his attention ahead towards the colossal anomaly growing in size and colour before his very eyes.

"Understood."

"Wait," said Dukas Myrrine, "Whose ship is that?"

She moved to the forward view. It looked like a drifting hulk, though at first glance it was an unlit dark shape, and might have been little more than debris. A number of small craft drifted around it, like flies attracted to rotting meat.

"Dukas," said Tactical Officer Eutropios, "Sensors show it's a damaged mercenary cruiser. Her weapons are gone, but the vessel appears mainly intact. She has power, and there are life signs aboard."

"Scavengers," said Agesilaus, "Make contact with them, and light them up with a few cannons. I want them gone from this sacred place. They have five minutes."

"Yes, Strategos."

He then licked his lips as he let the intensity, colours, and shapes of the nebula wash over him.

The battered old ship is of little interest to me, but I'll be damned if I'll let scrap merchants profane such a sacred place as this.

"The Nebula is a wondrous celestial phenomenon, is it not?"

"It is, Strategos. It truly is. I can see now why the great Warlord rallied his fleet here."

The ship dropped from FTL and appeared inside the centre of the Aulian Nebula with no pomp and ceremony. The flashing lights and clouds lit up every square metre of the ships as they moved into a dispersed column. Lightning crackled in the heart of the nebulae, each blast amplifying what already felt like a great religious experience.

"We have arrived," said Dukas Myrrine, "Scans show the area is clear of military vessels."

"Good. The Aulian Nebula is neutral space by treaty. We can stay here without issue, providing we're here on religious service. As per the treaty."

He looked to his right and gazed off into the clouds for something else. The bright flashes and arcing energy was enough to attract any Terran, but he was looking for something else.

"Where is my armada?"

He asked the question with great confidence, though as the seconds faded, so did the look of excitement on his face. It soon turned to suspicion, and perhaps even doubt. Agesilaus waited in silence, looking for any sign of his fleet, and still there was nothing.

"This cannot..."

Before he could say more, a series of alarms activated on the deck. He could not make out each station, but when the auletes turned to his commander, it all became clear.

"Dukas, the fleet is arriving! Every commander is reporting in for duty."

Agesilaus walked to the centre of the deck and stared out at the approaching shapes. With each second, another ship arrived, adding to the three he'd brought with him. There were vessels from small and large colonies, but as many arrived under no flag or colours. There were gunboats, frigates, dozens of armoured cruisers, and a good number of old battleships. It was a motley collection, but he was thankful that anything had arrived. This went on for almost a minute, and then the silence and stillness returned to the region.

"Excellent," he said to himself, "This is a very good start, more than fifty ships, and the same number of transports. We have numbers, and we have ships. This I can use."

He was so busy looking at the ships he didn't see what else was happening. Dukas Myrrine called to him and pointed to the imagery ahead of them.

"Strategos. The commander of the Black Spear light cruiser is offering to hand the ship to you as a gift for the campaign. He says they were there to try and help move it away because it was a shipping hazard. His crew is already evacuating the vessel."

"A gift," Agesilaus muttered, "A partially stripped ship. That can be of…"

Then he stopped, carefully reconsidering his words.

"Thank him, and tell him to move the ship into formation alongside our warships, with our thanks. And if they are so keen to help, offer him and his crew positions in the fleet."

"Uh…very well, Strategos. Oh…and can also confirm that Princess Kyniska is aboard the largest transport. It is of an unknown configuration, but bears the markings of Laconia on its flanks. She wishes to speak with…"

"Put her on…and show me this ship."

The image shifted as it transformed into the shape of his sister. In the background he watched the dark vessel seem to come closer as the system magnified the long-range view. It was a big ship, and little different in size to his own ship.

"Is it me…or is that an old Dorian assault ship?"

Dukas Myrrine walked to the tactical station and spoke with the officer. In seconds a number of schematics appeared.

"Strange," she said, examining the flanks of the ship.

"What is it?"

"The ship looks as though it was one of the modified troop transports used in the Helot uprising. If I'm not mistaken, this was the flagship of the Helot rebels."

Agesilaus looked upon the relic and almost gasped.

"The ship that Basileus Archidamus II himself boarded. Incredible."

He shook his head as he looked back to his Dukas.

"The stories say that of the forty Laconians that boarded the ship with him, only three survived, as well as the Basileus. I never realised the ship had been kept in order. Last I heard, it was supposed to be scrapped or sold to one of our allies."

"From the specifications, I would say it has found itself a new life as a warship," said Dukas Myrrine, "The armour is much more substantial than shown in the records, and it carries weapons taken from…Median escort ships. How bizarre."

The image on the main screen in front of Agesilaus rolled to the left, settling to show a crystal-clear image. Seeing her there put a smile on his face. As always, she was fully armoured and ready for a fight, and looked the spitting image of himself had he been an athletic young woman. Sometimes Agesilaus wondered if she slept in her armour, though that would hardly surprise anybody.

"Kyniska, I thought we'd lost you."

"Strategos. I have brought the mercenaries with me. The best three hundred I could find. They're not pretty, but they are good. And I found this old thing waiting to be scrapped on the station."

"How did you find such a relic? My Dukas informs me that the vessel has been heavily upgraded. I would dearly like to know more."

"All in good time, Brother. For now, just know that I've renamed her Archidamus II. We will have more than enough time during the journey to talk about her."

"Agreed. How did you secure the use of the ship, though? Our funds are somewhat depleted."

Kyniska winked at him.

"Leave that to me. I have ways of motivating people that you don't want to know about."

"Of that, I have no doubt. We will speak of it shortly. In the meantime, today is an auspicious day indeed. We will make a sacrifice to the Gods, right here where the ancient general did the same."

"You always were a sucker for the old stories, weren't you?"

Agesilaus did not appear offended at her insinuation.

"Indeed I was, and remain so. There is much we can learn from the legends and tales of old. Where do you…"

He stopped, realising his sister was doing what she always did.

"Kyniska. Even in times of war and strife you find the time for games and amusements. You'll recall what Father told us both when we were small."

Kyniska lifted a hand to stop him.

"Brother. Today is not the day for lectures. I've brought your mercenaries, and a prized warship for the fleet. Do we not have more pressing concerns? I, for one, cannot be the only Terran here that is a little concerned at your choice of name for your ship, and for assembling here."

"Oh?"

Kyniska could tell he was being coy, but chose to ignore

him.

"I assume you recall everything else that happened here before the great war with Priam? Because if you haven't, I can tell you now that every single commander in this armada of yours can remember what happened. "

That made Agesilaus' nostrils twitch. At the same time, he watched as each of the ships reported in on the command network. One by one they joined his pre-allocated squadrons and divisions until they were arrayed in battle order.

"Of course I remember, Kyniska. But I have no intention of sacrificing a child to allow us to leave safely. No, we are here on a mission from the Gods, and we will prevail."

"You have not checked the trade routes across the Great Expanse, have you?"

Agesilaus looked confused.

"What do you mean?"

"Wait a moment..."

His sister turned away and spoke with somebody out of shot. At the same time, Agesilaus signalled for Dukas Myrrine to approach. He was not nervous, but obvious concern showed on his face. The campaign was a massive undertaking, and if anything were to interfere with their mission, it could end it before it even started.

"What do you know of this?"

Dukas Myrrine shook her head.

"Nothing so far. I will get my people on it."

At that moment his sister returned.

"Look at this..."

She shifted from view and was replaced by a wide star map of the known galaxy. To the left were the scattered positions of the Terrans, and far to the right the jagged border of the Empire. The enemy home was so vast the mapping data displayed just the outer limits. The bulk of the map showed the void known as the Great Expanse, a massive region of space almost two hundred and fifty parsecs long at its widest point. This region of space was so inhospitable it would take eighteen separate FTL jumps. Each would then require the smaller ships to refuel from the larger vessels. Normally, this could stretch a journey from under three weeks, to over a month. There were small numbers of colonies scattered throughout, but most of the area was devoid of life. Lines showed the quickest and safest shipping routes, avoiding dangerous anomalies that could tear ships apart as they travelled using their FLT drives.

"Okay...I do not see the issue."

Kyniska sighed as her hand appeared in the middle of the map. She moved it along the three biggest shipping routes.

"A storm has arrived of the like not seen for a century. A rumour started in Thebes that it came because of Laconian actions against the Empire. They blame the rampaging of Terran mercenaries of the Black Legion, and their Laconian officers."

"What? Are they mad?"

Kyniska laughed.

"Does it matter, Brother? The rumours spread fast, and now the priests from the temple colonies are jumping on the chance."

"Priests," Agesilaus murmured, "Old men that will always change their minds when the temple sacrifices are large enough. If two men ask a priest the same question, the answer will never be the same."

"Perhaps. But a cruiser squadron from the colonies of Naxos Collective have sent reports of the damage. They sent three scout ships to investigate, and one has already been lost with all hands."

"You're serious? I didn't realise they even had military ships in their area. Weren't the Atticans supposed to be patrolling their planets?"

Kyniska nodded slowly.

"Yes, Brother. While you've been calling for volunteers across Terra, I've been looking for aid in other places. The Atticans are bankrupt, and their old allies are looking for new patrons. News of us heading their way is shifting them to our side. Every single ship we can muster will increase our chances of success."

A smile formed upon his face as he forgot about the priests and the stories, instead focussing on the news of the ships.

"You've been recruiting in the Great Expanse? It seems you've been more successful than I. You always were able to get people to listen to you. Maybe it should be you leading this campaign."

"Yes." She winked, "Maybe I should. Let's see how you do first of all. Perhaps you'll surprise me!"

She could see he was amused by her suggestion, but there were more serious matters on her mind at the moment.

"I was surprised to see so many were willing to help. The Expanse is uniquely vulnerable, and they know it. The colonies there are terrified of the growing military action of the Empire, and they have to make a choice."

"Of course," said Agesilaus, "They can either prepare to submit to the God King of the Empire, or they can side with other Terrans."

"And they have all heard of your plan, Agesilaus. Word is spreading quickly of a Laconian who leads a pan-Terran fleet. A man who will give them wealth and freedom, without the yoke of Laconia keeping them as little more than Helots."

"I see. And this great storm threatens our ability to travel to the Ionian Territories."

"The navigators and scouts from Naxos say they believe it will subside in three or four days. That will slow us down if we wait, or we can risk the ships…"

"No," replied Agesilaus, shaking his head, "This is a coalition of strangers. We must bind our people together through shared struggle, and losing ships before we arrive will end this before it can begin."

Even as he said the words, he knew what he had to do. Kyniska knew him well enough that she could tell he'd come up with a plan already. He was no ordinary Laconian, but a man that thought, as well as fought. He hesitated, and then signalled towards the ship's auletes.

"I want to speak with the entire fleet."

"Yes, Strategos."

Kyniska pointed to the displays at her brother's side, and he stepped closer to examine them.

"Look at the forces you have arrayed before you. Thousands of warriors are waiting upon your command. As well as the warships and transports, we have massed a force undreamed of. I assume you have a plan to keep them together?"

"I have an inkling of a plan. And for now, that will have to do. This is no Laconian host, and they will answer to me for as long as they believe I have something to offer them."

"True. You started with the Helots. You raised them yourself, twenty thousand freshly raised heavy infantry. But look to the transports of our allies. There are large numbers of volunteers from Arcadia, Mantinea, Lylos, Elis, Megara, and even Delphic star systems."

Agesilaus held his breath, finally asking the one question he desperately wanted an answer to.

"How many soldiers?"

Kyniska paused for effect; something she knew would annoy her brother.

"Sixty thousand volunteers. Three times as many as the Helot legions you've already arranged. Their colonial governments have not sanctioned war, but they have provided them with armour and weapons, as well as transports and warships to help get them safely to the Territories."

"Eighty thousand Terran warriors in total. That is quite a host. But they are not Laconian, though, are they? How many are veteran warriors?"

Before Kyniska could answer, he asked one final question.

"Are they even warriors?"

"You know the answer to that, Brother. Only Laconia can boast of a professional army. Every other Terran state can muster a levy in times of war. These are citizen soldiers, some of whom have experience of war, and a small percentage are mercenaries."

"I see. And the mercenaries you negotiated?"

"They are good. There are even Laconians among their number. Give it three weeks, and they'll have our new recruits beaten into shape and ready to take on the Medes."

Agesilaus nodded slowly, stepping into the centre of the deck, the point best suited for image capture and projection. He adjusted his crimson cloak and then pulled on his beard. Other Terrans ridiculed the Laconians for their attention to hygiene and their looks, but few truly understood the reasoning. It didn't take long until he was finally satisfied with what he had done. Others would spend time and money on accoutrements, ornaments, and other fanciful items. But the Laconians were famous for explaining that their hair was the cheapest of ornaments, and Agesilaus made it known that he was no different to any other warrior in his armada.

"Very well. I am ready."

"Beginning scanning and transmission now," said the auletes.

Agesilaus lowered his head and pulled on his heavy Corinthian helm. The tall horsehair plume reach up high, making him look even bigger than he already was. A blue light danced above him, and then a wide circle dropped down, scanning his body from head to toe. He remained still, upright, and calm, raising his gaze when ready to speak.

"I am Agesilaus II of Laconia, Eurypontid Basileus, and commander of this great pan-Terran endeavour. Some of you have already met my sister, Kyniska. Royal Princess of Laconia, she is my right hand, and will serve as one of my two deputies during this campaign. As Topoteretes, you will afford her word with the same authority as my own."

He then reached outwards with both arms. In his right he bore his weaponry, and in his left the shield projector directly attached to the generator pack still fitted to his back.

"Stratiotes of the Terran worlds. I thank all of you for volunteering for this grand campaign, one that will rewrite the history books."

He used the generic name for soldier, rather than calling them out by their specifics. In earlier times it had been used for everything from heavy infantry, through to skirmishers, snipers, and even the crew of vehicles. It was also the name frequently used to describe the forces that had fought in antiquity, such as the great siege of Ilium.

"I welcome you to the great Aulian Nebula. For millennia this place has been a holy place among Terrans. Though we fight each other, we have always kept this place free and as a haven to the Gods."

He gave his dekarchos a nod, and the man passed on his order to the other officers. Once satisfied his next action was underway, he looked back to the display and imagined the faces of the other Terrans. Thousands of them were out there, many having never even seen a Laconian before.

"Long ago another leader of Terrans came to this very place. He made a grave mistake and was forced to sacrifice to the Gods before he could leave. After all this time…another great fleet has arrived, and a mighty storm has come with us. This storm is a sign from the Gods that we must follow their natural laws and the paths laid out to us for centuries."

His eyes shifted for a second, and he could see the shaking head of Kyniska. She knew he was saying what needed to be heard, but he could tell she believed none of it. Yet it was the lip service he had to give if they were to continue.

"We cannot wage war against the Medes unless right is on our side. The worlds and colonies of Terrans do not seek war, but they will fight if provoked. We must prove to the Gods that this armada respects them, and respects their law. We will make sacrifice in the ways of old."

Now he could see the smile on his sister's face.

"We shall sacrifice a cruiser to the Gods, and ask for their favour in this difficult and arduous voyage. That will sate their appetite, and show we offer them the correct respect for our grand adventure."

He licked his lips before saying the next part.

"We will then know if the Gods honour our sacrifice and our objectives, by clearing the way to our enemies. I call upon you all to prepare your vessels for the ceremony. We will begin within an hour. If any of you have personal, family, or sacrifices of your own to make, now will be the time. Aulis accepts all offerings. May the Gods welcome our passage to the Empire!"

CHAPTER TEN

Battleship 'Agamemnon', Aulian Nebula

The hour passed much more slowly than Agesilaus had expected as the host of ships moved closer to the crackling energies of Aulis. The positive thing he could take from the experience was it had given time for several more ships to arrive. Most were transports, but occasionally another military ship would arrive. He found the most fascinating of all a contingent of Attican rebels who had arrived with a large squadron of Triremis cruisers. The ships bore no Terran colours, but instead the individual markings of their crews and officers. From memory, Agesilaus knew they carried double the crew of a similar sized vessel, and though flawed for long-distance operations, were regarded as some of the deadliest ships ever built.

"Our armada grows stronger with each passing minute," he said quietly, "Perhaps the Gods favour our campaign after all."

A noise from further back inside the ship announced the arrival of another officer. The Epilektoi bodyguards moved apart to let the man enter. He was dressed in Laconian battle attire and marched along the deck towards Agesilaus. He moved along the steps, and then bowed before the royal siblings.

"Komes Diogenes. I hoped you would join us. I take it Lysander was able to spare you for a few months."

The heavily bearded man chuckled.

"Lysander is not happy with his new posting. He has been sent to Thibron to relieve the colonial garrison. Apparently, the Medes have been causing trouble there, and only Lysander can save the day."

Agesilaus reached forward and grasped the man's forearm.

"It is good that you are here. It has been too long since we fought together in the Hall of Heroes."

"I am honoured, my Strategos. Or should I say, Basileus?"

"Strategos will do…for now, old friend. Do you know why I called for you?"

Komes Diogenes concentrated on the face of his friend for a moment before answering.

"You need volunteers, and where better to look for them than in your old sparring partners? I managed to bring a few of your old comrades along, too. Not enough to win this war for you, but more than enough to keep you out of trouble…Well, too much trouble!"

The two laughed together as Kyniska stepped in front of the man. He was almost the size, height, and build as Agesilaus, though at least a decade older. Any scars he might have were hidden below his armour and helmet, which he now removed.

"Princess. With you and your brother together, I do not see how this campaign can fail."

"Flattery will get you nowhere, old man."

Komes Diogenes wiped his brow and looked towards the vast command deck.

"Perhaps, but it was worth a try, eh?"

Agesilaus stepped to his side and then beckoned towards the rest of the ship.

"I have more than enough ships for now, perhaps more than I can afford to resupply. And there are tens of thousands of warriors in their holds, but few experienced commanders. I need experienced men and women to fight for me, and none is more important than the position of the leader of my personal bodyguard."

Komes Diogenes eyes opened wide. Kyniska spoke first.

"This is no Laconian campaign, and there are Terrans from a hundred worlds here. Most are honourable, but there are many that cannot be fully trusted. Laconia is envied by most, and hated by a few. To stand alongside us, is to risk death in foreign lands."

Diogenes shrugged.

"When has that ever bothered any of us? We go where Laconia sends us. One battlefield is as good as any other."

"True," Agesilaus agreed, "I do not want you to simply fight alongside us, old friend. I have something much more important to ask of you."

"Tell me. And if I can grant it, yours it shall be."

Agesilaus looked to his sister, and she gave him a nod, confirming he'd done the right thing.

"Good. I have brought all three hundred of my Epilektoi from Laconia. As Basileus it is my right, and it is also a good way of bringing a core of reliable warriors to the battle."

"A cunning move," said Diogenes, "More cunning than I might have expected to hear from…"

He stopped upon seeing the looks from both Laconians, and then wondered if he'd taken a step too far.

"My apologies, that was inappropriate of me."

Agesilaus was hard to gauge, but Kyniska looked as though

she was about to burst out laughing. So he looked back at the Basileus and said nothing further.

"I want you to lead my Epilektoi. You will protect both myself and Kyniska from any threat, external or internal. And when we are in battle you will fight alongside us, shield to shield. Will you accept this responsibility?"

Komes Diogenes dropped to one knee in front of them without hesitation. He'd done this before when he'd offered his services to Lysander, and now he did the same again before his new master. He looked down and waited for a moment, carefully considering what he had been asked. It was much more than a mere promotion, but a great responsibility. If anything went wrong, he could not expect to return home alive. The death of a Basileus in the field would mean the death of the senior Epilektoi as well. Any that returned could expect disgrace and dishonour. This did not worry him, but being responsible for the lives of two members of the royal household deserved at least a moment's consideration. He knew what he would say well before he said it.

"I would be honoured to serve you in any way, Strategos. If you want me to serve in your guard, I would be happy. To lead the Epilektoi is too much. There must be another that would be better served in this role."

Agesilaus leaned down and grasped his arm. With one firm tug, he yanked him upright and directly in front of him. They were now the same height, and yet Komes Diogenes appeared somewhat larger than he had been before, as though the very suggestion of the promotion had made him into an even greater man.

"Good. If you had not doubted yourself for a moment then I might wonder if you truly were my friend. This is no mere honour, it is a duty and a responsibility that I ask of you."

Agesilaus' attention shifted for a second as he watched the spaceships forming up alongside the rest of the fleet.

"Good. It is done, then. You will lead my Epilektoi, and keep both of us safe for as long as you're able. If you need anything, you will tell me."

Diogenes nodded.

"Of course, Strategos."

He then looked to the new ships, trying to lighten the sombre mood on the command deck.

"Triremis cruisers…I have to admit, I never expected to see them in our fleet."

"Indeed," said Agesilaus, "That is something I can make use of. There's nothing more dangerous in open space than a squadron of those ships. You might recall the trouble we had when we warred with the Alliance."

"True. Luckily, we were able to muster a large enough fleet to finally annihilate them at Fort Plymouth in the Aegospotami Nebulae."

"Yes." Agesilaus recalled the bloodbath, "And if I recall correctly, we did it with the help of a large Medes fleet commanded by Pharnabazus."

Mentioning the Medes Satrap made Diogenes' skin crawl.

"To have used Medes support to win the war was dishonourable."

"Perhaps, but while Laconia was and still is supreme on the land, the Alliance was always going to be one step ahead in space. It was the price for victory, and the price to end the war."

Both men remained silent for a moment, as they thought back to those bloody days. The Alliance fleet had been caught at anchor, and they'd swept in and crushed them without mercy. Laconian ships had gone in first, but there were as many Medes vessels in the battle, and a large number of mercenaries funded by the Satrap. The last few Alliance ships had made a stand to let the rest of the fleet escape. Agesilaus shook his head.

"Pharnabazus made a pact with us back then, a pact to hold back Alliance power and expansion. And it worked. We crushed them, and peace and stability returned to our colonies. The price was high, but it moved us to the forefront of Terran powers."

"Nonetheless, you have to admire those sailors. I wish we had men and women of that skill."

The two men watched in fascination as the agile ships moved with speed and elegance unmatched by any other vessels in the armada. Though technically cruisers, they were crewed by large numbers of professionals, with three banks of heavy weapons, powerful engines, and most incredible of all, a plasma ram at the bow. Agesilaus had seen them in action twice before, and knew how much damage the plasma ram could cause when slammed into the flanks of a ship. He'd watched an entire Laconian battleship break in half when rammed by two cruisers, only for the wreckage to been torn apart by broadsides from the triple decks.

"Agreed, they are impressive."

Agesilaus turned his attention to the crackling energies of the vast Aulian Nebula. The celestial phenomenon followed no logical order, the centre vanishing, and then appearing once more to mimic a great whirlpool in space. Anything that moved too close would be torn apart, much as the dreaded whirlpool monster rocks of Kharybdis did between Sicilia and Calabria. He waited at the rear of the elongated command deck, along with Kyniska and a handful of his personal guards.

"This is taking an age," he said with a grumble.

Kyniska turned from her position near the short ramp that dropped down to the main deck. They were positioned along the raised section, closer to the ceiling than the rest of the deck. Square in shape, there was a projected tactical table in the middle, and vertical displays rose from workstation desks positioned around three sides of the square space.

"Yes, it is. But you wanted your sacrifice to be done correctly."

"You disagree?"

Kyniska nodded.

"Yes. Victory in battle will give them a common cause. We waste time in this place while our comrades fight and die at the hands of the Empire."

Agesilaus shook his head.

"To send sheep against wolves will see a slaughter. We must be wise in this campaign."

He stepped down the first step back to the command deck level and looked out to the rest of the deck. It ran all the way to the vast oval window that was as wide as the deck itself. Similar virtual panels along the ceiling gave the impression of glass and let light from the nebula inside. More displays and crew were positioned along each side, and every one of them was busy. There was a murky look to the place, with many dark places near decks and bulkheads. This contrasted heavily with the bright lights from the displays. Dukas Myrrine approached and nodded slightly.

"The Black Spear is in position and ready to be sent into the whirlpool. There is more, though."

"Yes?"

"News has arrived of the storm and more ship losses. Rumours of dead and lost vessels are spreading fast."

Agesilaus shook his head bitterly. He knew this was likely to happen, and had hoped to avoid it by quickly making a sacrifice to the nebula.

"They are not panicking, though. I am as surprised as you are, Strategos."

Kyniska moved to her brother's side.

"What do you mean, Dukas?"

She pointed to the nebula. Trails of lights pulsed in rings as objects hurtled towards it.

"The other contingents wish to join in with this offering. The Helot units have sent in three landing dropships, and more are following. It is becoming something every ship is assisting with. So far fifteen small craft, and more than fifty containers of weapons have been sent into the nebula."

"What? Our numbers are limited enough as they are. We cannot afford to lose any more resources to this."

Kyniska reached out and pointed towards the old cruiser moving towards the nebula.

"Black Spear is more than a sacrifice, Brother. It has taken on their imaginations. Its sacrifice will mark the turning point in our campaign. It will…"

"Wait." Agesilaus he lifted a hand, "What is that?"

Something to the left caught his eye. He strained his eyes as he looked out into space via the VOB technology. The flashes appeared to be coming from ships, but he assumed more vessels were arriving.

Good. Then perhaps these sacrifices are having the desired effect. We must continue.

Seeing the flashes as ships arrived from FTL travel put fire in his heart, and when he continued to speak, there was a slight rise of excitement in his tone.

"From this place we will travel across the Great Expanse and come to the aid of our kin on the far side of the galaxy. As before, Terrans will make war against our common enemy, and we will do to them that which Agamemnon himself achieved…

their bloody and grim annihilation. The despicable war criminal and tyrant Tissaphernes is at this very moment bombarding multiple Terran worlds. The dead number in the hundreds of thousands, and our hard-built colonies lie in utter ruin."

He paused, letting those words sink in to the many thousands in the armada. As a Laconian he detested long speeches, and yet the majority in his fleet were not Laconian warriors. There were volunteers from dozens of different colonies, some of whom had warred with his own people in the past.

"I ask that each of you takes a knee as we remember the great deeds of our ancestors."

He bent down, and the armour at his knee creaked as he lowered his weight down upon it. One by one the other officers did exactly the same. Agesilaus closed his eyes as he looked at the ground and thought back to the stories of old. Of mighty Achilleus, bold Ajax, and the unstoppable warlord Menelaus. Even their enemies had been men of greater honour, more than the foes they faced today.

"We offer sacrifice to the Gods of old, to aid our campaign against the Great Enemy, and to offer each of us the chance to achieve greatness. We ask for Hermes to clear the shipping and communication routes to the Ionian Territories, and for Ares to grant us untamed violence and victory in arms when we come to blows with the Medes. And we ask for Athana for wisdom, intelligence, and strategy in our campaign, and to help us enforce justice upon our enemies."

He used the Doric name for Athena, a move that was a conciliatory position to make as a Laconian. To many other Terrans she was Athena, but he was not going to go that far. Not today, and not when he was trying to stamp his own form of command over the armada. He could have ignored the God entirely, but there were enough Atticans in the fleet to make this an ignorant move. So, he accepted the patron God of the Alliance, but in his own particular way.

"Strategos!"

Agesilaus opened his eyes and spotted the look of stunned horror from Dukas Myrrine. It was as though she'd seen the ghost of Tissaphernes himself standing on the deck alongside him. Agesilaus was so surprised he even glanced to each side, half expecting to find a blade moving towards him.

"Dukas ...this is not the time."

She shook her head and moved closer towards the shimmering figure of Agesilaus. The blue light continued to dance about his body as his image was transmitted to all the vessels in the mighty armada. Dukas Myrrine kept on moving and then reached out to grasp him arms. It was a bold move and caused his personal guards to materialise from the shadows, each pointing the razor-sharp tips of their Asgeirr-Carbines at her throat.

"What is it?"

Dukas Myrrine continued shaking her head, twisted about, and pointed off towards the centre of the great nebula. For a moment Agesilaus expected to see a great space monster, or even a god appear from the maelstrom. But instead it was little more than the flicker of dozens of lights. Kyniska was right there beside him, and spoke before the Dukas Myrrine could say even a word.

"They are here."

Agesilaus looked down towards the triple displays in front of his ship's tactical officer. The veteran naval officer, Penatarchos Eutropios pointed at the red icons flashing up to the left of the screens. Four large cruisers moved in around Black Spear, and without warning began to fire. Shot after shot slammed into the vessel, and soon it was burning. With no shields or weapons, the ship had little chance, and seconds later part of the stern broke away, followed by dozens of small explosions. Agesilaus' eyes shifted from his sister. At the same time a snarl spread across his face.

"They arrive without warning, and open fire without speaking a word. Black Spear is gone, and with it my sacrifice to Hermes. I knew they could never be trusted."

He rolled his shoulders, took in a long, deep breath, and walked along the deck towards the raised section. There the tactical map showed the disposition of his forces as they prepared to make sacrifices. The Black Spear was a long way from them, and the new arrivals seemed to be moving closer to it by the second.

"Prepare for battle. Our old enemy has returned. Assemble in menoeides combat formation. Activate shielding, and ready fighters for launch."

He glanced back to his sister. She nodded towards him.

"The way to move them on is to show them strength. They will not stand when they realise Laconians command this fleet. Not unless they want war."

The images showing on the myriad of screens stunned the officers on board Agamemnon. And yet for all their surprise, they acted without question or concern at their predicament. They were professionals, and proceeded to ready themselves for the coming battle. Agesilaus had fought for Laconia many times before, but he'd never commanded more than a squadron of ships or a few thousand warriors. Now he had an armada ready for battle, and enough soldiers to invade a single planet.

"The scum could not leave us alone, not even for one day, could they?"

The largest screen altered to focus down on the individual ships. Agesilaus took a step closer, and several of the officers watched as their intimidating commander examined the imagery. He was only interested in the iconography showing on the flanks of the bigger ships. Most were yellow or golden in colour. Yet the long diagonal clubs marked them out as coming from a single star system, and one that few Terrans would ever trust again. They were strong, and some said they might one day even challenge Laconia for control of all Terrans.

"Thebans," Agesilaus said under his breath, "They change sides faster than an Attican changes his mind. One day they fight with Terrans, and the next they fight alongside the Medes. Once more they prove to every Terran that they have no honour."

As he turned back, a number of the officers watched in silence for their commands.

"Show me my commanders."

The auletes took a moment to activate the projectors on the deck. One by one the commanders of each squadron appeared. There were six of them, as well as Kyniska whose figure dominated the group. She wasn't the biggest of the seven, but with her Laconian armour, clothing, and cloak she looked the part. For centuries Laconia had been the preeminent military power among the Terrans, and their style of dress and clothing always made them stand out.

"Strategos," each said in turn. It was all he needed to hear to know that they were ready and willing to do what needed to be done.

"It pains me to inform you of our betrayal. Even now, on the cusp of war, the Theban betrayers arrive and advance with violence in their hearts. They do this as our ships prepare to give battle to the Medes."

The large screen pulled back, showing the entire area around the fleet. Agesilaus' forces were arrayed in a menoeides formation, a large crescent shape, with the bows of each vessel pointed outward and towards the enemy. It was a simple, though relatively unwieldy formation, but did present the longest range and most powerful weapons directly at the Theban ships.

"Contact from their commander," said the auletes, "It is Strategos Photios Kosmas of the Theban Fleet."

Agesilaus nodded, but found it almost impossible to speak for a few seconds. The projection of the Theban appeared on front of him, dressed in typical Theban fashion. The armour mimicked the Laconian style, and he even wore a crimson cloak, much to Agesilaus' disdain. The armour was lighter, and the man's helm instantly marked him out as coming from the vast region known as the Boeotian Rift.

Photios. I have not met this man before. I will remember his face no matter what happens on this day.

The Terran commander looked as though he was sneering, and Agesilaus clenched his left fist with frustration as he let him speak. He'd rather have attacked, or performed some other action first, but his forces were not ready for war. Not yet.

"Basileus Agesilaus. We recently heard of your investiture. Reports suggest there is a great deal of discontent among the Laconian League since you were made Basileus. Perhaps it is wise that you left soon to ensure the safety of your own people."

Agesilaus didn't hesitate, choosing to ignore the words of the Theban.

"What do you want, Photios? I am not here to train whelps in the ways of war. My business is my own, and you should know better than to get in the way of a Laconian."

It was short, curt, and exactly as expected. Photios tried to look amused at the Laconian's words, but it was obvious to all that he was nervous. And he had good reason to be.

"Ah, Laconians, always the same. I thought you had come to heap praise upon my local Dekarchos. With one ship, he defeated an entire horde of pirates operating in this very place. Every Terran should be grateful for his endeavours."

Agesilaus laughed at the insinuation, and especially the idea that a local Dekarchos was worth of any kind of praise.

"Pirates? A Thespian hat maker could have achieved as much, perhaps with less."

That rankled greatly with Photios, and Agesilaus decided to push him further to hopefully reveal his intentions. Or at the very least buy his captains time to ready their ships.

"Every Terran should be grateful for his endeavours. Perhaps if more operated in this egalitarian fashion, our worlds would be more prosperous."

Agesilaus sighed, shaking his head. Any respect he might have for the man was quickly evaporating.

"A shoemaker is not a good craftsman who puts big shoes on a small foot."

Photios snarled at the insult, knowing it was especially targeted at him. The time for pleasantries was clearly over, and Photios straightened his back as he prepared to speak. Agesilaus derived some small measure of satisfaction in knowing that every one of his ships was now ready, their weapon and shield arrays charged and activated.

Here it comes.

"Basileus…" he said, almost spitting out the word, "You have come to the Aulian Nebula under force of arms, perhaps Laconian starcharts are as unreliable as your navy is. This area falls under our jurisdiction, and you have no right to be here without our agreement."

He crossed his arms in a defensive and provocative gesture.

"As commander of the Theban Star Fleet, I am under orders

to remove you from this place…immediately."

Agesilaus could see everything he despised of the Thebans in this man, arrogance, lack of respect, and an obsession with the façade of sophistication. The man's helmet was open, allowing good peripheral vision and unimpaired hearing when in battle, one of the weaknesses of the archaic helm worn by Agesilaus. It had a domed skull surrounded by a wide, flaring, down-sloping brim that could easily have been made from cloth. The brim came down at the rear to protect the back of the neck. It projected forward over the forehead and was worked into a complex shape at the sides, with downward pointing folds, affording some lateral protection to the face. It was an elegant design that favoured mobility and aesthetics over protection. Agesilaus forced himself to breathe slowly, even though all he wanted was to find the man's ship, board it, and personally choke the life out of him.

"Remove me? Let me check that. You're threatening to remove me, Photios?"

He might have laughed under any other circumstances, but chose to let his words express his amusement.

"That is an interesting suggestion from a Theban. Your fleet is adequate, but it is not enough to do any more than scratch the paint of my ships."

He licked his lips while watching the man carefully. He should have been nervous, but Agesilaus could tell he was up to something.

Damn the scheming Theban. Damn them all!

"Now. As my envoys have…"

Photios tried to interrupt him, but Agesilaus ignored him and continued. His voice was low and bristled with confidence.

"As did Agamemnon before me, I am here with my brothers and sisters to pay my respects to the Gods, to make a sacrifice, and to ask for their aid in my grand campaign."

Photios laughed, but still Agesilaus continued.

"I will complete my task before undertaking a grand campaign against our old enemy. It is time all Terrans took their vengeance upon them. Perhaps this would be a good time for you to offer up warriors and ships, and to prove your kinship with all Terrans."

"Our old enemy?" Photios said with a mocking smile, "And who might that be?"

Kyniska snorted, and Agesilaus threw her a withering stare that almost silenced her. Instead, she muttered an obscenity, and then gave him a mocking bow.

"Well, for the rest of us. Your scheming with the Medes has not been forgotten."

Photios shrugged.

"Better to bend the knee, than to burn and be forgotten."

With his right hand extended, he pointed towards the Laconian warrior. At the same time, more proximity alerts activated. Agesilaus looked to the screens, but Photios confirmed his fears.

"My ships now match yours in number, if not capabilities. I will fight, and with every hour that you stay here, more of my ships will arrive. In time, the Theban Fleet will destroy your plans of conquest against the Medes, and a state of war will exist between our peoples. Now…"

He rubbed his hands together in mock amusement at Agesilaus' predicament.

"You have ten minutes to leave before I give the order to attack. I will not…"

Agesilaus gave the signal, and the auletes cut the Theban off in mid-sentence. When he turned around, he found Kyniska looking right back at him. There was real fire burning in her eyes as she spoke.

"I say we arm weapons and open fire. How dare they interrupt this sacred gathering! I will burn every one of their ships to ash!"

A few murmured in agreement, but Agesilaus shook his head. He was a Laconian at heart, but there was more to him than that. He knew his people's history, and he remained convinced that intelligence was equally important in war. As he'd been trained to carefully lead troops into battle on foot, he would also have to exhibit the same tactical and strategic thinking in space.

"We did not come here to fight. Even victory will leave our ships damaged and weakened for the great voyage."

"You would yield the battlefield to the Theban collaborators?" Maxis asked, known as Lucky Max to his soldiers for a series of incredible successes over the last decade.

"I did not bring my contingent of Megaran volunteers and two fully equipped starcarriers simply to run from these cowards. Are you not a direct descendent of the Procles, the great-great-great-grandson of Herakles, and a son of Aristodemus and Argia?"

Few would dare speak to Agesilaus that way, but he needed the man and his ships more than ever. Those two vessels were not simply ships of war, but heavily armoured warships that each transported more than a hundred fighters to the coming battle. More significant, were the multiple squadrons of advanced fighters and bombers that came with the ships, and their Laconian trained pilots. An asset as significant as the Mega Battleships gifted from Lysander and would help make up for the lack of Laconian warships and soldiers.

"No, I will not flee. And never again will you question my ancestry or leadership, unless I expressly ask you to. Do you understand, Megaran?"

The mood shifted, and for a moment it looked as if a fight might break out on the deck of the ship, not that it was possible with only one of them actually physically present.

"Of course, Strategos. My apologies," said a suitably chastened Maxis.

"Nonetheless, I will not stop my campaign either. It is imperative I leave with my fleet intact, but also with Terran affairs left to maintain the status quo. Of what good will a war with the Medes be to any of us if the fires of war are spread at home?"

"A point well made," said Maxis.

Kyniska pushed past him and pointed to the tactical map. She moved her hand to the centre of the Theban Fleet, and to the largest ships they'd brought with them.

"We treat them as you treat any bully and his friends. We advance the fleet directly at them and hit their command ships. We threaten them in boarding actions, and send panic through their ships."

"I agree," said Maxis, "Perhaps this show of force will be enough to force their hand. The Thebans are all show, like a small dog with a loud bark. We scare them, and we break them."

Agesilaus had never met Maxis before, but he could already see he had been too hasty in his judgement. The man might be short and stocky, and dressed in the poorly fitted regalia of a Megaran Dukas. He was bald and overweight. Yet his physique told one part of his story, for all of them knew he alone had matched the Atticans in an infamous engagement between two Megaran starcarriers, and a fleet of fifteen Attican ships. It was a battle he'd emerged from victorious, and against all odds.

His judgement should be listened to, even if it is not acted upon.

Agesilaus looked to the rest of the small group. Two wore

traditional garb, the rest a mixed array of Terran armour, or did not bother at all, and looked little different to the captain of a civilian freighter.

"This is not how I expected our expedition to begin. Nonetheless, as my war council, I will listen to your suggestions. Maxis speaks wise words. We do not seek war, but these Theban animals may leave us little choice. Will you fight against your own kind?"

He ran his eyes along the group. They were a motley collection, and nothing like the commanders he'd intended to take with him. They were there by virtue of having been chosen by their own contingents, a common enough tradition among mercenaries and other non-professional armies. The group consisted of five Terrans, with none coming from Laconia. They remained silent as the sixth individual stepped forward.

"I have something to say," said Kaarja.

He was a half-breed from the nomadic Minotaurus tribe. Though outwardly Terran, other differences marked him out as a very different creature. His skin was dark brown, almost black, and his body well built and muscular. And yet for all the similarities, it was impossible not to notice the bullish face, with long snout, teeth, and glowing red eyes. He was a mercenary captain, yet wore a Terran breastplate and helmet.

"Go on."

"I do not care who my enemy is. Terran, Medes, Minotaurus, robot, or Mulac. They are my friends or my enemies. Their actions decide which they will be, not my opinions."

He wiped his long snout and then laughed.

"They threaten you and us with war. So show them who you are. What good is it warring against the Medes, if you are cowed by these Theban scum?"

Maxis gasped at the words coming from the creature. None

of them would dare say such a thing to Laconian royalty, and certainly not towards their Strategos. It was as uncouth as it was disrespectful.

"Forthright as I would expect from the Minotaurus," said Agesilaus, "If Terrans could use such clear language, we might avoid so much of our own strife."

He shifted his attention to his sister, and she simply gave a nod.

"Very well. If war is what they seek, then war is what they shall have. Open gun ports, and launch fighters. A few shots in their hulls, and the threat of Minotaurus boarding actions should be enough to send them rushing back to their seven gates."

"Yes!" Kaarja said, "They will run!"

CHAPTER ELEVEN

Megaran Starcarrier 'Gorgon's Bite', Aulian Nebula

Lights flashed all around Zax as the ship's exterior doors slid open. He gasped for a second as his cockpit filled with the glow of the celestial phenomenon of the great Aulian Nebula. He'd never visited this part of space before, and seeing the clouds of coloured dust and bright streaks could have kept him entertained for days, perhaps weeks. He was a veteran pilot, one of the small group of Megaran pilots that had volunteered for the battle, and though excited to take on the Medes, he had little interest in fighting his neighbours.

They won't fight, will they?

But then he spotted the long formations of distant shapes tagged on his viewscreen, baring the designation of the Theban Star Fleet. Each group was matched to heading, velocity, and hosts of other useful pieces of data. What interested him most was that one formation was moving rapidly towards them. At the centre was a pair of heavy cruisers, and a single massively modified battleship. It was an old design, and the onboard computer was unable to identify its class or configuration.

"This is Flight Commander Hasphio. We've been tasked with providing protection for the fleet. You will focus on corvettes and bombers. Leave the rest to the fleet."

Zax nodded to himself as he listened.

"The Strategos has tasked with us giving the Thebans a bloody nose. Be ready to do that."

More flashes of light marked the changing positions of ships, but then shots of plasma streaked past. Zax could do nothing, but wait. As he sat there watching the incoming fire, he felt helpless and impotent. Interceptor guns cut many of the shots down, but others slammed into the shielding along the flanks of the starcarrier. Every impact would reduce the power of that particular shield until finally the armour of the ship was vulnerable to damage. Zax prayed that by the time that happened, he would already be in space and in the thick of battle, or at the very least circling around the ships and able to avoid fire.

"Launch!"

The words were both terrifying and joyous to him, and echoed inside his head as the launch rails forced his fighter away from the hangar, and out into the blackness of space. The entire procedure was completely automated, yet he kept his hands on the controls, ready to resume control at any moment. The Hierofalcon II fighter was big for a one-man spacecraft, and the epitome of Laconian design. Most other Terrans relied on their own home-built fighters. They made up for quality by using large numbers of relatively simple spacecraft. Laconia, meanwhile, invested heavily in technology, and exported their weapons to their allies in the powerful Laconian League. Zax might not be Laconian, but he'd been trained by their best instructors, and flew an export model of their most common fighter.

The long, sleek nose extended out from the hull, and an angular crescent wing bent down at each side and out the sides of the nose. A pair of shot wings then pushed out from the flared sections. Two massive engines sat under the crescent wing armour and pushed out into a pair of wide thrusters. The fighter's weapons were hidden from view, positioned in front of the engines where they could fire and remain unseen. It gave the spacecraft a much sleeker design that might normally have been expected. Zax braced himself as his fighter blasted out into space, trailing fire and flame. He glanced left and then to the right to confirm his comrades were nearby.

"Ares Squadron," said the unit's commander, "Follow me in."

"Affirmative." Though Zax was now piloting the machine, the computer took over control of all other systems. It continually scanned the area for threats, while preparing the weapons for combat. Laconian technology was based upon small numbers of professionals, something few of the Terran states could match.

"Stay close to the battleships and then circle around to vector nine."

Zax ran his eyes along the computer screens. The Laconian ships and allies were spread out, their bows facing in the same direction. The Thebans were divided up into three separate divisions. They were less well organised, yet had more than enough ships to cause trouble.

"This is it. Watch your wingtips!"

The formation of nine fighters moved in close to one of the larger cruisers, and then swooped past along the upper superstructure of a Mega Battleship. Zax looked down at the thickly curved armour, and multiple gun batteries fitted to each flank. It filled him with courage seeing such a mighty ship on his side. An approach vector on the forward cockpit showed him the path to take, using the heavy ships for protection as they built up speed.

"Slingshot, now!"

One by one the fighters pulled around the raised communication section of the ship and off towards the line of Theban ships. The enemy vessels were in a broken formation, with many far ahead and close to the wreckage of the Black Spear. He looked for signs of the enemy, but so far all he could see were the cruisers and their escorts.

"New contacts!" Ares Leader said, "Fifteen fighters moving in from mark six. Boost forward shields, and prepare to engage them."

Zax removed the safeties on his weapons, and immediately felt a surge of adrenalin. He'd been on many patrols before and even tangled with fighters from other colonies. But he'd never been asked to fire his weapons in anger. They were moving fast now, and he could no longer see the ships of the armada. The Theban vessels seemed to be everywhere, their tracking systems lifting and scanning for threats. The first volley of shots came so quickly that Zax didn't even see them. Two Hierofalcon II fighters were instantly hit, and one broke apart in a series of bright flashes. The second managed to deflect the worst of the fire with its shields, pulling away before it could be hit again.

"All fighters…break and attack!" Ares Leader ordered.

Zax pulled on his controls and rolled his fighter to stay close to his comrades. They moved in a small group of three, each checking all around for signs of danger.

"Six Theban strike bombers below us and moving in on the starcarriers! They're moving in under a chaff cloud."

"Good eyes, Zax," said Ares Leader, "My scanners aren't

even picking them up yet."

"Wait," said Zax, "I see another group coming in from our right. They're all heading directly for the fleet."

"Let's see them burn!"

The trio rolled to the right and dropped down on the bombers from above.

"They're Haliaeetus Light Bombers," said Ares Leader, "Watch out for turret fire...They are more difficulty to bring down than a damned Hydra! But bring them down we must!"

The Hierofalcons screamed down towards the targets, with long streak of fire and flame gushing from their engines, and opened fire. The bombers were nearly twice as big as the Hierofalcons, their small cockpits dwarfed by the pair of massive engines that pushed out like fists on each side of the fuselage. Wings curved forwards in a crescent, and pushing out from underneath were a pair of low-velocity plasma cannons. Each matched the standard weaponry fitted to corvettes and light frigates. They were capable of destroying fighters, even small ships with ease. Small blister turrets, each fitted with a single pulse cannon, protected every approach to the bombers. They opened fire and filled the area of space around them with deadly bursts of energy.

"There are two more, watch out!"

Zax pulled on the controls before even checking to see where the bombers were. He rolled to the left, and then to the right, as shots tried to pluck him out of the air. A single shot struck the flat underside of his fighter, knocking out the shields. As he pulled up, he gasped at seeing his fighter remained undamaged.

"How did you make it out of that alive?" Ares Two laughed. Zax looked to his friend who was now flying thirty metres off to his right flank.

"I know. That shouldn't have worked!"

A stream of pulse rounds reached from below and scattered all around them, forcing each pilot to keep shifting to avoid being struck.

"I'm hit!" Ares Two yelled.

Zax watched in horror as turret fire cut through this cockpit and then ripped his fighter apart. Chunks of metal and fuel tore away as the fighter exploded. There was no chance that he'd escaped alive, and Zax covered his eyes with his hand to shield him from the explosions. He'd never seen a fighter destroyed before, and seeing it happen with one of his friends inside was a terrible sight to behold.

"Keep at them!" Ares Leader said sternly, "We've got work to do."

Their hidden pulse cannons hammered away. The shots struck the upper side of the nearest bomber, each hit flashing with energy as it broke apart against the shielding. More shots landed nearby, and in seconds there were gaps in the protection.

"We're through the shields!" Zax said, "Keep firing, not much more!"

The computer adjusted the focus of the guns and slammed shots into an ever-decreasing zone of fire. It was more precise than any Terran could handle, and maximised the damage in the shortest time possible. They passed right through the bomber formation as the damaged Haliaeetus Light Bombers split apart. Turret fire cut from left to right, but managed to completely miss the fighters, instead striking each other. The now damaged bombers broke formation, making it even easier to attack them.

"Perfect," said Ares Leader, "Come around for another pass. Don't let up until we've forced every one of them back!"

The two remaining fighters pulled up, rolling left and right to avoid gunfire. At the same time, another squadron of fighters moved in from the right, sweeping past and strafing the bombers. They formed up alongside Ares Leader and Zax. Half of them were from his starcarrier, the rest fighters he'd not seen before. Elongated, and with a single weapon turret fitted behind the cockpit, they looked more like strike bombers than fighters.

"Okay...this is it. We'll go right for..."

Ares Leader stopped talking as a thunderous volley from two Terran battleships ripped through the bomber formation. Most of the shots missed, but enough landed to destroy half of those remaining; the rest scattered while shots chased after them.

"Let them go," said Ares Leader, "It's time to move on their flagship. Focus your fire on the shield generators of their battleship."

The mixed formation altered course, working their way through the furious melee and right into the heart of the enemy fleet. The fighter battle had been so intense Zax had not seen what else was happening. The cruisers and battleships from both sides were a few kilometres apart, and still neither side was backing down. As he looked up, the Laconian battleships unleashed a horrific bombardment against the Theban flagship. A kaleidoscope of colours shrouded the vessel, its shields doing their best to protect it, but nothing could withstand the bombardment.

"All fighters follow your attack vectors," said Flight Commander Hasphio from deep inside the Gorgon's Bite, "Drive the Thebans from the nebula! Show them what we think of the betrayers and collaborators. No mercy!"

* * *

Battleship 'Agamemnon', Aulian Nebula

The battle for the nebula had been raging for more than thirty minutes, and five capital ships already burned as lifeboats raced away with survivors crammed inside. The powerful Battleship Agamemnon led from the front, her escort warships following close behind. No enemy vessels dared move to close should they expose themselves to her awesome firepower. Fighters from both sides circled almost continually, the heavy warships blazing away with heavy weaponry. For all the violence, the Theban Fleet continued to give ground rather than be sucked into a battle that would see every ship destroyed. It was a holding action, designed to waste as much time as possible.

"Strategos!" Dukas Myrrine called out, "We've lost shielding over twenty percent of our hull. We need to pull back and let the other contingents forge ahead. It will take time to refocus protection on the port side."

Before he could answer, a triple volley of plasma shells slammed into the heavily armoured hull of the battleship. The first few shots exploded in a shower of plasma, but the next volley hammered into the armour, ripping away great chunks of metal. Agesilaus growled as warning indicators soon appeared on multiple displays.

"No." Agesilaus shook his head, "We must deal with the Theban first of all. To pull back will let him believe he can hold us back. To do so will risk more loss of life."

Kyniska pointed ahead to the raging battle.

"He is intentionally spreading out and trading space for time. If I had to guess, I'd say he's dragging this battle out intentionally."

Agesilaus snarled as the siblings simultaneously came to the same conclusion.

"He's got more ships on the way," they said almost word

for word.

Agesilaus chuckled.

"And that means he is not serious about fighting us. I can use that…"

He looked back to Dukas Myrrine, who was managing the ship, as well as keeping a careful eye on the flow of the battle. She was the closest thing to an admiral the fleet had right now.

"What is the status of his ship, Fury of Herakles?"

He said the name of the ship with obvious bitterness. Though the Thebans might claim the ancient hero to be one of their own, every Terran considered him part of their national story. Herakles had travelled the world and touched almost every Terran colony during his adventures. Both looked towards the large Theban battleship. It was smaller than the Laconian vessels, though shared much of the basic shape and design. Its forward cutters activated in cyclic sequences, smashing a way into the shields of other ships.

"Does it matter, my Brother? We need to cut off the head of the snake, and fast."

Agesilaus smiled.

"Agreed, and it's about time we got our hands dirty. We will move on Fury of Herakles and end this battle before it drags on any longer."

He took a step away from his position on the deck and signalled towards Dukas Myrrine. He could see the tension along her forehead, but knew her reputation as a ship's captain and a fleet commander was second to none. There was nobody else under his command he'd rather have directing his ships in battle.

"You must keep us in this fight, Dukas. Bring us close to the flagship and keep hitting her hard. I need you to draw them in and hold them, as a trap holds a wounded animal."

The Dukas looked confused.

"Pinned? Will this not force us into a battle of attrition? Are you sure you want to risk damage to the entire fleet to win this battle?"

Agesilaus nodded.

"Yes, I want you to draw them in. Scare them, terrify them, and let them know that this is no mere skirmish; that I intend on destroying their fleet one ship at a time. I want every Theban to feel fear in their bones. Fear that they have unleashed the wrath of Laconia."

The Dukas nodded slowly.

"Very well."

"Good. Once aboard Fury of Herakles we will take care of the Theban chain of command. Eliminated, this Theban fleet will lose any sense of cohesion and break. That is the moment when we will send in our allies to mop up."

He said no more and walked back along the deck. Komes Diogenes moved to his side, and Kyniska marched at his left. Some of the ship's officers looked up, watched the three Laconians move past, and then turned back to their displays. More members of the bodyguard joined them. They headed for the corner of the deck, where pairs of express elevators were hidden behind lightly smoked semi-circular doors. They slid apart to reveal a platform, enough for twenty or more people.

"Operations Deck," Kyniska said to the computer. It beeped in acknowledgement as the doors slid shut behind them. Before the platform even moved, another volley of fire struck against the ship. It hit hard enough to send vibrations through the bulkheads.

"This isn't how I expected the campaign to begin," said Agesilaus, "Damned Thebans. I should have known they would cause trouble with Laconia. Do they not realise that we could crush them in a single year?"

The elevator dropped down multiple levels, working its way past multiple weapon decks, and down to the combined operation bays and flight decks. As it reached the final level, it began to slow.

"You intend on destroying the ship?" Kyniska asked, "You want to see Fury of Herakles left a burning hulk?"

Agesilaus shook his head as the doors slid open and revealed the massive operations deck. The place was bustling, filled with deck officers, engineers, pilots, and vast numbers of soldiers.

"Yes. Now this is more like it. I tell you, Sister. There is nothing better for the soul than to stand along side legions of Terran warriors."

Ahead were dozens of powerful Chelandion Dropships. For a moment he was transported back to the parade ground on Laconia, where he'd watched the thousands of Helot soldiers waiting patiently. The scene onboard this ship looked little different.

"Though for all that, I have to admit I would like a few more regular Laconian soldiers. They would transform this campaign in an instant."

Kyniska laughed.

"This was never going to be easy, Brother. If you had Laconia at your back, then this would be a war between us and the Medes. You said it yourself, this is not the case."

"True. For this to work, it must become something so much bigger. I am not heading to the Ionian Territories for mere battlefield victories. I intend on making our mark, and establishing Terran dominance for the future."

Kyniska seemed to like the sound of that.

"Perhaps this is the time to find out whether these people are really up for the job. Boarding a ship is not going to be easy.

But from what I've seen, none of the volunteers are weaklings. All have had a hard life, and every one of them chose to be here."

Komes Diogenes, who until now had been silent, finally spoke.

"Strategos. I can muster your bodyguard for this assault. I do not want to expose you to any more danger than is necessary. Three hundred elite Laconians can take any ship."

Agesilaus looked to his old friend and sighed.

"I would love to have them with me, but we have to start putting this armada together at some point. No, a fifty-man unit will be sufficient."

Komes Diogenes eyes opened wide in surprise.

"Fifty?"

"Yes, more than enough to fill my personal dropship. And I will take four Chelandion Dropships fully loaded with Neodamodes, and the same again with the Mothakes. That will give me…"

Kyniska laughed as she answered her brother's question.

"Five hundred and twelve warriors, plus your personal guard."

"Good. That should be more than sufficient. By the time this is over we will have turned them into soldiers."

"And if they fail?" Kyniska asked.

"Then they will die. One way or another, it is better to find out now, than during an orbital assault deep inside the Median Empire!" Agesilaus forced a laugh, "Nothing forges bonds better than a shared and difficult experience. It will be bloody, and there will be losses. But those that come back will have an unbreakable bond. Trust me."

He walked along the deck as the crew and soldiers of each dropship rose to attention. The Neodamodes looked the part, with their heavy armour, shield bucklers, and Asgeirr-Carbines at the ready. For a moment Agesilaus might have thought they were Laconians, but then some of them moved, revealing the lack of discipline and training. Next to them were the assorted Mothakes, though they seemed better organised than the units of Helot soldiers. Agesilaus stopped and looked to them.

"This will be your first time under fire. I intend on doing what Laconian armies do best. We will land onboard the Theban flagship and engage her crew in close-quarter combat. No other Terrans seek such close-range and bloody battle. And that is why we will win."

He looked at them carefully, trying to assess if they were up for what was to come. Had they been regular soldiers, he would never have asked them, but there was a palpable sense of unease among those waiting on the deck.

"Are you with me?"

A good number answered, but it was hardly a rousing cheer.

"I intend on taking Fury of Herakles in battle. I will personally land on her command deck, and I will take the ship for myself. The Thebans started this with their betrayal, but by the Gods, I'll have my revenge against them."

"Good," said Kyniska, "They need to know that you will lead them."

Agesilaus took a few more steps and faced the young Mothakes.

"I am putting my life on the line for this fight. I cannot take the ship alone. Will you stand alongside me, and share the danger as brothers?"

This time the shouting was much louder. Many lifted their weapons high as they cried out. Agesilaus could feel the excitement and the passion spreading through the deck, and in that moment, he knew they were ready. He lowered his voice as he spoke with his sister.

"Our armada would be hard-pressed to offer much in this campaign if they felt we'd let such attacks by the Thebans be ignored. It is a test of the fleet, and of its commanders. When the battle is over, we will have a fleet, or we will be heading home."

"Your bird is ready, Strategos," said Komes Diogenes, "Your unit awaits you."

Agesilaus nodded and looked out to his assembled legions.

"Board your dropships and remember. Today you are all warriors of Laconia."

They cheered again, and then as one filed inside the large spacecraft. It took some time for all of them to move into position, and Agesilaus waited until the bulk of them were safely installed. Then he walked towards the ramps resting down on the deck. Waiting inside were the fifty warriors that he'd requested. As soon as his feet touched the deck of the craft, they snapped to attention. Their feet cracked down onto the metal floor in a dull thud. None of them uttered a word as he moved to his fixed position, and for any non-Laconian, it might seem they were shunning his arrival.

"Epilektoi," said Agesilaus, "This is going to be fast and violent. I need you to push fast, even if our support units slow down. Time is critical in this fight. We cannot afford to be pinned down on the ship. Potentially, they could hit us with ten times our numbers in a stand-up fight."

"Ten times?" Kyniska asked, "Those kind of odds barely make it worth waking up for."

Komes Diogenes laughed, and then quickly caught himself.

"We will do what needs to be done."

The ramps lifted up, and before they locked into place, it was possible to spot the massive engines at the end of the extended wings rotating, ready to provide vertical lift. Two more crewmembers moved to their armoured control station towards the rear of the spacecraft, out of sight of prying eyes. Together they would manage the four powerful pulse cannon turrets that pushed out from the front and sides of the dropship's nose. Kyniska moved to her position at the front and pushed her body into the rigid harness. It locked her safely in place and would hold her there until released.

"Brother."

Agesilaus was so busy watching outside, by the time the doors and ramps were locked in place, the passengers were all locked and ready for launch. He joined his sister and locked himself in, as the spacecraft lifted and rotated within its own length. All five spacecraft surged towards the flank launch doors of the battleship. They made it to within metres before they slid open to reveal the nebula. Layered shielding activated, creating a thick seal along the launch doors. They could protect against gunfire, but their primary purpose was to keep the deck safe from the void as the spacecraft raced out of the ship.

"How long till we reach the target?" Agesilaus asked via the communications node fitted to his ear. There was a short pause before one of the pilots replied.

"Strategos. We're three minutes out..."

The pilot grunted as he pulled on the controls. The dropship circled around some unseen danger, and even Agesilaus briefly felt a little queasy. The engines then pulsed with power, and they raced away from Battleship Agamemnon, and towards the centre of the Theban Fleet.

There's a lot of flak out there," said the pilot, "I don't know if we'll be able to punch through with just these dropships."

"Understood. Just keep at it. I'm calling in help."

CHAPTER TWELVE

The Battle of the Aulian Nebula

Zax gasped as the last of the bombers tried to escape, crashing into the long spars extending out from the Terran starcarrier. The right wing ripped off, and the rest of the craft exploded in a cascade of burning fuel, exploding ordnance, and pieces of broken spacecraft. He was forced to make a sudden course change to avoid flying right through the destruction.

"That was close!"

"Cut the chatter," said Ares Leader, "Keep your eyes open. This ain't over yet."

"Sorry, Sir."

Zax was so stunned he could barely speak. The battle had transformed from a few fighters and bombers to more spacecraft than he'd ever seen in one place. Broadsides from battleships sent streaks of white-hot plasma against each other, while heavy cutters slowly burned through ships, destroying everything in their wake. It was a scene from some terrifying nightmare, yet there was a cruel beauty to the scene. The flashes of lights intermixed with the nebula to create a unique work of art.

"Form up in attack pattern alpha. We've got a new mission, and we're joining up with the heavy fighters."

What's happening now?

Waypoints and vector indicators appeared on the cockpit, and Zax made quick course changes to join in with the other craft. It took a few seconds until he realised they were joining a wave of assault dropships. He slid from left to right, and for a second was granted a clear view of the heavily armoured spacecraft. The thing looked tiny at a distance, but as he moved closer, he could see the gun turrets, and the powerful engines blazing bright and powerful in the cold void.

"We will provide advance escort for the assault teams. We're going in hard and fast. Our job is to help deliver the Strategos into battle. We must protect the dropships at all costs!"

Zax was shocked at the news. The Strategos was already something of an enigma, a man that led the fleet, yet seen by few people. He was a commander, and they traditionally stayed well back from the fighting. Joining in with a boarding action was the exact opposite of this, and though exciting; it also meant the life of the commander of the armada was now in Zax's hands. If he failed in his mission, the Strategos could be killed, and none of them would ever made it across the Great Expanse, and to the promised rewards.

"I'm on it," Zax said with greater enthusiasm than he expected.

He levelled off his fighter and lined up alongside the other spacecraft. They were close enough to support each other, but not so close to cause an obstruction. Zax began visual scanning of the area for signs of threats. The computer did the same, as well as utilising its array of electronic passive scanners. Correct detection of threats required visual, thermal, and radar scans, as well as a myriad of other sensors. No sooner was he in position when he spotted a trio of fighters moving in from above. They didn't show on thermal sensors, and that could only mean they were unmanned and running cold.

"Stealth interceptors!" he yelled excitedly, "I've marked them. They're moving in fast."

"Good eyes," said Ares leader, "Leave them to Theta Squadron."

"Affirmative."

Zax made additional course changes. The defensive fire was increasing in intensity, and the onboard computer worked overtime, constantly shifting power to the fighter's multiple shield emitters. Like scales of armour, the shield plates could be knocked out individually, or weakened, so the computer kept adjusting the system to ensure maximum protection to the front. It absorbed a lot of energy, but Zax was just thankful it was working.

"We're moving in on the enemy flagship. On my command, we will envelop the ship with a concerted assault on its turrets and defensive weapon systems. Move in close and move fast. If you dawdle, you'll be cut down."

Zax nodded to himself, as the targets changed before his eyes. Already the enemy battleship was big enough to fill his view from the cockpit, and with each additional second, it grew even larger. Five cruisers were alongside it, firing plasma broadsides almost continually. It looked like a fountain of water, except the water would annihilate his fighter with a single strike.

"Now!" Ares Leader ordered.

One by one the fighters activated their reheaters and accelerated towards the enemy flagship at greater and greater speeds. Each fighter left a trail of ionised plasma from their engines and twisted about to avoid gunfire from the cruisers. Shots crashed into the approaching fighters, and in seconds the first had been hit. One exploded in a bright fireball, quickly followed by two more that vanished from view.

"Damn it," he muttered, "That was too close."

Zax's chest pounded as he rolled to the right, and then dived between the battleship and its escorts. Defensive fire struck from both sides, but somehow he managed to avoid being hit, and lined up on one of the many aft gun batteries defending the battleship. He took aim, and then opened fire with every weapon he had at his disposal. At first the shields absorbed the bulk of his fire, but then as the turrets returned fire, the shields deactivated. It was for an instant, but enough to leave them vulnerable. Three bursts slammed into the battery, and they tore apart as Zax's fighter raced past.

"Yes!"

Lights flashed all around Zax as more guns opened up on him, and it looked like he was flying through an electrical storm. He and seven other fighters spun about and began strafing along the flank of the battleship. Each shot struck shielding, and a bizarre sequence of coloured flashes marked hits against active shielding. Missiles struck a short distance away as bombers joined in the attack. There was no way they'd cripple the ship, at least not yet, but it was enough of a distraction to buy the dropships time to close in.

"That's it," said Ares Leader, "One more pass. And this time hit the ventral turrets."

The fighters circled around the bow of the ship, breaking formation to strike the underside. More fighters came in at other angles, but Zax was only interested in his particular mission. The ventral turrets were fitted along a long armoured section, roughly a third the way along the hull. The turrets were manually controlled, and although accurate, they had a tough time tracing the fighters moving about like a shoal of tiny fish. Even so, several were cut apart by gunfire as they continued to blast away.

"Watch out!" yelled a pilot.

Even though Zax had no idea who it was, he instinctively rolled to the right. As he did so, a robotic interceptor raced past and then pulled up to give chase. Zax put his fighter in a spin and boosted the engines to take him closer to the battleship. The interceptor remained right with him.

"The dropships!" Ares Leader yelled, "They're under attack."

Zax rolled to the right, narrowly avoiding two bursts of fire from pulse cannons. One round glanced off the top of his wing, leaving a long black mark on the armour plating. His gut instinct told him to get closer to the battleship, and weave through its superstructure to avoid the enemy fighter, but then he spotted the formation of dropships. They were being harassed by a small number of fighters that had broken through the escort screen.

"I'm coming!"

Zax put everything he had left into the engines, and then shifted shield priority to the rear. Shots glanced off his shielding, and he was forced to slide left and right, trying to shake off his attacker. One round slammed into his starboard engines, and multiple alarms sounded inside the cockpit.

I have to do something!

Knowing he had to help the dropships limited his options, so he kept going directly towards them, but cut the main engines. Zax then hit the lateral controls and spun his fighter around so that he faced backwards and towards his enemy. The computer shifted shield power to the front as Zax pulled the trigger. His cannons opened fire at close-range and hammered the front of the interceptor. Shot after shot slammed into the spacecraft, and yet it returned fire with equal ferocity. Shots lashed back and forth, with the interceptor coming off worse. Finally, it split apart, but not before starting two fires aboard Zax's fighter, knocking out three of his manoeuvring thrusters.

"Critical damage," said the computer as he spun the fighter back around, "Targeting systems offline, engines damaged, weapons off line. Life support offline..."

On and on went the computer, but Zax ignored it. He took aim at the fighters continuing to strafe the dropships. Two in particular sat right behind them firing long, continuous bursts.

"This is Ares Six," said Zax, "I'm going in!"

For a moment Zax completely forgot about his damaged systems, and moved in to open fire on the fighters. He lined up his guns perfectly, but when he tried to activate them, he was greeted by warning from the computer.

"Weapons offline. Powerplant critical..."

Zax knew at that moment his fighter had seconds to live. Once the powerplant failed, it would explode with enough force to destroy the fighter and anything nearby.

Okay, then. Let's do this!

He aimed his fighter right between the pair of fighters still shooting up the Laconian dropships. He pushed the engine controls, and the damaged thruster instantly tore apart. The reaction was so great it threw his fighter into a momentary spin. Through great effort and skill, Zax got it back on a flat trajectory and headed towards the pair of enemy fighters. Sparks flashed through the cockpit as systems failed one after the other. A small fire broke out above one of the displays, and then every remaining warning light flicked to red.

Just a few...more seconds.

MICHAEL G. THOMAS

Two plasma fires erupted along the rear of the ship. Metal plates tore apart, and the fighter began its final stages of disintegration. From farther away it appeared to hurtle through space like some great meteor. Inside the cramped interior it began to shake violently, multiple forces pushing and pulling at the same time. Zax gripped the ejection handle firmly. The fighters were now so close he felt he could reach out and touch them, and yet with no weapons there was little he could do.

"Come...on!"

Fires inside the craft were so close he felt the heat through his pilot's suit. It started as little more than an itch, and then began to hurt.

"Now!"

He yanked the handle, and for a split second it seemed as if the thing had malfunctioned. Zax's heart could have stopped right then, realising he'd burn up inside the fighter. And then the fighter was gone, and he was hurtling through space in the remnants of his seat and part of the bulkhead reinforcement plates. He could see the battle, though as he spun, he had no control over where he was looking. Battleships and cruisers dashed by, and then he saw the dropships swooping down to their target. A pair of heavily damaged fighters spun out of control much like him. Only then he began to breathe.

It worked.

* * *

The dropships advanced towards the battleship. Their shielding deflected incoming fire as though it were nothing more than hailstones. The turret gunners fired continually, their supporting arcs of fire surrounding the armoured assault spaceships with clouds of pulse projectiles. Anything daring to come close

213

was soon chased away by the remaining fighters, circling the dropships like bees protecting their queen.

"Hold on," said the pilot, "We're going in hot!"

Agesilaus grasped the harness around his chest as the dropship performed a rolling manoeuvre he never would have thought possible. They then swept down towards the flank launch bays of the Terran battleship. He activated his communications node and spoke to every officer in the assault wave.

"This is the Strategos. Hit the ground running. We do not give them a moment to regroup. Ignore the wounded and dead, and concentrate the mission. The faster we are, the more lives we will save."

The final bank of turrets blasted away and managed to knock out one of the four engines fitted to Agesilaus' personal dropship. It wasn't enough to destroy the spacecraft, but more than enough to throw him off course, potentially forcing him to miss the landing deck.

"We're going down! It's going to get…"

The pilot stopped speaking, his voice replaced by barely intelligible grunts. Agesilaus needed no reminder as to the difficulty in flying the dropship, especially when so badly damaged. And he remained silent and calm, as the pilot managed to smash through the shielding and down towards the deck. It was a testament to the man's skill that he avoided slamming into the side of the ship. They shot inside like a bullet, crashing down onto the deck. The design of the Theban flagship shared much in common with the Laconian battleships, yet a few fighters were still present. The rest must either have been in storage, or already engaged in battle. They rose again before slamming into the metal decking for the last time. A great screaming sound of tortured metal announced the high-speed landing that was slightly dissimilar to a crash landing. And then it was over as quickly as it had begun.

"We're down," said the pilot, gasping for breath, "Get out... now!"

With the dropship stationary, and resting on the metal decking of the battleship, Agesilaus deactivated his harness. He looked like an armoured giant as he moved to the doorway.

"This is it, my stratiotes."

The door slid open, and the ramp dropped down with a thud. Before he could say a word, a volley of pulse-rifle fire slammed into the dropship. Other soldiers might have flinched, but not these Laconians.

"Everybody out!"

Kyniska was out first, and she spotted hundreds, upon hundreds of Theban stratiotes. Though lightly armoured, they all carried long-rifles and blasted away at the dropship. Small groups broke ranks and charged towards her and the dropships.

"Hurry!" she yelled, "They are going to overwhelm the landing ground before we can deploy into battle!"

Another soldier might have sheltered behind the large landing legs of the Chelandion Dropship, but not her. She moved ahead and met the Thebans face-to-face. Twenty metres away she stopped and activated her shield. She then opened fire with short, accurate bursts from her Asgeirr-Carbine, aiming at the nearest shapes just in front of her. As shots came in for her, they bounced off her shield generator. The gleaming circle flickered and flashed with pent-up energies. Agesilaus was next out, landing alongside his sister. Before aiming his weapon, he activated his shield projector to protect Kyniska. More Laconians joined them, and in a matter of seconds there were more than twenty, each shielded and blasting away.

"Form assault phalanx and advance!" Kyniska shouted

over the din of battle, not that it was necessary with the communication nodes.

Several Laconians were cut down by heavy gunfire, and still they rushed out from the dropship. The phalanx grew from twenty until it was quickly double the size. Agesilaus watched the Thebans with interest as the lighter armed soldiers tried to work around the flanks. At the same time their heavy infantry formed up. They were instantly identifiable by their unusual shields. The Laconians used hand-mounted projector units to create circular phased shields, the Thebans what was now commonly described at the Boeotian shield. Though similar to the aspis shielding used by other Terrans, it had the same overall circular shape, but differed in having scooped indentations at both sides. A small generator pack built into the metal shield created a phased barrier around the unit that could deflect gunfire at almost point-blank range.

"They're massing for the othismos," said Kyniska, "And they have the numbers."

Agesilaus snarled as the large numbers of Thebans faced off against the Laconians. Their own phalanx now pulsed with light as their shields activated. The small indentations in the sides of the shields provided loopholes for their Doru pulse rifles. Gunfire crashed back and forth, both sides trying to exploit gaps in the lines, weakened shields, or injured soldiers. Each impact on a shield would put pressure on its generator, and with a few more hits it would overload, leaving its wielder vulnerable.

"To the left!" shouted one of the soldiers.

Anyone would have lifted his shield to defend against this flank attack, but not these men and women. They'd been trained from seven-years-old to fight in the phalanx, and knew that individually they meant little. Their only responsibility was to the phalanx. It was better to leave the flank vulnerable to a few sharp shooters, than create gaps at the front that the Theban hoplites could exploit en masse. Two of the brave warriors were soon struck by gunfire, and though wounded, neither collapsed.

"Where are my Mothakes and Neodamodes?" Agesilaus shouted.

He looked off to his right and quickly identified the other dropships. All had made it inside, and their doors were open. Yet he could see large groups of the soldiers deployed around the craft as though defending the dropships with their lives.

"You must advance!" he snapped over his communications node, "Stay with the dropships, and you die with them."

Before he could say more, someone spotted something arcing above them, like an old arrow.

"Plunging fire!"

It was something Agesilaus had hoped to avoid. A quick and rapid assault would have given the Thebans little time to deploy their toys to the battle. It was a relatively recent development; a low velocity explosive dart launched from a special holder fitted to the front of the Dory rifles. The projectile sailed upwards, slowed, and then dropped down from above. Three were cut down before they could react.

"Defensive phalanx!"

One in four lifted their shield arms to provide partial coverage from above. It wasn't perfect, but it deflected the worst of the plunging fire, though at the expense of the phalanx's ability to move.

Agesilaus felt the unit slowing down. At this rate they would soon be surrounded and picked off.

I have to regain the initiative, and I have no intention of being beaten. Not today, and never by the Thebans.

"Ekdromoi!"

At once small numbers moved to the flanks. These were with small shield generators, and like the Thebans, they carried long rifles. Rather than fighting in the phalanx, they spread out in scattered groups, pinning down the lightly armoured Theban stratiotes who had moved out to the phalanx. Without warning, they broke ranks and charged at the Thebans, quickly putting them to flight.

Agesilaus allowed himself a moment of self-satisfaction, but then he watched the four large Theban phalanxes joining forces to create a unit close to a thousand strong. His Laconians were tough, but even he doubted that sixty or more of them could take on and defeat over a thousand well-motivated Thebans.

"Alala! Alala!"

Agesilaus looked to his right and towards the shouting. He knew the war cry as one commonly used by Terran mercenaries, but also often used by Laconia's enemies. For a second he sensed betrayal, but then he saw them surging forward. It was a ragged formation, barely a phalanx, and yet they were together, and in vast numbers.

"My fighting Mothakes and Neodamodes!"

The lightly equipped took casualties as they raced across the deck of the ship, but then the turrets of the dropships opened fire, sending a heavy bombardment of pulse cannon fire deep into the Theban ranks. Men and women were tossed aside, and gaps appeared in the phalanx.

"Yes!" Kyniska said excitedly, "The Neodamodes have found their courage!"

"And now it is time for us to go to work."

Agesilaus pointed his right arm out from his shield and towards the Thebans.

"To the othismos!"

The Laconians broke into a jog, still maintaining a perfect formation. Unlike any other Terrans, they moved silently, not one of them uttering a sound. There were no battle paeans, no cries, or shouts, nothing of any kind; just the silent and mechanical advance of soldiers that were drilled into the perfect fighting machines. The gap between both sides shrunk to a few metres, and Agesilaus was sure he could smell the fear of the Thebans. They still outnumbered his forces, and yet he knew they would win. The Laconians crashed into the front ranks with crushed limbs, broken armour, and exploding shields marking the point of impact. Soldiers fell on both sides. The Thebans started to break formation, but the Laconians locked shield arms and stepped as one machine-like formation.

"Othismos!"

Each Laconian advanced with one wide step, pushing hard with his shield arm. They pushed so hard, using their right arms to help push against the rear of their comrades' left arms. The Theban front rank collapsed, and the Laconians stepped over them, gunning down the wounded and fallen.

"Othismos!"

Again they stepped forward, and the second push collapsed the phalanx. Those at the front turned and ran directly into those behind. What started as a panic soon turned into a rout. As the Thebans ran from the deck, the wild and noisy Neodamodes pursued them.

"Victory," said Kyniska, "Hard fought..."

"And well won," Agesilaus agreed, "Now...let's find this Theban admiral and see if he feels quite as confrontational without his legions to back him up."

CHAPTER THIRTEEN

The Battle of the Aulian Nebula

The service passages were substantial, each easily capable of allowing the transit of scores of personnel at any one time. Agesilaus had little interest in sneaking about through shallow corridors, and he'd located the central passageway that led from the engineering sections to the rear and between the weapon battery deck. The passage shifted from left to right as it passed major bulkheads, but still managed to run almost the entire length of the ship. That major communication hub of the ship became a bitter battleground as the desperate Thebans attempted to hold back the advancing Laconians, and their courageous and violent Helot allies.

"Just a little further."

Agesilaus stabbed his razor-sharp Asgeirr-Carbine into the stomach of a Theban soldier. The impact lifted the man from his feet, and he crashed down lifelessly to the metal floor. More of his bodyguard fanned out, stabbing away in silence. They avoided using their guns as much as possible to mask their advance. They found the next double-width bulkhead doors hadn't been correctly sealed.

"They think we're coming at them from the gunnery decks. Keep moving! I want to be in front of their commander before they realise their mistake."

The elite infantry pushed through the partially open bulkhead doors and into the next section. Agesilaus used that short moment of respite to check the position of the rest of his units. His heart pounded in his chest, not from physical exertion, but from the stresses of the battle. His mechanical leg was causing him trouble, and the faster he tried advance, the harder he found it. Reports came in one by one, confirming that his forces were spreading through the battleship like a cancer. It was a long process, and one that could take hours.

"There they are!" shouted a man further ahead. Agesilaus squinted, but knew the accent before he could see him. A flash of light marked the firing of a rifle, but he was ready. He lifted his shield arm as the projectile struck the front. It glanced off to hit the ceiling.

"Yeah. This is the place. Form open order phalanx!"

They did as ordered and moved into a wide wall of warriors. Their shimmering shields provided protection to the front, though this time they were not locked closely together.

"Keep moving forward."

Small groups of six Laconians stepped forward, and when they stopped, another group of six would do the same. Simultaneously, they all fired their Asgeirr-Carbines at the entrenched enemy soldiers. It was slow, methodical, and brutally effective. In less than a minute they'd made it to the transit hub, a large interconnected point just before the command decks above. The main passageway continued on to the bow of the ship, but there were sub-passages to the sides, as well as ladders above and below to the next levels.

"Good work. This is where we will crush them."

Agesilaus knew from his reading of much older Laconian battles that they did best when forcing an enemy to commit to close-quarter battle. Even in space, the Laconian were a people optimised for boarding actions and bloody close combat. Training from childhood, there was nothing better for a Laconian than to face his foes blade to blade.

Yes. This is how it will end.

He was forced to duck behind his shield as a fusillade of fire slashed around him. Laconians guards formed up around him, but he ignored most of them, and opened fire with his carbine at the distant enemies. It was no show of bravado. He was one of them, and he had targets to attack.

"Kyniska. I've found the rest of their soldiers…"

Something whistled overhead and then exploded, showering them with pieces of burning plasma. It was an indiscriminate weapon, and succeeded in killing and maiming several of his soldiers.

"…or perhaps more accurately, they have found me."

A burst struck the ceiling above him, showering his scattered line with sparks and tiny pieces of burnt metal. He took that moment to examine the area more carefully, but the lights suddenly cut. What had once been well lit turned to pitch blackness, the only source of light the shield generators and flashes of energy from the guns still firing. Agesilaus took aim and opened fire with his carbine, putting a burst into his enemies as they huddled behind whatever cover they could find.

"The Thebans have rallied at the transit node."

"Understood." Kyniska moved via the narrower parallel passages. Though a few hundred metres away, she might easily have been on an entirely different ship. They could no longer see each other even though engaged in the same battle.

"So far the secondary shafts have been kept clear."

Though smaller, they worked as effective runs through the ship, bypassing the main routes. She travelled with a dozen of his people, relying upon two smaller groups of Helots. Their smaller frames and lighter equipment made them better suited for the race through the ship. At the next junction point, the passage widened into a double-width section, intercepting the major artery that ran most of the length of the ship. She was about to step forward when a group of heavily armed soldiers slowed, and then stopped directly ahead.

"Dammit," she muttered, "They're blocking up the smaller routes. I'll need to find another way through."

"No," said Agesilaus, "I can take care of this. I will call them to my position and buy you the time you need. Send any remaining Helot units to assist me. I am going to need the numbers."

"Very well, my Brother. Keep them busy. I will take the command deck for both of us."

Agesilaus tried to speak, but such a volume of fire was striking his shield, he needed both hands to hold it up. If he weakened, he'd be struck down and killed, and that would be the end of his great campaign. His shield started to push back, but then a heavily armoured spatharios pushed in alongside him. Others joined and spread out to thicken the line.

"Komes Diogenes…your timing is impeccable."

The older warrior chuckled to himself.

"Apologises for the delay. A unit of Theban mercenaries were attempting to outflank our positions. Now they've withdrawn and joined up with the hundreds of Thebans coming down from the upper decks."

Agesilaus grunted as another shot glanced off his shield.

"Half of these warriors must be their gunners. They're throwing the last of their crew into this fight."

"Not quite. We identified additional groups withdrawing to higher positions in the hull. They intend on making us fight for every deck."

Agesilaus shook his head angrily.

"I have no desire to spend a single minute longer than necessary in this forsaken place. No, we will bring them here, to deal with us."

A small group of Thebans broke ranks and dashed across the open passage, firing rifles as they ran. Rounds crashed into the Laconian line, forcing them to hunker down behind their shielding. To an inexperienced man it must have looked as though the Laconians were pinned down and weakened. The reality was brought brutally home to them as they reached a distance of a few metres from those sheltering.

"Osthimus!" Agesilaus roared.

The Laconian soldiers pushed with their shields, taking advantage of the dispersed phalanx to bring their carbines into play. A crackle of fire cut down the first of the Thebans, but then came the stabbing of the blades. Even the bravest Terran would tremble at the sight of so much carnage, and to the Laconians this was little more that training. Body after body fell, and then the Thebans broken once more. Agesilaus held his ground, lifted his arms up, and roared. He pulled off his helmet so that the Thebans could see his face.

"I am Agesilaus, Basileus of Laconia. I claim this ship in the name of Laconia!"

A shot hit his shield arm, and a knot of bodyguards rushed to his aid as more Thebans rushed in from different directions.

"You intended on calling their last reserves here, didn't you?"

Komes Diogenes asked, "We will be trapped down here."

Agesilaus grinned at him as the sound of shouting and gunfire increased by the second. He then nodded towards the open space at the centre of the hub.

"Rally around the ladder shaft, and form up into a circle. We make our stand here!"

The Laconians and the small numbers of nearby Helots formed up in rings around the vertical shafts. They could see the Thebans coming in from multiple directions. They lacked cover or means of escape, but they could no longer be surprised or ambushed. When the more confident Thebans started to fight back, Agesilaus actually relaxed.

"Kyniska. I have them all here..."

His shield arm shuddered as four rounds glanced off. For a second the shield deactivated, but a comrade stepped in, pushing his own shield into the breach. Agesilaus nodded to his comrade, and then reached out over his communications node.

"Now it is down to you...Sister."

* * *

Kyniska couldn't believe her eyes as the enemy soldiers in front vanished from view. She waited a few more seconds, and then looked to her small groups of bloodied, yet keen warriors. The Mothakes looked unlike any small army she'd ever seen. Most had lost or discarded some of their gear, giving them a dishevelled and ill-prepared look, and yet they were with her, armed and ready.

"Once we start, we do not stop till we reach the command deck. Understood?"

Those nearest nodded in agreement.

"Good. Now!"

Kyniska raced out from the passage and into the main hall. She crashed into a pair of Theban soldiers who were stunned at being leapt on by the Terran woman. Before they could react, she whipped out a kopis blade from her thigh and hacked down the first. The second pushed away and was soon swamped by a trio of Mothake volunteers.

"On...on!"

The next ten minutes turned to a blur as Kyniska led her bizarre rabble on a bloody rampage through the ship. Dozens of Thebans lay dead or dying, and by the time she reached the entry doors to the command deck, a mere handful of defenders were left. Kyniska charged at them together with her warriors, and either captured or killed every one of them. All that stood in her path were the vast and ornate doors, each of which looked like a vertical work of art.

"Open it!" she shouted.

Two of the Mothakes dragged a wounded Theban to the door and pushed him up to the metal plating.

"Do it!"

The man hesitated, but quickly decided that discretion was the better part of valour. He entered some kind of cypher sequence into the lock, and the doors slid open with a groan. Kyniska tensed her body. She was out in the open and facing a prepared command deck. Instead of legions of enemy soldiers, she found a small cadre of officers, plus a few dozen assorted crew and soldiers.

"You!" shouted the Theban commander, "You dare board my ship?"

Kyniska entered the command deck, and her soldiers fanned out on each side of her. All pointed their weapons ahead, while those carrying shields had them activated and ready for the coming fight.

"Dare? I come here to take your ship…"

She pointed her pulse pistol at him and smiled. Her bronzed helm glistened in the light of the command deck, making her stand out among the myriad of other warriors.

"…and your life. Strategos Photios Kosmas…And then I might take the rest of your Theban Fleet."

To the man's astonishment, Kyniska fired first. The pulse projectile should have hit the Strategos in the chest, but at the last moment one of his men leapt in the way. By accident or design, the man took the brunt of the blast and bought his commander time.

"Stop them!"

The remaining Thebans shouted to Herakles, drew their sidearms and blades, and raced along the deck towards Kyniska. They were easily outnumbered, yet surged forward in the knowledge there was nowhere to retreat to.

Kyniska took aim with her pistol, but there was little time to pick out targets. She managed three shots before they were on her. Two of her accompanying Mothakes were cut down, and for a second it seemed the more experienced Thebans would prevail. But then Kyniska went to work. She was as strong as she was elegant, and moved through the Thebans with ease. Her razor sharp kopis bit deep into her foes, while her pistol blasted almost non-stop. Soon she was past the main deck and heading for the raised commander's tactical station further back.

"Strategos Photios!"

A thin line of seven Thebans waited in her way, each drew long blades, spears, and glaives for the fight. It was an old fashioned approach, and one Kyniska relished. She was so excited by the prospect of the close-quarter fight she didn't notice that the Strategos was gone. Forgetting her training for a brief moment, Kyniska leapt into the fray and landed in the middle of the Theban line. One sword slashed her leg, embedding in one of her greaves. A glaive then glanced off her Corinthian helm and almost knocked her to the ground. Each strike seemed to goad her on to greater violence, and she began swinging her blade in wild slashes from the shoulder. They might look ungainly, but the cuts were well aimed, and followed in long-practiced sequences that cut against vulnerable target areas.

"I've got her!" laughed one Theban as Kyniska's blade swept down to his neck. It was a diagonal strike, and easy to parry. The big man took the impact on his two-handed curved sabre, but was stunned to see her sword simply drop down to her left, and then cut right back up. It slashed into his exposed armpit, removing his arm at the shoulder. He screamed as his arm, hand, and weapon flew away. He staggered backwards before collapsing.

"Wrong!" she laughed.

Kyniska dispatched the next Theban with a brutal fusillade of shots from half a metre away. No armour, not even the highest quality Theban gear could protect against such savagery. Before the wounded man could fall, Kyniska was onto her third victim. Her blade hacked down from the left, and a heavy glaive rose to meet it. As they made contact, Kyniska whiskered the weapon away, dropped down low, and slashed from right to left at head height. It was a perfectly executed cut and removed the man's head, along with making a show of blood as an eruption of red seemed to pulse out from the neck.

"Fight me!" she roared, her blade continuing to dance about in her hand.

The dark red blood sprayed across the face of Kyniska,

giving her a terrifying new visage as some female demon that could not be stopped. Two more Thebans tried to fight back, but the others quickly turned and ran. Those fortunate enough to realise what was happening threw down their weapons and dropped to their knees. Those that ran or continued fighting were chased down by the Helots and shown no mercy. Kyniska walked through the pools of blood, leaving thick footprints behind her. Once at the tactical station she snarled at finding a single dead officer. She activated her communications node.

"My Brother. Strategos Photios has escaped!"

* * *

Agesilaus could feel his artificial leg slowing him down, though what it lacked in speed it more than made up in power. He used it in his barging attacks against his foes. Each time they came close, he would hunker down behind his shield arm, and then thrust forward in a great surge of power. His strong legs helped, but the motorised limb pushed him that much harder.

"Out of my way!"

The news that Strategos Photios had escaped infuriated him. It was one thing to take his ship, but by escaping in the midst of the bloodbath, he'd managed to negate his victory. The man could transfer his flag to another ship, and the battle would continue. And the last thing Agesilaus needed was a long and drawn out battle. There was little time to dwell on the man's escape, as a small knot of Thebans tried to block his path. Using his entire body, Agesilaus crashed into them. The two nearest spun out of the way as he pushed through, and then he went to work with his blade.

By avoiding gunfire as much as possible, he'd managed to draw in the over confident soldiers. The closer they came, the less useful their rifle-armed comrades were. Gunfire still lashed back and forth, but with so many people from both sides engaged in hand-to-hand combat, it was next to impossible to safely identify targets. One stabbed at him with a bayonetted Doru rifle, but Agesilaus cut down into it as though it were little more than a toy. A second rifle stabbed past him, and he pulled away to avoid it striking his throat. He then grunted as a blade slid along his shoulder. It cut into the metal plating, and he felt a short glance of pain as it caught his flesh. He then pushed upwards and forced his own blade into the Theban's throat. The man dropped to the ground, and for a moment there was a gap in the enemy formation.

"Yes! Now push them hard!"

The small numbers of Laconians needed no encouragement and threw themselves into the fray. As before, they advanced in silence with mechanical skill and efficiency. The non-Laconians soldiers present tried to match their comrades, though instead of the cold and brutal approach used by the professionals, they howled with excitement, but as they stepped forward, the unthinkable happened. One by one the Theban crew and remaining soldiers dropped their weapons, and fell to their knees.

"What's happening?" asked one of the Mothakes.

The young man placed the tip of his blade against a Theban soldier's throat. The kneeling man continued to look down towards where he'd thrown his weapon.

"They're surrendering?"

"How is this possible?" Agesilaus demanded, "The battle is not over. Not until I say it is!"

Agesilaus paused for breath and glanced back towards his warriors. They were tired and battered, and every single one of them could not have looked happier to be there. And yet to their new and excitable allies there was bitterness to their victory. The surrender of the Thebans had robbed them of their chance of running down their vanquished foes. Every extra minute of fighting would magnify their success, and it was well known that the greatest damage to an enemy was always committed after their defeat in battle.

"There is to be no rout today."

Agesilaus walked along the deck. His warriors disarmed the few that were unsure whether to surrender or not, while others fitted manacles to their prisoners.

"The Thebans are not the enemy we assembled to fight. Seeing them crushed might be personally satisfying, but it does nothing for Terrans as a people."

He looked to the defeated soldiers, and they raised their heads to look at him. It was clear that most of them expected to be killed, or at the very least placed in chains and taken away to work in the dreaded silver mines of the League. Not one of them expected mercy, and certainly not from Agesilaus.

"I will not enslave you, but I will disarm you. Perhaps one day from now we will fight alongside each other, Thebans and Laconians against the common enemy."

An older woman wearing the insignia of a pentarchos laughed as he spoke. It was disrespectful, but at least a response. Agesilaus moved closer to her and opened his mouth to speak, when he heard Dukas Myrrine via his communications node.

"Strategos...we've got a serious problem."

Agesilaus shook his head while scanning the bloody field of battle. There were scores of dead and wounded on the ship, yet for all the fighting many Thebans were still alive.

"Long-range scout probes have detected approaching ships heading this way, and fast."

Agesilaus snorted. His blood was up, and seeing the capture

of the Theban flagship had pushed him to the edge. He wanted to see them suffer for interrupting his sacrifice, and perhaps to see their ships annihilated in lieu of his own.

"Whose ships are they?"

"Unknown, Strategos. But their path suggests they are coming directly from the Theban territories. There are at least twenty capital ships, all moving at maximum speed, and others are coming behind them."

Agesilaus shook his head and looked around the deck of the fallen ship.

"How long do we have?"

Dukas Myrrine answered immediately.

"Minutes. If you get to the dropships, we can redeploy the fleet to match them. I can have the fighters pulled back to provide a missile screen. We're ready for this fight..."

Agesilaus continued shaking his head.

"No, Dukas Myrrine. This battle is not to be ours, not today. Prepare the fleet for immediate departure. Set course for the Great Expanse."

"You are not staying to fight the Thebans?"

Agesilaus flinched at her words, the first time he'd flinched in this entire battle. He could feel the surprise in her voice, and the confusion.

"No. We have much bigger fish to fry. The Medes threaten our kin, and I intend on making them pay. Make sure the fleet is ready. We leave the moment I set foot back on Agamemnon."

"Yes, Strategos...We will be ready for you."

One by one his warriors redressed their ranks, while others continued to disarm the defeated Thebans crew and soldiers. It should have been a moment of celebration. They'd captured a Theban battleship, but there was no time to install a crew to take it as a prize. Agesilaus considered his limited options, neither of which he liked. He could destroy the ship…or he could try and take it with a skeleton crew, though he was sure they would need hours, perhaps even days to successfully pull that off. As he tried to decide, a familiar face appeared from one of the many ramps that descended from the next level up.

"Kyniska!"

She came towards him with her crimson cloak flowing elegantly behind her. Two columns of warriors moved with her, and in her arms she carried the discarded helmet of their hated foe, Strategos Photios Kosmas. It was completely intact, save for a large scorch march along the left cheek, and an indentation that ran from the nasal bar and up to the horsehair plume.

"It isn't much, Brother. But it is something."

He looked at her and sighed.

"This was supposed to echo the voyage of the Thousand Ships to reclaim Helen."

Kyniska laughed at that.

"She was supposed to have been a queen of Sparta. Perhaps if she'd fought like one, war could have been avoided."

Agesilaus looked at his sister, and then removed his trusty helmet. He was covered in perspiration, and though tired, far from exhausted. He reached out for the helmet, and Kyniska handed it to him as though presenting a great prize.

"What will you do with it?"

Agesilaus sighed.

"I'm certain of many things right now, but what to do with this thing? That is something else."

His communications node brought him instantly back to reality.

"Strategos. The fleet is ready. We just need you back onboard."

Kyniska looked to him with a questioning look on her face. "Well?"

"It's time. Let's go."

They began to move away, but then Agesilaus stopped and pointed towards one of the few remaining Theban officers.

"You!"

The man gulped, struggling to answer the giant of a warrior. "Yes, Basileus?"

"You can plot a course for this ship, can you not?"

The man shook his head, but then he saw the look on the Basileus' face. Though he continued to shake his head, he answered in the affirmative.

"Yes. I can provide a basic four-point course, with no additional waypoints. The battleship has sustained…"

"That's enough. Set this course, and then get to your lifeboats. I will give you five minutes."

He grabbed the man at the collar.

"My guards will assist you with this little enterprise. Fail them, and you fail me. And I can promise you now, that you do not want to try my patience. Do you understand?"

The Theban officer answered without giving it a moment's thought. He might be a member of the Theban Navy, but he was primarily a citizen, and like all Terran naval officers, it was a part-time posting at most. Only Laconians spent their lives at war, a consequence of their unique training and cultural system, as well as a complete reliance upon the slave labour of their indentured Helot workers.

"Yes, Basileus. It will be done."

CHAPTER FOURTEEN

Battleship 'Agamemnon', The Great Expanse
Nine days later
The journey through the Great Expanse was a testing time for Agesilaus. He wanted to get to grips with his enemy, and instead was faced with a never-ending journey through the void, the Great Expanse. He'd never travelled in this direction before, having spent all of his life either in Laconia, or fighting in the small skirmishes that seemed to pop up every year between the warring Terrans. Now he had to watch his great armada pass nebulae, storms, and other bizarre phenomena, all while they stopped, refuelled, and then moved on to the next location. It was long, slow, and tiresome, not how he'd expected a war to be fought.

So as he did each day, he followed his personal and group training regime, with most of the daylight hours spent honing with mental and physical skills; as well as working alongside his comrades to develop their team abilities. Today was going to be different, though. For the first time in his life he'd decided he would practice against people other than his peers.

"Strategos," said a firm voice as he entered the ship's gymnasium.

"Demokritos."

"Eyes on me."

Demokritos prepared his duo of fighters for their next bout. Agesilaus paused, and then looked about the place. Others were already training, and though they acknowledged his approach, they continued with their exercises. Two Laconians busily engaged in traditional Terran pankration particularly intrigued him. A dark-skinned trainer moved around them, shouting suggestions as they struck back and forth. He was utterly humourless, and a perfect interpretation of what a Terran god would look like. He was stripped down to training clothes, with bare limbs and chest. His body glistened, and every muscle seemed to function independently and with perfect control. He stopped the men, and then moved in to strike.

"Like this!"

Demokritos struck with open-handed blows, hitting with the power of a machine. One tried to circle around him, and he merely pulled back, avoiding the impact with a beautifully executed body void. The blow missed him by a fraction, and yet the counterattack hit like he was being struck with iron bars. The group then stopped fighting, and the trainer showed them his footwork once more. It was helpful, yet at the same time adversarial. Agesilaus watched and listened. The trainer was an expert, and everything he said made sense to him. Agesilaus was no slouch in close-quarter combat. But even he was no match for Demokritos, a man known on a dozen worlds as simply the Beast of Laconia.

Agesilaus nodded towards the aged man, and then moved to the side where a long set of benches extended out from the bulkheads. Demokritos was a Laconian trainer, and legendary warrior with a history of battles going back decades. His most famous of all stemmed back to the days of the great Helot Revolt, a time when the future of Laconia itself was at stake. Even now, after all of these days, Agesilaus still felt blessed for being able to recruit the man. He'd been travelling with a contingent heading for Lysander's fleet a day after Agesilaus had left the Aulian Nebulae. The man needed no encouragement to help his master in times of war, and now Agesilaus had the best trainer on hand to help.

"Now...fight again. And fight harder."

The man stepped back, and as before, the pair moved closer to fight. It was the common open-handed submission martial art practiced everywhere from Laconia to the barren regions of Makedon. The athletes used boxing and wrestling techniques, as well as kicks, holds, locks, and chokes. It was brutal for most to watch, and Agesilaus found their training rather therapeutic. Finally, the smaller of the men flipped his opponent onto his back, locking his neck in a deadly scissors position that began to choke the life out of him.

"Fight him!" The trainer circled around the pair.

The choked man should have been beaten, but he pulled in strength from somewhere, striking his fists into his assailant's ribs and stomach. Though he grunted, the man would not release the scissor grip.

"A few more seconds and you are gone...What do you do?"

The man struggled again, and then Agesilaus chuckled as the man did the unexpected. Rather than struggling, he went completely limp. For a second or two it looked as though he'd passed out. His foe remained locked around his body, but then relaxed, thinking he'd won. At that moment, the prone man snapped to life and twisted to the right. It was so fast and violent that he broke free, rolled the man onto his front, and dropped his knee down into his neck.

"Impressive," said Agesilaus, "From weakness, there is strength."

All three looked to their Strategos, but none did more than nod. He might command the armada, but here in the gymnasium there were other rules. While on the training floor only the instructor counted. To another Terran, the very mention of weakness might be laughed at, but not to them. Each was intimately familiar with the power of weakness, and how it could be harnessed to enable victory.

The two fighters grasped arms as they rose to their feet. There was no animosity or anger between them, and both discussed the highs and lows of the bout as they moved from the mats. The instructor remained, and as Agesilaus approached, he lowered his head.

"Strategos. You are here for your training? I was not expecting you this late."

Agesilaus stripped off his robe and placed it down on the bench. He wore the same training shorts as the others, and it was possible to see the marks and damage his body had sustained over the years. None stood out more than the artificial limb that whined and groaned as he moved.

"I have never fought the Medes before. Tell me, have you experienced their Immortals, the ones they call the…"

"Anusiyans?"

Agesilaus nodded.

"Yes."

"I have fought them on three occasions, Strategos. The Anusiyans are unique among their military forces, and the closest thing the Medes have to our Laconian regulars."

That seemed to make Agesilaus' eyebrows twitch.

"Regulars?"

"Yes. The Anusiyans are the only full-time regulars in the Median military. Their numbers are vast, and they are equipped with the best they have to offer. They are fast, well-motivated, and loyal."

"How do they fight?"

The man licked his lips and then whistled. Several seconds later a pair of doors slid open, and out stepped a mechanical fighting drone. It was tiny compared to those he sparred with at home. The thing lacked weapons or armour, and seemed almost naked as it walked in front of them both. The trainer then clapped his hands, and a dozen individuals appeared from the shadows. Some carried clothing, others weapons and armour. They moved quickly and efficiently, and soon dressed and equipped the machine in an utterly alien fashion. Finally, they slunk back into the shadows, leaving just the machine behind.

"Behold, the Anusiyan soldier."

Even Agesilaus was surprised as he looked at it. The machine adopted a fighting posture, and then moved through a series of odd-looking movements. They were very different to what he was used to, with more circular stepping, wider stances, and a lot of long-range work with the hands, feet, and spear. Finally, the machine came to a halt so that it could be inspected more closely.

"I did not expect this, Demokritos. From the stories I've read, the Medes are supposed to be weaklings, soft, and ill-suited to battle."

"Some are, but not the Anusiyans. They are not provincial soldiers of the satraps, but trained in legions in Imperial territories. They are professional soldiers, and carry the armour and weapons of the God King."

He pointed his hand towards the robotic demonstrator.

"As you can see here, they are more than a match for most Terrans, and in large numbers they are quite a threat."

He turned from the machine and back to Agesilaus.

"They are the ten thousand Immortals sacred defenders of their Emperor, their God King, and capable of great things."

"But what is your assessment of their abilities? Can they match a Terran shield to shield?"

The trainer almost looked amused by the question.

"That depends on whose shields they are pressed against, does it not, Agesilaus? They are skilled, and they have defeated many Terrans in open battle. And yet for their skills, they do not have the discipline or individual strength of our best soldiers."

He paused, letting that sink in for a moment.

"A Terran heavy infantryman will always have the advantage in the phalanx, but one-on-one these Anusiyans are a problem. And as for their numbers, the ten thousand Immortals is a misnomer. They field units of ten thousand, and based on combat reports, have the ability to field multiple armies of them."

Agesilaus didn't seem to like that news.

"That is something I did not know."

The trainer shrugged.

"Nothing is certain in war. I have heard of legions of these Anusiyans being fielded. There are even stories of there being more than fifty thousand of them in a single invasion force. That is what I heard from stories in the Robotic Domains."

"Interesting. That could be a problem."

Their eyes met across the gymnasium floor, and the trainer could tell there was something else.

"If these Medes are as agile and fast as you say they are, I need to work on my ranged work. Assuming your simulation is correct."

"It is. They will assault in formation, but looser than that of the phalanx. It gives them the advantage in one-on-one combat, at the expense of their own protection."

"Can you show me?"

Demokritos nodded, and then without warning he removed his tunic and cast it across to the others waiting on the benches. Now completely naked, he turned to Agesilaus. There was no hesitation on the part of the Laconian King, and soon he waited before his opponent. Other races might have recoiled at seeing them, but not the Terrans, and certainly not the Laconians. They viewed the Terran form as something to be praised, and to laud. With no armour, weapons, or clothing, it was a match based on skill, and both formed up into fighting stances ready for the battle.

"Now come at me with everything you have," said Demokritos, "And I promise you that I will offer you the same."

Agesilaus stepped in close, twisted to the right, swinging out with his mechanical leg. It was a fast blow, but impressive. The trainer leaned to the right and then chopped down into the limb. Agesilaus was instantly thrown off balance and hit the ground.

"Again!"

Agesilaus reformed his stance, and this time moved more carefully. His motorised limb whined and grated as he stepped. It was far from the elegant limbs of his comrades, yet he used its extra weight and heft to help move him in other ways. The kick was better timed, and though the trainer avoided the blow, he was forced to give ground as Agesilaus repeatedly punched. Finally, he moved in and snap kicked from the front. The impact was heavy enough to push the trainer back nearly a metre. Agesilaus stepped in for another attack, but the trainer dropped down low and swept in hard against his other leg. The impact came just below the knee, instantly throwing him off balance. Agesilaus hit the ground hard, and for a second he seemed to be stunned.

"That is better. Much better. Your limb is both a weakness and an asset, Agesilaus."

There was no animosity between them as Agesilaus rose to one knee.

"Against Terrans these techniques will be useful weapons in your arsenal, but against the Medes and their auxiliaries it could be a liability."

He rubbed his chin before grasping Agesilaus' arm.

"I can see the problem, Strategos. I have exercises we can work on. If you wish?"

Agesilaus smiled at the man.

"Everything you can teach me, Demokritos, will help. Thank you, old friend."

The old trainer's fist flew fast and directly towards Agesilaus. Not even the Strategos was fast enough, and it struck his cheek before he could move away. The blow was strong and sent blood bursting from his mouth. He nearly lost his footing, but then the motors in his leg stiffened up his posture, and he readied himself for the next blow. It came in hard, but he was ready this time.

* * *

Two days later
Agesilaus leant back in his high-sided chair and let out a long, slow breath. He did not enjoy playing this waiting game, and every additional day they spent in space was a day he was not righting the wrongs of the Medes and their brutal campaigns

against his kin. He was out of his armour, though still wore his tunic. At his thigh was a kopis blade, as well as a brace of antiquated looking pulse pistols. A beep at the door caught his attention, and his right hand instinctively dropped to his side.

"Come."

The door opened, and for a second a blast of bright light entered the room. It was enough to make Agesilaus squint as a figure entered his chamber. The door then slid shut.

"Kyniska. I thought you were busy drilling our soldiers into something I can use?"

She gave him a polite smile, and then walked towards the display on his wall. It was active and showed a paused video sequence of the Aulian Nebula.

"You're still watching that thing? I thought you be board watching her burn by now."

Agesilaus' eyes seemed to glow with energy at the mention of the Nebula.

"Oh...Sister. How little you know me. The burning of Fury of Herakles was the one piece of good news from the Aulian debacle. If it were not for that, we'd have nothing more than damaged ships for our effort."

Even Kyniska found her attention drawn to the looping videostream as the massive Theban battleship inched closer and closer towards the nebula. Halfway to the target, a large cloud of pods and lifeboats burst away. Other Theban vessels crowded around to assist, but they were too late to save their flagship.

"Yes. It was a minor victory. But a necessary one."

Kyniska pulled her attention away for a moment.

"Oh? And why is that?"

"Simple. If we'd abandoned her, and been chased away by the Thebans, we would forever be known as the Laconian fleet that ran. Now we are the fleet that arrived at the Nebula as planned and sacrificed a battleship in honour of the gods. We left on a high, and during the destruction of a large part of the Theban fleet."

"An interesting interpretation of events."

Agesilaus nodded politely to his sister.

"Why did you call me here? My duties require every hour of strength I can offer. The Helots are putting in the time, but they still lack skills and discipline. There is a reason they suffered almost four hundred casualties boarding the Theban flagship."

Agesilaus had seen the casualty reports, though he had to admit he'd not really paid much attention to the Helot dead and wounded. Back home they were effectively slaves, carrying little monetary, moral, or political value.

"Yes. Plus thirteen Laconians died in a battle that denied me the head of Photios or the capture of his ship."

"Yes. And I would argue they were utterly pointless losses that granted us no territory, ships, or concessions."

"That is not completely accurate. Their losses were necessary in giving our new soldiers the courage to attack. After seeing the courage of our own soldiers, were they able to find their own. That had a value that cannot be counted merely in terms of bodies and bullets."

Kyniska shrugged.

"Perhaps. But we need to be much smarter in the use of our soldiers if we're going to win this campaign. But I suspect that is not why you called me here, is it?"

Agesilaus tried to look serious, but with his sister he knew she could see right through him. His doubts were hidden from all but her, and yet there was no other he could rely on like Kyniska.

"I have a problem. A big problem."

Kyniska laughed at that, instantly irritating her brother. Though both Laconians, she had always had a more liberal view as to her role within it. Though allowed to train and fight alongside her kin, she would never have the chance to lead them in war. Only men were ever made Basileus. Years before she'd found it a painful thing to accept, but now she found it liberating. She could be a Laconian without having to worry about leadership and traditions. And that left her free to become involved in affairs that interested her more fully. She knew that serious look, though, and Agesilaus would never back down, not until he had said his part.

"I'm sorry…go on. You said you had a problem."

Agesilaus straightened his back, and then rose to his feet.

"Every few hours we're getting more reports and messages from the front. I've sent commands to the few mercenary squadrons still fighting to delay the Medes for as long as possible."

He rubbed his brow.

"But we're still a good few days out from offering any useful help. And the last video reports show that Tissaphernes is on the rampage. One minute he's in one place, and then seconds later he's somewhere else. It is not easy trying to understand his strategy."

Kyniska listened, though she had little useful advice for him. All of her training had been personal and small unit based. It was always assumed she would not lead an army to war, and until the last week, it was something she'd never considered.

"I have account after account of small fleet battles, raids, and then even planetary invasions. All I am certain of is that Tissaphernes has mustered quite a significant fleet and is operating independently of the Empire."

He shook his head, and Kyniska lifted her eyebrows.

"There's more?"

"Yes. Isn't there always?"

He tapped the screen, and an image of an elegant Median nobleman appeared. His clothing was exquisite, melded armour and weapons, expensive clothes and jewellery. There was no possibility of confusing him for a Terran.

"Pharnabazus? What does he have to do with anything?"

Agesilaus looked unimpressed as he showed her the map of the Empire's borders. Flashing lights highlighted the Terran cities positioned right inside its territory.

"Unconfirmed reports from Laconian traders say Satrap Pharnabazus is on the move. Apparently, he's been building ships for the last six months in his home territory. It's a war fleet, and I am certain he intends to use it to go to war."

"Pharnabazus," said Kyniska, disgust in her voice, "He hates Tissaphernes more than he hates any Terran. Is he planning on attacking his rival?"

Even as she said the words, she could tell there was more to what he'd heard. And with each passing second, her mind went into overdrive. In many ways Pharnabazus was an even more wily foe than Tissaphernes. He had provided funds and technology to assist the Laconians in their wars with the Alliance. He knew how to use money as effectively as soldiers to obtain his objectives.

"Hold on. His treaty with Laconia still stands, doesn't it? We've both agreed to avoid conflict with each other."

Agesilaus shook his head ever so slowly.

"No. I received a message from Agis himself from back home. He says that all diplomatic links with the Medes have been broken off. Pharnabazus has issued proclamations that he intends removing unsavoury elements from his borders."

Kyniska did not like this news one bit. She ran her hands through her hair as she read, and then re-read the message from Laconia's second king.

"This is rank stupidity. It has been our strategy to play them off against each other for years. That's how our noble Strategos Clearchus was able to make it so far in their battle for the crown."

"If only he'd succeeded, and put Cyrus on the throne, then we would not be here."

Kyniska focussed her attention on the images of the noble.

"If these two Satraps are able to put their differences aside, we will be in a lot of trouble. They control the entire flank of the Empire facing our worlds."

"My thoughts exactly. And if they work together, they will be able to bring a combined fleet of a hundred or more ships to battle. And that is without assistance from their God King. Just a few victories, and they will add the ships of those defeated, and then throw coin at any surviving mercenaries. It could be another invasion."

"I see. And this time our colonies are still recovering from our own civil war. It is the perfect opportunity to strike. You always said that the Medes thought long-term, while we Terrans thought only of the harvest. I think you might be right."

Her expression then softened as she tried to look more confident in front of her brother. Agesilaus clearly felt as though he now bore the weight of the world on his shoulders.

"I'm here, Brother. Tell me, what do you want of me? Name it…and it is yours."

He took a shallow breath, and for a second she half expected some terrible ordeal. Not for one moment did she think he would send her away from the coming battle.

"I will continue forward and face Tissaphernes, but I need

you to leave the fleet."

"What?"

Kyniska could hardly contain herself. She signed up for this war, and now she was to be sent away before it had even begun.

"I want you to meet with our Strategos, Thibron and his forces."

"Thibron? I thought he's been fighting near Byzantium for months now with small numbers of Laconian mercenaries. Why does he need my help?"

Agesilaus almost laughed at the suggestion, much to the annoyance of his sister.

"No, you misunderstand, Kyniska. Thibron was sent by Lysander to deal with piracy and some loyalist contingents that Tissaphernes had been backing, but since then he's been engaged with Tissaphernes in a series of pointless battles."

Kyniska had not expected that, and she leaned in for a better view of the screen. She'd assumed their campaign against the Satrap was the main event. Now it seemed half of the Terran colonies within the borders of the Empire were in a state of war.

"That wily Satrap is no fool, Sister. He knows the area, and he knows the people. So he's sucked Thibron into the Aeolian Territories and against a region of little significance."

"I see," she said with interest, "According to these ship logs, the fighting has raged for four weeks at the Phrikonis Star System. It started as a series of raids against the colonies orbiting Phrikonis Five, and then proceeded to the stations and facilities throughout the system."

"Yes. Tissaphernes has the time and the numbers to drag this out. Tissaphernes has managed to draw him into this month-long battle in a region he has little interest in."

Kyniska moved the mapping data about and tracked the

change in system-wide control over the subsequent weeks.

"Thibron is winning, though. He's taken a third of the ground lost by the Phrikonians since arriving, and his assaults are gaining ground."

"Yes. But I suspect Thibron has little interested in this fight. Look more closely."

Both examined the data, but Agesilaus had to tap the largest planet and then rotate it to show four orbiting moons.

"According to this, he lost three ships, and more than five hundred warriors fighting to take this single shipyard. And why?"

"Because he was ordered to?" Kyniska suggested.

"Exactly. He feels unable to leave, having been sent there by Laconian Command. And yet every victory is actually a defeat. He could win every battle in this system, and still lose against Tissaphernes. He's being slowly bled dry."

"What about Lysander? Surely he is best suited to assist Thibron? Has there ever been a battle or campaign he could not win?"

Agesilaus chuckled.

"He did not win command of this armada, did he?"

Kyniska found that to be most amusing.

"True...very true. But still. He could win in Phrikonis, surely?"

Agesilaus shook his head again, running his hand through his beard.

"Lysander is gone. He has been recalled home to help in case we fail. It seems our enemies at home heard about the Aulian debacle, and are calling for the League to prepare for a defensive war with the Medes...should an invasion come."

Kyniska laughed as she heard that.

"Scaremongering and war profiteering. You warned them all

about this before we left. Do they really intend on letting the Medes come to their front door?"

"I know. Thibron worries me, though. It is a battle I fear he cannot win, at least not without major help, and that is not coming for him. Phrikonis is a large system, with several worlds and dozens of moons. It must be taken, but not when it has been readied for siege by Tissaphernes. Thibron was a fool for being goaded in. The Medes are not to be underestimated."

He placed his forehead in his hand, thinking about the situation. It was something he'd have liked a good deal more time to think about, but time was now his enemy, just as much as the enemy legions.

"In the past, our ancestors would simply go to war wherever we found our foes. Our armies were confident, and they were right to be. We smashed our enemies, yet even when we beat the Attican Alliance, the real victors were the Medes. This is how they continue to beat us. We react to their actions, and not the other way around."

Kyniska knew exactly what he meant.

"Of course, Brother. The best way to strike your foe is to be where he does not expect. Target one area, but then strike another. Just as we practice every day."

"Exactly."

"But surely with this armada we could smash Tissaphernes where he stands. Let's go there now, and join forces with Thibron."

"No. Phrikonis is a distraction, nothing more. Tissaphernes is using it as a way of pinning him down while he has a free hand elsewhere. I will not fight a war based upon the strategy of the Medes."

"So tell me what you want."

Agesilaus looked at her carefully before explaining.

"There are rumours that Thibron has managed to locate the survivors of the Ten Thousand, or as they are now known, the Black Legion. Some of our new recruits even say he landed on Attica just after Lysander left, and made overtures for mercenaries to assist him. If true, it means he has some of the finest mercenaries ever put on the battlefield. And he's squandering them in a static siege."

"You want me to see if he will sell their services to us?"

Agesilaus continued to shake his head.

"No, not at all. I need them...all of them. Persuade Thibron to break off his siege, but to leave small contingents to harass the Medes in the system. I need him to prepare to join me in battle. When I call on him, I will need every ship, soldier, and weapon he can place a hand on."

Kyniska found her eyes drawn back to the video feed of the Theban ship, and this time Agesilaus had to reach forward to pause the video. It froze as the battleship entered the maelstrom and began to break apart. The forces in the nebula were colossal, and in a matter of three seconds most of the ship had been ripped open.

"Very well, I will do my best. I will need to take some vessels with me."

Agesilaus reached out and grasped his sister's arm.

"Of course. You do not need to ask. Take what you need, and return to me as soon as you are able."

"You will continue to Ephesus?"

"Yes," he replied with a twinkle in his eye, "but not before I send a message to Thibron confirming we are coming to his aid with our entire armada. I will give you four more days before I send the message."

Kyniska seemed to especially like that part.

"A feint. I like it. Tissaphernes will expect us to avoid

Ephesus, and move against his prepared positions in Phrikonis. Just do one thing for me when you reach Ephesus."

"What is that?"

"Smash anything you find carrying the markings of Tissaphernes and his Carian scum. It's time they paid for their betrayal."

Still holding onto his sister's arm, he gripped her even tighter.

"Don't worry, my Sister. I will never show Tissaphernes mercy. Of that I make my pledge before the Gods."

She finally released his arm and softened the tone of her voice.

"Not so serious, my Brother. We have a long road ahead of us. Keep your friends close, and remember that we are heading into uncharted territories. Laconia is not loved by all. We have as many enemies with the Medes as we do back home."

Agesilaus returned her polite smile.

"As always, you are right."

CHAPTER FIFTEEN

Megaran Starcarrier 'Gorgon's Bite', Phrikonis System
Light glanced off the hull of the two starcarriers as they burst into the Phrikonis System. At over four hundred metres in length they were big vessels, and some of the ugliest used by the Terrans. The triple catamaran style hull housed a short, squat design that was much bulkier than the cruisers and battleships used by the Laconians. Hangar decks and large armoured plates curved around the blast doors and shield generators of the side sections. The central hull was little bigger than the side sections, and hidden slightly behind the oversized hangar sections. Multiple flared engines pushed out from all three parts of the ships.

"Welcome to Megas Phrikonis," said Dukas Maxis, "The largest and most insignificant planet in the system."

Kyniska gasped with excitement as the massive Terran warship burst into the Phrikonis System, its engines burning brightly. They travelled with two escorts per starcarrier, creating a small but powerful squadron. These destroyers waited close at the vessels' flanks, their engines now beginning to cool down. The ungainly starcarriers left long trails of light and dust behind them as they forced their way deep inside the dust, then appeared within the thick dust rings of the largest gas giant in the Phrikonis System. If not for their powerful exterior lights cutting deep into the planet's rings, they would have been almost impossible to see. Kyniska looked at the unassuming man and nodded. She turned her attention to the ring of viewscreens.

"Insignificant, perhaps, but these rings also hide most of Thibron's fleet, do they not?"

The man shrugged.

"Perhaps. That remains to be seen. I remain unconvinced this is the best use of my ships."

Kyniska stared at the display as she tried to spot the hidden ships.

"Trust me, Dukas. If the Black Legion is here, then our mission will have not been a waste of time. They achieve victories in battle that are barely conceivable."

"Yes," he reluctantly agreed, "Their success is interesting. But times change, and so must we."

The bridge was a hybrid bridge, flight operations centre, and command and information centre. It was tall and square, unlike the long command decks on Laconian warships. A walkway ran around the outside, roughly a metre from the ground. Artificial windows were positioned on all four sides, those at the front reaching up almost to the ceiling. Computer panels hung down from the top, like arrival boards at an air station or aerodrome. The senior officers moved about the top walkway. The rest of the officers worked at their computer units positioned in a ring on the lower level. There were at least two dozen places for the officers, along with a myriad of screens showing everything from ship status data and weapons controls, through to complex command and control systems for the scores of fighters waiting inside the ship's cavernous hangars.

"Dukas," said a female officer.

Kyniska looked down at the moment she tapped her screen. The same data transferred to a display hanging from the ceiling, providing easy access for Maxis and the other senior commanders.

"Alpha and Gamma Squadrons have completed their sweeps. They confirm no immediate signs of the Terran vessels. They are requesting orders."

Maxis' nostrils flared as he listened.

"Widen the sweep, and launch another squadron. I want this area scouted. If there's a single ship out here, we must find it."

He looked back towards Kyniska.

"I was led to believe that an entire war fleet was out here and engaged in battle with the Medes."

"They are here," said Kyniska, "But they are also not here. These mercenaries are no mere guns for hire. They are men and women familiar with fighting some of the deadliest and most cunning warriors in this region of space."

Kyniska blinked and almost missed the shape of Megaran fighters launching in multiple groups. They were almost impossible to see, save for their engines and the bright beams of light projecting from their searchlights. For anybody not following the tactical plan for the system, it would look as though they'd flown into some kind of fog. There were no stars, and no sign of the blackness of space in any direction. They were in another world, and Kyniska loved every minute of it.

"I have to admit it, Maxis, that was an impressive piece of flying." She moved her attention to the overweight man and nodded politely, "I take back anything I've said about Megarans in the past. You people know how to fly."

The man performed a mock bow.

"Not all Megarans. But Starcarrier crews are the best we have. You Laconians have your soldiers. We have our starcarrier commanders. It is said that only our pilots can navigate through the hell that is Scylla and Charybdis."

"Indeed. Of that I have no doubt."

"Look!" said a Megaran officer.

Kyniska followed the man's outstretched arm, but she could see nothing more than the beams of light in the cloud, and the occasional flashes of light.

"I see nothing."

The man looked to her and shook his head.

"Look beyond the clouds, and feel the patterns of movement. Can you not see?"

Kyniska tried again, and for a second she wondered if the man was actually insulting her. The fighters now pulled up and vanished behind part of the cloud. At first it was nothing particularly unexpected, but then her mind told her the imagery was wrong. Something else was happening out there.

"Wait...I thought I saw something."

They all moved to the largest of the screens showing the view ahead of the starcarriers. No fighters were visible, the clouds of gas and dust continuing to make visibility impossible. They might have been able to see a single kilometre or a thousand; it all looked the same.

"Uh...wait. What is that?"

Kyniska narrowed her eyes as she concentrated. The cloud seemed to be moving like the tide on a river. Patterns shifted and pulsed, yet the swirling shapes remained. She was about to step away when a huge section split apart in two directions. A monstrous shape emerged from inside, as though a great beast was waking from the depth of an old ocean. The shape was dark and covered in towers, sculptures, and archaic patterns that would have been more at home in a Terran palace or temple. The thing continued to grow as its hull and finally its haunches emerged from the clouds. The vessel was so large that by the time it was visible, a good half of it had succumbed to the dust, once more fading from view.

"Contact from the ship," said the starcarrier's auletes.

"Is it them?" Maxis asked.

The communications officer hesitated and finally answered.

"Unknown. They say we're surrounded by forces of the Strategos, and that we are to return our fighters to their launch bays immediately."

"And then?"

The auletes licked his lips nervously.

"And then prepare to be boarded."

That sent a chill down the backs of those on the command deck. Not for Kyniska, though. It was exactly what she'd expected.

"Very well, Dukas. Recall your fighters, but bring the escort ships a little closer. Just in case."

"Wait, you're serious? You would let them come aboard?"

She flashed a smile at him, instantly disarming him.

"How can we expect any assistance if we refuse these people our hospitality? Prepare to receive guests."

The fighters circled back with speed and skill, racing towards the hangars that filled the flank compartments of the ship. One by one they landed, and the shielded blasts doors dropped into position, all save for one. Kyniska waited patiently on the starcarrier's command deck as a single dromon departed from the newly arrived warship. It moved slowly and deliberately, while the massed turrets covering the warship remained locked onto the starcarriers.

"Here they come," she said quietly.

The spacecraft performed a complete orbit around the starcarrier, before heading for the last remaining open blast door. Dukas Maxis looked positively bored as the seconds turned to minutes, and then continued on and on. Finally, he shook his head and turned to face her.

"This is..."

At that very moment, shapes emerged at the side of the square command deck. Both were dressed in dark grey uniforms, and decked out in armour from a dozen different cultures. One carried an alien rifle, and the other a pair of pulse pistols, one in each hand and slung down low to his flanks. They looked more like renegades than warriors, yet walked with a confidence that came from long experience and success.

"Who are they?"

Kyniska shrugged.

"No idea."

The two men stopped in the centre of the deck. Though on a lower position to the bridge officers, they still looked as cocky and confident as before. Each checked the room, scanning every hiding place until one spoke. His voice was so quiet it could only be meant for his communications node. More warriors entered, flanked by four senior officers. Each wore tall helmets topped with horsehair plumes, but there were differences in their armour and clothing. One in the middle struggled to walk, yet remained upright, ignoring the evident discomfort that he was in. Kyniska worked her way down the steps and stopped in front of them. They looked at her with interest.

"Greetings to you all."

She bowed just a little. It was enough of a move to show

civility and politeness, but not too much to show she was the passive faction in these talks. She was no politician, but knew how to behave around others, especially military commanders. There was an expected level of behaviour, but she would go no further than that.

I want, no need military help. But I will not beg for it. After all, of what help would that be? Agesilaus sent me for fighting men and women, people who will do whatever is needed to win the coming fights.

"I come with orders from my brother, Strategos Agesilaus of the Laconia." She sounded serious, yet friendly.

The Terrans stopped in front of her, and she looked at them, from one to the next. In the middle was a Laconian, heavily built, muscled, and tough. He wore a Laconian crimson cloak, and his armour bore light damage from fighting. His face was partially hidden inside his helm, and yet there was recognition in his eyes. He grunted as he moved, and though the injuries were not visible. It was obvious he was in a lot of pain.

"Strategos Thibron."

She offered no flattery towards the Terrans. It would have simply offended them, as it should. They both knew the other from personal experience, and reputation. There was no need to waste words on trivialities.

"Kyniska, a royal princess of Laconia."

The Laconian then turned to his left and nodded towards one of his companions. He was tall and carried an Arcadian half-shield on his left arm. The man was taller and stronger built than Kyniska, and yet she'd heard nothing of him prior to today.

"And you are?"

Thibron spoke before the man could answer for himself.

"Desma of Mantinea. One of the…"

Kyniska's eyes lit up with excitement at hearing the name.

For a second the two men were all but forgotten. Her focus moved entirely to the mysterious woman who travelled with two senior military commanders.

"Of course. I have heard of you many times. Your victories with the Black Legion are quite the legend back home. I've heard both the Atticans and the Thebans have staged plays in honour of your valour."

Desma did not seem very impressed.

"Are they not the same people that stage plays in honour of law courts, and a chorus of crying mothers?"

Kyniska burst out laughing.

"Indeed they are. There is a reason why in Laconia we have no tradition of theatre and stories. Our actions speak louder than any play."

The soldier looked back at her with barely an acknowledgement to her face. If she'd not been told it was Desma, she'd have though it was any other decorated soldier. But then the Arcadian pulled off her helmet to reveal a stern looking face. The woman's long hair had been tucked down into the back plate of her armour, but as she moved her helmet away, a small tuft pulled out. Then the hair spread out and dropped down to her shoulders. But then something changed. It was subtle, but as though something had clicked in her mind. Her expression softened into a questioning look.

"Kyniska you said your name was."

"Yes. And it still is my name."

Desma ignored the rebuff and continued her questioning.

"The same Kyniska that entered the Olympics on behalf of the Laconian state, and against the rules and recommendations of the festival?"

Kyniska laughed. She'd enjoyed competing a great deal, but the best part had not been the winning. It had been seeing the looks on her detractors' faces when they'd tried to stop her. That was the real victory, and she relished it with every opportunity.

"Yes, the one and the same."

The stern expression faded from Desma's face.

"Tell me, why did you enter when so many tried to stop you? Women were outlawed from participation for as long as I can remember."

Kyniska nodded along.

"Yes! That is exactly why I participated. Tell me I cannot do something, and by the Gods, I'm going to want to do it."

She then stepped closer to the Arcadian.

"Plus...there is another reason."

"Go on."

Kyniska looked to the other officers before shrugging.

"For years my brother has been complaining that the chariot events are there for the rich. He says they can pay to win the contests, instead of demonstrating true martial skill and form. So we concocted this little plan between us, a way to show that he was right, and that they were also so very wrong."

Desma laughed, and it was clear the two women had hit off an unlikely friendship on the deck of the ship. Kyniska was going to continue the conversation when her eye was drawn to the naval uniform of the next of the Terrans. She was a tall, confident woman with thick auburn hair and grey eyes.

"You're an Attican naval officer?"

"I was, but no longer. I've been with the Black Legion for some time now. I am Roxana Devereux, Komes."

"She is our best and most experienced naval officer. Where she travels, enemy fleets are destroyed," said the man next to her.

Kyniska looked to the man. He was not the biggest, but

seemed to ooze confidence. He was of average height and sported a beard similar in style to her brother's. His clothing suggested Attican, much like the Komes, but then he wore a Laconian cuirass and helmet. What made her gasp was the weapon in his hand. It was the standard issue Laconian weaponry, but this one was different.

"I've seen that before. Wait…isn't it the Asgeirr-Carbine that was wielded by…"

"Clearchus," said the soldier.

Kyniska was rarely silent, but at that very moment she was dumbfounded. The soldier watched with amusement as she reached forward and touched the marks on the metalwork.

"How?" It was all she could muster.

"It was at Cunaxa. Clearchus was negotiating with Tissaphernes and his officers when the animals turned on him. Five minutes later our entire high command was gone. I made it inside to help, but it was too late."

"Clearchus, the Laconian commander of the Black Legion gave you his weapon. Why you? This is a relic of my people."

"He was dying, with a glaive in his back, and surrounded by the dead and dying. His last actions were to stab Meno in the face, right after his betrayal. He dropped to the ground and handed his blade to me."

He paused, and then shook his head.

"Actually, he was already on the ground as it detached from his arm. He looked to me as he died, and he made me promise to him before he finally passed."

Others might feel sad, but to Kyniska this was as close to a beautiful death as could be expected. A Laconian trained for war from a very young age, and the intent was to fight for as long as the individual was capable.

"What did he ask?"

The soldier reached out with the weapon, so she could get a better look. Though similar to the weapon used by other Laconians, it was covered in additional details, as well as thicker energy coils running down the sides of the forearm clasp. Half-circle rings ran down the length of the barrels, each punctuated with small holes.

"Just three words. Protect the Legion."

"Protect the Legion," repeated Kyniska, "And then he passed?"

The soldier nodded slowly.

"Yes. There was no time to recover the bodies. Tissaphernes' troops hit us hard. The withdrawal was successful, but bloody."

That was all Kyniska needed to know to realise exactly who he was.

"Wait…we were told you'd returned to Attica."

She looked to Maxis who appeared none the wiser. He raised an incredulous eyebrow at her odd series of questions. She moved closer, as though examining some great statue or sculpture for the very first time.

"From the stories, I thought you'd be…bigger."

Desma laughed at that impertinent question.

"You're Xenophon? Aren't you?"

The man removed his helmet and grinned at her. There was a warmth to him rarely found among the men of Laconia, a warmth she found rather relaxing. And yet for all that, he carried himself as though a Laconian born and bred.

"And I'm very pleased to meet you, Princess."

"Call my Kyniska, please. I am not your princess. Unless you've renounced your Attican citizenship and come to us as a foreigner."

Xenophon chuckled.

"I've been tempted on more than one occasion, trust me.

Attica has not been good to me...or my family."

That piqued her interested, but she was well aware it was a conversation for another time. Nonetheless, an Attican with Laconian sympathies was something of a curiosity to her. Thibron cleared his throat, and spoke now that Xenophon had stopped talking.

"Now...Kyniska, perhaps you can explain what you are doing here? You may not realise it, but we've been fighting for weeks without support. We've destroyed seven ships, and taken a number of shipyards and stations. Are you here with reinforcements?"

Kyniska shook her head and pointed to a computer display that showed the Ephesus System.

"No, we're here to do much more than take a system. My brother is now Basileus. And he is leading the expedition to take on the satraps that threaten every colony out there. He will not stop until the Empire is on its knees. Are you interested?"

The four looked to each other, and then back to her.

"What do you mean, take him on?" Thibron asked, "I've been doing that for weeks. And my orders are direct from the Ephors and Lysander."

Kyniska smiled.

"He plans on doing a lot more than this. Agesilaus is taking the war deep into the Empire, Lydia, Caria, Phrygia and beyond. Each victory will encourage more cities, colonies, and soldiers to join us. His goal is to do to them what they have done to us for generations. He wants the heads of Pharnabazus and Tissaphernes on pikes."

The four looked to each other, but Xenophon spoke first after Thibron gave him a subtle nod.

"Very well. How can the Black Legion help you?"

Kyniska beamed happily back at him.

"So it is true. The survivors of your expedition are still up for mercenary work?"

"Of course. What waits for them back home? Poverty and unemployment. If they are paid, they will fight."

"And you?"

For the first time she noticed the Attican soldier flinch.

"Many of my friends died out here. Tissaphernes owes me a debt. And I would hate for him to cheat me of it."

* * *

Olympian Citadel, Ephesus Prime

The bastion looked more like an ancient ruin on a long abandoned world. Thousands of small holes marked where it had been hammered by burst after burst of pulse rifle fire, but still it remained. Every few minutes a fighter screamed overhead, and usually a moment later another would emerge and give chase. Neither side seemed to have much of an advantage as the battle had bogged down into a grinding war of attrition.

"I can't believe we're still here. Somebody needs to make a deal...and fast. Or there's gonna be nothing left of this planet."

She noticed dark shapes above, and when she looked up, she could just about identify the alien outlines of the Median warships. About half were of the same design, the rest Terran ships they must have paid for or captured. Occasionally, another transport or dropship would circle down, though with each passing hour the number of landers seemed to have dropped off.

"Another one, look!" said a Terran spatharios.

All eyes looked up. A Mulac assault ship dropped down from low orbit and was immediately assaulted by three Terran fighters. The fight lasted seconds, and soon the enemy craft was heading towards the surface, belching thick black smoke. Elli never saw the thing crash, but all of them cheered when the ground shook from the impact. Christoff, the second-in-command of the crashed Terran ship, slid alongside her and handed her a canteen. She nodded, and then pulled back her head as she took a sip. The cool water ran down her dry throat, though the taste made her gag a little. She handed the unit back, and he placed it on his flank.

"The rehydrate powder is not exactly the best drink I've ever had."

"Don't worry." She laughed, "Right now, I'm happy to get anything wet inside me. This fight is dragging on and on."

"Tell me about it. One minute we're in space, the next we're stuck down here in a war nobody expected. I thought this was a raid. We've been holding off these mercs for how long now?"

Christoff's expression shifted, and he ducked down, pointing to the bottom of the hill. Their position on the second level of the bastion provided a perfect view in three directions, even if it left them a little exposed. The vision slot was nearly two metres wide, but only a tenth of that high. Large chunks had been broken apart from the stonework, and now the slit looked more like a vicious mouth, with razor sharp teeth marking the impact points of pulse cannon fire.

"Yeah, I see that movement, too. One sec…"

Elli lifted her Doru Rifle and adjusted the sight to maximum magnification. The latest two Mulac ships had landed out of range, but she could still make out the armoured sections along their flanks. A number of them fanned out and began positioning weapons on heavy tripods.

"I don't like the look of this."

A unit raced across the open ground, trying to fall back

to what remained of the bastion. Their armour was broken, and some protected by nothing more than padded jerkins and helmets. Less than half still bore weapons as they ran as fast as their legs could take them.

"The poor fools." Elli watched them scrambling over the debris, "I told them not to go searching for survivors. Anybody in front of us is already dead."

Incredibly, they continued to push forward, perhaps saved by virtue of the cloud of dust and smoke permanently drifting across the battlefield. Alexis, Christoff, and Elli then waited, well hidden inside the dust and filth of the ruined bastion. To anybody but an expert hunter, they were all but impossible to see until the last few metres. Days of combat had reduced the bastion to a ruin, as well as providing them with an ample source of cover. They waited in silence, taking careful aim towards the broken rocks and rubble that lay off down the hill.

"There!" Christoff said, "I see the animals!"

He fired first and was soon joined by a dozen other people, the survivors pouring down fire onto the Mulacs chasing the surviving Terrans. They were supposed to have been there for a few hours, but that turned to days as the commanders deep inside the Citadel sent out teams to help the outlying fortifications. Now there were nearly twenty soldiers inside, as well as an assortment of heavy weaponry.

"Hurry!" Elli screamed as the retreating soldiers clambered over the rubble partially blocking the breaches in the wall, and then pushed inside. At that moment, Elli spotted something she never expected. At first the survivors looked like many of the other Terrans, but then she worked out why so many were not wearing their full set of body armour. Any other day that might not seem particularly important, but in the middle of the bloodbath, they needed every single piece of armour to survive. The second one in the group stumbled. That was when she spotted his arms. The skin colour was off, and so was his face.

They're not Terrans!

It was a subtle difference, but the harder she looked, the easier it was to spot the reptilian features. At that moment she knew she wasn't looking at Terrans, but another group of the fearsome Mulac mercenaries.

"Get down!"

Alexis dropped to the ground so fast it seemed he'd been hit, but Christoff and a few of the others were too far away to hear. As they turned to look at her, the fake Terrans charged inside and vanished in a bright fireball. Elli felt the heat even through her armour as the suicidal Mulacs exploded, opening up a large breach in the defences. She rolled to the right, lifting her Doru rifle as another wave of Mulacs charged inside. Using the confusion to cover their advance, they quickly made it inside the breached inner wall. A few vanished from view as they fanned out, some heading for the steps leading up to the next level. Then the dust cleared enough for Elli to see what was happening.

"They're inside!"

Her gun shuddered as she fired, and the remaining defenders opened up with their own weapons. Light danced back and forth from the energy weapons, both sides fighting tooth and nail to take the bastion. The slow crackle quickly turned into a powerful volley, but it was still too little, too late. Only four of the Mulacs were dead, and perhaps dozens were now inside.

"Get back!" Alexis shouted.

He stepped back, stumbling over the body of a fallen Terran. Two Mulacs appeared from nowhere and leapt upon him. One stabbed at his face, the blade glancing off the curved helmet.

"Drive them back!"

Elli stepped to the side of her new friend. Two weeks ago they'd never heard of each other, and now they were like siblings. She swung her rifle and caught the first in the face. In a fluid motion, she swung it around and fired three shots at the second. The pulse rifle pulverised armour and flesh with equal ease. More Terrans joined the battle, and before they could gain the initiative, the Terrans were pouring fire into the breach. The Mulacs never knew what hit them. At this range, it was barely necessary to aim the mixture of carbines, pulse rifles, and pistols at the targets. More Mulacs clambered over their dead kin, only for more hidden Terrans to open fire.

"That's it!" Elli fired a burst at a stumbling shape, "Keep up the fire!"

Five more Mulacs dropped inside, firing from the hip. Shots crashed into the defenders, and two Terrans fell to the ground. A third soon joined them, and the young female soldier screamed in pain. Shapes to the right caught Elli's eye, and she swung around to fire as a bloodied soldier appeared from the shadows.

"They've brought up artillery. We have to run...now!"

"How many are..."

Before the man could answer, the thick walls and stonework shook violently, shell after shell slamming into them. Elli and her small group of survivors threw themselves down, waiting for the shelling to slow. The seconds continued to pass as the heavy ordnance crashed down into the ruined bastion.

"I can't believe we held this place for more than a week."

An Arcadian soldier, along with five heavily armoured spatharii moved up alongside her own unit, positioning shield generators in the rocks at their feet. She shook her head as she watched them work.

"What are you doing? The walls are breached, the upper level is gone, and we have Mulacs inside."

As if to emphasise the point, a trio of the reptilian creatures moved from behind yet another piece of broken wall. Alexis opened fire on one, and she did the same to the second. The third dropped down into cover, not before lifting his rifle and opening fire. Pulses of blue light danced about the masonry, cutting down one of the Arcadians.

"The bastion is about to fall. We have to fall back."

The Arcadian officer shook his head and continued to issue orders. His helmet was long gone, and a bandage covered his forehead, as well as his left eye. When he noticed some of the defenders were ignoring him, he reached out and grabbed one by the throat.

"You'll listen to me. Now get on the firing line and..."

He stopped as soon as Elli pointed her rifle muzzle at his temple. The weapon was so hot from the gun battle it actually left black scorch marks on his armour. Another of the Arcadians gasped, and turned to point a weapon at her, only for Alexis to train his sidearm on his face.

"Fight the Mulacs, but don't start fighting our own people. We don't have so many friends that we can afford to lose them. Understood?"

The Terrans seemed struck in a trance as more Mulac mercenaries moved around the bastion from two directions. Sporadic shots glanced off the armour, but it was obvious to all of them that the place could not last for much longer. Elli nodded in the direction away from the Mulacs. A distant thin slit in the wall provided a view back up the hill and towards the major defences. From there she had the perfect view down the rocky slope, and towards the mighty Citadel.

"We're falling back, and you're not getting in our way.

Right?"

The Arcadian hesitated, and then nodded.

"Good. Now let's go, before these Mulacs turn us into lizard food."

CHAPTER SIXTEEN

Battleship 'Agamemnon', Ephesus System, Ionian Territories

Agesilaus rose up to his full height as he watched the shapes of the stars change. Some barely moved, but others flashed past so quickly they were little more than streaks. After many long days of travel, refuelling, and even the occasional sneak attack by Median marauders, his fleet was finally on the other side of the Great Expanse. He was now weeks away from Laconia, and the hundreds of other Terran worlds that littered the civilised, if perpetually warlike region of space. The journey had taken so long he could hardly believe he was now entering the Ephesus System, source of so much calamity, and home to the invasion fleet of Tissaphernes himself.

"Finally," he said quietly, though loud enough for those nearest to hear him, "We will strike at Tissaphernes as a lion strikes its prey. Hard, fast, and without mercy."

Dukas Myrrine walked across to him, nodding towards the tactical display table in the centre of his raised command position. It showed the vast forces arrayed under his command. Even he had to admit it was an impressive force.

"Thirty seconds, Strategos. Sensors show the Median Fleet is scattered through the system and in the middle of a massive redeployment."

"Redeployment? Interesting. If the Gods are with us, we might be able to tear them apart before they can deploy for battle."

He almost smiled, but then he recalled his foe. Tissaphernes was no fool, and each action taken by him was done for a reason. If he was redeploying, it might be because he knew the Terrans were coming. He gave a nod to the auletes, and waited to be scanned by the computer's projector unit.

"This is your Strategos. We enter the Ephesus System in twenty-five seconds. When we arrive, we will be far from home, and on the periphery of the enemy's territory. We can expect significant enemy resistance, but we will smash them, and continue to smash them until victorious."

He glanced at the countdown running on one of the larger displays. He knew they would arrive in seconds, and yet he barely moved. He was the epitome of calm, even before such a calamitous event as a full-scale fleet engagement.

"Ten seconds," said Dukas Myrrine.

Agesilaus could feel the tension in his body as the last few seconds ticked by. He'd never been to this system, but after spending so much time in planning for the battle, he felt he knew it like the back of his hand. He knew the location of all of its planets, moons, space stations, and shipping lanes.

"Fight hard, and fight well. Today we take Ephesus, and tomorrow we bend the Empire to our will!"

He nodded slowly to the projector and waited for the light to fade. No sooner had that happened than Dukas Myrrine gave him a subtle hand signal, and then indicated towards the forward view from the command deck. The VOB system provided a perfect circular view of the area, and everything looked peaceful and serene. For a few seconds, he doubted his strategy.

"We have arrived."

The planet transformed from something the size of his fist, to filling the viewscreens on three sides.

"Ephesus Prime."

There was no time to gaze at the massive planet, though. They were under fire as soon as they arrived. Scores of scattered ships fired on the exact arrival points of the Terran ships, showering them with powerful volleys of plasma fire.

"Shield!" Agesilaus shouted, though his orders were not needed.

Dukas Myrrine marched back and forth on the deck, issuing orders to the squadrons. The Terrans formed up into the formations she had already determined, along with input from Agesilaus. In seconds, it was clear they'd completely underestimated the defensive preparations the Medes would make. And yet as the Terran vessels made adjustments to their formations, the gunfire started to arrive. It began as a trickle, and then expanded to a torrent of laser and plasma fire. Two of the biggest ships, Agamemnon and Harbinger, took heavy fire to their forward sections, each impact slamming hard into the movable shield plates.

"What's happening?" Agesilaus demanded, "This does not feel like much of a surprise attack to me."

Dukas Myrrine stumbled as the entire hull of the battleship shuddered violently. The walls actually groaned under the immense stresses as the shield struggled to defend the ship. Agesilaus snarled as the light cut for several seconds, before returning to normal. The battleship was capable of sustaining a considerable bombardment, and yet in less than a minute of battle was showing signs of her limitations.

"Well?"

Dukas Myrrine shouted to the helmsman, and the battleship began a complex series of rotations, all of which were matched by the other battleships and heavy cruisers. It looked much like a dance performance, the rotations allowing the unaffected shielding to take over and give time for the rest of the protective layers to recover. Then she looked back at him.

"The Medes have deployed in a scattered formation over two hundred thousand kilometres. They are well spaced and ready for battle. Our forces are compressed into a much smaller area."

Agesilaus turned about as he watched the first stages of the battle via the VOB system. The Terran Fleet was big, and yet the Medes Fleet appeared equally massive. Both sides were relatively scattered and already blasting away with their weapons. Little would be decided yet, but any ships caught out in the open, or away from the protection of the larger ships, would soon be destroyed.

"Numbers?"

"We're roughly equal in numbers. I think it…"

Gunfire crashed back and forth, and Agesilaus grunted as an Archean cruiser pushed too far forward. It was instantly hit with fire from five separate heavy cutters. The beams made short work of its shielding, biting deep into its hull.

"They are scattered like a herd of surprised beasts, but it is a ruse. They knew we were coming, and they are as ready as we are."

Dukas Myrrine looked confused for the first time ever.

"But why? This formation is tactically weak. We can strike at any point and inflict significant damage."

"True. But they are trying to split us up, as they did on the ground at Cunaxa. This scattered approach will force us to break up into five or six units to deal with their open formation."

He then shook his head.

"No. I don't like it. What if they have a large reserve waiting for us this very moment?"

"It is possible," said Dukas Myrrine, "If I was in charge, I'd keep at least half of my fleet a single jump away, and wait until all Terran ships were in position. We are powerful when together, but they have speed and numbers on their side in most engagements."

Agesilaus rubbed his chin and nodded.

"Yes. I would also. Our current disposition is strong, and I suggest we remain in formation, and deploy with our bows forward. If they want to grapple with us, then they are welcome. We will not become entangled until we are certain of what lies before us."

Dukas Myrrine barely hesitated as she continued to issue orders. Agesilaus in turn continued to identify ship squadrons and pointed to the exact position in the fleet. His only experience of large-scale naval combat had been at the Aulian Nebula, but for now he treated it all as a variant of a large-scale ground battle.

"All ships are firing, Strategos. Heavy cutters are forcing the Medes to move from their holding pattern."

"Good. Keep up the fire. I don't want to give them more than a second to think about what to do next. Now that we're here, I need to maintain the initiative."

He reached out and began plucking shapes out of thin air. The computer system detected his movement and tagged the various objects as he did so.

"The main formation looks good. Push the cruiser squadrons from Arcadia, Mantinea, and Lylos to the left to reinforce our flank. Push the escort carriers into our reserve line, and the Delphic squadrons in front of us."

That put a smile on the Dukas' face.

"What is it?"

She glanced back and looked to the ceiling of the ship.

"You describe a two-dimensional battle, Strategos."

Anybody else might have been offended at the insinuation, but not him. He knew where his strengths were, and this was not it.

"Of course. I want the Atticans kept in reserve and above us. We'll keep their speed and mastery for when the time demands it."

"And the battleships?"

Agesilaus licked his lips before answering.

"Spread them out in open-order, but I want overlapping fire arcs maintained.

"Yes, Strategos."

For the next thirty minutes it looked as though the Terran ships were performing an odd ballet. The ships constantly shifted about, but always keeping their bows directly to the large numbers of Median ships. There were now close to a hundred and fifty vessels over the planet, and with the same number of fighters racing off to do battle. Dukas Myrrine pointed ahead.

"Four Median cruisers are coming right at us, with another ten in a double column behind them. No...wait...there are new contacts."

Shapes flashed near the column, and soon another six large warships joined the group.

"That's an Elamite battle squadron. Twenty ships coming right at us. I think they intend on breaking our formation by piercing our line."

Agesilaus was not remotely surprised to see them, and in some respects actually much happier to see them on the battlefield, as he knew from his experience in the Hall of Heroes, as well as on the battlefield itself. Often the greatest enemy of all was the enemy that was unknown. This squadron of Elamites was a major force, and could only have been unleashed in an attempt to perform a surgical strike against his command ships. But then a glimmer of doubt entered his mind. He imagined that he was on the other side and facing off against powerful Terran ships. Ships that might be slower, but would invariably be better armoured and armed than the majority of those fielded by the Medes and their allies.

"Those markings look like Carian ships. They are the vanguard of Tissaphernes' Fleet. It could be as you say, but they may also be trying to box us in, forcing us to expose our flanks so we can use our broadsides. Whatever they want me to do, I will do the opposite, for now."

His attention moved to the tactical control display of the vast arsenal of weaponry available on his ship. No other Terran class of ship other than a Titan could unleash such firepower as this one. He then double-checked on the disposition of the enemy. Their column extended out like a spearhead towards the heart of his fleet.

We'll see if you hold your nerve...Medes.

"Activate the torpedo cells, and give them a volley. Pass on the order to our torpedo boats. Let's see how aggressive they are with sub-atomic phased warheads moving down their throats. I want the front of that column sent straight to Hades."

"Strategos."

Almost half the ships in the fleet carried at least a single torpedo launcher to give them the ability to deal with larger ships. One by one they opened fire, every one of them sending a powerful projectile towards the ships. They accelerated almost instantly to more than ten thousand metres per second. A streak of light extended from behind them, giving each torpedo the effect of a shooting star.

That's more like it.

He watched with interest as the mega battleships launched their powerful warheads. Agamemnon and Harbinger, known as The Twins to many in the fleet, unleashed the most powerful volleys. Both ships carried a pair of twenty-eight torpedo tubes on each pylon, and in less than a minute they'd launched from every one of them. Between the two of them a veritable swarm of torpedoes hurtled towards the advancing Median vessels.

"Reload the cells and fire again! I want those ships hit hard and fast. Make them understand the true meaning of fear."

It took another minute for each cell to load in another projectile, and they fired again. Agesilaus turned his attention to the viewscreens where icons showed the position of each torpedo.

"Excellent. Let's see how they deal with this rain of fire. Send in the light squadrons to harass them. But keep our heavies back and in formation. Drown them in torpedo fire."

Dukas Myrrine passed on his orders, and soon scores of smaller ships raced towards the advance column of Medes warships while still firing. Defensive fire from the Medes ships was heavily reduced, due to their compact formation, though anything that strayed towards the flanks soon came under overwhelming fire.

"Now we wait and watch as our weapons do their work."

Scores of torpedoes exploded as they were detonated by defensive fire, but five times as many hammered into the front of the lead Elamite battleships. Each impact knocked out part of a shield, and then another, until three of the ships were stripped open and vulnerable. Agesilaus clenched his fist with anticipation as more slammed into the long pincer-like bow sections, exploding against the armour itself. In seconds, they vanished behind a long series of explosions.

"This is our moment," he said confidently, tapping his communications node.

"This is the Strategos. I am ordering a general advance. Move in and engage the enemy. Good hunting."

He relaxed his shoulders, watching with satisfaction as the Terran ships crashed into the Median formation. His own line of battleships moved in close. He felt the gun batteries striking hard, and his crew looked less confident as red warnings began appearing along different parts of the ship.

"Take us in close, Dukas," he said firmly, "We'll take this battle to the place that brings fear to the hearts of all Medes. Up close and personal."

Seconds became minutes as the second wave of Terran warships advanced slowly upon the Medes. Cutters sent bright beams vast distances, cutting at shields and armour with relish. Missiles raced back and forth, but cut down by weapon batteries. But then they moved close enough to fire at point-blank range. This was where the armour and heavy flank batteries worked best. Walls of energy crashed into the Medes' ships as they scattered before the onslaught.

"Six ships are powering up their FTL engines. The rest are massing in five groups," said Dukas Myrrine, "And they're trying to pull back from our positions. Should we break our formation and pursue?"

"Yes, but inform every captain that I want them able to redeploy in seconds. The Medes want us to pursue so they can break apart our formation. Let them think they've won what they want."

The line of battleships sank deep into the fragmenting Median line, and then they opened fire at a range of a few kilometres. Agesilaus watched with satisfaction as the seven port batteries on his vessel opened fire. Each battery was equipped with a pair of heavy-duty plasma cannons, as well as integrated auto-shields that deactivated on the impact of firing the weapon. Long blue streaks burst towards the first already damaged Elamite. The ship tried to turn so that it could present its powerful double heavy cutter array to his ship, but Dukas Myrrine was ready for that. Rather than alter course, she simply sent orders for a pair of the ungainly looking Thorakitai cruisers to move in from the other side.

"Nice work, Dukas. If they move away, they can expected a double volley up their backside. Very nicely played."

The Thorakitai cruisers were perhaps the most common type of Terran warships in service, a disparate class, with each colony producing subtle variants of the same basic design. At roughly two-thirds the length of the battleships, they were still big, though a good deal smaller than the Median Elamite. They were flat looking ships, with most of their hull taken up with the armour and support systems for the flank-fitted weapon systems. The bow was broad, consisting primarily of layered armour to allow the ships to take a beating from the front when entering combat. All Thorakitai cruisers shared the same basic hull configuration, four weapon bays on each flank, a short hull, plus a heavily armoured bow and engine section. These two ships carried four Prusak Mk VI Antimatter pulse thrusters that provided the same power as used by battleships, but on a smaller vessel.

"They are in position, Strategos. And an Arcadian cruiser wing is moving in from above. Another six Thorakitai Cruisers."

"Good. Very good."

Thorakitai ships were designed to counter the powerful forward weaponry of the Median ships with a traditional Terran response. Rather than fitting heavier weapons, they'd been given even more powerful engines, and were adequately armed with four plasma batteries on each flank. Together, a pair of the Toxotai cruisers could put out a little more firepower than Agamemnon. Their great strength was not in their flank gun batteries, but in their speed and armour, there to give them an edge in battle. Multiple layers of curved plate armour, as well as primary and secondary shield generators made them almost as tough as the battleships they escorted.

"There!" Agesilaus said, "I knew they couldn't resist. If they have a reserve, it will…"

As if on cue, an entire horde of shapes appeared from the left. They moved forward in a wide crescent of almost twenty-five ships, the majority forming up into a single, wide line.

"You were correct, Strategos. Their reserve includes the best ships in the sector. And if I am not mistaken, their flagship is the Median Battleship Vairya."

"Vairya?"

Dukas Myrrine nodded as she enhanced the imagery of the vessel. At first glance it looked little different to those nearby, but as they moved closer, the difference in size became more apparent.

"The flagship of Tissaphernes?"

Dukas Myrrine nodded.

"Yes, a great monster, with long pincers containing launch decks, and enough armour and weaponry to take on even this ship."

Agesilaus' nostrils twitched.

"They are trying to entice me in to attack, are they not?"

Dukas Myrrine shrugged.

"Perhaps. What are your orders?"

Agesilaus knew what his heart told him to do. There was nothing he wanted more than to engage the best ship his enemy had. But he also wanted to win the battle, and take control of the region.

"Maintain formation. Transfer the Thespians to our left flank, and send in the reserve to assist. We will follow with a single squadron of six battleships once we've dealt with the first formation of ships."

"Strategos."

He turned his attention away from the newly arrived ships and focussed on the now scattered Median warships. The first three Elamites twisted and turned, trying to escape the horde of cruisers. Plasma streaked from side to side as they put volleys into the armour of the Elamites. One managed to turn around enough to line up its guns on a battleship, but a cruiser swooped in front and took the full impact. The ship was instantly sliced in half by the powerful volley.

"Now push on towards Tissaphernes' flagship," said Agesilaus.

The battleships crashed through the broken formation of Elamites, leaving them to be dealt with by roving squadrons. His ship led the line as it circled and pulled away from the main host, redeploying into a triple stacked line, with the battleships at the centre. Their long hulls looked impressive, with layered armour, and banks of batteries on each flank.

"Perfect. Now it's time to..."

Before he could say more, the approaching ships activated their forward heavy cutters. Each battleship was well equipped with these weapons, and they streamed away, breaking down shield after shield.

"Shields are down to forty percent," said Dukas Myrrine, "We cannot survive a frontal assault like this for much longer."

The rest of the ships continued forwards, but the Terrans returned fire, with the battleships and some of the more heavily armed cruisers striking with their forward weapons.

"They want to deal with us at long-range, and with their greater numbers. We'll soon deal with that problem," said Agesilaus, "Send in waves of torpedoes as before, and then overload our engines. Let's get in close and personal."

Agesilaus then walked along the deck towards doors and shafts that would take him down to the launch decks.

"Strategos? Where are you going?"

He looked back at his Dukas and smiled.

"I intend on boarding her."

Dukas Myrrine moved closer to him and shook her head.

"They will expect you to do that, Strategos. We need to thin out this fleet first. Getting you onboard in one piece could prove difficult."

She pointed towards the enemy flagship.

"The remaining Elamites are moving in to encircle her, and they are readying themselves for a final assault."

"Good. Then this is the perfect time to attack."

"Is it?" said the Dukas, this time in a firmer tone, "Did you not say your strategy was never to act as your enemy intended. If they are preparing for a boarding action, then they will move in close together, and that makes our job easier. Let me circle them at close-range, and use gunfire and armour to reduce them to slag."

Agesilaus' body itched for combat, but he was no egomaniac. He wanted victory for his fleet, not for himself. Watching the enemy refinements forming up into a defensive formation, he knew she was right.

"You are as wise, as you are brave, Dukas. Your reputation is well deserved."

He looked at the large mass of ships. They'd pulled back for a reason, and he could not believe it was from mere fear. Tissaphernes was a shrewd commander, and he would want Agesilaus to act in a particular way.

"Move to medium-range, but no closer. And hit them hard. Do not advance to boarding range under any circumstances."

"Of course, Strategos. We will fight your way."

"Exactly." A smile formed on his face, "I will fight this battle the way I choose to fight it, not the way he encourages me. If Kyniska was back here with her ships, I could use her starcarriers, and as many extra mercenaries as she could persuade Thibron to give up. They have given up their space and speed to protect themselves. Now is the time to strike with gunfire. Carry on as you were."

He waited in the centre of the deck, watching impotently as the Terran vessel withstood heavy fire as they circled like sharks around a shoal of fish. The gunfire was heavy, but at close-range the better-protected Terrans had the edge.

"All heavy warships have been fully engaged. We are fully invested in this battle now."

"I can see that. Launch all remaining fighters to assist our ships. And send in the troops carriers and volunteers. They have more than enough guns in place for this fight."

"But, Strategos…they are ill-suited to such a conflagration as this. Half of them are inexperienced."

"Those that live will no longer be able to say that, will they? We cannot fight in all places at once. Buy me time with ships…and trust me. The battle will be decided here, between our heavies, and the Medes' battleships. I want any ship not currently in action to head this way."

Dukas Myrrine returned to issuing commands to the armada. Agesilaus focussed on the formation of Median heavy warships at the centre of the spherical defensive formation. Every time he spotted one of the enemy battleships, it was firing its powerful cutters. They were not so useful at close-range, but any time they caught a ship in the open, the effect was terrible to watch. Then to his pleasure and surprise, a vessel in the middle of the enemy fleet exploded. The resulting blast managed to catch a trio of cruisers. They scattered away, creating gaps in the fleet.

"That should not have happened," said the Dukas, "That battleship's shields were down, but its armour was intact."

Then she gasped as another began to break up; exploding in a blast so great it enveloped two nearby cruisers.

"Bomb ships. That crafty Carian! He tried to pull me in for boarding actions so that he could do this. The Medes have no honour. They would assassinate me, and any other warriors that tried to take his ships."

"A bold strategy," Dukas Myrrine agreed, "It would have crippled many ships, and wiped out our best warriors. At the cost of ships he can afford to lose."

"He would love the battle to win the war. I must say. I am almost impressed. Almost! Now, move in fast and fire everything we have left! But stay out of range of the blasts. Their ships are not as we expected."

The four powerful Prusak Mk VI Antimatter pulse thrusters flared blue, and then white as they activated to full power. They accelerated slowly, but in seconds hurtled towards a close orbit around the Median vessels. More explosions marked the loss of other vessels, and then ships began to scatter, as the entire formation collapsed.

"Just look at that," said Agesilaus, "We could have lost

everything, and instead we have victory."

More Median ships turned away; others activated their FTL engines and jumped out of the battle. The battle was so confused some of the Medes' captains actually activated their jump engines while their comrades were still in front of them. Two Elamites broke apart due to the lightspeed collisions, and then the battle ended in a flash, and turned to an utter rout.

"Strategos, look!" Dukas Myrrine pointed to the shapes directly ahead.

"Fleeing from battle, this does not surprise me," Agesilaus said as the Vairya disappeared before his very eyes. Left behind were the pitiful remnants of the Elamite squadrons and dozens of damaged ships. More and more vessels activated their FTL engines, and then the battle was over as quickly as it had begun.

"I…I can't believe it." Dukas Myrrine watched the rest of the Median fleet limp away. Dozens of ships were still on the battlefield, but all of them were moving away, or picking up landing craft and shuttles, "Should we send the main ground troops to the surface?"

Agesilaus shook his head.

"No, victory in space will seal their fate. I want these Medes chased from the entire system. No mercy, if they leave their gun ports open, hammer them hard. If they remain intact, then send in the boarding parties. Chase down every last warship until Ephesus is secured."

"And the transports? There are fifteen heavy troop transports and seven assault ships in orbit."

"Leave them be. I want them left there."

Dukas Myrrine appeared confused for a moment.

"Leave them? But they are vulnerable, and their escorts are leaving as we speak."

"Most of them are, but not all. I remember my lessons from

back home, Dukas Myrrine. One important lesson is to always provide your enemy with a way out. Put their backs to the wall, and they will fight like lions. Give them a means to leave, and many will break and flee."

He then licked his lips.

"But you are not wrong. And we have allies that remain unblooded. A little ground combat could be just the thing, and this is a useful opportunity."

"Yes? What are your orders?"

"Send the Argives and the Mantineans down to the Citadel. A thousand should do the trick. It's time to see if they're here for the booty or the fighting. I cannot afford any dead weight in this campaign."

"Only a thousand?"

He smiled at her.

"Trust me. When the Medes see the last of their ships leaving, they will think twice before pushing on with their attack. Self-preservation usually trumps all. They will leave."

If Kyniska had made it back here to see this victory. The war might already be over.

"And if they do not leave?"

Agesilaus clenched his fist. He wanted victory, and he wanted it as quickly as possible. But if a single ship wanted to hold back, he had absolutely no issue with continuing the battle.

"Then they will die."

CHAPTER SEVENTEEN

Olympian Citadel, Ephesus Prime
Elli adjusted the ocular scanner built into her helmet's visual targeting array and checked the distant defences. Dawn had broken minutes earlier, and much of the area was still shrouded in long shadows. The Medes and their Mulac lackeys had pushed hard over the last few days, and now it was almost impossible to see more than a kilometre due to the thick columns of black smoke rising upwards.

This is what the depths of Tartarus must look like. Dark and veiled in horrors.

She leaned back for a moment and looked back at her new home. The bastions were nothing but ruins, replaced by the great machines of war brought by the Medes. The Citadel wall was slightly curved at this point and functioned much like a long curtain wall of a fortress. Each end of the mighty wall buttressed directly into the side of the mountain, giving the effect of being one stone structure. Elli's hidden gunnery position was one of hundreds that allowed defenders the ability to fire down in relative safety. She was protected by over three metres of metal and stone to the front. An angular roof sheltered them from strikes overhead, though much of it was now cracked and partially broken.

I cannot believe we're still alive. This place should have fallen days ago.

The flicker of dozens of lights betrayed the rough position of machines and hardware now installed in a vast ring around the Citadel. It was more like something from an ancient siege than a fixed battle. Every few seconds a single shot fired from the Citadel as a sniper tried to push back the encircling enemy, and each time a powerful response from dozens of guns would crash back into the defences.

"How does it look?" said a voice from behind her, and hiding in the shadows.

"Same as before," she replied without moving.

Using the device, she could see hundreds, perhaps thousands of shapes moving, individual people as well as machines and armoured vehicles. Tracked artillery rotated slowly searching for signs of life along the wall, and heavy bombard machines fired every ten minutes, hurling massive shells against the defences.

Not good. They're massing for a big…a really big attack.

Something glinted light, and her reactions instantly kicked in. She ducked down behind tower thirteen of the bastion, and a powerful volley of fire hammered into the stonework.

"Head's down!" shouted an officer.

The survivors at the defences had managed to live through multiple brutal firefights. More than merely men and women who had survived the impossible, they were all now combat veterans. Each had heard the thunder of artillery, the crack of Doru rifles, and the howls and screams of Mulacs smashing their way inside. Komes Andronis, commander of the Arcadian contingent, slipped down beside her, and tapped the top of her helm. She instantly spun around and almost struck him.

"Well?"

Elli deactivated her faceplate and wiped the sweat from her skin.

"They're massing for another assault."

As she slid into position, an entire line of spatharii opened fire. Dozens of them waited along the battlements, yet their numbers seemed insignificant compared to what faced them. At her side, Kentarchos Alexis struggled to fit a new coil into his Doru rifle. He struck it for the third time, but rather than fixing the thing, it started a low pitch whine that quickly increased in intensity,

"Throw it…now!" shouted one of the soldiers.

Kentarchos Alexis looked confused as he stared back down at the thing, so Elli reached over, yanked it from his hands, and tossed it over the wall. It made it halfway down before exploding violently. The blast tore open yet another hole in the defences. She gasped at spotting dark shapes climbing up the wall. They looked different to the others, with strange hooks fitted to the hands of their armour, and metal spikes they embedded into the stonework to provide grab holds.

"Everybody back!" Elli cried, "Mulacs are coming up the walls!"

She stepped back as the wall in front vanished in a flash of light and energy. The intensity forced her to look away. A few Terrans returned fire, but the Mulacs had succeeded, and burst onto the top of the fortification. Many jumped down and opened fire with stunted carbines, showering the battlements with blue and red light. Many Terrans were hit and in seconds running for their lives.

"Hold the line!" Alexis shouted, but panic had set in. One

Arcadian even barged at his flank, knocking him to the ground in his haste to escape. The man then clambered over rubble, taking a hit in the back. He fell down face first, not before the pulse-carbine burnt a hole through his back and out through his chest. Elli had met fear before, but as the black armoured Mulacs swarmed over the walls, she felt it once again. She lifted her weapon and fired, but no sooner had she hit one Mulac, another clambered up behind it.

"Down!" said a voice to her right.

Without thinking, she instantly dropped to one knee, and a unit of oddly equipped Terrans pushed on past. Their uniforms and armour gleamed, and their Pilos style helmets different to the more archaic helms worn by most of the Arcadians along this part of the wall. They advanced and formed into a line. One in three carried shield generators, and soon a scattering of shields appeared in front of them.

"Front rank kneel!"

Fifteen or sixteen dropped to their knees. Some lifted up their shield projectors to create a loose barricade of protective energy.

"Second and third ranks close up."

Elli watched in astonishment as the hundred or more soldiers formed up into a dense line, three ranks deep, and every single one of them pointing their weapons towards the horde of Mulacs.

"Volley fire…on my command."

Shots glanced off the formation, and two of the soldiers were cut down by heavy Mulac fire. At the same time, enemy snipers tried to pick off individuals.

Fire!"

A massive boom shook the ground as each of them fired. Most carried pulse rifles, but a good percentage also carried much more powerful weaponry. These plascannons were not the same weapons she was used to, but the very short-ranged weapons used by some Laconian and Argive heavy infantry in siege warfare and ship boarding actions.

"Wow!" Elli kept her head down.

The volley of pulse rifles was impressive, but the plascannons were horrific weapons of war. Each shot obliterated anything standing in its path, continuing onwards, and finally exploding in a bright flash of collapsed matter.

"Keep firing!"

The plascannons barely looked like guns, with their square shapes and four hexagonal muzzles used to generate the pulse of plasma energy. Cables ran to the shield generator units carried by others soldiers, providing energy for the weapon, as well as their personal Aspis shield projector. It was a strange sight, seeing them advancing in pairs. Yet what they lacked in individual flexibility, they made up for in protection and firepower.

"Cease fire!"

The fire and smoke cleared, and Elli gasped at the scene of destruction. The morning's sun streamed through the myriad of holes and cracks in the Citadel. She sat down on what could have been the floor, or just as easily a piece of the wall, and closed her eyes. The sound of battle soon faded, though the crackle of gunshots served as a reminder that the enemy was not surrendering on the spot.

"Look," said Alexis, "They're being recused by their landing ships."

She rose to her feet and moved to the side of the firing position. It was completely open to the elements and covered in the bodies of Mulac, Medes, and Terran alike. Scattered groups of black armoured soldiers leapt into small spacecraft, trying to escape. Some fired back at the Citadel, but it was sporadic and with little real intent. By the time the last of them had left, the sun was a good deal higher in the sky, and Elli could feel its warmth against her skin. Alexis leant again the wall and drank from a flask handed to him by an Argive soldier. He then reached out to Elli.

"You need to stay hydrated."

She took a sip, and then closed her eyes, letting the moment wash over her. The brutality of the fighting had been terrible, but now the absence of it seemed equally odd. Finally, her breathing slowed, and she felt calm spreading through her body.

"I don't know how you survived so long," said the officer, "But you'll be pleased to know that the Laconian Agesilaus, the new Basileus has arrived. He's here with more than a hundred thousand warriors, and an entire fleet."

Elli opened her eyes, but before she spoke the officer had gone, leaving her with the few survivors of the Citadel defence. Two were speaking with Alexis, before finally moving back into the wreckage of the Citadel. Alexis moved to Elli's side and looked at her carefully. He could see she'd taken a beating in the fight, although her armour remained intact, and she appeared lightly wounded from the gunfire and shrapnel.

"Some of my people are looking for new ships to crew. But the others…they want payback."

He looked into her eyes and tried to gauge what she was thinking.

"What are you going to do?"

"I'm not sure. Ephesian Command will need at least three months, maybe more to start construction on new light cruisers. Until then, I can help train the officer corps…or look to other things."

For a moment Elli was confused.

"What do you mean?"

He shrugged.

"My ship is gone, and my crew are dead or being invalided out for injuries and time served. The rest are thinking of joining this armada to get some justice against the Medes."

"They can do that? I thought you were all Navy?"

"Kind of. We're contracted to crew ships. No ships, no work."

"Like me," said Elli.

"Yeah, I thought as much. Look…I'm thinking of going with them. This place has seen too much destruction for my liking. It's taken a lot of my friends with it."

He winced as he said that, and she reached out to hold his forearm. The two were complete strangers, or had been until this great calamity. Any other pair might want to stay well away from ships or war, and yet the very idea of travelling on some great expedition seemed to appeal to them on a deep, almost philosophical level.

"We'll get paid for the duration, and after that…who knows? It could be quite the adventure…they reckon."

"Maybe. Or quite a way of getting killed."

The naval commander grinned back at her. Alexis missed his ship, but his lost crew he missed most of all. Staying, while they left on new adventures was the last thing he wanted right now.

"Perhaps. But it could be interesting finding out. Want to come with us?"

Elli looked at the bodies all around them and the ruins of the Citadel. Ephesus had been little more than a way station to her for the last few years. And now, in the middle of all of this, she'd befriended the crew of a ship she'd never even seen before. Today, of all days, that seemed important.

"Why not? If we stay here, we'll probably get press-ganged into the city's levies. I'll come with you."

* * *

Olympian Citadel, Ephesus Prime
Agesilaus walked through the ruins of the Citadel, while his warriors advanced in groups to check for signs of the enemy. Ephesian flags and banners were already flying high, now joined by those of his forces.

"So this is what victory looks like."

His heavily armed boots crunched on the rubble, his mechanical leg whining. It didn't take long to reach the final structure that was built into the cliffs. The roof dome was broken, and large chunks of it scattered along the floor. Bodies of Mulacs were even now being dragged away. There were many battered and wounded soldiers, yet they watched in silence as Agesilaus joined their commanders on the raised part of the senate floor. They waited patiently inside the shattered structure. Agesilaus had never seen the place in its heyday, and now the place was an utter ruin.

"Hail, Basileus. Welcome, victor of Ephesus," said an Ephesian Dukas.

It could have been abandoned for a thousand years based on the damage he could see. Leaders from each of the Terran factions waited in a loose group, while Laconian Epilektoi protected every entrance to the facility. At Agesilaus' side was Komes Diogenes. The man's eyes never seemed to stop as he looked for signs of danger to his Basileus.

"Thank you. The victory was not mine, but that of every man and woman that stood in the phalanx, both in space, and here, on your sacred soil. It is…"

He stopped as one of his trusted auletes approached.

"The Emissary has arrived. He will be here within the minute."

"Emissary?" asked the Ephesian.

"As I expected," said Agesilaus, "The Beast of Caria is here to negotiate."

"Tissaphernes?" asked the man in horror, "He is here?"

Agesilaus nodded, but focussed his attention on his own warriors.

"Keep your eyes open. You will recall what happened the last time a Laconian commander met with this scum."

Komes Diogenes nodded as an Ephesian junior officer rushed into the grand old building. The Epilektoi raised their weapons, and the sound made the Ephesian stop in his tracks.

"He is here, Strategos."

Agesilaus look away from the Terran, and towards the small group of Medes soldiers. They were not Imperial foot soldiers, but a group of Carians, the nobility to which Tissaphernes was a member. They were armoured and carried firearms at their sides. Moving ahead of them was a single grand figure.

Can it be? Is our hated foe before us?

Agesilaus reached down to his side, seeking a blade to fight with. A single slash and cut could end this war right now, in the opening few days. But then he remembered what his sister Kyniska had told him.

Never act as the enemy wish, my Brother.

So he waited and let the group approach. With a simple hand gesture, his bodyguard moved back to give them space. It left him vulnerable, a risk he was willing to take. To his astonishment, standing in front of him was a robot, crafted to look the spitting image of his archrival Tissaphernes. Its face was a curved display that almost looked real, though the illusion was lost whenever the thing moved.

"We have no issue with Laconia, Great King," said the artificial Tissaphernes with a mock bow, "We wish a peaceful coexistence with our Terran kin. The violence in this sector is merely an internal policing issue."

It was enough to send Agesilaus into a rage, but he managed to restrain himself. Attacking the projected image would do nothing for his reputation, and there was simply nothing he could do that would affect his foe.

"Policing? And yet you rain down fire on our colonies."

"Our?"

"Yes. Every one of the twenty-four colonies houses large numbers of my kin. I am here to ensure their lives, and their futures."

"Of course. And I am here to maintain the peace. What do you propose?"

Agesilaus licked his lips before issuing his demands.

"You will leave this system, return to your Satrapy, and leave the peoples of the Territories to themselves. You will not raise another fleet, to do so will incur my wrath."

"And you will leave also?"

Agesilaus smiled.

"Not yet. I have sustained losses, and each colony needs a thorough inspection and engineering assistance. I will remain for as long as is required to ensure this peace is maintained."

The robot paused, and for a second it looked like it might agree.

"I cannot agree to these terms."

Agesilaus placed his hand on the hilt of his blade, but the machine spoke before he drew it.

"Only the God King can agree to such terms."

Agesilaus tried to assess whether the robot was telling the

truth. It was hard to tell, as every gesture could have been pre-programmed in advance. He didn't even know if he was actually talking to Tissaphernes, or if the machine was speaking on its own behalf.

"Very well. Until you return with an offer from your master, there shall be peace between us. Neither of us will prepare for violence against each other, and neither will move against the other."

The robot bowed ever so slightly.

"I accept."

"And how can I know that this is you, and that you will honour your deal?"

The machine's face vanished, and in its place appeared a complex and detailed shape for all to see. It shifted continually, but they all knew exactly what it was. A Laconian bodyguard stepped forward and scanned the shape.

"It is confirmed. It is the seal of Satrap Tissaphernes."

"I offer my seal as proof of my acceptance. Until the God King makes his decision, there shall be peace between us."

The machine turned and walked away, but not before Agesilaus called after him.

"Break your word, Tissaphernes, and I will rain down hellfire on Caria."

* * *

Median Battleship 'Vairya', The Ionian Territories
Tissaphernes opened his eyes and gazed at the remnants of his fleet. Inside the command chamber there was room just for him. All around him was open space, a projection of the reality of his situation, one he was not overly happy with. Far, far away was a small dot that represented Ephesus. It was close

enough to see, but now well and truly out of his grasp.

"Enough."

The device opened up slowly, and revealed him to the long command deck filled with automaton officers. As always, his Sarvan was present and busily issuing commands to them. Waiting at the top of the steps was the immaculately dressed Darbabad Forouzandeh. At her side, a single exquisite Makhaira blade. Something Tissaphernes had not noticed before.

"I gave you more than fifty ships, including Carian and Lelegian vessels. And now we have lost Ephesus. I have been forced to concede to this Laconian. Tell me this is where I need to be."

She looked at him with an expressionless face.

"This is exactly what you needed, my Lord. The enemy is now here, far from home and vulnerable. Their supply routes are long, and their list of allies is short."

"Perhaps. But now I have two enemies to deal with, the Laconians and their lackeys to my front, and Pharnabazus snapping at my heels. I can deal with one, but not both."

"True," said Darbabad Forouzandeh, "Agesilaus has brought more troops and ships than you implied. I suggest the best course of action is the one you already know. It will take time, but time is how we will grind them down. Time, and coin will erode their power."

"So you suggest I wait?"

Darbabad Forouzandeh shook her head.

"No. We must prepare for the real battle."

Tissaphernes seemed to like that.

"Yes…that is true. I will act as though I am contacting the God King for aid, as promised. And in the meantime, you will help me assemble every ship from here to the Core Worlds."

He nodded to himself as another idea sprung to mind.

"You will take a squadron of warships to the Phrygian Territories and notify Pharnabazus that I intend on calling upon our treaty. He must prepare his forces to join me in battle."

"What if he refuses?"

"Tell him that if I fail, the Terrans will be coming for him. And I will ensure every surviving Median soldier and officer joins Agesilaus against him."

Even Darbabad Forouzandeh seemed surprised to hear that.

"A bold move indeed, my Lord."

CHAPTER EIGHTEEN

Olympian Citadel, Ephesus Prime
One week later

The games were an impressive occasion, and even the Laconians seemed to enjoy the festivities. Most of the military commanders from the expedition were there, and though nearly all the buildings on Ephesus Prime were clear of rubble, it was evidently the scene of a great and terrible battle. In front of the assembled dignitaries were more than a hundred men and women, all stripped down to the bare minimum of clothing, and competing in dozens of events.

Agesilaus should have been enthralled by what was happening, but his attention was drawn to a detailed mapping module he held in his hand. It showed the status of the nearby territories near to Ephesus, as well as known ship positions. Try as he might, he could not pull his attention from the reports of ship movements in the Phrygia System, home to the mighty Satrap and warlord, Pharnabazus.

"What is it?" Komes Diogenes asked.

Agesilaus looked to the leader of his bodyguard.

"Tissaphernes is gone…and has retreated back to Lydia and beyond. If I act against him, I will have to enter the Empire. And then I risk open war with the God King himself."

"We can deal with him, and anything the God King can muster."

"Perhaps, but what of Pharnabazus and his fleet? While we fight each other, he continues to build ships. If these reports are accurate, his shipbuilding programme is colossal. Soon he will have enough to match every Terran fleet…combined."

"A problem. But a problem merely waits for the solution to be found."

"Indeed."

Agesilaus turned his attention to the fighters. To the left nine individuals were all pushing their bodies to the limits, lifting heavy objects and weight. To the right two groups were engaged in mock battles with synthetic blunted weapons.

"An impressive sight," said Kaarja, indicating towards four pairs of fighters. They circled each other before rushing in with a series of strikes and grapples. One group in particular consistently threw their opponents to the ground, to the approval of the baying crowd.

"It would appear even your Laconians struggle in the Pankration against my warriors."

"There is no dishonour in being bested in physical combat against a strong opponent," said Diogenes.

At that moment, one of the naked Laconians ducked passed the much stronger Minotaurion and slammed a foot hard into his opponent's stomach. The powerful Minotaurion dropped to the ground, and before he could regain his balance, the Laconian was on top and punching away.

"Strength is not the only decider in battle, my friend," said

Agesilaus.

Shouting spread through the great exhibition space as a runner entered, rushing past all of them and towards the stand filled with dignitaries. Dozens of soldiers moved to stop him, yet on he came. One guard swung a blade and struck the man in the face. He went down hard, gasping with pain as he lay there.

"Leave him be." Agesilaus stepped down the steps to the open ground, "I know this soldier. Bring him to me."

Two helped carry and drag the poor soul towards Agesilaus, dumping him unceremoniously on the ground. The man struggled to breathe, and Agesilaus shook his head, signalling the others to back away.

"Get a breath, young man. Ready yourself before you speak."

The man bent forward, gasping several times as he inhaled far too much air. Seconds ticked by until finally he straightened up and shook his head.

"Apologies, Strategos. I came as soon as I heard."

"Heard what?"

The entire exhibition space was now silent, as hundreds listened to what was being said. The man looked about nervously, and then tried to move closer.

"There are ears all around us."

"It doesn't matter, son. If you can tell me, then you can tell my friends gathered here."

The man licked his lips, took in a deep breath, and spoke as clearly as he could.

"One of Strategos Thibron's deep range scout ships has made contact from outside the Median Core Worlds. Imperial ships pursued them, but they bring news of Tissaphernes, and his betrayal. Thibron himself sent this encoded signal directly to this system...to warn you."

"Yes?"

The man seemed unsure as to whether he should continue. So he handed a small device to Agesilaus. He took it and examined the data carefully. It was logged and marked, confirming it was authentic and coming directly from the Laconian commander.

"Fascinating, Thibron confirms that Tissaphernes has made no attempt to contact the God King, as promised to me. Instead, he is raising vast forces in his satrapies."

Agesilaus' nostrils twitched as he lifted his gaze to the man.

"Tissaphernes has broken our treaty?"

The man nodded feverishly.

"Yes, Strategos. Tissaphernes is calling upon his levies to mobilise as for war. He must be preparing to return here to finish what he started."

Agesilaus looked out towards the myriad of men and women.

"Did you all hear that? Our deep-range scouts confirm that Tissaphernes has betrayed us, that he has broken his promise, and prepares even now to wage war against us. Will you let his betrayal stand?"

Most shouted back all manner of bitterness and insults towards the Satrap.

"Auletes!" Agesilaus called out.

The officer moved up to him and nodded.

"Yes, Strategos?"

"Contact Tissaphernes, and pass him this message."

Agesilaus spoke loudly so that every Terran present could hear him. The officer took a deep breath as he waited for the momentous words from his commander.

"Tell him that he has broken his scared oath to me, to the Ionian Territories, and to this fleet. I give him three weeks to surrender himself to me, here on Ephesus Prime, for trial and sentence."

"Is that the entire message, Strategos?"

Agesilaus shook his head.

"No, it is not. Tell him that if he does not present himself to me within twenty-one days, I will come and get him myself, but not until I have burnt every colony in Caria to the ground. I will leave his cities nothing more than ash, and his people sold into slavery. Then I will enlist those that wish to join me and travel to the Core Worlds, and destroy the Empire... personally."

The auletes gulped, and then nodded. "Yes, Strategos."

He turned and left, leaving Agesilaus and his entourage in silence.

"Walk with me."

Agesilaus moved from the open floor and along the grand hall. Many watched him, but then he stopped and called out to them.

"Continue with the games. Trust me, you will thank your officers for it when we come to battle with Tissaphernes once more."

Some of the senior officers barked commands, and the games continued. Agesilaus, however, walked out through an arch that led outside to a wide viewing point. He kept going until reaching what was left of the stone wall. On the other side was a huge drop of several hundred metres. Smoke columns still rose to the skies from the many remaining fires throughout Ephesus.

"Close the doors."

Four of his bodyguard stepped in to push the mighty doors shut behind him, so that it was just him, and two dozen of the most senior men and women in the fleet. They waited for him to speak, but he remained silent. Agesilaus glanced at each in turn, assessing their state of mind based on what they had just heard and seen. Finally, one of the Mantineans spoke.

"Agesilaus. We cannot go to war with the Empire, not yet. The rest of the Territories require our protection."

Agesilaus laughed.

"I have no intention of attacking him...not yet."

That stunned every single one of them. Kaarja, the leader of the Minotaurus contingent grunted and growled, saying what each of them was probably thinking.

"You will back down on your threat?"

Agesilaus' expression turned as he looked at the aged warrior.

"No. We will do what the Medes would never expect. I will point my spear in one direction towards Tissaphernes. He already knows I will be coming for him. I want every captain, trader, and soldier to know my destination."

He then grinned.

"But then we will strike in a completely different direction. Tomorrow we mobilise every ship available and head in a direction the Medes would never expect. I plan on hitting Pharnabazus while his fleet sits at anchor. Knocking out a Satrap from this war tomorrow, and we will be in a stronger position than at any time in our history."

The others gasped at the audacity. Kaarja in particular seemed positively thrilled at the idea.

"Destroy his fleet, and he will be impotent. Terrans and Medes alike will flock to join this armada. Tissaphernes will have little chance of victory. It is a bold, and unexpected move. I'm with you."

It took a second, but eventually each of them extended their arms to grasp his.

"Good. Then go back to your people and enjoy the games. For tomorrow we go to war, and we will see the ships of Pharnabazus burn at their moorings."

CHAPTER NINETEEN

Battleship 'Agamemnon', Phrygian Territories
Five days later
The fleet crashed through the dust clouds of the Phrygian
Territories as they travelled towards their destination, each ship
leaving long trails that would last for months to come. There
were new ships with them now, with two large formations of
Ephesian warships in the armada. Leading the fleet were the
elegant and deadly looking Triremis cruisers, moving like razor-
sharp spears through enemy territory. Agesilaus paced about
on the deck as the hours finally turned to minutes. He was
dressed head-to-toe in his full battle attire, and every officer on
the deck was ready for the fight to come.

"Show me the tactical map again," he said to Dukas Myrrine,
"I want to see what this so-called warlord has waiting for us."

Dukas Myrrine nodded patiently as she brought up the
imagery of the Dascylium planetary system. He'd gone over it
hundreds of time before they'd even left the Ephesus System,
and it looked no different now.

"This is with the latest updates from our scout ships?"

Dukas Myrrine walked to the side of the table and pointed to the planet.

"Half of Pharnabazus' Phrygian fleet is at its moorings, with the rest spread throughout the system. Even moored, there are more than enough ships to deal with us. As soon as we arrive, they will come at us, hard and fast."

She moved her hands to pull back from the star system. It showed the entire area with planets, moons, and space stations.

"But over half of their heavy warships are not accounted for."

Agesilaus pointed to one of the platforms orbiting the planet.

"Each of these is capable of handling multiple capital ships. I still cannot neutralise them all with gunfire. We will have to send ground troops against some of them. It's going to happen fast, and we'll lose a lot of soldiers. Once we're entangled, these missing ships could jump in and hit us hard."

"Perhaps. That is why I think we should use the backup plan."

Agesilaus started to speak, and then stopped when a single image appeared in the middle of the deck.

"Brother."

He turned about to face her, and sighed with relief at seeing her face. Like him, she was dressed for battle. Other officers were nearby, and though wearing unfamiliar armour, he already knew it as the style worn by the infamous Black Legion. He knew she'd manage to muster a number of ships, but still had no idea of exactly what forces she'd persuaded Thibron to hand over.

"You made it."

"Made it? We're fifteen minutes away from the target. And

before you ask, yes, I've brought quite a few friends."

"I never had any doubts. Based on our scout's reports, we'll need every ship and soldier we can muster. The threat is bigger than any of us ever expected."

"First one to get to Pharnabazus gets to be Strategos for the month. Deal?"

Agesilaus laughed back at her.

"Kyniska, how could I argue with that?"

"I've brought quite a host. We might even take the planet before you can climb off your throne and get involved."

She was making light of the situation, but Agesilaus could tell there was tension in her body. She was never worried about combat, but this was something so much bigger than the two of them. They'd brought half the mercenaries in the Terran colonies to this fight, and if they failed, they'd leave their homeland permanently weakened.

"I want you to attack first. Send the Black Legion against the Phrygian Fleet and pound them hard. I need them to believe this is everything we have."

Kyniska took a step closer, and part of her vanished from view. Then she lowered her head so that it seemed twice as big to her brother.

"I will bring fire and fury against them. The Black Legion are all veterans. I will make one ship seem like ten, but don't take too long, Brother. Eventually, their numbers will overwhelm us."

He smiled at her, and then cleared his throat.

"I'll be there. And my ships will shatter every vessel they have at their moorings. We will cause massive damage, and then we leave. I don't want to linger in this system."

"Agreed," she sounded disappointed.

Agesilaus could see she wanted more, but both knew how

precarious their situation was.

"Now…you were missed at Ephesus. It was quite the fight."

"Don't worry. There are more than enough battles ahead of us. I will see you soon."

Agesilaus clenched his fist, and then pressed his forearm to his chest.

"Fight well, Sister."

"And you…Brother."

* * *

Bactrian Grand Battleship 'Aegospotami', Dascylium, Phrygian Territories

The battle over the fire-swept planet of Dascylium began as many battles did, with surprise, confusion, followed by utter devastation. The planet was not just the most powerful planetary colony in the star system, but the capital of the Phrygian Territories. The Median Warlord and Satrap, Pharnabazus called this place his home, and it was an area no Terran would dare travel unasked for. Yet on this very day the Terrans arrived in overwhelming numbers. And they were arrayed for one purpose only, war.

First to enter the area was the ancient Terran battleship. She burst into the heavily defended Dascylium sector with all the brutality and violence the Terrans could muster; right behind her came four Terran battleships, each almost as big as the much older vessel, and baring the insignia of their native states. They were all different, though shared the same basic hull design.

A series of small flashes marked the denotation of numerous mines that littered the system, providing a defence against stray ships jumping into the system. Against any other vessels they might have caused damage, but not against this mighty behemoth. Aegospotami. These were not raiders or pirates, but the lead ships of the Black Legion, the most famous mercenary flotilla in history. And they had been tasked with the difficult job of tackling the largest ships the Empire could muster. They travelled into battle as only they knew how, engines on full burn, and gun ports wide open. The stars slowed down, and then they arrived in high orbit over the planet. Their shields activated, and the entire region filled with fire and flame.

The Median Empire might have the largest fleets in existence, but they could not be everywhere at once. The planet was still well defended from most attacks with an entire division of seven Elamite battleships and their escort cruisers, all baring the colours of Phrygia. It was an impressive force of fifteen ships, more than enough to beat off even the bravest marauding pirate or corsair. Many times more ships were moored to the dozens of orbital platforms, stations, and shipyards, and so far none of them had moved. The Elamite battleships might be half kilometre-long behemoths bristling with weapons, but they paled to insignificance as the larger vanguard of the Terran invasion force arrived. In the first ten seconds, three more squadrons of Terran ships arrived, and more joined them with each passing second. The battleship squadron and its flagship, the Bactrian Grand Battleship led them. No sooner had they arrived, than they boosted their engines and accelerated directly at the Medes ships.

Komes Devereux, the commander of the Grand Battleship paced about inside the ancient and lavishly decorated combat chamber. It was designed to be the perfect setting for a prince or other noble to command from. But she was neither, and nothing more than a naval officer. What she lacked in nobility and bloodline, she more than made up with a decade's worth of experience in war. She looked at her targets with interest, quickly identifying the strongest and most capable of her foes. Images of the defensive force over the planet were visible in all directions, but the formation of Elamites drew her ire. Her nostrils visibly twitched as she looked down at them. She was so busy she almost missed the sound of her tactical officer.

"Komes. The enemy are deploying into line of battle. They're firing." said Dekarchos Icarus, "I'm seeing a lot of plasma fire coming this way. More ships are launching from the orbital shipyards. They believe they can stop us."

"As expected. These Medes are used to always being at the top of the tree. What they don't know is that we're just the beginning. If they had half a brain they'd jump, and get help... fast."

She then turned to her chief engineer.

"Direct all energy reserves to the forward shield emitters. I'm going to ram Aegospotami right down their throats."

Dekarchos Icarus nodded as he moved his hands rapidly over the displays. Like most of the officers on the Grand Battleship, he was a veteran of countless battles, and had served with Devereux for the last two years. They worked like a well-oiled machine.

"Shields are active and overloaded. Nothing is getting through... for now."

"Excellent, Icarus. As always."

Her line of sight shifted along to the next officer on the deck.

"Dekarchos Patras, are the forward cutter arrays ready?"

"Yes, Komes," he quickly replied, "The coils are fully functional, and reserve units charged and ready. We're ready to fire on your command."

"And our plasma batteries?"

He checked the displays for what must have been the fourth time.

"Every deck is reporting as active and ready for battle. Gunnery officers await your command."

"Excellent. Target the lead ship and open fire. Send these coordinates to the other battleships so we can coordinate fire. I want saturation fire to hit every vessel in their arsenal."

A gentle shudder ran along the length of the ship as it opened fired one deck at a time. A smaller vessel might struggle with the gunfire, but the Grand Battleship was barely affected due to its thick bulkheads and heavy armour.

"Auletes. Put me on with Princess Kyniska."

"Yes, Komes."

The communications officer brought up a direct connection almost instantly. The holographic image of a woman floating slightly above the deck; Kyniska was an impressive looking warrior, even in her distorted state shown over the communications system. As usual, she was dressed in full Laconian battle attire. From the long flowing cloak, and gold and crimson detailing, it was obvious she was an elite Laconian, the cream of Laconia, and only a small number in the entire League.

"Komes. What is it?"

It wasn't so much a rebuff, but it did serve as a reminder that to the Laconians, she was still considered an outsider, and always would be.

"The vanguard has arrived. The Arcadian and Thessalian contingents are in position as agreed, and I am ready to engage the enemy taskforce. I am sending in my ships directly at them."

"Good...as we planned it."

"Where is the rest of the fleet? The Laconians have not yet arrived under the command of the Strategos. They were supposed to assist me in this attack. I…"

"Komes. You understand your part in this operation, do you not?"

She hesitated before answering. The Strategos was effectively a god on the battlefield, and every single commander in the fleet followed his orders without question. Nonetheless, she remained ever suspicious of his motives in this battle.

"Of course, Princess Kyniska. My division is to draw out the enemy fleet from the protection of the planetary orbital platforms. I thought that…"

She stopped speaking as warnings sounded.

"We've got trouble. They are launching fighters and moving in to engage. It looks like they were not as slow to respond as we thought. I have also…"

Both stopped speaking as a bright beam as wide as a battleship extended out from the planet below. It raced up into space and struck the side of a Thessalian Toxotai Cruiser. The ship's shield turned bright white, and then vanished a moment before the entire vessel exploded in a sub-atomic blast. When the light cleared, there was nothing left of the ship, other than a growing cloud of dust and micro fragments.

"What in the name of Zeus is that?" Kyniska demanded.

Komes Devereux stumbled backwards as she watched the beam extend out again, this time cutting an entire battleship clean in two. In seconds, the Terran fleet began to lose cohesion as ship commanders changed course to avoid the devastating weapon.

"I've…I've never seen anything like it. Not even our Titans can unleash firepower of that magnitude."

Kyniska shook her head while snarling.

"It came from the surface, did it not?"

Komes Devereux turned her gaze to her tactical screens,

while her senior officers sent her the latest, and most detailed analysis of the information.

"It's a shielded weapon installation on the planet. It appears to be coming from the palace."

Kyniska leaned forward, as though that would provide her with a better view. But then more warnings activated around them.

"What is it now?"

Komes Devereux concentrated on the nearest screen, and began counting the number of new groups arriving.

"Pharnabazus must have called for help. I'm detecting more ships entering the system. He must have recalled every ship in the Phrygia Territories for this battle."

"I expected as much," said Kyniska, "He sent panic into our fleet with this wonder weapon of his, and then brought in his reserves. He wants to scare us into leaving."

"He has a point. If we stay, we'll lose a good many ships."

She then pointed towards something out of sight.

"You may be right, but check the platforms," said Kyniska, "And try not to smile too hard. If I'm not mistaken, we arrived well before they were ready. They may have a reserve and heavy weapons on the surface, but they are still vulnerable. I say we stay and end this...right now. Next time we try, he could have three times as many ships here."

Another beam reached out, but this time the ships were looking for it. One cruiser caught part of the attack and its stern tore apart and off into space. Luckily, its secondary thrusters propelled it away from the next burst of fire from the planet. Dekarchos Icarus gasped.

"Komes. I count at least forty vessels at their moorings, and none of them are powering up. We seem to have caught them with half of their fleet unable to join battle. It's a miracle.

Well…almost a miracle."

Kyniska laughed once more.

"No miracle, my friends. This is what happens with good planning. Concentrate on the fleet…they still have enough ships to cause us a problem. We need to keep moving, and put everything we have into shields."

"You can say that again…" Dekarchos Icarus said, before realising he was answering the Princess.

"I…uh…they have almost a hundred active vessels in this system."

"A hundred?" Komes Devereux asked in horror, "That is double my number."

She looked back to Kyniska.

"Your brother had better have the forces you promised, or this will end the same way Ilium ended for the Trojans."

Kyniska smiled and nodded directly ahead.

"Prepare to be dazzled."

Dozens of lights flickered above the enemy fleet as a huge Terran armada appeared before their very eyes. Dekarchos Icarus and Komes Devereux gasped at the sheer enormity of the force powering into the system. There were cruisers galore, and at least a dozen powerful battleships. Coming in right behind them were scores of assault ships and transports, each crammed with warriors.

"As I promised. My brother will deal with the platforms and moored ships."

"And the weapon below us?"

Kyniska simply smiled.

"It's part of the palace complex. I suggest we send our ground forces into battle. With our combined forces, we can together take the planet. We'll take the palace, the weapon, and the Satrap's head in one swift move."

* * *

Battleship 'Agamemnon', Phrygian Territories
"Excellent work."

Agesilaus watched the vast number of ships from the Black Legion. They were heavily engaged in the system, and he was actually enjoying watching the battle unfold.

"Put me on with my sister, and the commanders of the Black Legion."

His auletes worked quickly to bring up the images of both on the nearest displays. They looked less significant on these units compared to the three-dimensional projections, but it was more than enough for him. Dukas Myrrine moved to his flank and activated the tactical table.

"It's up to date."

"Good."

He then looked up towards the face of Komes Devereux, and the shimmering shape of his sister.

"How is my fleet?"

Komes Devereux shook her head as alerts sounded in the background. The ship was clearly under attack, yet she remained upright and calm.

"Scattered, but fighting. Each passing second sees more of our Legion ships embroiled in close-ranged battles. The Medes are putting up quite a fight. They're learning quickly. Much more quickly than I've seen before."

Komes Devereux then looked pained as her face lit up red. A nearby display filled her face with the warning markers. At that moment, Agesilaus knew they'd lost another ship.

"Another," she said bitterly, "The weapon on the planet is devastating our capitol ships. Either we deal with it now…or we leave this system."

Agesilaus looked stunned as his eyes shifted to the status indicator for the fleet. More than a dozen ships were outlined in red, showing that they had been crippled or destroyed.

"Our ships are heavily engaged," said Komes Devereux, "The Medes have more ships in this fight than we have. Xenophon is preparing the assault teams for the boarding actions. He's selected twenty units to spearhead the strikes."

"Xenophon. I would have liked to talk to him."

"If he survives this fight, you will. Right now, he's seconds away from launching."

Agesilaus uncharacteristically smiled.

"A man after my own heart. Perhaps there is more Laconian to him than he would ever believe."

The image of Komes Devereux flickered once more, and her voice crackled as she spoke.

"We've stuck to the plan and drawn them out to fight Legion ships. It would appear they are keen to tangle with us."

"Of course they are. You have quite the reputation. And trust me, it's exactly what I need."

"Perhaps, but I cannot keep this up forever. Weight of numbers will turn this into a battle of attrition. And it's a battle they seem willing to fight. If they can pin us here, that super weapon will kill us all."

"That's because it's their homeworld." Kyniska, had been relatively quiet until now, "They will fight, because if they lose here, they lose the entire Satrapy to us. The shame and dishonour will probably mean most will be executed, or sold into slavery."

"That is why we will not fight them to the last man," said Agesilaus, "I wanted to knock out their moored ships, but the plan is going to have to change. The only way to stop their weapon is to hit the planet."

He looked to each of them, and Kyniska quickly answered him.

"I agree. Most of the Legion is embroiled in this battle now. You will need to take the palace and the weapon with your own forces. Take the head of the Satrap, and take this fight to them. When he is in chains, the Medes will yield."

"And if they do not?" Komes Devereux asked.

"Trust me. My sister is correct. They will yield, or I am not Basileus, Strategos of this Armada. The Legion will remain engaged and keep their ships busy. I will take our Helots and one bandon of Minotaurion shock troops directly to the palace."

"Most of those troops are still green," said Kyniska, "Xenophon is about to launch, I can divert some of his troops to assist. He has the experienced in the fleet. Thibron gave him access to most of the Legion, on the promise that we send him twice as many troops within three months to help in his own campaign."

Agesilaus hesitated, and then nodded.

"Very well. Send in Xenophon. But tell him to get a shift on. If he takes much longer, he'll find nothing on the planet but bodies and ash. Any ground units that are not engaged need to be sent to the surface."

Both saluted with their arms across their chests.

"When we next meet, it will be in the ruins of the capitol."

Their images vanished, and once more he felt alone even though the men and women crewing his battleship surrounded him. His sister was on her personal ship, and though a few thousand kilometres away, she might have just as easily been in a different system.

"It is time," he said to Dukas Myrrine.

His formation of battleships moved into high-orbit over the planet. One by one they fired broadsides into the trio of orbital platforms that acted as defensive bastions for the planet. Each volley knocked down shields, and then tore apart armour in seconds.

"Now bring us lower," he said firmly, "I want to blast a path through their defences."

He turned to his right and nodded towards Pentarchos Eutropios.

"Double-charge our starboard batteries and burn them. We don't have..."

He stopped speaking momentarily as one of the platforms activated its integral weapons. Multiple heavy cutters slammed into the dorsal decks and crashed deep into the ship's armour.

"We've got problems!" said the Pentarchos, "Shield breached and fires on decks four through eight."

"Fires do not interest me, Dukas. This battle is time dependent. We have to reach the surface before the Satrap can escape. Smash through!"

Dukas Myrrine flinched as another volley crashed through the same damaged section, and more red warnings appeared on multiple displays. Even Agesilaus stumbled as the ship's artificial gravity system fluctuated before the Chief Engineer was able to stabilise the situation. Dukas Myrrine grabbed onto one of the grab rails that extended out from the sides of the command deck.

"Redirect fire against the platforms. We have to create a breach for the squadron."

Lances of lights continued smashing into the ship, as well as the three battleships following close behind. All were now burning in multiple locations, and yet they remained in the fight.

"Torpedoes!" Dukas Myrrine yelled, "Smash the platforms… now!"

"We're too close!" said Pentarchos Eutropios, "If they detonate at that range, we'll sustain damage."

"Irrelevant," she snapped back, "Either we knock them out, or this ship will burn. Remove all safeties and fire double-charged plasma. Now!"

The ship's internal lights continued to flicker as the column of ships steamed past the platforms. Shells and plasma fire crashed into the thick armour of the ship. But then the massive torpedo cells rotated and opened fire, each torpedo covering the short distance and exploding in bright sub-atomic flashes.

"Hold on!" Pentarchos Eutropios shouted.

Torpedo after torpedo struck the station, exploding against its armour. It took fifteen direct hits, plus seven volleys of plasma gunfire before the shield generators on the upper decks finally collapsed. At that point, a pair of assault transports swept into the docking gates.

"Is that Kaarja?" Agesilaus asked.

Dukas Myrrine nodded.

"Yes. He's going to board the station."

"I almost feel sorry for them. Hundreds of Minotaurion shock troops, I doubt most Terrans would stand against a horde of half-breeds. I'm glad they're fighting for us."

One display showed a live camera feed from a Minotaurion officer, a wide platform with a burning landing craft sitting in the middle. Scores of Minotaurion soldiers charged ahead of him; at least half swinging swords and axes, the rest using a variety of different small arms. It was close-ranged and brutal, and they were covering a lot of ground, fast.

"We're moving through, Strategos," said Dukas Myrrine, "Hold on!"

The ship vanished in a cloud of gunfire, flames, and smoke as it surged past to low planetary orbit. The rest of the squadron were right behind, firing short bursts of heavy fire to support the Minotaurion boarding parties.

"Excellent," said Agesilaus, "Now we move to the real prize. Take us lower."

The squadrons of ships moved quickly, as low as they could before the thick atmosphere interfered with their armour. Even so, flames began to spread along the underside of the ships, creating long fiery trails behind them. Small numbers of Median cruisers and heavy fighters rose up from the surface, but they were swatted aside like flies. Two were already burnt hulks, while the other three raced away as fast as their engines could take them. There was no time to bask in the success, though, as another of the dreaded beams extended out from the planet, this time striking Agamemnon in the centre of her hull.

"Brace!" Dukas Myrrine screamed.

But it was too late. The powerful weapon sliced into the ship, setting off dozens of secondary explosions. Incredibly, the ship remained intact, though many of her systems were offline.

"We're going down!" Dukas Myrrine said.

A great howl from twisting metal spread through the innards of the vessel. Agesilaus knew it was over. Any other ship would have been annihilated in the blast, but not this ship. He tapped his ear communications node.

"This is the Strategos. Agamemnon has been crippled, but this fight is not over. Everybody to your dropships, shuttles, or lifeboats! Set course for the enemy capital. I will see you all in the ruins of their palace. Good hunting to you all!"

The lights finally cut as a great blast of fire and smoke tore through the command deck.

CHAPTER TWENTY

Bactrian Grand Battleship 'Aegospotami'
Dascylium, Phrygian Territories

"The Agamemnon is down. I repeat; the Agamemnon is down!" Komes Devereux said.

The words repeated in Xenophon's ears. He could barely believe it. The Agamemnon was the biggest ship in the fleet after his own vessel, and the flagship of the combined venture.

"Understood, I'm on the way. What about lifeboats? Did he escape?"

There was a pause before his old friend answered.

"Xenophon. Three cruisers are helping take off survivors. But the Strategos and Kyniska...they have ordered them all to the surface. They're going to hit the palace."

Xenophon licked his lips as he considered that.

"We're scattered and in trouble. If we leave, we could lose half the fleet. I agree with them both. We need to disable that weapon and make this sacrifice worth it. Too many have already died in this fight."

"Very well. I'm as low as I can push it. I'm screened from the weapon for another six minutes. After that, they'll have a clean shot and will blow me out of the sky."

"Just do the best you can. I'll take it from there."

"Come back alive, Xenophon. I lost Glaucon, and I'm not ready to lose you. Not yet!"

He smiled as he acknowledged her request, and then cut the connection.

Agesilaus and the Agamemnon may be down before the battle is over.

Unlike the Laconians, he was not a man born to war, and found no great pleasure in large battles and violent engagements. He was a thinker, and as content at home with a book and pen as he was out here. He tensed his muscles as the battleship hurtled towards its destination. They'd split away from the massive space battle that now engulfed the system, and were escorting two huge formations of ships towards the planet. He couldn't see what was happening outside, but the reports continued to arrive on the viewer inside his helmet, and it did not make for comfortable viewing.

We've broken the back of their fleet, but the planetary weapon system is killing us. One ship gone every five minutes! In an hour there will be no fleet left!

He walked quickly past the units of warriors. Each looked at the strange man, with his mismatched armour and tall plumed helm. He was clearly one of them, yet something separated him from every other warrior on the ship.

They would be in position over the industrial world of Dascylium soon, and he hoped beyond hope that the diversion had worked. He walked along the deck resplendent in his heavy armour, along with the other fifteen men and women of the unit. They moved quickly towards the line of waiting Skylla gunships. Standing in front of the machines was a massive warrior. His armoured plates gleamed, and the tall horsehair plume from his helm made him look even taller.

"Dukas. Your ship is ready, and I've found the best pilot in the fleet to take you to the surface."

Xenophon smiled back at him, but as he looked at the spacecraft, he found words eluded him. He turned his gaze back to the man, but found his attention drawn to the columns of warriors heading to their predetermined vessels. There were some mercenaries in this unit, but the majority were professionals, and every one of them meant business. This was an army on the move, and one focussed on a single mission, the devastation of the world of Dascylium, a move that would represent the first phase in Laconia's war with the Empire.

"Excellent. And my equipment?"

"Your weapons are onboard, Dukas."

He nodded, and then approached the side door built into the hull of the gunship. It was big enough for two to enter at a time, and unsuited for the rapid deployment of a large combat unit. What it lacked in storage it made up for in ferocity.

The Skylla gunship was actually a variant of the common Dromon, a vessel used by all the Terrans. It was an ugly fusion of armour and firepower, creating a spacecraft that could give even the most stable individual nightmares for days. It was completely black with a low and angular hull capable of carrying dozens of soldiers in cramped conditions. The short, stubby wings extended out on each side to a massive thruster assembly, containing three separate engine units. Intakes above the narrow two-man cockpit ran along the top of the ship and out between the pair of angled tailfins. Four bulbous turrets pushed out from the side of the craft's nose and flanks, making it a deadly foe to face from the front.

He entered the ship, and at once the assembled warriors

moved to attention. He'd only met a few of them before, but that shouldn't matter with regular soldiers. They were all career soldiers and would follow their orders to the letter, no matter the cost.

"Dukas!" they shouted as one.

". Are you ready to ravish this world?"

"Yes, Dukas!"

"Are you ready to bring glory to the Black Legion?"

"Yes, Dukas!"

"And are you ready to teach these cowardly backstabbers what it means to threaten Terrans?"

"Yes, Dukas!"

"Excellent. Then in the name of sacred Terra, we will bring civilisation to these barbarians. We will remind them of our victories of Marathon, Salamis, Plataea, and Cunaxa. And that we can do this whenever we choose to."

Xenophon then moved to his allocated place near the doorway, so that he could be first out of the door.

"Launching!" said the pilot.

The gunship burst out of the forward launch bay, and was quickly followed by dozens of similar craft. They were well spaced apart, yet close enough to provide mutual supporting fire as they passed the Phrygian defences. Fighters were everywhere, hurtling towards the Terran craft, in an attempt to stop them reaching the surface. Xenophon held onto his harness as the Skylla's pilot expertly avoided their shots, and then opened fire with its array of power pulse cannons. Shot after shot cut apart the Zafar Imperial fighters that made the mistake of crossing its path.

"Beautiful flying," said Xenophon, with a mixture of praise and relief in his voice.

He could see the seating position for the pilots, as well as a partial view ahead. Three Median warships were in their path, and several Terran cruisers were blasting them with broadsides, trying to keep them occupied. One, baring the iconography of Plataea, made a mistake and found itself in front of two Elamites. They opened fire with a repeated burst of heavy cutters, quickly triggering dozens of explosions.

No... There must be five hundred souls aboard her!

"That ship is about to go nuclear."

Xenophon watched the ship try to escape, but its stern vanished in a bright fireball. Now completely out of control, it twisted about, moving into the path of one of its comrades.

"A bad way to go."

The combined impact tore both vessels apart, scattering wreckage and fire in all directions. He lifted his hand to block out the bright light, and for a second completely forgot that the windows inside the spacecraft would do that for him.

"We're through the blockade," said the pilot, "Hold on. This is going to get rough!"

Bright flames of fire and flame reflected on the smoked visor of Xenophon's antiquated helmet, as the formation of spacecraft dropped away from the invasion fleet. The light danced about, mirroring the violence and tortured surface of Dascylium. He lifted the visor of his helmet to reveal the face of a young man, with a light beard and a multitude of scars. Of the sixteen warriors on the spacecraft, he was the only non-Laconian, yet the most experienced of them all in this part of space. He twisted about in his seat, groaning as the harness pulled against his armour.

"What a sight."

The combined Laconian League battle fleet and Black Legion fleet was a sight to behold. Every kind of warship, including a dozen of the finest battleships ever sent to war.

There were also large numbers of cruisers plus scores of transports. Almost as many smaller craft travelled with them, including armoured assault ships and escort vessels provided by the smaller worlds of the League. A young spatharios, one of the Laconian heavy infantry, chuckled. All the others bore the marks of many battles on their armour, but not this one. Xenophon was no old man, but seeing this newcomer reminded him of how arrogant and cocksure he'd been just a few years earlier.

"You've never seen a Laconian war fleet before, Sir?"

Xenophon sighed and then shook his head.

"I was present at Aegospotami, soldier. Trust me, I've seen more than enough fleets in my life. It is still quite a sight. Combined with our forces, it is a fleet only the Gods could imagine."

The man looked surprised, but was then grabbed by one of his comrades. They exchanged stern looks before another leaned across the narrow gap in the centre of the spacecraft, and almost laughed at him.

"The Dukas was with Clearchus at Cunaxa. The two were friends."

Another then tapped his arm, and when he twisted about, he found a spatharios with five indentations along his chest armour. Like all Terran soldiers, they repaired but never hid the marks of battle. Each dent, crack, and burn mark was a symbol that represented their experience, and the armour worn by Xenophon was true to form. It was a curious mixture of Laconian heavy infantry armour, along with an assortment of light infantry plating, and even a few key pieces taken from the fallen enemy in the Cunaxa campaign.

"Hold on!"

The pilot rotated about to avoid more wreckage. For a brief

moment the change of course gave Xenophon the perfect view of one of the larger Laconian armoured transports. It was as big as a battleship, but instead of weapon arrays, it was equipped with double launch decks that ran from bow to stern. Dromon gunships, and the slightly larger Chelandion Dropships launched, and then formed up in groups before joining the attack on the surface. For a second, Xenophon was taken back to the assault on Cunaxa, the bloody battle where he'd first seen the Laconians engaged in a full-scale assault. It was an image he would never, ever forget.

"We're entering the planet's atmosphere. We're in for a rough ride. Gunners, be ready!"

Xenophon watched the spacecraft's crew move to their stations. The Laconian Dromon carried sixteen fully armed warriors, but it also had positions for four gunners, two on each flank. These turrets looked like translucent spheres, each fitted with double pulse cannons, and with enough space for one individual inside. The rear face was made from layered armour plate to maintain the integrity of the ship. Xenophon gritted his teeth, and watched as they crashed through the upper atmosphere, and down further and further towards the surface. The Laconians were masters of orbital assaults, and it didn't take long for the flame and smoke shrouded dromons to burst out into the sunlit sky of Dascylium.

"Look," said the pilot, "It's the Princess."

Even Xenophon felt a thrill at hearing mention of the woman. He looked to the right of the cockpit and spotted a large formation of Chelandion dropships moving in the same direction as them.

"Kyniska," he said under his breath. He then looked to the others in the spacecraft.

"How can we lose this fight with such a woman at our

sides?"

There was no time to answer, as a fighter screamed past them with its guns firing. Several rounds glanced off the dropship's armour, each impact sounding like a sledgehammer smashing into rock.

"Fighters!" said the pilot.

The Median spacecraft might be small, but they were fast, and all around them in seconds. The fuselage was small and shaped like a spearhead. Thin wings bent down on each side, so much so that they were almost vertical. At their tips were multimode thrusters, capable of propelling the craft at hypersonic speeds. An extra vertical winglet hung down from the nose, thus negating the need for any kind of tail. Small pulse cannons extended out from the thruster mounts.

"Look!" said a soldier, as a Laconian Dromon ripped apart under the combined fire of five fighters. It exploded, and the wreckage dropped down wreathed in flames.

"They will die in the fire," said Xenophon, "It will be quick."

The words stunned a few of them, yet not one seemed frightened by what was happening. They were not Helots or green volunteers.

"This is where it all gets interesting."

They all looked ahead as they dropped through the clouds. For all his knowledge and experience, he still gasped at the sheer brutality and violence of the planet. Several of the other heavily armed spatharii spoke in hushed tones as geysers of fire and flame reached up into the sky. Any normal pilot would pull up and travel back into space, but this was a military ship, and they were on a mission.

"Hold on, we've got trouble ahead. Air-defence installations have activated their tracking systems. They've got us!"

One by one the transports dumped clouds of radar

absorbent material, and some dropped bright star flares to draw the attention of scanners. Xenophon instinctively grabbed his harness and held on tightly. He knew what was to come, and felt as helpless and vulnerable as he always did during an orbital assault.

"Taking evasive action!"

The heavily armoured dromon rolled twice to avoid incoming gunfire. It was an impressive piece of flying, and not just because they avoided being hit by gunfire. They'd also managed to avoid crashing into the dozens of other dromons moving in the same direction. And these were not the light spacecraft he'd used over the last few years. These were Laconian League dromons and much bigger, tougher, and more powerful than anything he'd flown in before.

"On the ground in three minutes, Komes. There's a lot of fire on the approaches to the palace."

"Then get lower." Xenophon sounded irritated, "It's our job to secure the landing grounds. Without us, the rest of the army will be stuck in orbit."

"Yes, Komes."

Small windows fitted throughout the vessel provided a limited view of the planet, and it was unlike anything he'd ever seen. Dascylium was the closest a planet came to a literal hell. Volcanoes and lava pools covered large swathes of the planet, silhouetted by the bright red of lava pools.

"Look at that thing!"

A tall triple tower made from what looked like black marble or obsidian rose up from the rock, so high the tips vanished into the clouds. Halfway down from the tower was a wide hexagonal section with landing platforms on each of the six sides. Angular sections ran down for at least a thousand metres until they reached a series of flat buildings and structures. From here an identical area to the hexagonal platform extended out ever further, offering space for large transports and ships. Directly below the platforms was a great moat filled with molten lava.

"Dukas Xenophon. I am detecting a transmission from inside the palace. It is on an open channel to any listening ships."

"Put it on."

"...ten minutes to leave Phrygia. Turn back now, or I will unleash the full might of my fleet."

Xenophon's eyebrows rose in interest.

So...now he knows fear. Good.

"This is Satrap Pharnabazus of the Median Empire. My palace is impenetrable, and protected by shielding and weapons developed by the best Terran engineers. I will destroy each and every ship in this system if you do not leave immediately!"

"Cut the signal," said Xenophon, "I've heard enough."

"The God King will..."

Before he could say more, the pilot cut the feed.

"Sorry, Sir. It took a little longer than intended."

Xenophon chuckled.

"That's okay. It is good to know he is scared. He'd not have contacted us unless there was doubt in his mind. He knows who is here, and he knows what we have done before."

Xenophon turned his attention to the impressive defences. There were plenty of defended facilities on the planet, but the palace lay alone and exposed to wind and fire. And that interested him.

"More than a hundred turrets, landing pads for warships, and garrison buildings," said the pilot, "It is a palace and fortress. If you..."

He stopped speaking as a great sphere of energy appeared at the centre of the tower, and then raced up the towers and into the sky above. The clouds changed colour as the energy reached out to destroy yet another ship.

"The Satrap. He says he will target our transports if we do not turn around."

Xenophon shook his head as he watched the growing energy build up deep inside the tower complex.

"The weapon. It cannot be allowed to endure!"

A dozen Skylla Gunships raced in from the East and opened fire with their arrays of powerful pulse cannon. Hades missiles dropped from hardpoints under their hulls and accelerated at the massive black fortress.

"Go on!" said a spatharios in the gunship, "Smash it!"

The gunfire struck first, creating a pattern of coloured pulses.

"Dammit," said the pilot, "Nothing got through."

Next were the missiles, and one by one they simply vanished in puffs of light.

"The palace is heavily shielded, Dukas. It's weird, but the energy signature matches Arcadian phased shielding technology."

"Yes." Xenophon looked at the data inside his helmet, "And it looks suspiciously similar to the technology used onboard the Titan Olympia, Xenias' old ship. If that's the case, we'll have to get a lot closer and blast open entry points in the grid to get inside. We won't be able to destroy the palace from here. Not in the time we have left."

Xenophon looked up at the cloud, and the shimmering light from the weapon, as it finally subsided. He didn't dare check the fleet channel for fear of hearing of the loss of yet another ship. Instead, he concentrated on the palace ahead of them and activated the command network. To his surprised, it was answered immediately.

"This is Xenophon. This is not going to be easy."

"Agreed," said Agesilaus, "You have suggestions?"

Xenophon was shocked at being asked his advice from the man. He was so used to Laconians telling him what they wanted, and rarely asking for suggestions.

"The tower has enough air-defence turrets. I don't think we can get within five kilometres of the tower."

Xenophon looked out towards the black tower, as a trio of Terran fighters moved in too close. They strafed the buildings on the lower levels as the guns opened up at close-range. Two of the fighters exploded instantly, while the third pulled up to try and get away. Gunfire tore into the sky, and several shells exploded above the fighter, catching its left side engine. It spun out of control with smoke belching from the machine.

"If we hit it from three directions, we might have a chance," he said, though none of them sounded convinced.

"We could lose half of our soldiers in a third attack," said Kyniska, "We can't take these losses in a single fight. Perhaps we…"

Kyniska stopped speaking as a dark shape appeared above them. A voice filled the airwaves with a grim howl.

"This is Kaarja. I'm coming down. Clear the way!"

Xenophon visibly pulled his head back in surprise, and then pushed forward to get a better view from inside the gunship. He could see the massive form of the huge Minotaurus assault transport. It was heavily damaged, and yet remained under full control. The extended engine pylons pulsed with energy as the crew pointed the nose directly towards the palace.

"Where do you want my troops?"

Xenophon looked at the palace, and then back to the ship.

"How quickly can you evacuate your ship, Kaarja?"

"Who is this?" demanded the alien warrior.

"Xenophon, commander in the Black Legion."

Kaarja grunted, and then answered.

"My troops are already waiting inside their craft. The ship's crew can be in the lifeboats in seconds. Why?"

Agesilaus answered for him.

"I already know what Xenophon is thinking, and he might be right. Will it be enough to knock down the shields?"

Xenophon nodded to himself, though deep down still not entirely convinced it would work.

"Yes, it will do the job."

Agesilaus' communications was jumbled for a moment, and then his voice returned with a series of crackles partially breaking it up.

"Kaarja, you'll send your ship to the structures on the lower levels. Evacuate your ship, and follow the vessel in."

Kaarja sounded as though he was laughing.

"You're serious?

"Always, Kaarja."

"I see. Very well. I will see you on the ground."

"Anything else, Xenophon?" Agesilaus asked.

Xenophon rubbed his chin as he double-checked the tower. It was now wreathed in flame as scores of powerful turrets fired in all directions. It looked as well protected as a Terran Titan, and perhaps even tougher to damage. Doubt ate at his mind, but he knew he was right.

"We will move in ten kilometres behind the ship. Once the shields are down, we need all Chelandion Dropships to converge on the platforms along the upper parts of the weapon complex. Skylla Gunships will remain in the air and provide tactical fire support."

The image of Xenophon crackled and faded inside Agesilaus' helmet, and he thought communication had been lost. But then the infamous senior officer in the Black Legion appeared again.

"The Minotaurion assault ship is seconds away from impact. Are you ready?"

Agesilaus licked his lips with relish. He could imagine the upcoming battle, and both his body and mind ached for the thrill and the violence of a clash such as this.

"I am ready, and so are my loyal troops. I will send additional Helot units to strike the lower levels right behind us. May the Gods grant us their favour in the assault. Good hunting to each of you."

Xenophon brought up his forearm against his chest and nodded, just as his image began to fade.

"And to you all."

Agesilaus moved towards the assault doors fitted to the side of his massive Chelandion Dropship. The four bulbous turrets chattered continually as the gunners poured fire into the circling fighters trying desperately to force them away. A tiny image in the corner of his helmet repeated the forward camera view from the dropship. He could see the massive bulk of the Minotaurion assault transport hurtling towards the palace. It was big, and capable of tackling a heavy cruiser on its own. Today would be its last battle, and as hundreds of shells and laser blasts slammed into it, he imagined no better send off.

"This is the Strategos," he said over the command network, "Begin the attack."

The Chelandion Dropship's four pivoting engine mounts swung around and activated simultaneously. It moved fast, above and to the right of the huge ship. Dozens and dozens of similar craft were all heading directly for the palace. Both sides fired back and forth, but the palace shields remained active, and impervious to attack.

"Strategos. The weapon is about to fire. The targeting matrix is shifting to point at us."

"Stay on course. One spot is as good as any other. We cannot avoid our fate."

Here it comes.

The beam struck the massive Minotaurion assault ship, burning through it from bow to stern. The impact was so great the ship crumbled into five separate fragments, and each continued forward at the same speed. Turrets around the palace focussed their fire on the debris, but it simply wasn't enough. One by one they smashed into the tower and the lower structure, bursting open parts of the shielding.

"Yes!" Agesilaus watched the bizarre kaleidoscope of colours, "On the ground...now!"

The gunship dropped down in a tight circle, striking an upper landing pad on the partially damaged hexagonal array.

"Everybody out...Now!"

The doors dropped open, and a bright red glow filled the interior of the dropship. For a second, it seemed as though the tower was on fire, but then Agesilaus realised it was the reflected heat and light from the lava lakes and rivers.

"With me!"

The Laconian bodyguard leapt out, while more dromons and gunships moved in. Hundreds of Terrans were crawling over the upper and lower levels, their numbers growing by the second. Agesilaus spotted flashes of light and lifted his shield arm just in time.

"Phrygian stratiotes. Drive them back!"

The enemy soldiers wore gleaming black armour, and though unshielded, made use of long and powerful rifles that blasted holes in anything they struck. Round after round glanced off their shields, but some found their mark, or struck so hard they knocked out the generators. Laconian soldiers fell from the fire, and still they surged ahead in open formation. Their shields fizzled and crackled as sporadic gunfire from inside struck them. Agesilaus was with them, and as he moved ahead, he could see the platform was connected directly to the tower. A huge section was now missing, and revealed the glowing interior, filled with black causeways and tall staircases.

"Keep moving!"

Shapes raced past, and he twisted to the right to find a trio of Black Legion dropships moving to the other side of the tower complex. He didn't know who was inside, but it filled his heart to see so many Terrans in one place, and working to a common goal.

"Everybody inside, hurry!"

The defenders were well positioned, putting down heavy fire against the Laconians as they struggled to get away from the landing platform, and into the outer ring of palace. One by one they were struck down, leaving a crowd of dead and wounded on the field of battle. Still Agesilaus pushed forward until finally a small group managed to reach the vast breach in the outer wall. They clambered through, but found dozens of Phrygian soldiers waiting on the other side.

"Phalanx!"

Laconians dropped to his left and to his right, but still they came, and with each passing second, the phalanx grew. Its powerful shields protected them from the gunfire, while they identified targets, and then fired with short, well-aimed bursts. Agesilaus was now well inside, looking to the left and right, trying to assess what was happening.

"I need help!" said a voice in his communications node. Even though they had never met, Agesilaus knew immediately who is was.

"Xenophon! What is it?"

"I've found him, on the twentieth level, the lower landing platforms. I need help…fast! If you…"

The channel filled with white noise as it was suddenly blocked. More shots struck around him as enemy soldiers fired down from a hundred different positions. He looked around for his officers and found Komes Diogenes stabbing a Phrygian soldier lying on the ground. He opened his mouth to speak just as a great beam of energy filled the centre of the tower. The sound was deafening, as was the heat it generated. Those too close were lifted from the ground, as it seemed to affect their weight. Many stopped firing and watched the bizarre phenomenon unfolding before their eyes.

"Incredible," said Agesilaus, "I have never seen anything like this."

The light faded, and those that had been lifted, crashed to the ground in a heap. The light vanished and was instantly replaced by more gunfire. He looked back to his trusted bodyguard and grabbed his arm.

"Komes. What level is this?"

The Terran looked at him, but then a round whistled down. It missed their shields and struck Agesilaus in the side of his helmet. The pulse bullet exploded and sent the Strategos flying through the air. As he lay there, more rounds slashed back and forth, both sides fighting a desperate and bloody battle. He shook his head, and then laughed as he looked up to the ever-reliable Komes Diogenes.

"What level is this?"

The man looked stunned by the question.

"Forty-five," he answered in a questioning tone.

Agesilaus struggled to get back up.

"We need to go down twenty-five levels, and fast."

The Komes looked at Agesilaus' artificial leg, and then back to his face.

"Is that leg as good as you say it is?"

Agesilaus raised an eyebrow.

"Why?"

"I have an idea. And it's a little crazy."

"I like it already. Show me."

* * *

Kyniska shook her head in amazement at the vastness of the tower's interior. It was bigger than any ship she'd been inside, and shaped in a vast ring around the glowing and pulsing power that rose and fell at the centre. A long, black walkway ran around the outside and continued upwards, vanishing in a haze. She spotted bursts of light arcing back and forth from each side of the tower, as Terrans engaged in brutal combat many levels above her. She could tell the gunfire was coming from Laconians, due to the hue of the pulse rounds, and the discipline and accuracy being used.

"Agesilaus!"

A round reached across, glancing off a shield carried by a Mothake. The man looked at her and laughed with relief, but only for a second. It missed the shield and struck him in the forehead.

"Fool," she muttered, "A man is never safe, not even in death."

Then she spotted something she never thought she would see. Off to her right, and three levels above her, was a man clad in golden armour, and flanked by what must have been a hundred soldiers. There were also many combat drones, the large, heavily armoured fighting machines often employed by the Imperials.

"Pharnabazus!"

She activated her communications node, but found nothing but white noise, mixed with random static. Snorting with frustration she pointed up towards the man.

"Stop him!"

Kyniska moved quickly to the circular walkway that ran in a very wide ring around the palace. It took longer than expected, as she ran so fast her comrades could not keep up. They moved up two levels until finally they were one level below the Phrygians. There were two more rings, each connected by dangerous looking metal walkways with no fencing or protection on their sides. The rings shrank down until meeting the point where the energy beam would fire upwards, as though it were a great pole made from fire and light.

Some of them spotted the pursuing Terrans, and began firing across the wide-open gulf that led down to the mouth of the weapon. Shots glanced back and forth, and soldiers on both sides fell to their deaths, hit by a fusillade of fire.

"We have to go on," said Kyniska, "We cannot let him escape."

She tried to move further, but dozens of rounds struck around her, forcing her to shelter behind more shields.

"I will not be held back by mere pulse bullets."

She broke away from her guards and ran along the walkway. Bullets slammed into the black material all around her. On and on she went until finally she was on the same level as the Phrygians. She could see they'd reached the inner ring, and were waiting in a large group, protected by some kind of ring energy shield that completely encircled them. Devices on the ground flickered with energy as it powered the shield ring.

"It's projected from the tower itself!" said a spatharios as he ran back to join the others. He was too slow, and a volley of fire struck him in the back. Unshielded, he was no match for their rifles.

"Bring it down!" Kyniska shouted.

Terran soldiers moved in against the ring from all sides, but the shield proved impossible to breach. Most shots glanced off the shielding, the occasional shot managing to breach a weakened section. Kyniska was about to call out an order when five shapes rose out from the black platform extending out from the central ring.

Five massive combat drones lifted out of the hatches, turning as they tracked targets. Each was permanently attached to their base like a turret, yet the upper bodies were identical to those used as combat drones on the battlefield. Their low sunken shoulders and heavy armour marked them out immediately. They twisted back and forth, blasting the Terrans with their low velocity guns. Those inside were somehow able to keep firing as the ring ebbed and flowed for long enough to create small gaps to fire through.

"Surround them, and keep firing. We have to breach that shield."

"Good idea," said a familiar voice.

She looked to her right and found a unit of Black Legion. They were hunkered down behind their shields, and pouring fire into the ring shield. Standing in the middle of the unit was the man she'd heard so much of over the last few years.

"Xenophon?"

"Yes. Get your head down. We need to find a way through."

She leapt to her side and moved behind a shield She was so close to Xenophon she could feel his breath on her arm, and she lifted her pulse-pistol.

"What are they doing?"

Xenophon shook his head.

"No idea. They seem to be stalling for time. They're waiting for something."

"Look!"

A shape flashed on by to their right. It quickly vanished from view, reappearing as the outer walls of the tower began to slide away. They'd been stuck inside the massive black structure, and now multiple levels were exposed to the elements.

"That's a Median cruiser!" Xenophon said, "Get down!"

Hundreds of white lights flickered along the warships as it poured fire through the open structure, shattering the ranks of the Terrans.

"It's a trap!" Kyniska screamed.

"We have to fall back. We can't stay here with that ship nearby."

Even as he inhaled more air before speaking, a pair of Terran gunships strafed the cruiser. Their pulse rounds glanced off its powerful armour, but they were able to pull away in time before being shot down.

"I can't believe we made it this far," said Kyniska bitterly, "I will not leave the field of battle. Not today!"

Xenophon watched her draw a blade from her side. He tried to grab her, but she pushed him away.

"I decide when I fight, and only the Gods will choose when I die."

Xenophon shook his head and pointed to the next level below them. Dark shapes stormed up along the walkway, brandishing axes, blades, and firearms. They looked like demonic creatures, snorting and bellowing as they ran. At their head was a heavily armoured figure holding up a pair of axes and howling wildly.

"Kaarja!" Kyniska said, "That crazy beast!"

The Minotaurion warriors reached the same level as Kyniska,

and soon ran into a wall of gunfire. Dozens were cut down, and most of them scattered to find cover. Some opened fire, while others used the cover of their fallen comrades to keep firing. But then a small number crashed into the ring shield and began hacking away. There were only three of them, but to Kyniska's surprise, they were able to breach the shield with each strike. They managed to cut down a single Phrygian soldier before the robotic combat drones gunned down all three.

They walked slowly along the ring platform, and both continued blazing away at any targets they could see.

"The shield can be breached with blades," she said quietly, looking to Xenophon.

"We have to get closer."

He nodded, and then gave a hand signal to his unit of spatharii.

"Close rank and advance!"

The Terrans formed a loose phalanx, though nothing as impressive as the Laconians. Shots glanced off their shields as they moved, but then the combat drones unleashed their bombardment of shells. As each shell exploded, the shells ripped open the line, killing or maiming any too close to the blasts.

"We can't get close enough," Xenophon said through clenched teeth.

Kyniska took aim with her pistol and fired one shot after another into the nearest machine. It swivelled about at its waist, and then fired a short burst towards her. She ducked down behind the shields of her comrades just before more rounds slammed above her head.

"Stay down..." Xenophon said, "And close up the ranks!"

That was the exact moment the cruiser appeared behind them. Multiple turrets swung around as the gunners took aim.

"Behind us!" screamed one of the Terrans.

As some of them turned around, they created gaps in the line that were immediately exploited by the Phrygians. Gunfire from the cruiser lashed across the tower, picking off any unshielded soldiers. In ten seconds there were another forty dead or wounded Terrans, for the loss of no Phrygians.

"We need something," said Xenophon.

"Like a miracle."

* * *

Agesilaus reached the edge of the platform and looked down.

"Are you insane, Komes Diogenes? That fall will turn us into jelly."

Shots crashed back and forth, and when he looked back, he could see nothing but Phrygian soldiers and Laconians engaged in a brutal melee. Some of the Neodamodes had even made it up this far and doing their best to match the Laconians in battle. A league apart, yet still they fought with rifles and carbines. Agesilaus was impressed by their tenacity, if not their skill.

"Look!" Komes Diogenes pointed to the bottom of the shaft, "It's about to fire. Do you trust me?"

"Of course."

"Then…jump."

To his astonishment, the man leapt over the ledge and plummeted down the central section, a few metres from the centre.

"You fool!"

Without giving it a moment's thought, he leapt from the ledge and began the terrifying fall from high. Level after level flashed past, and then he spotted the glowing shape far below.

It grew in intensity almost as quickly as the platform with the enemy soldiers.

What am I doing?

Then the weapon fired, and he felt his body shudder as it pulsed up into the skies. He felt lighter and lighter, and then he was a hundred metres above the platform. His descent continued to slow until he was almost hovering a dozen metres above them. Then the light vanished, and he fell into the centre of their formation. Four Phrygian soldiers were knocked down by the impact, and three more had been knocked aside by the falling Diogenes. There was no time to think, only to activate their shields, and to start fighting.

"To the death!" Agesilaus roared as he stabbed with his Asgeirr-Carbine. The blade punched into the chest of the nearest soldier, and without withdrawing it, he fired the carbine. The pulse rounds tore through flesh and armour, bursting out of the man's back and into the next soldier.

"Your left!" Diogenes yelled.

Agesilaus lifted his shield arm and beat aside a rifle barrel, and then chopped down with his own weapon. It slashed through the pulse rifle, triggering an explosion that killed several soldiers, as well as knocking Agesilaus to the ground. He rose back up in an instant just as a blade whistled past his face.

"I don't think so, Phrygian. He lifted his arm and blasted the armoured soldier in the face. As the dead warrior dropped away, he spotted the man he'd come to fight, the fully armoured shape of a Median Satrap. The armour was beautiful, the perfection of function and form. The noble's face was hidden behind a golden mask, yet for all this protection, he carried no weapons.

"End him!"

Two-dozen black armoured Phrygians charged at him, their weapons blazing. They were about to run into him when shapes dropped from above and landed in the middle of the fight.

"To the Basileus!" Diogenes said.

The Epilektoi moved with great skill and precision. Rather than fight individually, they formed into small groups around their leader, creating a solid wall of energy in front of them. Guns blasted away, and the Phrygians began to scatter.

"Yes!" Agesilaus said excitedly, "Bring down the shield."

Several Epilektoi split from the phalanx and cut their way through the scattered Phrygians. No sooner had they reached the shield emitters, than they stabbed their blades directly into the units. Three exploded on contact, and breaches opened up immediately in the shields. Pharnabazus became visible for a moment before being swamped by his own soldiers. Phrygians formed up around him to present a solid wall of armour and flesh.

"I want his head!" Agesilaus roared.

The Epilektoi pushed on, but they were still heavily outnumbered. Shots crashed around their leader, and they were forced to close ranks to protect him. Then he spotted shadows moving through the shields. The great robotic combat drones were on fire, and through the gaps came something completely unexpected. A great horde of Minotaurion warriors crashed through the breached formation, swinging blades and axes. Dozens of Phrygians fell as they crashed into the formation, and soon they scattered as prey before a predator.

As bodies fell on both sides, more Terrans managed to reach the fight. Kyniska, Xenophon, and his entourage were next, and they moved to within fifty metres of the Phrygians before pouring volley after volley into the enemy's broken ranks. She pointed her blade at the survivors and screamed at the top of her voice.

"Charge!"

As they smashed into the heart of the battle, Agesilaus began searching for his prey. He could see the golden figure running from the fight, with just a dozen guards at his side.

"Stop him!"

Without showing care for his own life, he charged through the middle of the skirmish and chased after them. Two stopped to try and hold him back, but he blasted them apart, leaping over their bodies. The ten that remained formed a line and opened fire. Agesilaus lifted his shield arm and charged. Round after round slammed into the shield, three striking his artificial leg, and one his shoulder. He staggered, and then lost his momentum as his wounds slowed him down. The remaining Phrygians circled around him, their weapons drawn and pointing at him.

"Don't touch him!"

A blade slashed into the soldiers and instantly decapitated the nearest warrior. Komes Diogenes moved in next, kicking away another soldier that was about to blast his leader.

"Stop him!" Agesilaus said, spitting blood.

As he looked up, Pharnabazus reached the edge of the platform. There was nothing but open air behind him as he turned around and looked towards the Laconian commander. For a brief moment there was open space between them. The Satrap pointed at him, and then laughed.

"This is not over."

He then leapt from the ledge and vanished from view. Kyniska raced to the edge and gasped as the massive Phrygian cruiser swept into view. A ramp hung down and atop the structure was the shape of the Satrap. He staggered inside, and the armoured doors began to slide shut behind him. Kyniska lifted her pistol and took aim, but Xenophon stumbled towards her, dragging her away as the engines pulsed with light.

"Get down!"

The engines grew brighter, and then with a thunderclap, followed by a roar of light and flame, the ship vanished into the ether, as it jumped away at faster than light speeds.

EPILOGUE

Dascylium, Phrygian Territories

Kyniska waited at the edge of the damaged platform, looking back to the rest of the skirmish. There were few Phrygians left fighting, and with their leader gone, they quickly threw down their weapons. Multiple dead Phrygians lay across the black floor, a bloody reminder of the cost of Pharnabazus' escape. Waiting for them at the end was Agesilaus. He moved slowly, and his battered and bruised body forced him to wince. Yet when he looked back to the pair he smiled.

"He might have escaped...but what a victory."

The sound of battle faded as the Phrygians finally gave up the fight. Kyniska placed a hand on her brother's shoulder.

"The entire system is ours, Brother. It is a glorious victory."

"And so is half of their fleet." Xenophon moved to a few centimetres from the edge of the platform. Agesilaus pointed down far below them.

"Look. Our unblooded Neodamodes are still fighting in the lower levels, and thousands more are running rampant throughout the palace."

A loud crack made them all look up. A dark shape split apart and fell down from the heavens, each piece trailing a long line of black smoke.

"Agamemnon," said Kyniska, "She was quite the ship."

"Indeed she was," said Agesilaus.

At the same time, a pair of massive Megaran Starcarriers appeared in the upper atmosphere. In seconds, they deployed vast numbers of fighters that raced off into the distance to do battle with the few remaining enemy fighters.

"Too late," said Agesilaus bitterly, "Pharnabazus has used his jump drive."

He turned his back on the raging planet.

"We've taken Ephesus, and forced Tissaphernes back to his homeworld. And in this brutal battle we've taken Pharnabazus' fleet, as well as his palace, and all of his wealth. I'd say phase one of our campaign has just begun."

His eyes shifted to the senior commander of the Black Legion.

"We have more than enough funds to pay for your services for years to come. Are you with us?"

Xenophon looked to Kyniska, who gave him a subtle nod that he should accept.

"I would be honoured. But tell me, Basileus. What is phase two of your plan, the destruction of the entire Median Empire?"

Agesilaus laughed, a low booming laugh that echoed through the shattered hulk of the dark, black palace. The longer he laughed, the louder the sound. Finally, he stopped and moved closer to the two of them.

"I'm sure we can find something in the middle. Will you and your commanders stand at my side as we bring war to the

Medes? Together, I believe we can achieve the impossible."

Kyniska nodded, but Xenophon looked up to the wreckage of the falling battleship. He remembered the betrayal of Tissaphernes, and the death of so many of his friends.

"For as long as you can fight this war, you can count on me and the Black Legion at your side, Strategos. And if you need them, I know of others that retired who would welcome a chance for some retribution."

"Excellent," said Kyniska.

Her brother gave her a nod, and she pointed out to the legions of soldier swarming across the planet.

"Send out the signal, Xenophon. Call back every mercenary that will answer the call. The great war of our time has come. Riches, fame, and fortune will come to those that join us."

Agesilaus lifted his blood-soaked blade to the sky and called out in his loud, booming voice.

"To the future!"

Kyniska and Xenophon joined him in raising their own weapons. Like the Strategos, their blades dripped with the blood of the fallen.

"The future!"

THE END

APPENDIX I: THE GALAXY

APPENDIX II: PEOPLE

Agesilaus
He was a big man, at almost two meters in height and encased in bronzed armour.

Agesilaus bore the traditional weaponry of his people's spatharii, the heavy infantry of the Laconian state. One of the two Basileus, the Kings of Laconian, and a military warlord in his own right. Brother of Kyniska.

Ariaeus
Median general and Cyrus' second-in-command. The young rival of Tissaphernes but powerful and ambitious. He commanded a fleet that was double the size of the Legion as well as over 20,000 automaton stratiotes. Famous for leading a series of revolts in the border lands against central Median control. He was a loyal friend of Cyrus but never fully trusted by the Terrans.

Artaxerxes II (Emperor of the Medes)
The half-brother of Lord Cyrus and leader of the most powerful Empire in the known universe. Also known as the God King Artaxerxes. He was a shrewd tactician and ruthless in ambition. His personal fortune and Royal Fleet were the envy of every Terran world.

Artemas of Caria
The beautiful daughter of Lygdamis, one of the Median governors of the independent Ionian Territories and niece of Cyrus. Lady Artemas walking towards her. As usual, she wore her unusual hybrid of corset, armour, and Median clothing while carrying her weapons at her side.

Ezekiel Manus
The Kybernetes of the Black Legion cruiser Vendetta, who took over command of the ship following the death of the kentarchos.

Komes Diogenes
Veteran Laconian soldier, and a senior member of the elite Epilektoi. He was almost the size height and build as Agesilaus, though at least a decade older. Any scars he might have were hidden below his armour and helmet which he now removed. He was a classic Laconian, strong, honourable, reliable and utterly without humour. Diogenes was usually found standing alongside the royal siblings when in battle.

Kallinos
A half-breed Medes mercenary from the Ionian Territories.

Kaarja the Minotaurion
A mercenary from the nomadic Minotaurus tribe. Though outwardly Terran, there were other differences that marked him out as a very different creature. His skin was dark brown, almost black, and his body was well built and muscular. And yet for all the similarities, it was impossible not to notice the bullish face, with long snout, teeth and glowing red eyes. He was a mercenary captain, and yet he wore a Terran breastplate and helmet.

Kantos
Fencing instructor from Attica. Served with the Black Legion. Had not been heard of after having been exiled for sedition after fighting the Thirty Tyrants on Attica. His brother was killed prior to him leaving Attica to join the Legion.

Kyniska
Sister of Agesilaus, She was the epitome of Terran beauty. Tall, athletic, and with a mischievous look in her eyes. Her limbs were strong from the same physical training as the others in the Agoge. Unusually her hair was not black, but instead a dark red, with hints of blackness at the roots. Kyniska was a young woman in her mid-twenties and a perfect example of the strength and skill so regarded in Laconia, and yet she remained single and unattached, a reminder of her fierce will and independence.

Roxana Devereux
Officer in the Alliance Navy, friend of Xenophon. Met on Attica before enlistment. A confidant and tall women with thick auburn hair and grey eyes. She was almost the same height and build as Xenophon and spent time both in the Alliance military and working as a mercenary prior to the expedition.

Tissaphernes
Median Satrap and high lord of the rich regions around the Cilician Gates. Close friend of the Emperor and major rival of Cyrus. His power and influence was second only to his scheming and politics.

Xenias (Dukas)
An Arcadian soldier and commander of the Olympia. He took a vast contingent of 2,000 mercenaries with him to join the Ten Thousand. His junior commanders included Komes Pasion, leader of the Night Blades.

Xenophon
A citizen of Attica and rumored to be a pupil of Kratez. Saw

limited service during the Terran Civil War. Prefect of the Inner Wards on Attica. Eventually forced into exile with Glaucon. Blamed for death of his father Gryllus, who fought for the rights of the citizens with the Thirty. Joined the Ten Thousand mercenaries that fought for the rebel Prince Cyrus against the Empire.

Though an ardent Attica loyalist, he showed sympathy towards the Laconians and argued against continuing hostilities with them all his life. Famously single for most of his life, avoids getting too involved with any one person. He was tall and slender, with cropped blonde hair and dark blue eyes, and known for being introverted, highly conservative and intellectual.

APPENDIX III: PLACES

Aegean Expanse
A vast and desolate region of space. It is a three-week journey through nebula and other anomalies between the Terrans colonies and the mighty Median Empire.

Aeolian League
Twelve rich and successful colonial star systems that run along the border of the Empire. Though Terran worlds, they are inside the territories claimed by the Empire, and are technically Imperial border worlds. They have the same confused status as the Ionian Territories.

Arcadia
A Terran world famous for its stoic warriors and weak stability. Many Alliance politicians would joke about the elections not being needed on Arcadia, this was apparently due to the number of coups.

Attica
The heavily populated homeworld of the Atticans and the capital world of the old Terran Alliance. It was one of the earliest colonies established by the Terrans in their earliest years of expansion. Home of Xenophon, Glaucon and Roxana.

Boeotian League
A loose coalition of Terran colonies including Thebes and others powerful colonies. Rivals to the power of Laconia, and one of the oldest and most respected groups of colonies among the Terrans.

Citadel of Cunaxa.

Built on top of a natural peak in the centre of the capital, it was surrounded by a dozen star-shaped fortresses and joining walls of thirty meters in height. Behind all of this was the Citadel itself, a mighty structure covered in domes and pillars that reached up into the clouds. Landing pads, weapon turrets and shield generators covered the entire site. It was the most impressive defensive structure on the planet of Cunaxa Secundus, the second most important planet in the Median Empire and guarded the route to the Imperial homeworld of Babylon Prime.

Corinthian Collective

A single massive star system with multiple inhabited colonies. Famous for the quality of many of its spatharii soldiers.

Fort Plymouth

The most distant and powerful of the Alliance Olympus class outposts. It was situated within striking distance of the border worlds of the Empire. It was the home of the Armada during the last war with the Laconians. With thousands of personnel and hundreds of ships, it was impregnable to all but a full invasion. Stationed over 200 parsecs from Attica and nearly 230 parsecs from Laconia. 14 jumps were required for the trip, a journey that would take 2 weeks from Attica if stops were made at Alliance refueling stations. With tankers, the trip could be conducted in half the time.

Ionia Territories

A disputed area of twelve systems that had once been under Terran control. It had now been carved up into a dozen separate territories, each controlled by a powerful Ionian warlord.

Several of the colonies are home to high gravity worlds that have helped breed a swarthy but short people who specialized in shipbuilding and high-energy weapons.

Laconia
Ruled by seven men that included a dual kingship, knows as the two Basileus, five Ephors and a vocal 'popular assembly'. In reality the planet was controlled by the Ephors who were elected for life as tyrants. The Basileus were little more than generals with little political power. The manpower for the state was provided by a complex series of indentured workers who were little more than slaves and commonly revolted. The capital world of the massive and heavily populated Pelopon Cluster.

Laconian League
The pre-eminent Terran Empire lead by the military colony of Laconia, and the Congress of Allies. An equal to dozens of Terran powers on its own. The master of the League is the leadership of Laconia, though technically this could be any of the colonies in the League. All of the Pelopon Cluster is part of the League, as well as more distant locations recently captured by Laconian fleets.

Median Empire
A massive Imperial state of over a thousand worlds spread through the galaxy. Its capital, Babylon Prime, was based in the heart of its territory and protected by an elite navy of a thousand ships. Its worlds included hundreds of races from primitive farming worlds to the death worlds and the advanced robotic domains. The dominant race were the Medes who inhabited the Core Worlds of the Empire.

Naxos Collective
A region in the centre of the vast Expanse, and consists of dozens of small, lightly populated worlds. Haven to pirates and smugglers.

Su'bartu Maelstrom
A vast cluster of star systems populated by dead planets. Situated between the fertile border worlds and the rich inner systems close to Median territory. An extremely dangerous area to pass through, due to lack of fuel and supplies for dozens of jumps. Even a Titan would take two to three weeks to make the journey. The Maelstrom was dangerous only one in three ships ever makes it through. At the Median side of the maelstrom is the massive Babylon Starfort, home of the Imperial Fleet; the fleet in the known Galaxy.

Terran Alliance
Also known as the Attican Alliance. Formed following the historic victories of the Terrans against the Empire. Money and ships were provided as a tithe and in turn the Alliance provided security and trade. They were the arch rivals of the Laconian League, headed by Laconia. Much richer and more diverse than the Laconians. They were famous for their use of Romanesque titles in civilian and military life. The homeworld of the Alliance is Attica, positioned in the rich and populous Attican Binary System. The Alliance is far flung, and includes colonies throughout the Expanse and even along the border of the Median Empire. This is only possible due to the size and power of the Alliance Navy.

APPENDIX IV: GLOSSARY

Anusiya

The elite royal military of the Median Empire. Known as Anusiya in their own language, it means something akin to immortals due to their large numbers that never dwindle.

Asgeirr-Carbine

Laconian close quarter weapon. Fits in the fist and lower arm of a warrior and combines a razor-sharp blade and a cut down pulse carbine. The entire unit is compact and very light. Short ranged but very powerful, its blade can punch through most armor.

Boeotian blasters

Also known as Xiphos Assault Carbines. It was smaller than the Dory rifles, though looked much heavier. A thick strap system hung form his armour to help take the weight of the weapon, and its integral shield generator. It was also a pulse weapon, but shorter and squatter. The front was covered in a cowling that hid all but the three muzzle that pushed out to the front. The weapon's magazine extended up from the top and curved slightly forwards.

Combat Drones

War machines built on the worlds of the robotic domains for defensive purposes throughout the Medes Empire. The standard models were of a similar size to a Terran but much broader in the upper body. They lacked complicated hands, and instead were equipped with low velocity pulse weapons and blades. They were designed to be resilient, but lacked tactical awareness or planning capabilities.

Dekas
A small unit of ten soldiers, commanded by a Dekarchos.

Doru Mk II Rifle
Arcadian, standard weapon used by the light infantry for scouting and special operations. The Doru MK II used a high velocity pulse round and was capable of long distance interdiction and could penetrate most modern amours.

Dromon
Generic name for small transports, assault ships and rescue ships. One of the most popular types of craft used throughout the Terran planets. Most were capable of atmospheric flight.

Elamite
A Scythian Class heavy battleship of the Median Empire. Almost half a kilometer long, and frequently used as a command ship for Median fleets. One of the largest ships ever seen outside of the Median Empire's own territory.

Epilektoi
The elite bodyguard unit of the Laconians used to defend senior commanders at home and on campaign. A full company of these warriors were stationed on the Titan Valediction under the command of Komes Artemis. The unit contained ten elite Dekarchos, each promoted from the ranks of Laconian bodyguard units.

Hydra class destroyer
A common Alliance destroyer. At a length of one hundred and fifty meters, and with a crew of one hundred and ninety-five,

the vessels were the smallest self-sufficient ships in the Alliance Armada. The destroyers had the look of large predatory fish from Ancient Earth, with large frontal sections and long tails that carried a multitude of antennae and sensors.

Laconian Infantry
Laconian spatharios were the traditional heavy infantry of Laconia. They wore their traditional crimson Laconian uniforms, topped with their iconic helmets. Unlike most other Terrans they also wore the common infantryman's breastplate, an archaic looking device made of an advanced polymer compound that was proof against many common weapons. Only the senior commanders and the elite bodyguard unit were entitled to wear the red tunics and armor. Other Laconian units were allowed to wear the crimson cloak but only for ceremonial purposes.

Laconian Army Structure
Tourma (1500-2100 warriors), A Laconian military unit
tagma (900+ warriors), 3+ banda
Bandon (300 warriors), Five to seven banda form a tourma
Allaghion, (64 warriors), made up of four lochaghiai
Lochaghiai (16 men), Sixteen lochaghiai per banda, led by lochaghos, assisted by *Dekarchos* (leader of ten), pentarchos (leader of five)

Mothakes
Neodamodes who were the sons of Laconian citizens. Classified as indentured workers, they were the elite of the Neodamodes volunteers that fought with the armada commanded by Agesilaus.

Mulacs

A generic name for several species of mutants, pirates and mercenaries. These creatures were often used by the Medes as scouts and raiders for their own forces. In more recent years they were found carving out their own territories in the border regions.

Neodamodes

Helot indentuired workers, who had been offered their freedom and a wage in exchange for their military service.

Night Blades

The elite special forces reconnaissance unit on-board the Olympia. Commanded by Komes Pasion. Their specialisms were raiding, recon and assault.

Olympia

The renegade Titan from Arcadia, commanded by Dukas Xenias. The first ship that Xenophon and his comrades served on in the expedition under Lord Cyrus.

Ranks

The Ten Thousand under Clearchus used the traditional system of military ranks of the Laconian military. This system dated in part back to the system used thousands of years earlier on Earth. They were a bizarre mixture of naval and army titles that had become mixed over the millennia. These ranks include:

<u>Senior Ranks</u>
Strategos, General of a campaign
Topoteretes, sub commanders of the *strategos*, usually two per *tagma*

Anticensor, leader of engineers

Akolouthos, leader of the general's bodyguard, known as the Epilektoi. Allowed to wear red uniforms

Dukas, commander of a multiple *tagma* (group of professional *bandon* or ship squadrons, usually 1,000+ warriors)

Komes, leader of a small fleet (5-10 ships) or 300 infantry (a *bandon*)

Kentarchos, ship's captain or commander of infantry company of 100 warriors (*kentarchiai*)

Kybernetes, ship's executive officer

Junior Ranks

Dekarchos, commander of 10 warriors (*Dekas*) or junior command position on a ship

Pentarchos, commander of 5 warriors (*Pempas*), or junior command position on a ship

Auletes, communications officer

Satraps

Regional governors in the Median Empire. These men were the most powerful nobles and controlled their regions of space with an iron fist. They answered directly to the Emperor himself and were responsible for raising and commanding the Imperial fleets.

Spatharios

The spatharios (plural: spatharii) was a Terran heavy infantryman, used frequently by the Arcadians and Laconians. They wore the grey uniform adopted by all of the Ten Thousand but each contingent wore their own armour. The Laconians, like Clearchus, wore their own Laconian breastplates and greaves over the top. Their helmets were tall, crowned with an imitation of an ancient plume to increase their height and foreboding. On the left arm of each warrior was the body shield device. When activated, the device created a meter-wide disc of energy that was proof against all man portable weapons.

Stratiotes
A common Terran solder, frequently used to denote the light infantry in Terran armies or the heavy infantry of non-Terrans.

Titan
The largest capital ship used by the Terrans. Capable of carrying tens of thousands of crew and warriors. Five Titans accompanied the Ten Thousand. Each Titan was commanded by the senior Dukas, selected based on the man with the largest contingent. Titans in the fleet included Valediction (under Clearchus), Olympia (under Xenias)

Topoteretes
Senior commanders that would normally commanded half of the military forces at any one time. Also the personal sworn bodyguards of the Strategos.

Taochi
A race of terrifying warriors that had swept through large parts of the Median Empire before being crushed by a vast Imperial Armada. The refugees from these worlds numbered in the millions. As with all conquered tribes, the Taochi now served as part of the Imperial Army. The race was bipedal and of similar shapes, built like an upright bull but with a strongly muscled upper torsos and arms. They famously eschewed firearms in combat.

Virtual Observation System (VOB)

The inner surface of a deck was controlled at a molecular level to give it the characteristics of a flawless three-dimensional video display. Standing on the deck was like flying through space, with the full ability to see outside of the ship, past the armor and into space itself.

www.ingramcontent.com/pod-product-compliance
Lightning Source LLC
Chambersburg PA
CBHW051319250626
47155CB00007B/2379